REQUIES
DAWN

a novel

J.L. Forrest

Books I and II of *Eternal Requiem (Requies Dawn, Requies Day,* and *Requies Dusk),* originally published under a single title—*A Requiem Dawn*—in 2014 by the Robot Cowgirl Press.

SECOND EDITION. Amazon.

Published by the Robot Cowgirl Press. http://robotcowgirl.com

Design and Cover by Forstå and Shana Cordon.

Library of Congress Cataloging-in-Publication Data has been applied for.

ISBN 978-0-9989492-7-7

For who we were.

Foreword

*I*n 2014, the first edition of *A Requiem Dawn* was published by the mysterioso co-op house known as the *Robot Cowgirl Press.* I am quite happy, now, to see Robot Cowgirl revisit the *Requiem* stories, this time with major adjustments and all apologies to dear readers who may have purchased the 600-page behemoth which was that novel.

Things have changed—slightly.

The first "part" of *A Requiem Dawn* was roughly 74,000 words, by itself, with another 80,000 words belonging to the remainder of the book. One hundred fifty-four thousand words was, for our purposes, simply too long. Worse, while *A Requiem Dawn* was received generously, the story in my opinion felt rushed, and its development suffered—600 pages actually needed to be 1,000.

Not one book, but three.

Nyahri et Sultah and Sultah et Nyahri deserve no less.

In that same year, *Analog Science Fiction and Fact* chose to publish a novelette titled "Sentience Signified". (Grammarians can argue with me about the use of that last period at jlforrest.com or at facebook.com/jlforrest.) Contracted in 2014, "Sentience Signified" earned my entrance into the Science Fiction and Fantasy Writers of America, SFWA, and it appeared in bookstores for the May 2015 edition. That story now appears in the collection *Minuscule Truths,* under the title "Sapience Signified" because, damn it, the title really was wrong.

Similarly, the title to *A Requiem Dawn* wasn't quite correct either. The word *requiem* is Middle English and comes from the Latin *requies,* all those vowels in the second syllable pronounced something like the *eese* in *geese.*

In English, we've come to think of the *requiem* as an act of remembrance or, more specifically, as a musical composition in remembrance for the dead. This overarching series of books retains the title *Eternal Requiem.* The individual novels, however, are now titled *Requies Dawn, Requies Day,* and *Requies Dusk.* (There may even be a *Requies Night*—time will tell). *Requies* means here, more broadly, *rest* or *repose*—perhaps in death, but perhaps in some other sense.

I will leave it to you, the reader, to decide what the themes of the *Eternal Requiem* might be. Like so many writers, I fear I've only struck an inch beneath the surface, and you'll see through the smoke and mirrors immediately. All writing is, after all, little more or less than legerdemain.

As a last note: In October 2016, *Analog* kindly published a novelette, by the title of "Progenesis", which is a prequel of sorts for the *Eternal Requiem.* In case you're unable to find out-of-date copies of *Analog,* you'll be able to read "Progenesis" in *Peculiar Declarations,* my third collection of short fiction, due out in late 2018.

J.L. Forrest
Mt. Princeton, Colorado
2017

A Note on Languages

*T*he languages of Nyahri's world—following the Eventide, the *life blooms* of the Hive, and the recovery of humanity—are necessarily simplified as presented here; e.g., Rosian isn't Russian. At a time so far removed from our own, the common languages of the E'cwnii, Inwnii, and Oudwnii would be only a vague mishmash of contemporary languages, influenced by the tongue of the Atreianii, which is itself a blend of English, Italian, and other language structures. Given the length of the recovery after the Eventide, languages would have diversified more than this tale can allow. Sometimes storytelling prefers simplicity.

For the most part, pronunciations are also simplified, except where they steal from contemporary and historical sources (e.g., Gjørg or Kepler). A few of the more common letters are:

a: A soft *ah,* as in the word *soft.*

c: A hard *k,* as in the word *kleptomaniac.*

dh: A soft *d,* pronounced with the tongue tip just behind the upper teeth.

e: A soft *e,* as in the word *elevator.*

i: A soft *i,* as in the word *tin,* except at the end of nouns, where it follows the rules for singular and plural forms.

i: (singular noun) At the end of many Atreian-influenced nouns, the singular *i* is pronounced as a hard *e* sound, as in the double *e* of the word *tree.*

ii: (plural noun) At the end of Atreian-influenced plural nouns, the double *ii* is drawn out with the tongue at the back of the mouth. The change is not one of type but of length and accent. The practiced speaker and listener would know precisely whether an individual specimen was referenced, as opposed to the plural. Sometimes this can occur in names: *Sabi* is from the Atreian word meaning a single falcon; *Marii* is from the Atreian word for a multiplicity of seas, meaning "all waters."

j: A soft *j*, as in the second *g* of the word *gorge*.

o: A short *o*, as in the word *home*.

u: A rounded pronunciation of the double *o*, as in *moon*.

w: A soft pronunciation of the double *o*, as in *coo*, drawn out longer than a single *u*.

y: When at the beginning of a word, it is a hard *e* sound, as in the first *e* of the word *concede*. Within a word, it is a hard *i* sound, as in the word *pie*.

Examples

Sultah yw Sabi is pronounced Sŭ•ltă ū Să•bē. (*Yw* combines from ē and *oo* and shortens merely to ū.)

Nyahri is pronounced Nī•ăr•ē. *Nyahri* is from the E'cwn word for *antelope* or *gazelle*.

Dhaos is pronounced Dhă•ōs.

Atreiani is pronounced Ăt•rā•ăn•ē. (The *ei* combine to form a nasal *e* as in the English *hey.*)

Book I of the Eternal Requiem

Requies Dawn

I love thee with a love I seemed to lose
With my lost saints—I love thee with the breath,
Smiles, tears, of all my life!—and, if God choose,
I shall but love thee better after death.

Elizabeth Barrett-Browning

isky to light a flame where enemies might spot it, but Nyahri kindled a small fire to offer herbs and dried venison to the Atreian devils and the hosts of the E'cwn gods. She plucked night-falcon feathers from her braided hair and cast them to read her foolish cousin's fortune—*Suhto, proud Suhto,* the feathers said, *doomed from the start.*

The night deepened and, at moments, the triplet moons hid their cold faces behind clouds. Called Lwn, the largest waxing- crescent moon shed a frigid glow, overwhelming her pallid little sisters. In that light the violet-shaded foothills silhouetted the lower boar-back hills of the Abswyn range.

After making her offerings, Nyahri tamped out the embers. She led Suhto's black stallion and her russet, Kwlko, to a hilltop overlooking the Red Valley and the pinnacle of Abswyn, House of Hell. She fussed over the horses, checking their hooves and teeth and ribs, healthy as they were, anything to distract herself. Over many hours she refused sleep, at last sitting on the ground with her stallion's saddle behind her.

Why must I be so stubborn? she thought. *Why must he be so stubborn? If I had found a way to make him understand, we would not be here.* Her thoughts circled, *If I had accepted his offer, we would not be here either.*

The marriage, though, would never have lasted.

So here we are, she thought, *and maybe I have killed him with stubbornness?*

At daybreak she crawled to the hillock which overlooked a sandstone valley. Two days before, Suhto crossed the valley and entered Abswyn, past the colossal stones of the red Gate, where no one should go. Midday passed without sign of him and, at last, sleep overcame her.

When she woke again in the late afternoon, she stared across the valley as far as the pine-blanketed foothills. Would Suhto run toward her, his smile proving he'd won her challenge? Yet he appeared nowhere in that hallowed place, that cradle of the dead.

At the center of the valley the devils' slender pinnacle jutted a thousand handspans straight into heaven, though at its base it measured no more than five paces wide. A beacon glowed at its gray point, an unhurried white-red light which pulsed eternally.

A tower built by devil-gods, Nyahri thought, *an aeon ago, a place where good men and women do not go, a forbidden place.*

Dusk came, the moons scarcely brighter than the night before. At next light she sipped water, not wanting to blink in case she missed some sign. Nyahri kept her eyes open through most of the day but, with warm afternoon sun on her back and grass against her cheek, she closed her eyes again.

With her heart in her throat, Nyahri woke to a violent shrill, her skull rattling. The din centered upon the devils' pillar, and it filled her ears, a noise made solid. Both horses neighed, bucked, and circled on their tethers. She fought to saddle them and mounted the stallion.

Then the shrill quieted, replaced by a deep, earthen hum. The horses attempted retreat, eastward from Abswyn toward the open plains. Instead, Nyahri drove the stallions west, riding downhill. The sun, nestling against the foothills, blinded her even as the Abswyn tower loomed overhead, its light no longer pulsing but flickering.

She rode over the flat, between sandstone cliffs which cast shades of rust and dried blood. Nyahri galloped through the bone-laden bowers of her ancestors. For a hundred generations, the E'cwnii had laid their dead at Abswyn, and now she desecrated their remains, knocking bones from their places, crushing others under hoof.

Nothing like this, Nyahri thought, *has ever happened before.*

Below the tower, the great mass of the devil-gods' home hid beneath the earth, only its uppermost shell at the surface. Nyahri directed the horses across its vitreous metal, an unyielding gray roof exposed piecemeal through the quaking red sands.

She returned to a familiar mesquite-rimmed draw—where she'd left Suhto to his challenge—and Nyahri scrambled from the saddle. An erosion revealed a glassy wall and a single rounded door, an entrance into this House of Hell. At the start of Suhto's challenge, it had shut behind him.

Now it stood open.

"Suhto!" Nyahri screamed until her throat burned. "Suhto!"

The earth-shake worsened. Choking dust washed the valley in a bloody haze.

Soon the horses will run. Nyahri turned back to the stallions, but she found more than horses. Her stomach fell.

A woman stood before her.

Not a woman, Nyahri thought. *A devil.*

A hand taller than the tallest E'cwn men, her hair blacker than the darkest E'cwn hair, the devil appeared humanlike but could never pass for human. Her opalescent skin glinted, human-like but for her coloring, for the long litheness of her arms and legs, for her slender fingers.

The devil staggered toward Nyahri, catching the stallion's reins. She clutched a large bag to her chest, wiping her eyes with the back of her hand, a smear of dust crossing her forehead. The devil blinked, then spoke a few incomprehensible words.

"I do not understand," Nyahri said.

The devil tilted her head, adjusting some thought, some perception. She uttered other words with different sounds.

"I am sorry," said Nyahri, "I do not speak your language, Atreiani."

Another tilt of the head, an adjustment. The devil tried another speech, another language entirely. In succession she attempted idiom after idiom, recombining tones and grammars, all the while gesturing to the horses.

At last the devil's words carried meaning: "You understand me, girl?"

"Yea." Nyahri nodded.

"I've never ridden a horse, but if we don't flee fast as we're able, we're dead. Understand?"

"You *are* an Atreiani?"

The devil blinked. "Yes."

"Gods!" Nyahri covered her mouth, raising her other hand in a sign against evil.

"No time for superstitious bullshit," the devil said, her voice urgent but trembling. "We've half an hour. Get us out of here."

Nyahri pointed to the subterranean orifice, to the crimson lights pulsing from it. "My cousin! He is inside the House of Hell—"

"No man's left alive down there."

Tears flooded Nyahri's eyes. She shook her head, willing Suhto to exist.

"I must get him!" Nyahri screamed.

"Try and you're dead too," the devil said.

Is that a threat? Nyahri wondered. *An explanation?*

"Nay—"

"Listen!" the Atreiani said, her accent thick. "We go now or we're both dead."

Nyahri tried to understand. *Why will we be dead? How is Suhto dead?*

"I've never ridden a horse," the devil repeated.

"What?"

The Atreiani took another pained step. Nyahri reached to steady the devil's arm but at the last moment withdrew, fear besting her urge to assist, to serve an obvious divinity.

"Aid me!" the devil said, grabbing Nyahri's wrist, the Atreiani's skin as smooth as sun-warmed, polished stone.

Her hair drank the sunlight, no rays reflecting from it. Her gaze fixed upon Nyahri, the devil's coal irises encircling black pupils, depthless but for a grieving panic.

Nyahri shuddered. *A viper's eyes, but something more.*

The horsewoman helped the Atreiani to the black stallion's saddle. She strapped the devil's bag to the cantle, jumped onto her own horse, and the stallion bolted. Nyahri drove the horses across the Red Valley till they frothed, passing between the red stones of the Gate. They charged into the forests at the feet of the boar-backed hills, leaving the hell-spire behind, following long arroyos and cottonwoods to lower ground. The earthen hum quieted. A thousand strides fell behind the riders, then two thousand, then three, until only hoof beats sounded on the leaf litter. Nyahri looked over her shoulder: the hollow-cheeked devil slumped, clutching the blanket and saddlebow.

She possesses strength though, Nyahri thought, *and she will not fall. How beautiful she is, gods protect us! An Atreiani, one of the old ones, the enslavers who bring blessings and destruction.*

The sun fell beneath the horizon—but in a flash the fledgling darkness seared into reborn light. The west erupted to heaven with Abswyn's death-throws, a mushroom of fire silhouetting the foothills and boar-backs and trees. The air boomed, carrying an ashen cloud faster than any horse, throwing everything before it, razing trees, lifting stones.

Another explosion followed, then another. The horses screamed and a shockwave threw Nyahri from the saddle. She tumbled, clambering to grasp anything. Her head struck the ground. Then nothing.

reamless, Nyahri lay beneath the ash, the taste of dust and fire on her tongue. Her memories echoed, the passing of hours, the spilling of moments:

Days before, the firm winds caressed the open prairie east of Abswyn, the plains' golden horizon upholding a generous blue sky. Armies of giant grasses marched, sweeping unbroken except by a half-empty arroyo whose goliath cottonwoods shaded a creek. Locusts droned in the afternoon heat, and crickets trilled beside cool currents, where silverfish danced.

Nearby, low-domed hide tents squatted in a clearing, hedged by scrub oaks, hidden from a distance. Cooking fires unfurled aromatic white smoke, drying venison strips on woven willow stands. Boys and girls kicked a leather ball between them, tumbling and colliding. They ran naked or dressed in simple cloth, their skin tinted in hues from tea leaves to burnt sienna.

A mottled dog lay in the shade beside men who wore their earth-dark hair in tight braids. Night-falcon plumage fluttered from the longspears braced across their laps.

The dog raised its head, cocked its ears, and ran to the water.

Riders approached the opposite bank, young men standing in the saddle with their longspears held high, their bows slung at their backs, quivers at their sides. They crossed the river and dismounted, clasping arms with adolescent boys who accepted the reins of the sweat-lathered horses.

The riders gathered at the communal fire. An old man, the tribal Ahtros, stepped from a tent, naked save for a blanket cinched around his hips. Dark feathers adorned his white hair, fluttering against his engraved face as he sat with the riders.

They passed a water skin from man to man, quenching their thirst, eating their fill of roasted violet maize. The old man played a flute, the others listening.

"Mournful," one hunter said, his head bowed by the music.

When the old man finished his tune, he said, "The spirits of your fathers. I am grateful to have you home."

"The spirit of your father," the hunters said. Each cast dust into the fire.

"What have you seen?" the old man asked.

A wiry man sat forward, taller and stronger than the rest. "We met Inwn spearmen in the north," he said, "at the wide bend of the Heron, where the gray cranes nest in the short grasses. It is the first time in two summers any of us have spoken with the Inwnii. They were peaceful, trading water-bone ivory and beads for our foals. The Inwnii spoke honestly with us. When we left them, we scouted west. Our tribe has come faster than we thought—Abswyn is only two more days, following the sunset."

A young woman brought boiling water in a clay pot, and she sprinkled herbs into it before passing earthenware cups to the men. They let the tea steep, poured it, and sipped it, nodding to her in gratitude.

The speaker continued, "At the forest's edge, near the boar-back ridges, we spotted Oudwn archers afoot along the riverbank. We followed them to the mouth of the Red Valley, and they slipped into the foothills. They saw nothing of us."

"Abswyn is untouched?" the old man asked.

"Yea, Ahtros. Our ancestors' bodies rest on their palanquins. The devil's pillar, the hell-spire, stands as tall as ever. The House of Hell never ceases its ghost-fire."

"A place of death and dying, you see?"

"So everyone says."

"I do not wish to insult you, Suhto," the old man said, "but you still insist on doing this thing?"

"Your daughter demanded her bridal challenge."

"I might speak with Nyahri, change her mind."

"It is not how I would have it with her, her father speaking for me."

The old man frowned. "I might speak with *you*, change *your* mind."

"Nay, Ahtros, my resolve doubles every day."

They drank, emptying their cups, and a young hunter refilled them. The frowning old man closed his eyes.

"She is undoubtedly foolish," he said. "You are foolish too. You are foolish *twice*."

"Twice?" Suhto asked.

"Once because my obstinate daughter is a safi—everyone seems to know this but you and she—and if you accepted this fact, you would not be going to die for her. And twice because you are actually *going* to die for her."

"You are so certain?"

"That Nyahri is one of the safii? Yea. About your death? Nay, but your odds are poor."

"She is no safi and I can win through. I am not afraid."

"I *am* afraid, Suhto. I have a right to be afraid for you."

Suhto studied the old man's eyes, their color the rare jade of high mountain water. The Ahtros already grieved Suhto's death, though the young man sat alive at the campfire, teacup in hand, kinsmen around him. Suhto tipped his spear into the blaze, which scorched away its beaded black feathers.

"I do not believe in the Atreianii," Suhto said. "I have never seen one. Neither have you. Neither did your grandfather or his grandfather. If there ever were any Atreianii, they are long dead, and we have no reason to fear them."

The old man's eyes glittered in the amber dusk. He turned to the sun, his shadow lengthening behind him.

"Would you are right, Suhto."

Tribal life went on. Two women stretched antelope skins on racks, mothers looked after newborns and toddlers, and three young huntresses returned from a morning's work with a brace of rabbits. Seated on a log, a bowyer wound sinew into strings. At the grasses' edge, tethered horses grazed, flicking their ears. Bright beads and feathers decorated their manes, declaring one horse's owner from another's.

Nyahri rode, her stallion's hooves drumming the sward. His mane flew, and he flew, and she flew upon him. His lungs filled and emptied as she worked her knees against his flanks, no stirrups or reins, her hands clenching his russet hair. At a high crest she shortened her grip and Kwlko lowered his haunches, kicking dust.

Stroking his neck, she clicked her tongue by his ear.

A tempered longknife rested at Nyahri's hip, its blade carefully oiled within its beaded sheath. A trade-coral necklace hung around her throat above a turquoise-embroidered serape, its silver-worked edges across her shoulders. A long leather riding skirt draped her waist and thighs, her figure as much a girl's as a woman's.

She dismounted, only a short distance from the encampment, and let Kwlko wander. Thought the scent of evening campfires lingered, the swelling hills hid the firelight from her.

Good, Nyahri thought.

She wanted the darkness, as she lay in the grass, her hands clasped behind her head. The stars glittered, the White River overarching the dome like salt spilled on slate.

The heavens filled her wide eyes, reflected in irises green as her father's, tapered like pawpaw leaves. Freckles peppered Nyahri's nose and cheeks, patterned like the constellations, a decoration of dark stars on her cinnamon skin.

Lwn hovered overhead, a late crescent moon with its obscured face decorated like dew on a spider web, a thousand-thousand twinkling lights upon it. In Lwn's wake followed Stashwn, the lesser orb a meager silvered disc. At the edge of the sky hovered the smallest, Trwl, the dark-gray maiden. Stashwn never journeyed distantly from Lwn but, over the course of years, Trwl wandered wide from her sisters.

Nyahri meditated on these celestials.

The Atreianii taught the three sisters to soar, she thought. *The devils did terrible things, but they are also gods of beauty.*

She thanked those sleeping devils for the blessing of the moons, watching the sisters until Lwn chased the sun past the horizon. Then Nyahri stood, calling the stallion with soft coos, and she cantered back to the encampment, where most everyone already slept.

Nyahri scrubbed her horse, then tethered him on the herd line, where he contented himself on fresh grass. As she crossed the camp, Suhto gazed at her from the men's fire, where his brothers and cousins laughed at each other's ghost stories.

At her tent, Nyahri swept open the door and crawled inside. Soft lamplight greeted her, along with acrid bison-fat smoke, which hung in the shadow.

Her younger sister lay on their shared sheepskins, gazing at the roof, the corners of her mouth notched downward. Nyahri attempted a smile before setting her knife aside. The long ride's ache remained with her, obscuring deeper pains, though she tried to stretch her muscles. On her stomach, Nyahri folded her arms beneath her cheek, staring at her sister until the girl met her gaze.

"Cirje," Nyahri began.

"You stink like horse," her sister said.

"Angry?"

"*You* are a prideful hag and everyone knows it."

"Cirje—"

"A *hag,* I say." Cirje huffed. "You will be a lonely old crow someday."

"What are you saying?" Nyahri grimaced. "I will be an old crow if I do not marry Suhto?"

"You will be an old crow because Suhto is going to *die,* and no other man will ever dare being with you. That will be *two* men dead because of you—Suhto *and* our uncle."

Nyahri winced.

"To think," Cirje added, "every other girl in the nine tribes wants to share Suhto's tent."

"Let some other girl have him."

"He wants *you.* Think you are too good to bear his children?"

"I do not *want* children, his or anyone else's."

"You really *are* a safi. It is true."

"Am not and, even if I was, that has nothing to do with children." Nyahri shook her head. "I had the right to set my challenge for him."

"Such a stupid challenge! My heart breaks for you." Cirje laid her hand on Nyahri's shoulder. "Whatever were you thinking?"

"Thinking?" Nyahri's shoulders fell. "The words simply poured from me—there was no *thought* in them."

Cirje sighed. "Poor sister! There *is* a way to end this, to save Suhto's life, and you know it."

"Nay."

"Accept his proposal and *bed* him."

Nyahri raised her voice. "I have offered to release him from this challenge many times these weeks!" She clenched her jaw. "Every time, he persists. Which is easier? For me to marry my good friend, no matter my guilt for leading him on, for too many thoughtless kisses? No matter that I do not wish him as husband? Or for him to simply *let it go?*"

"You had to challenge him, on tribal ground, in front of *everyone?* The dishonor of it! He *cannot* back down." Cirje rose to her knees, hugging her sister.

"Mayhap I will end up his wife after all? Men have gone into Houses of Hell before and come out again."

"Only in legends, and you know it. No one *truly* survives where the ghost-fires burn, and at Abswyn they *burn*. It is a house of the gods, not meant for men."

Nyahri closed her eyes. "Our brother's remains rest there," she said, "as do our grandfather's and his father's, and all the healers of generations past. Their spirits will look after Suhto."

Growing quiet, Cirje turned onto her side.

Nyahri stripped away her own garments, wetted a cloth in a bowl of water, and washed the sweat from her skin. A short while later, with the blankets over her, she listened to the camp.

Perhaps forty paces away, a man and woman moaned together in their tent, their whispers and gasps indistinct.

The woman crescendoed and, with the rise of her voice and a few shouted words, Nyahri recognized her. The man peaked soon after.

Is that Cahlia's usual lover? Nyahri wondered, the detail irrelevant but blessedly distracting.

Every day, a thousand such details presented themselves to her, endless familiarities. Since Suhto proposed marriage, since she set her challenge, she noticed these details all the more, and she bristled at them. Of course, a third choice occurred to her, many times. Perhaps Suhto could never have refused, a dishonor too great for him to bear. Perhaps Nyahri could never marry him, not so willingly, so contrary to herself.

Yet she *could* flee, put Suhto and all the rest of them behind her.

Would that not also be a dishonor?

The fire crackled. The hunters recited their stories. Suhto's restrained voice sometimes rose above the conversation.

Her childhood friend.

It is not my fault he fell in love with me.

Thoughts of him circled with dreams of flight, of another life, of some escape. On these, she drifted to sleep.

At dawn the tribe awakened, broke fast, and packed. The E'cwnii disassembled tents and loaded gear. Like the others, Nyahri bundled her litter for the packhorses and, before the chill fled the morning air, scarce sign remained of camp.

The tribe loped westward, huntsmen and archers at the fore, unsaddled horses and watchmen at the rear. Foothills now crowned the western horizon, upturned ridges and their valleys blanketed by violet-green woodlands of bitter-pine and magiswood.

Close to the mountains, with tall grasses touching the horses' bellies, Nyahri rode beside her father. Cirje trailed behind them. Two years younger than Nyahri, Cirje still preferred her pony, though she rode like a chieftess upon it.

Throughout the day, Nyahri spotted Suhto a half-dozen times. Always wary, he appeared on hilltops or in vales, he and other hunters scouting ahead. The tribe's danger grew with each pace, each step closer to the forests of Oudwn archers. Despite this danger, despite herself, Nyahri smiled when she glimpsed Suhto.

The vulture god, she thought, *the lord of death, could not catch Suhto unaware. If anyone could enter a House of Hell and live—*

She too kept a keen eye for Oudwn archers or for border-land reavers like the Bk'ferii, remembering what her beloved brother, Erhde, once taught her: *Watch the horizon for death afar, the ground for death below, the sky for death above.*

Of course, his own death had come unlooked for.

Nyahri's chalk-haired father sat straight in his saddle, but he had moved slower in recent months, and each new day settled on him like a pebble. Each added to the weight of his years, and one day would crush him. Nyahri pressed her lips together.

His time nears, she thought, her heart aching.

The tribe reached a stream, scarcely enough drink for the horses. Escaping the sweltering midday, the E'cwnii shaded beneath a sparse copse. The Ahtros sat on blankets, near the water, and Nyahri joined him. She picked a grass blade, stripped it, and chewed it, rolling it between her teeth.

Her father gazed at the horizon, his eyes glistening. With embers, he lit his pipe, inhaled a few puffs, and handed it to

Nyahri. She drew on it and passed it back. Their smoke rings drifted over the water.

"Father—"

"Nyahri, my son—"

"Your *daughter*."

"You act like a son."

"Father," she said again, exasperated.

"Your father without sons or grandsons. Thus you are my son."

She understood.

Women do not ride warriors' stallions, she thought, *or learn so well the bow and spear and longknife. They do not take the pipe. Women marry, lay aside childish interests. Even young huntresses eventually take a husband.*

"Could you not dissuade Suhto?" she asked. "Any other woman would have him."

"That is not the way of it."

"He would listen to you."

"I tried. Shall I ask for his cowardice? His wishes are clear."

"I was sure he would refuse the challenge."

The Ahtros's eyes widened, his jaw clenching. Seldom had her father berated her, but now he verged on it. She readied herself, waited for his command: *Marry!*

What will he do if I deny such a decree? Banish me?

Yet he sighed and curled another line of smoke into his mouth.

"You must become a better judge of men's hearts," he said, "before I die."

"I will do my best."

"Tell me, *are* you one of the safii, daughter?"

She grimaced at him. "Everyone should stop asking me that."

"They will stop if you will answer."

"I do not know."

"Might change things if you did."

"*I do not know.*"

Upstream, playful children hollered and the horses raised their heads, listening for trouble. Finding none, they returned to grazing. A colt pranced and nudged its mother for milk.

"When Suhto departs for the House of Hell," she said, "I want to ride out with him. To witness."

The Ahtros's thin lips stretched, neither a smile nor a frown. "When you send a man to die, it *is* polite to see him off."

Nyahri gritted her teeth, stood, and walked to the arroyo bank. There she gathered flat stones to skip across the water.

{03}

By early afternoon the scouts returned and the troop moved once more. The terrain undulated nearer the foothills, though the stark peaks remained distant, their lengthening shadows filling the valleys. Within a wide hollow, a scalloped lake reflected the few clouds which still dared the sun.

Nyahri wiped her brow, shielding her eyes from the west, heeling her horse to her father's side. From a knoll at the lake's far edge, Suhto galloped to them until he rode abreast the Ahtros.

"Nyahri," he said, "will you be my wife?"

"You know my mind," she replied for the hundredth time, "enter the House of Hell, come back with proof of the Atreianii, whether they are alive or dead or nothing at all, as you think they are. Do that, and I will be your wife."

He smiled. "That I will do."

"You know I would release you from this duty?" She said this as a matter of course. "Go find another woman, Suhto."

"My mind is set."

"A brave man," the Ahtros interrupted, "might enter the ghost-fires and return."

"Yea," Suhto said.

"Might."

"Yea, Ahtros. When Nyahri and I come back from the Red Valley, we will find you at the old camp, and we will feast."

"Would we will, Suhto."

Suhto gave his stallion rein and kicked. The horse leapt, opening his gait through the grasses. Nyahri quelled an urge to ride after him, her dear friend, to go upon the hunt, to cross the plain with him as equal hunters, as they had many times before—

Eager for distraction she looked over her shoulder. Cirje gloomed at her, the girl's brown irises smoldering in the sunlight. Nyahri held her sister's gaze for a long moment but, as she turned away, her heart fell.

As a matter of tradition, the whole of the tribe never entered the Red Valley. As it had hundreds of times before, the tribe camped short of the forested mountains. The old campground nestled in a floodplain of sweet grass, cottonwoods embracing it by the thousands. Cherry and crabapple trees grew nearby. The women raised shelters and picked fruit. Dogs chased each other. Hunters established a perimeter.

Cirje pouted, refusing to emerge from the tent.

At dark, the vigilant hunters traded their watch. Other men sang death songs, told tales, and made obeisance to their ancestors—and to the Atreianii in whom Suhto refused to believe.

Many matrons glowered at Nyahri, their thoughts easy to guess: *What kind of woman sends a good man to die? Why not make children, the Ahtros's grandchildren, which he might hold before he dies?*

She sighed, leading her horse into the open grasses. The stallion carried full saddlebags, a bedroll, and a blanket. Nyahri brought her weapons. Her best serape adorned her, pale silverset turquoise and amber sewn with fine whispering wool. Hunter's breeches replaced her skirt, matched by thick-soled sandals. Charcoal spirals whorled across the horse's ribs and haunches, emblems to protect against the devils of Abswyn.

She slept that night far from camp, sheltered below an apple tree heavy with sweet fruit. At daybreak, Kwlko nuzzled her awake. Nyahri worked a trade-ivory comb through her hair, saddled the stallion, and crested a hillside to await Suhto's departure. A few of the tribe followed, close enough to witness her leave, but she acknowledged no one.

A thousand strides ahead, Suhto waited on a hilltop for his younger brothers, Uhlo and Ehteh, to mount a sleek gray mare and a black bay. Even from such a distance, white mud showed on Suhto's face and hands—the color of death—and he'd smeared his dark stallion's flanks with it. Together the three brothers set heel, riding toward the foothills with sunrise at their backs. Nyahri gave a slow thousand-count before following.

BY EVENING SHE ENTERED the woodland. The Bhar River flowed beside her, leading into the hills. Nyahri tensed, alert to the stallion's every sound. His ears pricked and his nostrils flared, seeing and scenting what she could not.

Moist air touched her skin, the season's first frost kissing the forest's yellow-tinged leaves. On the plains the sun had scorched the land but, only a few hundred paces uphill, Nyahri shivered.

Squirrels chattered and unfamiliar birds sang. Twice during her climb, Nyahri startled day-bedded deer which darted into the underbrush, their white tails flickering. She followed the hoof prints left by the brothers' horses, who made straight for Abswyn.

It has not been so long, she thought, *since my dear brother's funeral procession. Ill luck to follow so impatiently on the path of the dead.*

Nyahri rode until last light, then tethered the stallion to a sapling, unsaddled him, and brushed him. She unpacked a blanket and lay on the ground, trusting the cold to keep her sleep shallow. She drowsed, waking now and then to some sound—passing porcupines or skunks or deer.

THE STALLION SNORTED AND sidestepped. Nyahri opened her eyes, her fingers around her knife hilt. Leaves rustled.

As she moved, a man yelled. He leapt at her but she rolled, kicking his groin, swinging him to the ground. Her blade angled for his throat even as his sinewy hand gripped her wrist, and he kneed her gut, pinning her to the earth.

"How could you?" he pleaded, his voice breaking. "Witch!"

"Uhlo!" she said.

"Go to Suhto, tell him to stop!"

"I cannot."

"Witch!"

"I will not!"

Uhlo's tears wetted his cheeks. "Why?"

"He can back down."

"And be dishonored?" Uhlo spit on her.

Nyahri's wrist tingled and pain shot through her stomach. Then his knee drew away—

She smashed her palm into his nose. As he swung back, longknife in hand, she brought her foot against his knee. It popped and he collapsed, groaning in the dust.

"You dare?" Nyahri said. She spit on him, snorted phlegm, and spit again. "Hobble back to your brothers, tell them whatever story comes to mind! What will you say to Suhto? A woman beat you?" She circled him. "Will you lie? Weave some fable, how Oudwn woodsmen sported with you?"

As he held his knee, sobs racked him. Blood smeared his cheek, glistening in the new moons' spider-webbed light.

"A man," he said, "should not die in Abswyn, not there. You can stop this, Nyahri."

She sighed, her heart aching, already sorry to have kicked Uhlo so hard. Nyahri picked up his knife, slid it into her belt, then sheathed her own.

"Your knee is broken," she said, "likely as not, but I am not coming anywhere close to you till you promise to behave."

"Do you not love my brother?"

"Keenly. I care for you too, idiot—I might have killed you."

"Why refuse him?"

"My mind is on our ancestors, on the ride and the hunt, not on motherhood and babies. My mind is on the Atreianii, and I know their lore as well as any elder."

"Still—"

"I am a huntress. One day I will be a priestess—"

"Your mother was a priestess, still wed, still *your* mother."

"Her rite may have been motherhood, but mine will be the kill. I am a better archer than you, Uhlo, and by horseback too. I am no tent wife."

"Suhto never wanted a tent wife—he *wants* a huntress."

"Sooner or later I *would* become a tent wife." She resaddled the horse and tightened his girth. As she lowered the stirrups, guessing the length of Uhlo's legs, she closed her eyes against her doubts. "Let us try to put you ahorse, get you to your gray, and your little brother can ride back with you. Leave Suhto to his fate."

"Let me go with him." He laid his hand on his knee. "You have a healer's skill—"

"I never finished my training," she said.

"You mother was the best healer in memory!"

"Stop talking about my mother." She scowled. "My mother is dead."

"Please let Ehteh and I accompany our brother to Abswyn."

"You will be on a stretcher for a fortnight or longer, and with a splint for two months. I can only send you back to other women and their better medicines."

Nyahri helped him up. Uhlo grimaced, balancing on his good leg, and he drowned a scream. Kwlko shied from him.

"Now," she said, "up."

Uhlo swung to the saddle, straining the unbending leg over it, catching his breath.

"Take us to Suhto's camp," she said.

Uhlo nodded. Nyahri tapped the stallion's rump, following on foot.

They headed west under the sliver moons. Nyahri minded Uhlo but kept an eye and ear to the woods, holding her breath to listen, to be certain no one followed. She preferred wide-open spaces where a horse could stretch its legs.

If Oudwnii set upon us here, she thought, *their bows will outmatch mine. What an awful risk we take, coming here.*

uhto fretted over Uhlo, who'd snuck away without a word. Any search would need to wait until morning. Ehteh, their youngest brother, a boy of thirteen, slept in a bedroll obscured by undergrowth. Suhto smiled at him, his heart aching for both his brothers, for the thought he might not see them again. Resting on his heels, Suhto strained his ears hour after hour, his spear clenched in his pale-knuckled fists.

A hollow of horse hooves approached on the moist earth—
One moons-lit rider.

Suhto glanced to the horses and to Ehteh, praying for his younger brother to stay asleep, for the horses to remain still. He feared an ambush, Oudwnii in numbers, or worse.

The rider whispered, "Suhto? Ehteh?"

"Uhlo?" Suhto clicked his tongue, easing forward with his spear raised, alarmed by his brother's bloodied face. Then he recognized Nyahri's red stallion.

She emerged from the shadows, laying her hand on Kwlko's flank. "Your brother's pride is broken," she said, "as is his nose. Mayhap his knee too."

Uhlo lowered his eyes. Suhto shot his brother a reproachful glance, then nodded to Nyahri.

"Best if your brothers head back at dawn," she said. "The knee will need care."

Suhto took his wounded sibling by the waist and Uhlo dismounted, trembling into his brother's arms. "Please, Nyahri, he grows cold."

"Shock," she said.

"You *must* have something?"

She dug through her bags and tossed a pouch at their feet. "The brew must be hot, but cover your fire well out here and keep it small. Only a pinch of herb. Keep him covered and warm."

"Will you not camp with us?"

"Nay, Suhto."

"Where then?"

"Abswyn."

"You go before morning?"

"I do not feel like sleeping." She frowned at him. "I will watch for you."

"Too dangerous." He stood tall, the shadows seeming to carve him, his dark hair swept behind his ears. His eyebrows lowered over his glistening eyes. "You should stay here with us."

"Oudwn bowmen," she said, "will have a hard time shooting me by starlight, nay?"

Nyahri jumped into the saddle and tossed Uhlo's knife to the ground. Suhto watched her disappear westward through the trees.

Uhlo hissed through his teeth at a swell of pain. "Why devote yourself to *her?*" he asked his brother.

Suhto gave him a wistful look, then returned his attention to the trees. "Last time the winter wapiti came onto the western plains, she dropped a bull from fifty paces. A week later she slew another from five—it never knew she was there. During the southern raids, two summers ago, we fought back the White-hands. You remember? She never flinched, even while E'cwn hunters, older than she, pissed their breeches. When she is fierce, she is fierce. When kind, kind. You question why I love her?"

"Eh, brother," Uhlo said softly.

"Do not ask again."

{05}

Nyahri rode many thousand strides without hurry. Crickets kept her company, unalarmed by Kwlko's pace. Moist air filled Nyahri's lungs and softened her face.

Strange to ride here, she thought, *strange to come alone.*

The last time she traveled that path, she rode in full daylight with her entire family. They had carried her brother's corpse at the fore.

Before dawn she chose a game trail, parting from the main route. It veered uphill, tangled by fallen trees and washouts. Kwlko complained, hesitating until Nyahri dismounted, leading him by the reins.

The hill crested over a valley framed by two sandstone monoliths. Known as the Gate, they stood hundreds of hands high, coppery and coarse. Past the Gate, at the valley's heart, arose a straight and unnatural pillar, the hell-spire. At its dizzying pinnacle, a luminescent beacon burst into being, then died, then lit again over and over as it had for Nyahri's entire memory, as during the memories of her father and her father's father. Between and beyond the stones, encircling the hell-spire, stood thousands of carven ponderosa frames, the palanquins of the dead. For generations, they had hoisted the bones of Nyahri's tribe.

The wind blew against her face, and Nyahri gripped her spear, studying the rhythmic ghost-fire of the devils' pillar. Tears blurred her vision, but before she descended to the burial grounds, she dried her eyes.

I come to Abswyn, she thought, *a House of Hell, where many tears have fallen.* Nyahri harbored no wish to add to them.

NYAHRI WAITED FOR SUHTO at her brother's hatchet- hewn palanquin. The season had bleached his bones, and his funeral clothes fluttered in the breeze. The base of the Abswyn hell-spire stood an arrow-shot away, its glassy metal flat and gray in the daylight, its pinnacle a thousand hands above.

Nearer stood the Feather Stone, a slab of golden granite like no other in the mountains or on the plains. Long ago, the gods had carved this stone themselves. They chiseled a circle into it and, in the circle, inset a doublet of feathers in black granite, highlighted with white quartz.

Night-falcon feathers, Nyahri reminded herself, *the emblem of the goddess Sultah yw Sabi.*

The goddess once worshipped by Nyahri's mother, whose own grave stood not far beyond the Stone. Nyahri prayed then to the night-falcon goddess for some good fortune that day.

Before noon, Suhto arrived. He dismounted and sat with Nyahri on the cracked red clay. The cousins ate bread and drank cold tea, surrounded by their tribesmen's remains. Wandering a short distance, the horses grazed on dry grasses, unbothered by that place's ghosts.

"I miss your brother too," Suhto said.

Nyahri nodded. "How is Uhlo?"

"His knee, only dislocated. His nose will never be right."

"He deserved it."

"Probably." Suhto tore another piece of bread and chewed it. "We do not have to do this. We can go back."

"You withdraw your proposal?"

"Nay."

"To bed me might make you Ahtros after my father dies."

"That is not why I want you."

"You would make a good Ahtros." Nyahri tucked a strand of her hair behind her ear.

"And you an *excellent* Ahtras, as is your right."

"You know how I feel about that."

He grunted, nodded.

"Can you not love me without making me yours?" she asked. "I have loved *you* since we were children, but I do not need to *bed* you."

"I *want* you in my tent."

She stood and kicked the ground. Stones clattered and Suhto closed his eyes against the dust.

"Forget having me," she said.

"You made your challenge, according to the old laws." He attempted a smile. "If I enter the House of Hell, you said, and tell you of the Atreianii, bring back some bauble of proof, you *will* be my wife."

"Into your embrace, to accept babies and whatever else would come, but this is madness, Suhto! Do you not understand? I set this challenge because no sane man would take it."

"Did you not know me better than that, Nyahri?"

She folded her arms. "You will not turn back, seek some other woman? If you want none of ours, there are good women among the Inwnii. Consider?"

"Nay. You will not be mine?"

"Nay."

He sighed, looking into the wind. Shying from something, the horses stamped. A coyote fled across the distant brush.

"I confess," Suhto said, "I do not remember where the entrance lies."

"On the west side. I will show you."

They circumvented the burial grounds, their strides echoing between the red cliffs. Where the soil wore thin, a gray metal showed through, unmarred by seams or edges—the roof of Abswyn, the house of devils beneath the earth. The horses' hooves rang deeply on it as if on an unfathomable glass bell. Nyahri flinched, unhappy to drum on the devils' home. Yet she remembered Suhto believed nothing of living Atreianii, and she felt foolish, turning her face from him.

What if he is right? What if the House of Hell is empty, filled with nothing but the corpses of gods?

She led Suhto beyond the pillar, the beacon now dizzyingly above them. A round portal existed at the its base, half buried in sand, but no one had ever learned how to open it, so she passed it by.

Farther west, a sandstone wash exposed more gray structure. Beside it, the cousins tethered the horses on a tangle of mesquite, and on foot the two E'cwnii climbed downward. On one side stood only the vitreous metal, now rising vertically. Nyahri's heart pounded. Sweat gathered on Suhto's brow, his lips drawn tightly.

"Here it is," she said.

A smooth gray door of metallic glass—or glassy metal—sat within a thick frame. The gray deepened into a translucent black along a single rectangular slit, a window no spear or rock or hatchet could break. Nyahri knew men had tried, for generations, using all their strength and their finest weapons. None had left so much as a scratch.

Yet *something* had once scored it, a scribble of graffiti, an ancient text of the Atreianii. Nyahri understood a few of its words, taught to her by her mother: *Atreianii* and *Sultah yw Sabi* and *Absolution*.

In this place Nyahri's senses both focused and widened, a mortal fear's yawning and pitching, and she could take not one more step.

"I do not believe in the Atreianii," Suhto said, "but if you cast feathers and offer *them* something to let me pass, I will be grateful."

"I will."

His voice quavered. "Wait till sunset tomorrow, agreed?"

"Atop the hill, hidden inside the tree line. I will stay, a day or ten, however long it takes."

He stepped toward the door. "How do I open it?"

"Look into the black, give it some time, and the door opens itself. The old priestesses sometimes left offerings in the fore-chamber, though nothing ever claimed them. You will walk beyond this chamber to the second door."

"It too will open?"

"Yea, but no one has ever walked beyond it, not since the time of our great grandfathers."

He gripped his spear with both hands, bent his knees, and gazed into the dust-smeared glazing. The slab clanged, the door rolling aside. For a moment, shadow lay within, then an undiluted ghost-light filled a narrow hall. Stale air wafted from the enclosure, Suhto wrinkled his nose, and he turned back once more.

"I love you," he said.

She mustered her will. "Yea, I love you too."

Suhto entered Abswyn and the door sealed behind him. Nyahri waited outside in the cliff shade. The sun reached its zenith, and the House of Hell offered her only silence. She climbed back to the mesquite and rode to the hilltop, leading Suhto's stallion to a grassy clearing. Nyahri removed the horses' saddles and blankets. She ate a cord of smoked antelope and, by the gloam of the sunset, she watched the ghost-fires glow as they always had.

{Interim: Graffiti}

Men polluted the earth and turned the sky to poison. They raped life and vomited forth their genetic follies. As they teetered, men assumed in hubris to have ended the world.

Humankind lost the right to rule.

The Magisters wrought their progenesis, and then they created us. Together we Atreianii perfected ourselves, wresting control of the Earth. We countered human recklessness, making pets of mankind, chaining Nature as our handmaiden, we mistresses and masters of molecules and chromosomes, aided in time by the Hive. We trained the sun and said, 'Let there be light,' certain such limitlessness could never fade.

Yet Nature would not remain a whore. She turned Her dark eye against us, blackened the heavens, and refused us the light. Sultah yw Sabi was right—the Gallatin eruption marked our defeat. All life withered as we descended into the Citadels to wait through the catastrophe, until the world might live again. We bequeathed desolation to men. For that we must recreate God to give us a true Absolution.

Abswyn Entry Inscription
E'cwn burial ground and House of Hell
(Now lost)

{06}

here am I? Nyahri thought. *Waiting for Suhto? Nay, Suhto—*

She woke on soft bedding, on her back, her own blanket warming her, tucked beneath her chin. Broad-leafed oaks spread sheltering foliage over her, dappling the sky. Somewhere nearby a campfire crackled, and its smoke sweetened the air. Nyahri tried turning her head, but a pain stabbed her skull and, hissing through her teeth, she lay still again. Her thoughts flowed like syrup, the drying sap of her confused memories: her father's judgment, injured Uhlo, and vanished Suhto, then the horses' screams, the hellfire, the devilry.

Footsteps approached and the Atreiani knelt beside her. Nyahri met the devil's gaze, black eyes, evoking her every inborn reverence and her every childhood nightmare.

A dweller of the House of Hell.

"Stay still," the devil said, her voice feminine but deep, "stay silent."

At the devil's touch, Nyahri repressed a scream, not because it hurt but because Nyahri thought it *should,* like the lick of fire or the bite of a rattlesnake. Yet that touch conveyed warmth, a surety like any healer's, and a tingle slithered along Nyahri's spine.

The devil examined Nyahri's wounds with neither malice nor any marked concern, tapping Nyahri's head left and right. She moved Nyahri's shoulder and arm. She prodded tender ribs.

The devil's long hair brushed Nyahri's cheek, hanging in her eyes. Its strands distinct only at their ends, locks dark as void, they reflected no sunlight.

Like the feathers of night-falcons, Nyahri thought, *mayhap even darker.*

The Atreiani's complexion softened whatever light fell upon it, its translucence like milky quartz. A cloth suit fit her like a second skin, covering her from her neck to her wrists and ankles.

Her palm rested against Nyahri's forehead. "No fever."

"Horses?" Nyahri said, speech bringing pain.

"I said *stay silent.*" For a moment, the devil's eyes narrowed. "Your big russet is fine. The other broke two legs and I finished it."

The Atreiani sat cross-legged. She swept Nyahri's hair from behind her head, reaching beneath Nyahri's neck, testing vertebrae, no expression other than a casual focus. When she seemed satisfied, the devil fetched a dark metallic cup from beside the fire. She tipped it to Nyahri's lips, a bitter fluid pouring from it. Nyahri swallowed, warmth infused her, and her discomfort lessened. She calmed and her head cleared.

"You mustn't move awhile," the Atreiani said. "There's inflammation, and you've a concussion."

"You come from Abswyn?"

"Abswyn? You mean *Absolution?* The Citadel?"

Nyahri realized the Atreiani might use words other than those she knew, even names unfamiliar. "Yea."

"No, I don't *come* from Abswyn, as you call it. Abswyn was my jail cell, nothing more. What about you, girl, where're you from?"

"The grasslands."

"Any particular grasslands?"

"E'cwn lands, the plains of my fathers."

The devil tested Nyahri's pulse. "Strong."

Once more, Nyahri cringed at the devil's touch. The devil had stripped her of clothes and weapons, of every defense, leaving her naked beneath the blanket. Despite that, the drugs unraveled her anxiety, leaving behind only a supernatural uneasiness.

Nearby, at the banks of a murmuring brook, birds sang in the trees.

Nyahri turned her head enough to see her stallion, still wearing his saddle. She furrowed her brow. Following Nyahri's gaze, the Atreiani looked back at the horse.

"I'll not care for him," the devil said. "Never handled animals much. I thought he might've run by now, but it seems he knows his owner."

"His name is Kwlko."

"He'll do without care till you can tend him yourself."

"Why save me?" Nyahri asked.

"You saved *me*, didn't you?"

"Why have you come?"

The devil gave a noncommittal shrug. She stood, turned away, and tended other things. Nyahri glanced around timorously, guessing the danger of her injuries, though now her neck and skull pained her less.

Nearby, her shortbow hung on a branch, her arrows and spear beside it, piled with the longknife and serape and necklace. Bloodstains darkened the right leg of her breeches. In reflex she moved her aching legs, relieved she could move them at all.

She studied the terrain—a depression nestled between a cluster of low hills, ash trees, and aspens. The brook, Nyahri figured, flowed from the larger Bhar. The Atreiani's bag lay emptied, its wondrous contents strewn across the grass, bundles marked with fay symbols like those of the Abswyn door. Utensils of glassy metal sat in a row, some in recognizable shapes, some not. Among these a few tiny lights glowed, red or blue or green ghost-fires. Several dozen sharp black pins rested in dark cloth, tied together, separated from the other gear, along with cylindrical stacks of silver-gray discs.

Devil things, Nyahri thought, sensing danger in them.

The Atreiani lingered over two items. A golden-hued strip of fabric, two fingers wide and four handspans long, glittered like gemstones. The devil caressed it as if recalling a precious memory, then folded the strip into a pocket of her suit. The second item, a rod of dark metallic glass, measured longer than the Atreiani's forearm. She clipped it to her belt, and it weighed against her leg. Then she inventoried the rest of the gear, repacked it, and set the full bag near the stallion.

"How far to the road?" Nyahri asked.

"Enough to keep us hidden. You carry a bow, a spear, a knife. Are they for food or protection?"

"Both."

The Atreiani caught Nyahri's gaze, and Nyahri's pounding heartbeat quickened. Shade and light played in the devil's muted, black irises.

In the legends the Atreianii gave glorious gifts but exercised horrific power. That the devils killed, no one disputed; that human life availed them little, no one doubted.

Does she let me keep my life out of goodness, Nyahri wondered, *or for another reason?*

The Atreianii gazed into the forest. "Is there something you fear in this region? Something besides *devils* like me?"

"This is the Oudwn border. We and the Oudwnii are not so friendly with each other."

The devil sat again beside Nyhari, rolling back the blankets, prodding Nyahri's ribs and legs. The plainswoman studied her caretaker's skin, its surface like softened, living opal.

Not a wound of any kind on it, Nyahri marveled, *only the faintest scratches. Yet we suffered the same blast!*

"You called Abswyn a *House of Hell,*" the Atreiani said. "That's what you believe it was?"

"Is it not a house of devils?"

"*Was* not *is*—Abswyn is gone."

Gone? Nyahri gasped.

"It was just a Citadel," the devil said, "one among many *houses for devils.*"

"Atreianii *are* devils," Nyahri said, *"You* are a devil."

"Your stories tell you this?"

"For many ages the true gods and goddesses abandoned the world, giving their thrones to you. You ruled men. You set the moons in the sky and remade all life to your liking. And you were cruel."

"*Clinical,* I'd say, for most. Some cruel." She rested back on her heels. "I don't recall any *gods* or *goddesses.* What else do you believe, hmm?"

"When you came, you found free men and women, and you enslaved them."

"That we did. Do I seem *cruel* to you?"

"I—" Nyahri held her lip in her teeth. "My mother worshipped your kind. Her mother too. They thought you something more than *cruel,* and I learned the rituals when I was young. My mother believed there could be a truce between devils and men, that there had been such truces before."

"You evaded my question." The Atreiani unwrapped venison from Nyahri's bags and added sticks to the fire. "Eat," she said, giving Nyahri the food. "You've a name?"

"Nyahri."

"Where is it you think I come from, Nyahri?"

"Hell."

The devil let slip a smile, either in annoyance or amusement. "When I was a child, I came from this very region, a short way north. For most of my life I traveled the world, even going beyond it, far from here." She looked around her at the land. "Why and how am I here? In Abswyn the alarm sounded and I woke before the others—the *how* is simple. The *why* might be harder." The Atreiani stared into the fire, appearing then passing lonely, until she blinked and shook her head.

"Will the others awaken from Abswyn?" Nyahri asked, guessing the answer.

The Atreiani started. "Other Atreianii? As I said, Abswyn is destroyed, along with everyone in it."

"All the other devils are dead?"

"Everyone who was in stasis, everyone sleeping in Abswyn, yes."

"And Suhto?"

"The man who entered the Citadel? The one you thought to save? I told you, he died before the explosion."

"Did you kill him?"

"I didn't."

Nyahri's gut doubted.

"Consider," the Atreiani said, "why kill him and heal you? Think on that. How're you feeling?"

Unsatisfied by the answer, Nyahri stared a moment. "Less pain. Perhaps I could ride."

"Good, but not quite yet."

"I feel well enough."

"You feel *drugged*. I thought I'd find your brains on the ground, so much of your blood was on it. Rest, and we'll have more questions later. I'm lucky you lived—I need to know things, what kind of time I'm in, the state of the world."

The devil poured tea from a small vessel into a clean cup, sipping, cradling the drink in her long-fingered hands. Nyahri smelled the infusion: her own, taken from her saddlebags. She stared at the devil, hoping to bait conversation, but the Atreiani focused through the golden aspens, her cup raised every so often to her lips.

"What is your name?" Nyahri finally asked.

"Sleep, girl."

"Please?"

"Sultah yw Sabi et—" the devil said, stopping on some uncomfortable word. "My name is Sultah yw Sabi."

Nyahri lowered her gaze. "I *know* your name."

"Unsurprising, I suppose. There must still be *some* records of me in your world, even if only tales. Interesting." Sultah yw Sabi licked her teeth, a peculiar gesture, rounding canines which at a glance seemed too many and too large. "Now, we won't speak again until you rest, Nyahri, *so go back to sleep.*"

The Atreiani walked the camp perimeter, checking vantages. Nyahri sighed, a girlish expression she once used to annoy her parents into speaking, but the devil gave her no notice. At last, with the leaf-filtered sunlight on her face, the E'cwni closed her eyes, the drug-warmth soon overwhelming her.

WHEN NYAHRI STIRRED AGAIN, night reigned and the White River glittered across the sky. The campfire danced in a soft breeze. Nyahri ventured to turn her head, and a dull ache lumbered from her skull to her toes. Behind her neck and at her side, her skin itched.

The Atreiani sat against a nearby log, hands in her lap, staring into the fire. Save for some hollowness in her cheeks, she appeared stronger even than she had that afternoon.

Was it this afternoon? Nyahri wondered. *How long have I slept?*

Sultah yw Sabi looked at her and Nyahri froze.

Gods, she is *as a viper, the moment before it strikes.*

Then the devil blinked, breaking the impression. "How do you feel?" she asked.

"Better," Nyahri said.

"Hungry, thirsty?" Yw Sabi retrieved meat and flatbread, as well as unfamiliar round wafers. Nyahri flinched from these.

"What's the matter?"

"Tainted food," Nyahri said, glancing at the wafers.

"Tainted?" Yw Sabi turned one in her fingers, sniffing it. "It's perfectly preserved."

"It is devil's food."

Yw Sabi rolled her eyes. "Eat it."

Nyahri took it reluctantly.

The Atreiani scoffed. "Eat! Before I lose my temper." She leaned forward. "First, girl, I'm not a *devil* and you'll stop referring to me or anything about me that way. Second, when *I* was young, devil's food was a *good* thing. Spongy chocolate. Delicious. This is neither devil's food *nor* spongy chocolate, but it'll give you some strength."

Devils can deceive with such talk, Nyahri thought, *trying to convince others they are not devils.*

She nibbled the flavorless ration, knowing nothing of *spongy chocolate.* The venison and flatbread sang better on her tongue.

"Try to sit up," yw Sabi said.

Nyahri did. A throbbing flared behind her eyes.

The Atreiani brought water, offering it in a translucent bowl which felt like the smoothest iron, looked like lightning glass, and weighed as much as a child's laughter.

"Water's from the stream," the devil said, "but I ran it through a filter."

Filter, a word which did not quite translate, which sounded to Nyahri something like *withholding.* She wrinkled her nose, scenting the water before sipping.

"I kept you under while working on you," yw Sabi said, though Nyahri didn't understand this either. "You might feel groggy. Let's continue our questions and answers, hmm?"

"Yea, Atreiani, I *do* feel stronger. I am much more myself tonight."

"Quaint way of putting it. You ever encounter another like me?"

"An Atreiani? Nay."

"Heard of one near or far?"

"In dreams and visions."

"Never in the flesh, never walking the world?"

Evening birds flittered on the tree limbs, their chatter an angry din of diminutive feathered creatures fighting for food and mates and territory. An old, old dance. Then the birds scattered to other boughs.

Nyahri shook her head at the Atreiani's question.

Yw Sabi continued, "You've family, a people. Tell me of them."

Nyahri hesitated. "Yea, Atreiani."

"You know their number?"

"To the person, one hundred eighty-seven." Nyahri glanced away. "Nay, one hundred *eighty-six.*"

"A tribe," yw Sabi said. "Large compared to others?"

"There are larger. Thousands of E'cwnii live on the southern plains, in many tribes, all part of the Great Tribe. Thousands more of our Inwn cousins live in the north."

"Thousands live?" Yw Sabi caught a falling leaf, turned it, and studied its pinnate ridges. A momentary smile touched her lips. "Amazing anything survived at all. All this life, as beautiful as I remember. You too, Nyahri, are wondrously beautiful. I thought none of you would still exist when I finally woke."

Wondrously beautiful? Nyahri thought. *She speaks like I am a sunset or a good horse.*

"None of us?"

"Humans," said the Atreiani.

Nyahri finished the water. Nearby, Kwlko snorted, shaking his mane.

His saddle yet on him! The plainswoman startled. *Far too long now.*

She looked back to the Atreiani, who brought Nyahri's clothes from where they hung on a willow branch.

"I washed these," yw Sabi said. "They're stained, but clean. Tend the horse."

Nyahri climbed from the blankets, stretched, and examined her naked legs.

"Atreiani, how long have we been here?"

"This is our third night."

I slept days, and how I have healed! Nyahri made a sign against evil. *Atreian witchery.*

Deep cuts had opened Nyahri's leg, that much remained clear, but now only faded reddish scars crossed her skin. Hard as chitin, a film clung to the injuries on her side and neck, these too almost mended. As Nyahri examined herself, the Atreiani's gaze lingered on her.

The way Suhto looks at me, Nyahri thought. *The way he used to look at me. The way the other men sometimes look at me.*

Nyahri slipped her serape over her shoulders and placed her sandals on her feet. She walked, with only the slightest limp, to Kwlko. The horse nuzzled her and kicked, a spry and impatient shake. Nyahri loosened his girth before pulling the saddle and blanket free. Mats tangled his hair. She prodded him, checking ribs, face, legs, and hooves.

A few nicks. No real harm.

She set a brush to his hide, stroke after stroke. The stallion raised his head joyfully while Nyahri peered over his back. At the other side of the camp, the devil washed the cups, packed them, and walked to the camp edge, folding her arms and stargazing.

I could jump to Kwlko's back this instant, Nyahri considered, *and flee the devil, leave her behind.*

Little would stop her.

But why? Have I not worshipped the Atreian spirits? Here stands an Atreiani, an ancient myth in skin and bone! Have I not denied my people, turned aside motherhood and tent wivery to outdo my mother, to outdo every Ahtras who ever lived? Ay! Would I learn whether this devil is worthy of worship? Whether she is a goddess or a horror? Whether she is a friend or enemy? Whether her heart beats?

An obvious answer.

Nyahri sighed and, after she completed her work, she returned to sit by the fire.

{07}

Nyahri propped her feet against the stones of the fire pit, rubbing her hands together. The moment for fleeing came and went, and it would not come again.

"Do you know of other Citadels?" yw Sabi asked, still standing at the camp edge.

"Yea."

The Atreiani gained her bearings, pointing northwest, deep into the forested mountains. "That way there would be one. You know it?"

"I have never been to it. Too far into Oudwn lands."

"What do you call it?"

"Swyn Templr."

"Swyn? Its proper name was *Sojourn Temple*. Do you know of the Templarii?"

Nyahri nodded. "The keepers of records. They live among the Oudwnii. We call them *flesh walkers*." She curled her lip, recalling stories. "Thank the gods for it, it is said there are not many of them."

"There wouldn't be. Flesh walkers? Something to that."

"It is said they keep the Oudwn sacred grounds, mind their libraries, teach their chieftains sons. The flesh walkers are holy demons, nay?"

"Holy? Demons? Neither." Yw Sabi touched her forefinger to her chin, a thoughtful gesture. "Tell me the trouble between your people and these *Oudwnii?*"

"We have fought for many reasons. Longer than I remember, since before I was even born."

The Atreiani's dark eyes reflected the firelight. "What do the Oudwnii think of the Atreianii? You have some reverence for me. Would they?"

"Mayhap."

"Tell me more of them."

"Most are no more than hill farmers, but their archers are deadly. When my father was a boy, the Oudwnii opened the mountain roads through their lands. They traded with us. Now they do not."

"While they traded, did your father travel those roads?"

"Long seasons ago. The feud is old and my father is aged, but he remembers more than I can tell you." Nyahri regretted these words at once, realizing the Atreiani's intent.

"Go on."

"Nay, I would not—"

"*Go on.*"

"Many years ago," Nyahri said, "an Oudwn chieftain claimed Abswyn, where we have buried our dead for many generations, and we fought the Oudwnii for it. That is how the worst killing started."

"Who is their chieftain now?" Yw Sabi paced slowly, her arms crossed.

"Shwn Jhon Oudwn," said Nyahri. "When my father first knew him, they were both boys. When my father was older, he led a war party and burned the Oudwn lodge in Cohltos. Some of Shwn Jhon's family died."

"If these Oudwnii stumbled upon us tonight, they might choose violence?"

"They might."

"We *will* meet them, tonight or soon. Three days ago, Abswyn exploded, its annihilation visible for a hundred kilometers in every direction. You comprehend this?"

Nyahri shook her head.

"A *long* distance." Yw Sabi plucked a swollen water skin from a tree branch and emptied it on the fire, which guttered, hissed, and died. The camp darkened. "Men clearly still care for the Citadels, even if they don't remember why. These Oudwnii will come. Would they attack for the sake of it?"

"Who knows what any man will do?" Nyahri fought a shiver. The dark shown only the Atreiani's faintest outline, her hair blacker than the night. "Forgive me, yw Sabi, but are you *afraid* of the Oudwnii?"

"Last night, a firelight appeared upon the mountain ridges to the west." The Atreianii fetched another container of water and doused the last of the embers. "A encampment, I'm certain."

"Oudwnii."

"To answer your question, I'm not afraid, girl, but *cautious*. I've slept long and woken to a changed world, a world I never expected. I *must* go to Sojourn, but first I'd learn more about these Oudwnii and their *flesh walkers*. The Templarii were wretched cockroaches when I knew them—not *my* creations— and I bet they're cockroaches still."

Not her creations, Nyahri thought, having heard in ritual of Sultah yw Sabi's more horrifying *creations.*

Cricket chirps grew louder. Somewhere an owl called.

Nyahri clenched her jaw. "You wish to go to my father."

"I do." Yw Sabi's lips curled upward, an expression visible in the dark only for the paleness of her skin.

"I fear, goddess, you might harm my people."

"So it's *goddess* now? A promotion from *devil*." The Atreiani sighed.

"Promise me, Atreiani, you will not hurt my loved ones, my cousins, nor anyone in my tribe."

"Promise?" The devil's voice rasped. "I promise no one anything. They're not far from here, are they?" The Atreiani stepped close, crouching on her heels, touching one of the feathers braided into Nyahri's hair. "What do you call this bird?"

"A night-falcon."

"We called it *Aquila umbra*."

"The stories say *you* created the night-falcons."

The Atreiani nodded. "An engineered fancy." She studied Nyahri. "I surmise something of you, E'cwni, with night-falcon feathers in your hair and barely disguised worship in your eyes."

I have worshipped mere ghosts, Nyahri thought, *and here now, she is more flesh than spirit.*

The Atreiani's skin smelled fresh, not merely bathed in the creek, but scented with soap or oil, something rare, something E'cwnii seldom encountered.

"Is worship what you wish?" Nyahri asked.

"No," yw Sabi said.

"What *do* you wish?"

"I told you—to go to Sojourn." The Atreiani pulled the feather from Nyahri's hair. "The night-falcon was my demesne's crest, and I'm guessing this is one land where you might encounter such a crest from time to time. You've seen it before?"

Crest faltered in translation, but Nyahri understood the concept of any symbol. "Everyone in our tribe has, in the old places. It appears cut in stone, scattered throughout the plain. We wear the feathers to honor the Atreianii."

"Many Atreianii *hated* my emblem before the end, *despised* the umbra feather."

"I do not understand." Nyahri shook her head.

Yw Sabi shrugged. "I tested you when I sent you, a horsewoman, to your horse. I would've let you go."

Nyahri swallowed, her heart pounding at yw Sabi's every movement, gestures sometimes smooth and slow, other times quick, the movements of a snake or bird. Thinking of cats, Nyahri remembered how lionesses might sleep, languid and lazy, so easeful until an antelope wandered too close to them.

"I felt your friendship for Suhto," yw Sabi said. "You would've died to save him. I suspect such devotion's not *your* character alone, but your people's, hmm?"

"In my heart I still fear you a devil."

"You think I might kill your family, everyone you love?"

"Did the Atreianii not do such things once?"

Yw Sabi nodded. "Will your people try to kill me?"

"Nay."

"I must relearn the world, who to trust. You're smart. Think it through."

"Think what through?"

"We've spent some hours together now. I've tended you, looked after you these days. You watched me, as well." Yw Sabi folded her arms.

Nyahri inclined her head. "You will not harm them."

"Not likely."

"What *will* you do?"

"Whatever I please."

Would my mother have trusted her? Nyahri sighed. *Mother would have prostrated herself—*

"All right," said the plainswoman, "I will take you."

The devil gathered her possessions. "Come. Those Oudwnii make me think we should leave before sunup. *You're* a known factor—*they* are not. You feel well enough?"

"I do."

"Take your weapons. Harness my bag, as well. Can your horse carry us both?" yw Sabi asked, nodding toward Kwlko.

"At a walk."

"Let's be on our way."

Nyahri rolled her blankets and tied them, moving slowly, her body still aching. She adjusted Kwlko's tack, smoothed his padding, and set the stirrups forward. Last, Nyahri strapped the Atreiani's black bag to the cantle, hesitant to touch the fabric, a cloth alien to her. Her knife regained its place at her belt, and her bow and quiver hung at easy reach. She kept her spear in hand. As Nyahri eased into the saddle, yw Sabi stood beside the stallion, running her pale fingertips over his hide.

The Atreiani's skin reflected the barest moonslight, even to her white lips. Her long limbs and fingers reminded Nyahri of an antelope; her corded muscles, of a mountain lion; her neck, of a bird; and always, the serpent.

Something in her walk, Nyahri thought, *not quite human. Her mouth, the frame of her face.*

"You are not tired?" Nyahri asked.

"No."

"How is that possible?"

"I'm supposed to be a goddess, right?"

"I have not seen you so much as close your eyes."

"I slept long enough in Abswyn."

"How long, yw Sabi?"

"Too long, for certain, but I don't know the answer to that question. I'll seek it at Sojourn."

NYAHRI HELPED THE ATREIANI climb behind her, for the devil showed no skill with the horse. They rode from camp at an easy gait, beginning the trek to the plains, stopping often to listen and look.

They paralleled the smaller stream, back to the river, following it downward. Once Nyahri discovered a clear path east, she increased their pace, trusting the stallion's keener senses to keep the way in the predawn darkness. The Atreiani studied the woodland by starlight.

The witch-scepter, hanging from yw Sabi's belt, brushed Nyahri's leg. The plainswoman pushed the thought of its unnaturalness from her mind, its black-magic taint, along with the wicked possibility she rode with a devil at her back.

Soon, the sunrise cast a golden light on the lowest foothills and rocky boar-backs. Dew glistened on the trees, and birds burst into chorus. The undergrowth thinned and, on the rises, the prairies appeared.

As they cantered over open ground, the Atreiani tapped Nyahri's shoulder. "On the ridge to our left, do you see them?"

Two hooded men stood in full view, too far for a bowshot. Deerskin cloaks wrapped them, and they leaned on longbows, watching awhile before melting into the forest.

"Oudwn archers," Nyahri said. "Others will know soon."

"Couldn't be avoided," said yw Sabi.

They rode on and, after some hours, yw Sabi took a thirsty drink from the water skin. She licked her lips as if relieved, as if the water meant as much to her as to any mortal.

Nyahri felt some relief. *More proof of her flesh.*

Having paused, they took an opportunity to stretch and eat. The Atreiani helped herself to Nyahri's flatbread and roasted grains. Once more, she tipped back her head to drink.

Nyahri glimpsed the Atreiani's teeth more clearly: four canines above and two below, long and sharp. Yw Sabi wiped her mouth with the back of her sleeve, handing the skin back to Nyahri.

Fangs, Nyahri thought, *at least six.*

By the creekside, Nyahri refilled the skins, glancing over her shoulder. Yw Sabi waited at the widening path, facing away. Several times, the Atreiani turned her back on Nyahri, easy prey for a knife or spear—

Nay, she is no easy prey. She reminds me also, she *is the predator. It is a test as much as sending me to my horse was a test. She feared death at Abswyn, but I doubt she much fears me.*

They continued downslope and, by afternoon, the pines blended with cottonwoods. Golden grasses mixed with the greenery. The scent of a cooking fire reached them, Nyahri reined the stallion, and a breeze carried distant voices to her ears.

"My people," she said.

Kwlko stamped and turned, anxious to reach the horses and humans and dogs he knew. Yw Sabi's lips brushed Nyahri's ear, an over-familiar gesture, disconcerting and warm. Her unnatural hair tickled Nyahri's cheek.

"Let us go to them, girl. I will *not* harm your family."

At those words, Nyahri set heel to the stallion's flanks. They rounded a bend and the land opened. The camp lay before them, the E'cwnii watching them come.

{08}

Cries arose, many voices calling her name, "Nyahri!"
Women and young men rushed forward but
stopped short before the Atreiani. They blanched at her,
their arms slack. The hunters, those few Nyahri counted,
put their hands to their weapons—a hatchet loosed from its
sling, a spear raised—and they gawked.

The mottled dog ran beside Kwlko, barking and tail wag-
ging, playful but careful of the horse's legs. Children, less fearful
than the adults, sprinted past their horrified parents.

As the children approached, Nyahri tensed. To bring
the Atreiani to her cousins, their children, and their infants.

Have I made a mistake? she wondered. *Did I have a choice?*

Nyahri kept her hand on her longknife.

"What was the boom?" the children asked. "The bright
light in the west?"

"Has Suhto come back?" A girl looked past Kwlko,
awaiting a rider who would never arrive.

A boy asked the Atreiani, "Who are *you? What* are you?"

Yw Sabi leaned down to muss his hair. Her closed-lipped
smile vanished as quickly as it appeared, a brew of sadness
and joy.

She nodded to him. "A friend to you, child."

As she entered the camp, Nyahri's foreboding grew. Defensible shelters encircled a central fire, its smoke rising across
the river into darker clouds which rolled from the west. The
horses stood near the water's edge. Prepared saddles hung
on stands, bags packed and sheltered by half-folded woolen
blankets. Too few adult men appeared with too many skirted

women, not huntresses but tent wives, and too many babes and young boys.

Where have all the hunters gone?

A few elders prostrated themselves before the Atreiani. After a moment, the younger men and women dropped to their knees, touching their foreheads to the earth, extending their hands along the ground.

Leaning on his spear, a thick-boned, tan-skinned young man stepped forward. Braver or more foolish than the rest, a hunter still in his trials, he was Nyahri's second cousin.

This is who remains to speak for the E'cwnii?

"Greetings, Muuteh," Nyahri said.

He looked beyond Nyahri to the Atreiani, and he bowed his head to her, though he kept to his feet. One woman sobbed. The children, so spirited before, echoed their parents' dread, and some ran crying to their mothers' arms.

"You are not the leader here," yw Sabi said to Muuteh.

"Nay," he said, "but I have the watch."

A few bolder women crowded the horse, touching yw Sabi's clothes. Nyahri's father emerged from his tent, wearing only his breeches, standing with his arms folded, his white hair aflutter.

He raised his hand. "Welcome, Atreiani," he said. "Do you wish for the Ahtros of this people to prostrate himself?"

"I'd rather *speak* with you," the devil replied.

He beckoned, disappearing again inside.

Yw Sabi dismounted clumsily, turning on her heel instead of her toes, balancing by strength alone. Nyahri swung her right leg over the horn and slid from the saddle, handing the reins to Muuteh.

"Your father has sat and smoked and sang to spirits," he said to Nyahri, "and done little else since you went. He sang so hard for your return—" Muuteh glanced at the Atreiani. "—a spirit came back with you."

Yw Sabi walked toward the tent, and Nyahri hurried after her. When they reached the tent door, yw Sabi turned, her gaze stern.

"Stay out here."

"But I—"

Yw Sabi's eyes narrowed to razor lines. *Stay out here.*

"Why?"

"Because I *tell* you to."

"You cannot *tell* me—" Nyahri began, her voice trailing. The Atreiani's countenance told her otherwise, that the goddess could command anything she wished. Nyahri stepped back. "Do not harm my father."

The Atreiani's expression sharpened before she swept the door aside. Nyahri glimpsed her father, seated by his sacred fire, adding incense to the coals.

Nyahri retreated, stung by the rejection. She tromped back to Muuteh, who stared at the Ahtros's tent, and the tribe gathered to hang upon every moment which followed. Nyahri stood beside her cousin, her attention also transfixed.

"What is happening?" Muuteh asked.

"In the world? Or here in our camp, now?"

He shrugged.

"I do not know," she said.

"It has been almost a week since you departed. Seems much has happened in so few days."

"Yea. The other hunters, where are they?"

"To Abswyn, looking for you and for Suhto. They play hide and seek with the Oudwnii, who infest the plains like termites since the western night lit with hellfire."

"Have the Oudwnii come here?"

"They test our defenses, and three came to speak with the Ahtros."

"And?"

"We told them we knew no more than they."

"Did you tell them we went to the House of Hell?"

"We played dumb," Muuteh said, "telling them only that you had a simple rite to perform. You would be a priestess, nay? They need know nothing of our affairs."

"They believed you?"

"Your father thinks so. I am less sure."

"They will believe no longer—their scouts spotted us this morning and must have seen the Atreiani for what she was, even from a distance."

After a long while, the tent door opened, the flap held aside by the Atreiani's pale hand. She waved Nyahri toward her.

"Brush Kwlko," Nyahri said to Muuteh. "Touch *nothing* else."

Muuteh scowled at yw Sabi's bag, at its unnatural fabric, and he turned his nose up at it. "You need not tell me to stay away from witchcraft. You should heed your own advice."

Nyahri entered her father's tent. The central fire's white-hot embers nestled in a hollow, a cooking tripod set over them, sage smoking in a censer. Nyahri took her place on the floor rugs with her legs crossed, one knee against her father's, the other near the Atreiani's, forming a triangle between them.

"Pour us tea," her father said.

Nyahri passed the cups, and the Ahtros lit his pipe, smoke wreathing his brow. Politely, patiently, they drank their teacups dry before speaking.

Her father broke the silence, "The Atreian Sultah yw Sabi and I have talked. I have learned a little. She has learned a little."

Nyahri listened.

"Suhto is not with us," the Ahtros said, "and he is not with you. Our scouts out-rode you twice over, bringing news of a deep void where once Abswyn watched over our E'cwn palanquins, and everything in the Red Valley is destroyed. Oudwnii ask us questions for which we have no answers. They test us and, soon enough, testing may become fighting."

"Yea, father."

"Proud Suhto is dead, or so the goddess tells me. She tells me it is neither your fault nor hers, but only the way of things—men cannot enter the Houses of Hell. If our legends said otherwise, well, Suhto was not a legend."

"Suhto *is* dead, father. I am sorry."

"Who are you sorry to? Yourself, I think. Suhto was one man, and now you have the rest of your tribe to think on. These have been tidings of ruin and rebirth, nay, for all of us? The Oudwnii accuse us of witchcraft at Abswyn." His sleepless, bloodshot eyes settled on the Atreiani. "*Have* we done some witchcraft for which the Oudwnii might be angry?"

The devil refilled the cups and passed the first to him. "One thing of which I am quite certain, Ahtros, is no E'cwni has committed any witchcraft. You've never seen an Atreiani before me, have you?"

"Not in my years. None have. You are creatures of dream."

"Do I look as you dreamed?"

"Less of nightmares," he said matter-of-factly, "but you are no woman."

She laughed dryly, taking another sip. "Depends how you define *woman*."

"Are you evil, Atreiani? Do we need fear you? Beg our lives?"

"Everyone should fear me." She gave again her uncommitted shrug. "That's the truth."

The Ahtros filled the pot with water and mint, the odor sharp as he crumbled the leaves. He set the pot to boil.

"What do you remember of Swyn Templr?" yw Sabi asked, using the E'cwn name.

"I was there twice—once as a small boy, once in war. Its pillar is as Abswyn's was, but taller. Its ghost-fires lit a wide valley between peaks which touched the sky. There stood a stone house, a fortress as I never saw elsewhere, with a village and a forked river below many orchards."

"What was the fortress called?" asked the Atreiani

"S'Eret, the Oudwnii name it."

"From some older word." Yw Sabi narrowed her eyes. "Maybe *turrets?* What about the Templarii, details you remember?"

"Not well, but the Oudwnii revere them."

"You call them *flesh walkers.*"

"Demons who walk in the skin of men." He nodded. "Demons or not, when I was a child they traded fairly with my father and treated me well. They wrote the ancient letters on fragile leafs, and it seemed their main occupation—filling their house of books with words."

"They wrote in *books?*" The Atreiani creased her brow at this. "What is that settlement called, where the flesh walkers dwelt?"

"Cohltos," he said. "Oudwn families work its valley from one edge to the other, their huts touched each day by the shadow of the pillar. We used to trade bison for bear hides, fat and pelts, otter and beaver for silver and coral and shells from the waters over the mountains. The Oudwnii bartered with people still farther west."

"Tell me about Shwn Jhon Oudwn?" she said, sitting motionless as a sayi snake, a sudden and unnatural stillness.

Human or not, Nyahri reminded herself, *she is still flesh.*

"Ay," the Ahtros said, "*he* will hold grudges till he dies."

"Because you killed his family?" yw Sabi asked.

"It is true." The Ahtros frowned as if tasting something bitter. "Since his father failed to take Abswyn, since our raids on Cohltos, there have been starvation-times when the Oudwnii and E'cwnii warred outright for game trails, or when our arroyos ran dry and only the Oudwnii had any water. We would fight them for it and there has been plenty of death. Other seasons our hunting herds gave us just enough to eat while the Oudwnii starved. During the worst winters, they murdered aplenty for food."

"When was the last time?"

"Nyahri was a child, last time it grew serious, but these skirmishes have happened so many times before." The Ahtros hesitated, weighted by memory. "My raiders burnt a portion of the flesh walkers' house of books, torched many Oudwn houses. Shwn Jhon was a young man, and his wives and most of his children died, though I hear he has long since had new wives in an old hall in the lower valleys. For nine years we and our cousin tribes warred with the Oudwnii for Abswyn."

"That was a long time ago?"

Long for a human, Nyahri thought, *not for her.*

"Twenty-six years," the Ahtros said. "What is that time compared to wives and children killed in flames? During those years, you resided in your house in the ground, yea? You resided there long before."

"*Resided* isn't the word." Yw Sabi tried another term, but neither the Ahtros nor Nyahri caught it, something outside their experience and language. Trying other phrases, the Atreiani said, *"Tied up, bound, kept.* In any case, I slept."

"How long did you sleep?"

"I don't know." Her jaw tightened, her eyes narrowing. "If even your grandfather had no memory of woken Atreianii, if it was your father who retook Abswyn from the Oudwnii, if it was your ancestors' remains piled up around it, so many thousands of bones? A few hundred years. Longer than I should've."

"Why do you awaken now?"

"Again, I don't know."

"Suhto awakened you, put all this into motion?"

"That would be impossible." Yw Sabi shook her head, considering for a moment. "I'm going to Swyn Templr. As much as I dislike the *flesh walkers,* the Templarii might have answers for my questions."

He nodded. "As for your journey to Swyn Templr, you are faith made real to E'cwnii *and* Oudwnii. My guess, you will find welcome in the woodsmen's lands, but take care, and if there is some word you can give the Oudwnii to keep them from warring with us, I beg you do."

The Ahtros forced a polite cough and Nyahri read his pain in it.

"You leave tonight?" he asked.

"I've need to hurry," yw Sabi said, "but not so quickly as that. For the next night or two, I'll want a tent."

"You are our guest."

Silent moments passed. The Ahtros sipped his tea, easing his lungs.

He added, "Would you tell us what the world was like when you went to sleep?"

Yw Sabi sighed, moving her body at last, leaning on her knees. "Darkness and shadow and immolation and terror," she said, "desperation and disagreement and madness."

"Was your world ever anything better than mad?"

"There existed," she said, "between two great eras of horror, a time of unparalleled beauty and achievement. Nothing I wish to speak about."

The fire crackled, the Ahtros adding a pinch of sage to it. He relit his pipe, its smoke thickening.

"If that is all," he said, "then I ask more to our purpose. What danger are we E'cwnii in, now you are walking the world? What should we do?"

"My advice? Move your people east, as far from here as you can go. My business at Sojourn Temple is dire."

The Ahtros's eyes widened, his words hastening. "You mean to do evil?"

"Evil is already there."

He nodded, an acknowledgment. "Did my daughter tell you the story of Suhto?"

Yw Sabi looked at Nyahri.

"She should recount it," the Ahtros said. "Nyahri intended no evil for him, I am sure, but nonetheless he is dead."

Nyahri flinched, bowing her head.

"I will do what I will do," the Atreiani said, "because it is my *will* to do so, evil or not. In the end that is all there is to it."

E'cwn maidens raised a decorated tent for the Atreiani and they brought the best morsels for her to eat. They sang sacred songs, and Nyahri almost joined them. The women also left long-legged breeches for the devil, along with a wide serape adorned with malachite-set silver, new boots, and fleeces. The Atreiani packed these. Standing among the horses, keeping her distance, Nyahri observed all who came and went from the Atreiani's shelter. Yw Sabi nodded her thanks to every E'cwni who offered gifts.

The afternoon waned and cooled, clouds thickening and darkening on every horizon. A storm approached.

Cold rain, Nyahri thought, *mayhap wet snow.*

After she brushed the stallion, Nyahri retreated to her own tent, pausing inside the door, faced with her sister. Cirje's eyes glistened and flashed, and Nyahri braced for a tirade, for insults and accusations. Instead, Cirje embraced her, gripping her so hard Nyahri's tender ribs pained her. Nyahri offered no complaint, stroking her sister's hair.

"I am sorry, Cirje."

The girl shook her head, wiping her nose. "I thought you dead."

"Only injured."

Cirje pulled away, her expression limned with concern. Nyahri showed her the gashes at her side and neck, where the Atreiani's unnatural film still clung like egg yolk. Cirje touched it but withdrew as if from a flame, filled with witchcraft-fear.

"There must have been so much blood," she said. "It is all over your breeches. You are healed so speedily!"

"Medicine-craft, the Atreiani's—"

"Yea, *her.*" Cirje shuddered. "You entered Abswyn?"

"Nay."

"Suhto?"

"Yea."

"Did *she* kill him?"

"She would not answer me straight. She likes half answers."

"She *is* a devil."

Nyahri shrugged. "She is Sultah yw Sabi. She is an Atreiani."

"*The* Sultah yw Sabi? I cannot believe that." The priestesses' rituals mentioned the *Mistress Sultah yw Sabi* only once, an Atreiani feared by her own kind. "What is she like?"

"Dangerous, but she showed care enough for me."

"What happened at Abswyn?"

"Only yw Sabi knows, but she has not told the whole tale."

"I am glad you are back, Nyahri."

Raindrops pattered the tent. The sisters lay beside each other, Nyahri stroking her sister's hair. She blew out the lamp, stretched, and closed her eyes. Sleep eluded her, though Cirje's breaths soon deepened.

When at last the rain ceased, the odors of mud and wet grass permeated the air. Horses snorted and someone added logs to the fire.

Too anxious to remain still, Nyahri donned a cloak and climbed from the tent. A frigid evening breeze wrapped her, raising gooseflesh on her arms, and she warmed her hands at the campfire. The firmament cleared, its relentless stars twinkling.

Lwn and Stashwn and Trwl hovered as crescents in quarter light, and upon a hillside they silhouetted a lone figure, too tall and lean to be E'cwn. The Atreiani shouted at the sky, repeating a name from the ancient tongue:

"*Borea!*"

Nyahri shivered, setting out through soaked grasses to the Atreiani, who watched her come.

"What were you calling to, goddess?"

"Difficult to explain," yw Sabi said. "Something you might think of as another god."

"Does it answer you?"

The Atreiani clenched her jaw. "Much to my frustration, she doesn't say a damn thing."

"You expect her to?"

"Yet another change in the world. Borea won't answer."

Nyahri looked into the heavens. "I was taught you put the moons on their paths."

"We only put the lesser two up there. Ehl-Seven, which we called Vo Misa after its designer, or simply the *Station*. Then the smallest, Ehl-Thirteen, which I think you named *Trwl*." The Atreiani glanced at Nyahri. "Interesting to listen to your syntax, the words your people use. Your language is quite lovely."

"You did not speak our language before?"

"Cobbling it as I go—a skill, and good algorithms."

Not knowing what to say about such a remarkable *skill,* or a new word like *algorithms,* Nyahri asked again about the moons. "Lwn was there before your kind came into the world?"

Yw Sabi nodded. "We Atreianii covered it with the pattern of lights you call the ghost-fires, but it was there from the world's beginning."

"Those lights are the Web, the house of the Great Spider."

"Interesting story."

"It is no *story,*" Nyahri said, then remembered with whom she argued. The cold numbed her thoughts.

"There's no spider there," yw Sabi said, "unless some of the ordinary variety stowed upon a shuttle. No great spider web. The *web* you see is the network of industry." The Atreiani spoke more to herself than to Nyahri. "The Moon—near thirty-five hundred kilometers across, marked by our handiwork to *this* age—and its little sisters, our children, the larger a *mere* five hundred clicks wide and completely artificial. Either someone up there is alive, which I very much doubt, or the Stations' automatic systems are still doing their job. So far I've counted four OpNet satellites too, tiny ones, orbiting up there, but I'm sure they're many more whose trajectories are still strong. You must have names for those?"

Nyahri knew, at least, the name of the fast-moving star to which yw Sabi pointed. "We call that one the *Little Rabbit*."

"*Little Rabbit* is a self-maintaining communications satellite. We launched those models in twenty-eighty." She smiled, someone pleased with her craftwork. "It's part of a network with which I'll need to communicate. Borea won't answer me, though, and I've no satcom. What am I to do?"

"I do not understand *anything* you are telling me, goddess."

"I suppose you wouldn't." She looked briefly at Nyahri, a flash of annoyance, and then toward the darkened edges of the hills. "This world's climate has changed. It had warmed before, but this region had still been short grasses and pines. Now, bounty! Ferns and fruit trees and pampas, some of it engineered for a dynamic biosphere. Pumice smothered everything here, massive earthquakes, all altered the mountain line." She pointed toward the night-hidden hills, sweeping her hand to encompass the horizon. "It wouldn't surprise me if the atmospheric carbon dioxide has dropped—"

So many unfamiliar words. *Biosphere, atmospheric, dioxide.*

"Atreiani?" Nyahri's teeth chattered, fresh rain soaking her cloak, weighting her hair.

"You know what a volcano is?"

"A peak of fire."

"You've seen one?"

"Nay, only heard of them."

"Imagine volcanoes so great their ash blots the sunlight for years. We Atreianii existed to fix a broken world. Little good it did." Yw Sabi laughed.

A bitter laughter, Nyahri thought.

Yw Sabi returned to stargazing. Nyahri sidled closer, basking in the Atreiani's warmth, but her shivering grew stronger.

"The Gallatin had risen for over two centuries," yw Sabi said, again talking to herself, "its pressure compounded by our own machinations. We thought we tamed it, if only just enough. We thought we had control, and perhaps we did—"

"Mistress—"

Yw Sabi turned, drawing a sharp breath through her teeth. "You *mistress* me! Not a word I guessed your people knew."

"We use it only to speak of the Atreianii. It was what some men called you?"

"These are mysteries to you, aren't they? The word *mistress* has special meaning between an Atreiani and a human, and you're using it incorrectly."

"Teach me to use it correctly?"

"Willful girl." The Atreiani shook her head. "You've no idea how ignorant you are, how foolish that is to ask."

"Then teach me why it is foolish."

"How much would you learn?" Yw Sabi folded her arms, regarding Nyahri.

Danger in the invitation, but promises too.

For a moment Nyahri ceased shivering, not daring to breathe. She had learned the histories with her father, hunting and warfare with her brother. Nyahri learned of the Atreianii on her mother's lap, her mother who made herself the devils' deepest devotee, who swore that in her own childhood the gods told her to worship the Atreianii above all others, to bind herself to them.

What learning I did at my mother's side! Nyahri thought. *But what questions she had!*

A pale scar crossed the back of Nyahri's arm, a cut reminding her of her mother's death, the day she'd no longer hear her mother's stories, learn what her mother had to teach. A cut self-afflicted.

My uncle's death followed, no great loss. Then my brother's, too great a loss. Now Suhto's! I never wished for the tribe to depend on me. Mother was their healer. Brother was to be their leader. Gods how I miss them! Gods how I could exceed them!

"I would learn everything," Nyahri blurted.

"What if I told you I killed Suhto?"

The hairs tingled along Nyahri's arms, at the back of her neck. Her stomach dropped and she reached for her longknife, only to realize she had left it in the tent.

"I didn't kill him with my own hands," yw Sabi added, "not with any weapon I wielded."

Nyahri stayed light on her toes. "What do you mean?"

"The world I helped create—that's what killed him."

Nyahri clenched her teeth, in part to show her anger, but mostly because the cold seeped the last of her warmth. "No riddles—tell me."

"You want to learn? See more with your own eyes?"

Nyahri nodded.

"Hmm. Tell me," the Atreiani said, turning back to the stars, "who among your people will guide me to Sojourn?"

"To Swyn Templr?" Nyahri's teeth chattered as she spit the words. "No good men are left. Who remains? Muuteh?"

"I'd like *none* of your men—I was rather thinking *you*."

Again Nyahri nodded.

"And perhaps," yw Sabi said, "you'll discover a thing or two along the way."

The Atreiani set her hand at Nyahri's cheek. The gentle motion came without warning, and Nyahri flinched, her skin warming where the goddess touched her.

Yw Sabi's brow lowered, a sign of concern. "You're freezing."

"I am fine," Nyahri said, shivering to her core. "If it is warm enough for you, it is warm enough for me."

"You'll never see me shiver in a frosty autumn rain. If it's cold enough for *me* to shiver, *you* will be dead. Let's get you some warmth and furs and a good night's rest."

They walked back to camp.

"I want to hear more," Nyahri said, "about the night sky. These *sah tel ites?* You could teach me that?"

Yw Sabi accompanied Nyahri to the communal fire, then left her, starting toward the guest tent.

"Get some sleep," the Atreiani said, and no more.

IN THE MORNING THE E'cwnii feasted. The campfire roared, with corn roasting on hot stones. Yellow squash with sugar beet, prairie chicken, and wild long-horned cattle stewed in iron pots with potato and sage. Dogs begged and stole scraps from the meal.

Whenever anyone neared the Atreiani, they bowed or prostrated themselves.

Near the flame, yw Sabi sat at the left hand of the Ahtros; Nyahri, at his right. Beyond the camp, frost coated the grasses, melting only after the blue sky brightened. A few E'cwn women dared smiles at the Atreiani, who only nodded in reply.

As the meal concluded, Nyahri ate honeyed bread surrounded by those she'd lived among all her life, brave young men, bright children, and concerned matrons. Youths danced to flutes and drums, and the Ahtros smiled to watch them.

The tribe celebrated Sultah yw Sabi. Nyahri clapped to the dancers' rhythms, breathing the plain's heady air, sweetened by autumn's first currents. For a moment she allowed herself a measure of respite, an instant to forget Suhto had died, how everything had changed. Then, from the corner of her eye, a flutter of supernatural hair stole the daylight; the Atreiani's gaze followed the dancers too, but her focus sought something distant.

Nyahri recognized the expression—the same as her own, when she missed her mother or brother, when the longing overtook her. "You well, Atreiani?"

Yw Sabi started from her reverie, blinking at Nyahri. "Well as can be."

"Missing someone?"

For an instant, yw Sabi betrayed surprise. "You presume my business? To have any right to it?"

Nyahri sat back. "I—I did not mean to offend."

"You didn't *offend*," the Atreiani said. "You *presumed*."

"I am right?"

"I should put it from my mind." The Atreiani gave a scantly perceptible roll of her eyes. "Now is now. Here is here. I don't take the generosity of your tribe for granted." She turned back to the dance.

The Ahtros laid his hand on Nyahri's.

After the feast ended, Nyahri walked him to his tent, slowly, too slowly. The cold mornings bit his limbs, and Nyahri ached in sympathy for him, to see his face, always masking his pain. The Atreiani followed and they sat in the sunlight outside the door. Nyahri lent her arm to her father, helping him settle. She warmed his tea and, as she did, the Ahtros retrieved a stick and on the ground he drew a map.

"Major rivers here and here," he said, pointing, "the Wyst and Bhar. Broken ruins in the north—from your time, Atreiani?"

She nodded. "Likely."

"The Inwnii call those ruins the *Devils' Teeth*. You may approach Swyn Templr two ways—west of Abswyn or more northerly by the ruins and across to the Wyst. It has been too long for me, yw Sabi, so I cannot suggest one road over another, except the Bhar is more direct."

"I understand."

"Cohltos valley is here," he pointed, "high in the mountains. This time of year there may be snow on the way, who knows? Prepare for cold weather. You will be deep in Oudwn lands and their archers guard the path, so you *will* meet them—it is no small ride."

"I'll walk."

"I do not recommend you do."

"I've never tended a horse. Before this week I'd never ridden one—I'll walk."

The Ahtros scratched his chin, then sipped his tea. "Even on horseback it could be weeks before you reach Swyn Templr. Too slow to walk. Winter will catch you."

"I don't fear the cold."

"Do you fear avalanches? Drifts? The pass will be unreachable and there are other reasons to ride."

"Such as?"

He bowed his head. "I wish no offense, Atreiani. Perhaps you fear no men? But if a woman ahorse may be said safer than one afoot and, it follows, an Atreiani ahorse is safer than one afoot. Oudwnii are not the only tribe in the lands. While they are our enemy, they are more civilized than most—in the north there are the Gabarii and C'naädii and even more violent tribes. You should ride, unless you *do* wield all the powers of a god."

"What's to say I don't?"

"Then you need fear no man," he said, "but still to have a horse is better than not."

"Doesn't change anything. Whatever I am, I'm not a horsewoman." The Atreiani shifted her gaze to Nyahri.

Nyahri realized yw Sabi's ploy and cleared her throat. "I could tend after her in the saddle, care for her horse."

His eyes widened as he wrestled back his panic. "The Oudwnii would like nothing better, daughter, than to capture you. An easy thing to do if you ride straight into their arms."

"Father, I am capable."

"Capable, yea! But were you a strong man, full grown, I would still doubt, and you are a young woman."

Nyahri's face flushed and she tightened her fists. "I earned the right of the hunt many times over, I have *killed* men—"

"Yea, but—"

"It was my mother, your wife, who taught me of the Atreianii."

"I sometimes wish she had not—"

"It was *I* who yw Sabi came to first. It is I who should accompany her to Swyn Templr. It is I who am most able of us here to find what portents this brings and to follow it to its end."

His voice deepened, "Rein in your pride—"

"She has some reason for pride," the Atreiani said, "don't you think? Your daughter seems capable—she's no delicate flower."

"Ay," he grumbled.

The Atreiani continued, "And I am certainly no *young woman.* Nyahri will not be a lone E'cwni on the road, but an Atreiani's guide."

"Revered Sultah yw Sabi," he said, "goddess or not, can you guarantee her safety in this world?"

"No." The Atreiani shook her head. "Can you?"

He frowned bitterly but at last let go, sighing, raising an eyebrow at his daughter. "You made up your mind to go," he said to her, "before we had this conversation."

"I will guide the Atreiani to Swyn Templr. Would mother not have gone?"

He flinched at this and Nyahri regretted the words.

Before she died, Nyahri thought, *he learned to resent the gods.*

"You will have all you need," he said to yw Sabi, "and Nyahri shall go with you."

The Atreiani nodded.

"When do you leave?" he asked her.

"Tomorrow morning," she said.

He raised his hand. "I know you make no promises, not for my child nor for anything else, but please favor my tribe. Favor my daughter, for an old man's sake."

"As soon as we leave," yw Sabi said, "take the tribe east."

She nodded to the Ahtros, then to Nyahri, and left for her own tent.

"You are your own woman," the Ahtros said to his daughter.

"Thank you, father."

"Do not *thank.* The last man I said was *his* own is now dead."

"Yea, father."

"You will not, I believe, come back to us."

"I may survive."

"Survive or nay. I am reminded of the old stories, of the tales your mother used to tell. You will leave us and on this road you are likely to become *hers*—" He gestured after the Atreiani. "—at least as much as your own."

"Nay, I will come home."

"Nyahri, please, follow the goddess's example and *make me no promises*—"

"Yea, father."

"—except to make me proud of you. Follow the course you believe best."

Nyahri kissed his cheek and left him.

The encampment's business carried on. A handful of women and young men knelt near the Atreiani's tent, singing the ancient songs. Nyahri's heart aching, she looked to all the faces she knew.

What could I give them? she asked herself. *What Ahtras would I be to them, when I am the death of all my suitors? What would one more moment here accomplish?*

Nyahri went to the horses and soothed Kwlko; or he, her. She scratched his ears, saddled him, and for hours rode alone on the plains, a full quiver at her side, her bow strung across her back.

{09}

hat afternoon, Nyahri slew an antelope, which she gutted, quartered, and brought back to camp. After washing, she brushed the stallion, whispering to him, and left a blanket on him to ward away the cold. Long after dark, as Nyahri passed the Atreiani's tent, she noted lamplight through the door. She stood noiselessly on the grass-bare earth, thinking to call out, but decided instead to turn away.

"Nyahri?"

She froze. No mortal could have heard her.

"Yea, Atreiani?"

"Come."

Inside, yw Sabi sat with her legs folded. Nyahri settled across from her.

"You needn't accompany me anywhere tomorrow," the Atreiani said.

"Yw Sabi, my father has said I am my own woman. I go where I choose."

"Your own woman?" Yw Sabi hinted a smile. "Then you should choose to stay here."

"Why?"

"Because I've seen your father's health and I gather, sooner than you'd prefer, you might be somewhat more important here than you like to tell yourself."

Nyahri's cheeks flushed, something like anger swimming through her, something like regret. She swallowed it.

"I will go with you," she said.

Yw Sabi sighed. "Perhaps some good will come of it. In a few months you'll be back home with a lifetime of stories to tell."

"I will help you the best I can," Nyahri said. "For now I am yours."

Yw Sabi took a darker disposition, her head tilting upward. She looked down on Nyahri, her gaze heavy.

"How much," yw Sabi said, "do you really know of our ways? Last night, *mistress*—tonight, *I am yours*. You say it casually, as if 'for now' had anything to do with it. Your mother must have heard fairytales passed through the generations, and you heard them too?"

"She repeated the rituals, the words, to me, to my sister." Nyahri bowed her head. "I know enough, yw Sabi, to know what I say."

"I think not. You're toying, pretending to know. Language is important. We reserved these words for the highest servants, our seconds, elevated between *Homo sapiens* and *Homo atrean.*"

"Did you ever have such a servant?"

"Yes."

"Where is he?"

"She," yw Sabi said, as if breathless for that moment. "I don't wish to talk of her."

"Did all Atreianii have such servants?"

"No, but it was a well-considered system—it bound them to us and us to them, created a bridge between us and humanity. Our laws prevented the joining of our demesnes with one another, and unions between Atreianii never lasted. The need for total commitment, for unyielding devotion, and for trustworthiness demanded another kind of companionship. Shifting allegiances were no allegiances at all and we had to know who to trust. Not that it mattered in the end."

Nyahri fidgeted, glancing aside, searching for something to say.

"See?" yw Sabi said. "You don't understand at all. You don't mean, 'I am yours,' repeating things half heard and barely understood, distorted by time and culture. You mean only, 'I am going along for now.' It isn't the same thing."

Nyahri raised her chin. "You are right. I do not *know*. For all my mother's stories, I know less with each new thing you say. I *do* know how long I looked upon the night sky and wondered at those patterns—the Web of Lwn, the quick stars, the errant stars, and all the heavens—and now you tell me they are something even more wondrous! How long I wondered after you, Sultah yw Sabi, your name on Abswyn's door! You figure at the heart of our tales, *the Atreiani feared by Atreianii,* but now you are here and I find you not so terrifying—"

"Do not presume me kind."

"Yet you have treated me with some kindness. I know the gods brought me to you—"

"There are no gods."

These words cut Nyahri. "Yw Sabi, the gods—"

"*There are no gods,* though it sometimes serves me to play the part. We'll discuss it in due course. Until then you *will* follow me, and you *will* guide me. Believe me, Nyahri, you puzzle me almost as much as I puzzle you, and I too would like to learn more."

"*I* puzzle *you?*"

Yw Sabi nodded.

"I will follow as you wish," Nyahri said.

"You called me a devil and I reprimanded you." Yw Sabi touched Nyahri's cheek, a perfunctory gesture. "Devil I probably am."

Nyahri drew away, a fraction, from yw Sabi's fingers.

"Hmm?" Yw Sabi raised her eyebrows.

Do not touch me so, Nyahri thought.

The Atreiani withdrew her hand. "Get some rest. We should depart early tomorrow. Goodnight."

Nyahri hesitated, wanting to stay as much as to leave, flustered by the unexpected caress. Then she headed to her own tent.

Inside, all was dark, Cirje gone, and Nyahri lit the lamp. On the bedrolls lay a coronal of darkest night-falcon feathers, a band of leather threaded with sinew and crimson cloth. The feathers hung in braids of silver wire and finely wrapped red twine. Nyahri ran her fingers over the headpiece, its plumage and beaded cords, and she slipped it over her hair. Feathers cascaded down her back.

She knelt, closing her eyes to gauge the coronal's weight, the strands waiving gently back and forth. Behind her the tent opened, Cirje crouching at the threshold.

"It is beautiful," Nyahri said. "It reminds me of mother's."

"A priestess's coronal. I made it with Suhto at midsummer, but I hid it with our aunt. It was a gift if—"

"If I accepted him?"

Cirje nodded. "I was angry. But now—"

"Ay, I remember—there were cuts on your fingers you would not explain to me."

"The unwrapped wire is sharp."

"You went to so much trouble, and I have hurt you with all my deeds, all my thoughtless words."

"It is nothing, Nyahri. Let us not be angry again, nay? We are caught up in miracles and this is a dreamtime. Should we not be together in it?"

Somewhere toward the horizon, coyotes called, their songs punctuated by the occasional horse's bray or dog's whine. Nyahri braided Cirje's hair, and the girl cried until she slept. Setting the coronal aside, Nyahri rolled onto her back with her eyes open to the blackness, and she laid her hands on her stomach.

I will do as I know my mother would have done, she thought, *I will follow the Atreiani, but I will not follow so blindly. Yw Sabi is no great killer of men, nay? Not so frightening? Perhaps all the legends of her are wrong. Yw Sabi, do not touch me so—*

Nyahri smiled and thought, *Eh,* do *touch me so. That was nice—*

SHE OPENED HER EYES, staring across her sister's vacant bedding. Cursing to have overslept dawn, Nyahri bolted upright, threw on clothes, and burst from the tent. A clear sky overarched the frosty plains. The E'cwn men and women tended their tasks, and a woman disassembled the guest tent, laying the hides and poles on a litter. Dread settled in Nyahri's heart and she looked in every direction.

Has the Atreiani left me anyway?

Girls gathered water at the river, elders warmed their hands at the fire, and a woman smoked the antelope which Nyahri had slain.

Nay! Where is she?

After a frantic search, Nyahri found yw Sabi standing on a westward-facing knoll, dressed in her Atreian clothing, the strange gray fabric covering her to her ankles, wrists, and neck. Beneath her pant hems, she wore light black boots.

Nyahri crossed the encampment to her side. "Yw Sabi, I thought you abandoned me."

The Atreiani kept her eyes on the mountainous horizon. "I considered it."

"Forgive me for oversleeping."

"For sleeping? When you're probably still anemic, still recovering, cracked ribs and all?" Yw Sabi waved her hand dismissively. "You give me other reasons to leave you behind. Not the least is a good family who'd be fortunate to keep you, this winter and every winter after it."

"Yw Sabi, I wish to go with *you.*"

"If I say no?"

Nyahri furrowed her brow. "Yesterday you asked me to guide you. My father gave his leave—"

"Shush." Again, the dismissive wave. "I gather you'd just follow me anyway. We're not delayed because you slept late, no, nor because I question taking you from your family. We delay because your father insists on choosing me a *proper* horse. Some monster, no doubt, full of fire. I'd prefer something docile. I'll need you, Nyahri, if for nothing else than to teach me how to ride and care for a horse."

"The Atreianii never rode?"

"Many kept horses. I had other—" She paused, savoring some memory. "—amusements."

At the campfire they ate a hot but simple meal of beans, potatoes, and sage trout. Soon, a gathering of children brought to the camp a charcoal-hued gelding, chosen from among the Ahtros's fastest horses. He had bridled the horse in silver, and new-oiled saddlebags hung at his flanks, with blankets and winter clothes strapped behind the cantle. A master-tooled saddle of dark leather rested on his back, and Nyahri recognized it too as her father's. The saddle, Nyahri feared, would be a poor fit for the Atreiani, but it would have to do.

After their meal, Nyahri lashed the Atreiani's bag to the gelding's pack and tethered him aside Kwlko, who she burdened with her own gear and the foodstuffs.

Yw Sabi mounted, her ankle once more turned too much in the stirrup, her hands too near on the saddlebow. She patted the charcoal's neck as though she might touch something unclean.

Uncertainty, Nyahri thought, *the same which children show the first time.*

Nyahri watched wide-eyed, somewhat reassured by yw Sabi's doubtfulness in the saddle, a quality which lent her some vulnerability. The plainswoman felt as if she kept a talley, counting qualities of the Atreiani which made her more or less human.

Nyahri sprang to her stallion's back.

"What do I do?" yw Sabi asked.

"Nothing. Your horse will trail mine."

"His name?"

"Turo."

They observed no ceremony for the departing, no long goodbyes. The E'cwn community gathered, the Ahtros raising his hand in parting. Behind him, Cirje watched but made no sign. For a short time the children paced the horses, the mottled dog barking beside them. Nyahri slipped the silver coronal onto her head, its feathers dancing in the breeze, and wearing it her mane now appeared almost as dark as yw Sabi's. She rode Kwlko along the arroyo, upstream toward the trees, and the gelding followed.

Among the elders a few turned their backs.

"What're they doing?" the Atreiani asked.

"They do not believe they will gaze on us again. To turn the back is to mourn the dead."

The Ahtros lowered his hand and entered his tent. Nyahri turned from the camp, bracing her spear across the saddle, and she did not look back again.

§

SHE LED THEM BESIDE the Bhar River until afternoon, when she stopped to drink and eat, stretching to test her injuries. The clinging film had washed away, with water or sweat, but faint scars remained on her thigh and across her spine. A dull ache reminded her how deep the wounds had gone, damage which might have killed her, which should have taken months to heal.

Throughout the day the Atreiani asked no questions about horses, but Nyahri felt her watching: how Nyahri tilted her hips in the saddle, how her legs angled against the stirrups, the exact press of the reins in her hands. Nyahri waited for some sign of saddle-soreness in yw Sabi, but she suspected it would never appear.

Behind them the plains opened beyond the treetops. A distant storm darkened the yellow horizon, blowing eastward with a rainbow in its wake. To the southwest, temperate forests blanketed the foothills.

"Two roads, nay, Atreiani?"

"North and west."

"Which?"

"West. We'll keep to the Bhar."

"It will bring us past Abswyn. There may be Oudwnii there. The valleys will be thick with them."

"Let them see us. In any case we *must* go this way—I must return to Abswyn, find what remains of the Citadel, if anything. It'll be instructive."

"Yea, mistress."

Yw Sabi frowned at Nyahri. "That's twice now—don't *mistress* me, Nyahri, you haven't the right."

"How might I earn that right, Atreianii?"

The frown deepened into a glare. "Not now, girl."

"Yea, Atreiani." Nyahri grumbled.

Before dark they followed the familiar path, passing the glade where yw Sabi had sheltered them to tend Nyahri's wounds. Nyahri glanced toward it, then back at the Atreiani, who showed no sign she recognized that place or, if she did, that she cared.

Soon after, the way worsened. Fallen trees and branches barred the path, debris cluttering the woodland.

In the evening they camped off road, eating a cold meal, lodged in the cleft between two boar-backed hills. They burned no oil or wood. Only a thousand horse strides lay between them and the Red Valley, the heart of Abswyn's destruction. Here, while many trees still stood, detritus covered the ground, and the explosion had stripped most branches of leaves. After dark, cricket songs trilled through the valley, a chorus of night insects in millions, and early-autumn wapiti calls resounded from the far hillsides, a whining tune first high and ending in lower cries.

"Colder weather will come soon," Nyahri said.

After she filled the water skins and tended the horses, she sat beside yw Sabi.

"If you wish to rest, Atreiani, I will watch."

"You'll sleep."

"I am not tired. The ride was an easy one."

"No matter, *you'll* sleep. If I'm weary, E'cwni, I'll let you know."

Nyahri cleared wood chips and splinters from a patch of soft grasses. She lay down, curled within her blankets, her coronal on the saddle with her bow and spear beside her. Yw Sabi sat calmly, and the crickets lulled Nyahri to sleep.

THE ATREIANI NUDGED NYAHRI into wakefulness. Bright stars clung to the sky, soon to be swept away by sunrise.

"Day's coming," yw Sabi said.

"You never slept?"

"It was good to sit and think." The Atreianii stood and stretched. "I almost forgot—traveling with humans, how it makes me take time to reflect."

Does she sleep? Nyahri wondered, but she withheld the question. The Atreiani, it seemed, answered few questions outright.

They ate, then departed with the sunlight crowning the treetops. Yw Sabi rode with a measure more confidence, and Turo responded to her reins. Soon they broke into the open, Nyahri marveling at a great clearing where none had existed before.

Trees by the thousands littered the landscape, flattened away from Abswyn, their trunks broken like grass blades and their limbs stripped of bark. Deep cracks scarred the sandstones of the Gate, which had once flanked the House of Hell, boulders crumbled at their bases. Of the palanquins of the dead, none remained, nor any sign they had ever existed— no bones, no staves, no tattered remnants. The Feather Stone had ceased to exist. Blackened earth and burnt mesquite radiated from a crater wider than an arrow shot, its edge swollen and bowled with disgorged stones. Slag, shattered more like glass than iron, lay twisted on the fire-scored ground.

The horses struggled to cross the beaten terrain, but Nyahri brought them to a vantage which overlooked a deep void, its basin charred and wrecked.

"Abswyn!" Nyahri said.

"Indeed." A smile fleeted across yw Sabi's face.

Satisfaction, Nyahri thought.

The Atreiani gestured to the basin. "It'd be foolish to go closer." She retrieved a device from her bag, ghost-fires lighting its surface. "No radiation."

"Yw Sabi?"

"The cores of the Citadels aren't nuclear, but I worried there'd be free isotopes—" Her voice trailed.

"I still do not understand?" Nyahri shook her head.

"Perhaps you'll need lessons in particle physics someday, but not today."

Yea, Nyahri thought, *much to learn.*

They took two hours circumventing the crater's edge, past the debris and half-burned animal corpses and still-smoking spot fires. On the far side, human footprints appeared in the ash.

"Those," Nyahri said, "are recent."

Yw Sabi shifted in the saddle, turning, looking in all directions. "Today?"

"Within hours."

"Oudwnii?"

"Yea." Nyahri studied the hillsides and loosened her longknife in its scabbard. "Let us get out of the open."

"Lead on," the Atreiani said.

Nyahri gave a quick nod, choosing the best route.

{Interim: Love Letters}

Beloved Ekaterina—
  The steppes, golden green.
The shadowed falcon which lives over her, who never leaves her ranges, can hunt everything which lives upon her, every mouse and roe

  But she cannot hunt the steppes themselves.
    They touch the infinite sky,
    And who can hunt the sky?
  The steppes below, the sky above,
    These you are to me.
I am only the falcon. I can never be anything more.
Why would I ever want otherwise?

     Love,
     —S
     From *The Collected Letters*

TSARITSA—

What but the first time I saw you? What would be better than when you entered the great hall in your splendor and I knew beyond reason I'd be yours? What could exceed this, except all which followed, every season of your claime?

Mistress, though you host Council in Giza and I play the Sydney concertos, we're never apart. Borea threads us: I listen across half a world to your heartbeat; I feel your struggle to out-politic the Congress; I share your frustrations, weariness, thirsts, lusts; I know these when no one else dares presume your slightest mood.

You are with me this moment, yet I write with quill on vellum a letter you'll not receive for days. You'll open it, smell my perfume, and smile at the mess which is my handwriting. Every thought we entertain, everything we do, is a love letter to one another. How beautiful this is! You may declare, mistress, that you never were a Romantic, but I know better.

Love,
Ekaterina
From *The Collected Letters*

{10}

Nyahri guided yw Sabi into the still-standing trees, climbing the western foothills. Spear in hand, she walked Kwlko, finding yet more Oudwn sign: an abandoned camp, a broken arrow. The forest thickened, broad ferns overhanging the path.

Before nightfall, cold clouds descended, and Nyahri pulled a pelt coat over her serape. Yw Sabi wore only her own clothing and a light cloak, its hood shielding her face from the mists. An E'cwn gift, the cloak seemed at odds on the Atreiani, something of one world wrapped about something of another. Relaxing more in the saddle now, she still grimaced at Turo's unexpected sidesteps and canters. She was learning the horse quickly, true, but Nyahri worried as the tapered canyon grew steeper.

We have seen no true test of horsewomanship yet, mistress—

"We could go on," Nyahri said, "but there has been a sharp drop or two and, without light, the horses will know this path no better than I."

"The Bhar is below us to the left. You may not be able to see it, but I still can. Nothing but rocks and cold water down there."

"You make my point for me."

"I could give us light."

Nyahri wondered what light would be so bright as to help. *It will not be a torch,* she thought, and she wished no witchcraft that night.

"Nay, mis—" Nyahri caught her words and reined them back. "Please, I would we draw no attention."

"Very well, but our visibility's worsening."

"We should move out of this weather."

"Can we find a copse, thick evergreens at the least?"

They followed the ruins of an ancient highway, crowded with pine. The path's cut and fill had washed down the mountainside, torn by the ages. Nyahri dismounted, walking ahead, testing the way. She discovered a wide plateau, too open for her liking, but they crossed into a stand of dense ponderosa.

"We can stop here," yw Sabi said.

After Nyahri unsaddled them, the horses stood abreast, hindquarters turned to the wind. Nyahri sat beside the Atreiani, her back to a granite slab, and the dry ground beneath the trees offered meek comfort as they ate their cold rations. After their meal, Nyahri paid homage to her ancestors, thanking the heron god that the storm blew without more malice.

"You wish me to keep watch?" Nyahri asked.

Yw Sabi scowled at the clouds, her shoulders dropping. At last she closed her eyes.

"I *am* a little sleepy. Just a few hours' rest, no more, then wake me."

"Yea."

Yw Sabi laid back her head, with her blanket, cloak, and scarf wrapped around her. After more than a week, it was the first time Nyahri had seen the Atreiani tire. Nyahri moved from the rock and, exposed, the cold sharpened her senses.

Yet after an hour she also faded, her mind wandering, and she shut her eyes. Forcing herself to wake, she planted her spear in the dirt, fighting to keep it upright as the mists wetted her face, the wind blowing in her ears.

Kwlko startled and Nyahri's eyes snapped open at a soft, quick rhythm in the trees.

Perhaps wolves.

No need to fear wolves, who'd find guarded horses too risky a meal and look elsewhere. The stallion snorted and stepped. A tree branch cracked.

Not wolves! Nyahri crouched, her spear in both hands.

"Lo, Atreiani," she whispered and, a moment after, yw Sabi knelt beside her.

"Three men downslope," yw Sabi said, her lips close to Nyahri's ear. "They're nearer the river, under some pines."

"How do you know?"

"Because I can see them."

Nyahri strained her eyes at only spruce and mist and darkness. "Weapons?"

"Bows."

"Nocked?"

"They're only watching. I'm not sure they can see us."

"What do you wish to do?"

"Give them time."

For long minutes, nothing moved save the worried horses and the bitter gusts. Then a rustle, mistakable for wind. Nyahri tensed, raising her spear.

"Relax," yw Sabi said, "they're going."

"By tomorrow night we will have permanent shadows."

"I'm sure you're right."

The horses settled. As yw Sabi reclined again by the stone, Nyahri stretched and yawned, for the moment reassured.

"Go back to sleep, yw Sabi. I can watch awhile longer."

"I'm rested. I want you alert come morning. Lay down. Keep warm."

Three hours' sleep in a week! A notch for the *inhuman* in Nyahri's talley. She frowned at this, but settled into her bedroll with her blankets packed about her, and her mind turned toward more immediate and practical considerations. *If the weather worsens, we will need lean-tos and windbreaks.*

On those plans, though, the thick skins warmed her and she slept.

DESPITE NYAHRI'S CONCERNS, THE weather cleared the next morning, light snow melting by midday. On horseback she and yw Sabi rounded a series of wide meadows, the pines walling the short, dry mountain grasses. The valley led them for three days and, all the while, Nyahri sensed the Oudwnii following them. A tumble of stones down a slope, a sudden alarm of starlings: the land told a story.

"There are men at our flanks," Nyahri said. "Not sure how far or how many."

"There were three last night," yw Sabi said. "I count six now, give or take."

"They are surrounding us?"

"They're only pacing us."

"We could outdistance them. Give the horses their heads. The lea is open."

"And ride headlong into what?"

"We could lose them."

"Or blunder. We never believed we'd get anywhere close to Sojourn Temple without meeting the Oudwnii, did we?"

As they crossed wider fields, Nyahri appreciated the Atreiani's better judgment. Rivulets fingered through the grasses, stagnating in marshes. What seemed solid ground sometimes hid mires, the stallion and gelding struggling till Nyahri brought them higher into the trees. With swamp-stink on the horses' legs, she thanked the cottontail god, lord of lucky choices.

A gallop might have been the death of a horse.

Yet she cursed the trees too. They confounded her sense of direction, and she lost the path. Only after a noontime stop did she rediscover it along an expanse of golden aspens. At last they made better time.

We are quick, she thought, *but not so quick the Oudwn trackers will not catch us.*

While they could, she pushed the horses faster.

During the afternoon's ride, Nyahri shot three hares. That night she made camp within a glade of spruce, a sheer granite cliff guarding them from the north wind. Knowing the Oudwnii already trailed them, she lit a fire and roasted the rabbits.

"You seem well, Atreiani."

"Why wouldn't I be?" Yw Sabi sat with her back to the granite, hands folded in her lap. She looked up from the fire at Nyahri.

"A handful of hours' sleep in more than a week, and you have been some days in the saddle? Most people, when they have not yet learned the horse, they can barely stand by the third day."

"Uncomfortable animals. Smelly. Dirty. I don't much understand the point in them."

"A horse is a precious thing, Atreiani. Tribes without them are always worse off."

"*Worse off* is a relative term. In any case, Nyahri, I'm fine."

A guttural huff sounded from uphill. The horses raised their heads. The trees swayed, creaking in a gust, and a half-fallen ponderosa cracked against the boughs supporting it.

Yw Sabi stood, gazing into the darkness between the pine stands.

"Do you see anything, mistress?"

The Atreiani shot Nyahri a glance but suffered the title. "Not in my line of sight."

"I smell it."

"It'd be hard not to."

The huff sounded again, a low, emptying bellow. Foliage shook, nettles rustling, and something heavy hit the ground. Stones rolled downhill.

Nyahri rushed forward, snatching her spear from its place by the fire. She grabbed the horses' leads and walked them between the fire and the high granite wall. The horses kicked nervously, pulling their tethers, and Nyahri tied them to the closest tree.

"I see it now," yw Sabi said.

"Coming?"

"It is."

Gods! It sounds big. *And the Atreiani stands there without a weapon—she is strong but not* so *strong.*

Nyahri returned to the Atreiani's side. The pungent stink of wet fur weighted the air.

A bear, Nyahri thought, *but no black bear.* Small bears often wandered the edges of the open plains, but the beast in the darkness outweighed a black bear by many times.

Nyahri raised her spear, bracing for a shattering blow. The bear lumbered closer. Yw Sabi stood with her hands at the back of her waist, head tilted, a gesture of pure curiosity.

First the firelight glistened against the bear's nose and jowls and teeth. Then the rest of it emerged from the shadow. Its brown-black coat rippled as its forepaws swept before it, scraping the dirt, claws more than a handspan long. It raised its head, drawing long breaths, scenting.

"Atreiani," Nyahri said, "get behind me. I will protect you."

The bear stood, twice Nyahri's height, and when its forequarters hit the earth, the ground thumped. Sweat chilled Nyahri's skin.

I might get one strike, she guessed, *maybe two, before my spear breaks.*

Yw Sabi laughed, truly delighted. "*Ursus spelaeus!* You are beautiful!"

"Atreiani, step back."

Yw Sabi stepped forward, studying the animal.

She is mad!

Nyahri rushed to put herself between the bear and the Atreiani, and it rose again. Nyahri bent her knees, setting her spear at a stronger angle.

The Atreiani raised her witch-scepter before her, its ghost-lit patterns following her fingertips. A soft chime filled the woodland, clear even through the rising wind. The bear dropped to the ground, shaking its head, turning its nose away. At last it mewled, snorted, and lay on its side.

"Gods." Nyahri stepped away.

"Ah, you *are* beautiful," yw Sabi said to the beast, approaching its back. She knelt, laying her hand on its thick pelt. The bear stretched its limbs.

"Atreiani—"

"Come here, Nyahri. Be slow. Make no sudden movements."

"I do not—"

"*Come.* Do as I say."

Nyahri inched forward, spear still raised, until she stood beside yw Sabi. The bear sprawled, so she might lance its heart with a single blow. Instead, she too knelt and laid her hand on its fur. Its cavernous breaths shuddered under her hand, its generous coat muting its thunderous heartbeat. The bear gave a gentle shake of its head and pawed the air.

"*Ursus spelaeus*," yw Sabi said, "the cave bear. They existed for hundreds of millennia, but they died out twenty-seven thousand years before I was born. *Homo atrean* brought *spelaeus* back to life."

"The cave bears live because of you?"

"Yes."

"Why did you give them life?"

"Because we could. We decided the resurrection of many mammals would cause little harm, and in most cases it proved important theories of superabundant biodiversity and the role of top-level predators. Wherever we brought megafauna back to life, ecosystems recovered more quickly."

"Recovered from what?"

"Human folly." Yw Sabi ran her hand across the bear's flank. "This fellow is a long, long way from where we first seeded them. Wrong continent actually."

Nyahri understood *continent* as little as *superabundant biodiversity.* "You say that with some concern?"

"Concern he's here? No, he seems quite happy here. Does it raise more questions for me?" She nodded.

"You do not wish to kill this beast?"

"No."

"What shall we do?"

"Ride farther up valley, enjoy the meal you cooked us somewhere else. We'll leave him to recover. I doubt he'll follow."

Nyahri looked at the bear, then at the chiming witch-scepter, then at the face of the Atreiani. She set her spear on the ground, tucked her knees beneath her, and bowed her forehead to the dirt.

"You *are* a goddess," she said to yw Sabi. "You raise hellfire and command the greatest beasts. Forgive me if I doubted."

"Many have bowed to me," yw Sabi said without the slightest pride, "but I'm no goddess. I tell you again—there are no gods."

"I know what my eyes tell me."

"Raise your head."

Nyahri met the Atreiani's gaze.

Yw Sabi hinted a smile. "I'd rather *other* offerings from you, Nyahri, than groveling."

"Yea, mistress."

"Though if you keep *mistressing* me, we'll need another serious conversation about it."

"Yea."

"*Yea?*"

"Yea, mistress."

"Hmm." The Atreiani started to frown, then shook her head. "Come, let's leave this bear to his forest and put a few kilometers more behind us."

THEY ATE THEIR MEAL colder than Nyahri would've liked. The rest of that night they caught sign neither of beast nor men.

The next day they rode through the morning without event, and in the early afternoon crossed into larger stands of aspens clinging to their last golden leaves. The forest floor shone with gold, crisscrossed by the trees' white columns.

Yw Sabi pulled another device from her tools. She examined it, turning in the saddle, and she watched a tiny dial in her palm, adjusting it in increments. A smile touched her lips.

"Atreiani?"

"Checking our bearing. The poles aren't where I expected. Maybe some change at the beginning, maybe while I slept? Enough for the axis to flip."

"Eh, yw Sabi?"

"This is a compass, a simple device. You know loadstones?"

"We use them."

"The magnetic pole is near south, off by a few degrees from the axis. You realize it once pointed north?"

"Nay."

Yw Sabi raised her hand toward the horizon. "North sat at zero, adjusted by declination, varying from region to region. It always moves, but now it points south. One hundred eighty-seven centesimal degrees—that's a *big* change."

She slipped the compass back into its place, clicked her tongue, and tapped her heels to the gelding. With a cinch of the reins, Turo drew beside the stallion.

Nyahri smiled. "You are learning."

"Yes, I am."

For several hours they traveled through the aspens, stopping only a brief while during the afternoon. Nyahri unsaddled the horses, resting them too. Afterward, they left the white-wooded forest, merging with sweet-scented cedar groves and spruce. Another long dell opened, this one free of bogs, and beyond them arose sharper snow-crowned peaks. Nyahri drank the vision, her first sight of the highest alpine slopes.

Yet yw Sabi frowned.

On the path ahead, twenty men waited at a distant outcropping of gray stone. All carried longknives and stickbows and razor-pointed arrows.

"They are watching for us," Nyahri said.

"Thus far, they haven't seen us."

"We could ride the ridge, try to circle around them?"

"No need. They're practically inviting us. Let's not spurn the gesture."

{11}

As Nyahri and yw Sabi descended into the shallow meadow, the sun grew hot and Nyahri stripped off her warmer clothes, leaving only her breeches, serape, and coronal. Yw Sabi wore her cloak forward, the hood veiling her eyes. Seeing this, Nyahri understood her intent and trotted half a stride ahead. She held her spear where she could best defend the Atreiani, becoming now not only guide but guardian.

They approached the outcropping at a walk. The archers, most full-bearded men, spotted the riders as soon as they left the trees. The men wore woolen cloaks, their dark clothes in browns and grays. They tightened rank aside the road, resting their hands on their stringed bows. Though none touched an arrow, Nyahri respected Oudwn archery, knowing she might kill only one man before the arrows flew. She raised her left hand, spreading her fingers in a gesture of peace, her longspear skyward in her right.

Nyahri and the Oudwnii studied one another until a square-jawed, stubble-bearded archer stepped forward, his hair like sun-faded sand. His bow slung, his weapons sheathed, he held forth his palm in answer to hers.

"Two E'cwn women," he said, "deep in the Oudwn valleys? You have bigger balls than your so-called men."

"Who are you?" Nyahri asked.

"Dhaos Shwn Oudwn."

"The chieftain's son?"

"The chieftain's son, yea." He shrugged. "Who are you?"

"Nyahri."

Dhaos cocked his head. "Only Nyahri?"

"E'cwnii use short names."

"And your companion?"

"Does not speak."

He stepped forward, reaching for Kwlko's bridle. The stallion nipped him and Nyahri pulled the reins.

"I must insist," the archer said, "she speak for herself."

"My business," yw Sabi said, "is mine. We're riding to Sojourn Temple."

The Oudwnii exchanged glances and Nyahri grimaced at yw Sabi's heavy accent. A few Oudwnii reached slowly for their arrow-filled quivers.

Do they guess, Nyahri wondered, *what is among them? They must—*

"The Templarii will have something to say about that," Dhaos said, "as will my father."

"No doubt," said yw Sabi.

"You traveled by Abswyn?" he asked.

"We rode by it," Nyahri said.

"It was as if the gods themselves lit the sky and burned Abswyn from existence. What happened there?"

"I do not know," Nyahri lied, though she assured herself she also told the truth. *What do I really know of Abswyn's end?*

"Those were grounds sacred to the E'cwnii, eh, Nyahri? Quite a loss."

"Now we are on our way to Swyn Templr."

"Swyn Templr, as you E'cwnii call it, is *not* Abswyn. Just because your sacred ground is wasted does not mean we must share ours." He folded his arms. "Our elders are on war footing, worried over black magic, of woken Atreianii and demons afoot." He glanced toward yw Sabi. "Would you have any explanations to calm their fears?"

Yw Sabi's voice sharpened, "I'll have news for the Templarii, not for you."

"Makes no matter to me," Dhaos said, "what you have for the Templarii. For my part I do not care *where* you go, except you should take precautions, especially farther west."

"Why?"

"Too many raiders these last few years, this side of the peaks." He gestured toward the far heights. "Dangerous for anyone traveling these paths, women most particularly."

"We can handle ourselves," Nyahri said.

"We Oudwnii are civilized—do not look so disdainful, E'cwni—but these are not civilized lands. You should come with us. We can escort you."

"I have no fear," Nyahri said, "of anyone, civilized or otherwise. Will you let us pass or nay?"

"*Makes no matter to me.* My father, though, would know the business of the E'cwnii, and we are ordered as of late to bring any strangers to him."

"To what purpose?" yw Sabi asked.

He smirked. "Some of our men spotted a *strange woman* near Abswyn. Did you happen upon one in your journey up the valley? My father wishes to know more of her."

"We might speak with Shwn Jhon Oudwn nearer Sojourn."

"Save he is not there anymore, not for some years. He no longer makes his home at Cohltos."

Yw Sabi jerked her gelding's reins, the horse half turning. She laid her hand on the witch-scepter at her side, and Nyahri grimaced at it, remembering its power over the bear.

What would it do to these men, or to me?

"I don't wish any delay," yw Sabi said.

"Apologies, but we and our bows demand your delay," Dhaos said, and at that a few men loosened arrows from their quivers, setting them to their bowstrings. "South of here, my father keeps Orÿs Lodge—"

"We're not going to Orÿs Lodge."

"It oversees the Province of Aukensis, well sheltered and stocked. While you are there, we can resupply you, and I promise good hospitality."

The Atreiani's tone deepened, soft but animal and throaty. "I doubt that's a promise, young Oudwni, which is yours to give. By some accounts, your father doesn't have a hospitable reputation. What would you do if I refuse your invitation?"

The men traded nervous glances. Dhaos squinted, trying to pierce the shade beneath yw Sabi's hood.

"You, woman," he said, "are *not* an E'cwni."

"I'm also no one who suffers hindrances. We're two women traveling alone, so what threat could we possibly be? We wish only to go our way."

"You *must* be the woman my father seeks."

Three archers put tension in their bows. Nyahri reared the stallion, bringing him before the gelding, setting herself between yw Sabi and her would-be enemies.

"Who are you?" asked Dhaos, focusing past Nyahri to the Atreiani.

Yw Sabi slipped her hood. While her skin caught the bright afternoon sunlight, an impression of warm but living quartz, her hair reflected no light at all, a flat void which defied any sense of depth or texture. None could mistake her as human.

The archers' eyes widened. Some signed or cursed, and a few lowered their heads or dropped to their knees. Nyahri swept the spear across her flank, thrusting its point within a finger's width of Dhaos's neck. He jolted back, unsheathing his longknife.

"I *might* not survive a fight, Dhaos Shwn Oudwn," Nyahri said, "but I *know* you will not."

Dropping his blade, he raised both palms, his gaze flicking between the spearhead and yw Sabi. A half-dozen archers recovered their composure, nocked, and drew, their arms trembling.

Fearful men, Nyahri thought, *liable to stupidity.* She prayed again, this time to the falcon god, who guarded against the follies of cowardice.

"I am not an idiot," Dhaos said.

Nyahri kept the spear point at his throat. Yw Sabi nudged the gelding forward, heedless of the arrows leveled against her.

To the archers, Dhaos shouted, "What would you do? Shoot the devil? Stay, weapons down."

They obeyed, backing to the rocks.

"I must go to Sojourn Temple," yw Sabi said, and she spit the word, "*boy.*"

"Nay, Atreiani," he said, "I understand your earnestness, but my oath to my father is my oath—I must bring you to his lodge. You may kill us all, go your way with this land bent against you, or you may go to my father and perchance he will put the land in your favor."

Yw Sabi rode around him. Nyahri cursed under her breath; the Atreiani blocked her view, baiting the archers.

Yet Nyahri remembered the old stories. The magics of the Atreian devils destroyed men, devastated armies, transformed the earth and sky.

If she fears them, Nyahri thought, *she does not show it.*

"We'll visit your father," yw Sabi said, "but when you deny *me,* Oudwni, you should know what you deny."

"You are an Atreiani," he said, "the divine, and what fool would offend a goddess?"

"You do understand. Good. Now lead us where you may."

He nodded to the archers. Brave men, proud men, but their fear showed. Some exhaled in relief. They too knew what they saw: a wakened of Abswyn, who they'd no desire to fight.

Dhaos led them southward, over the broad meadow, toward a line of cedars. Nyahri's heart thumped in her ears, and she thanked the falcon god anew that she yet breathed, riding ahead of the Atreiani, watching the Oudwnii all the while for treacheries.

SOON, OPEN GROUND SEEMED only a memory, the blotchy forest light confounding Nyahri's sense of direction. She doubted the road back, the path underfoot sometimes nothing more than hard-packed earth, but yw Sabi betrayed no alarm.

All the while, Nyahri wondered what would have happened if she had punched her spear through Dhaos's throat. Who would yet live? Who else would have died?

Yw Sabi is *flesh,* Nyahri thought. *Can she bleed too?*

Keeping pace with the horses, the men jogged. They traded hand signs—a craft of the E'cwnii too—but Nyahri recognized none of their cyphers. Instead, she watched their body language, the slant of a shoulder or bend of the knees which might prelude betrayal or ambush.

None came.

In the late afternoon they stopped at a hollow in the hillside, sheltered among the cedars. Dhaos laid his cloak on the ground and sat on it, catching his breath.

"The men need rest," he said to Nyahri, "and here is as safe as anywhere."

"It *is* defensible," Nyahri said, sliding from horseback. "You expect trouble?"

"Nay, but trouble often comes anyhow."

"Atreiani," Nyahri looked to yw Sabi, "this a good enough place for you?"

The Atreiani's gaze followed the depths of the hollow and forest. "Decide on such things as you will."

The archers lit a fire and gathered around it. They set their guard beyond the firelight's edge, apart from the horses and their riders.

Separate from them, Nyahri sparked another campfire for her and yw Sabi alone. Though the men offered, Nyahri accepted no Oudwn food. Instead, she blackened dried venison over the cedar flames and warmed flatbread. Yw Sabi kept her back to a tree, watching all.

A few Oudwnii talked quietly, casting respectful glances toward the Atreiani. Breaking from their banter, Dhaos unhooked his longbow and quiver, carrying them to Nyahri's fire. He knelt on the ground, smiling boyishly, his bright eyes keen. Nyahri gazed at him longer than she meant to, then looked away, poking a stick at the embers.

Measuring his next words, Dhaos licked his lips, but yw Sabi shook her head at him and his smile faded. He fidgeted with his bow.

At last he said, "My father thinks of little but the Citadel at Cohltos—"

"You call it a *Citadel,*" yw Sabi said.

"It is what the Templarii call it, nay? They tease my father with promises, tell him what the Citadel might do for us, but he's begun to lose faith in them."

"What promises?"

"For years the Templarii spoke to him of a better world, as if they might find a way to open the Citadel, raise Atreianii like you from their slumber, bring about a new era."

"That would end badly for your father," yw Sabi said, "and for every other human, you included."

"I do not understand?"

"You wouldn't." She leaned forward. "The Templarii certainly have *not* managed to open a Citadel, Sojourn or any other?"

A moment of confusion crossed Dhaos's expression. "They have tried, many times, to unlock it. Always they have failed."

It appeared and vanished in a blink, but Nyahri caught a shimmer of relief in yw Sabi's eyes.

"My father loves his clan," Dhaos said. "Sternly, yea, but loves his people still. Yet some years the snow drives hard. Some years there's no game. We have too much disease. While my father can be a harsh man, in the end he wants what's best. We know the old magics could cast aside many of our problems."

Yw Sabi watched him unflinchingly, and Dhaos waited for a shrug or gesture of sympathy from her. She gave him no such satisfaction.

"Father believes," Dhaos continued, "if we could unlock Sojourn, he might change the world."

"What do *you* think, boy?"

"I agree with him." Dhaos bowed, pressing his palms to the dirt. "Atreiani, we know what *influenza* is. We know of *pneumonia*—the Templarii have taught us that much. Have you seen a man under the fever? A loved one's waxen skin, cold sweat, and ramblings? The racking cough and every time your mother or brother or child cannot breathe, their pain is yours and you dread and also pray for the end."

Yw Sabi leaned back, hands on her knees. "Don't seek my sympathies. Don't seek to master Sojourn, either, even to cure every disease you ever suffered or to pile food on your tables. You would lose far more than you would gain, not that any human can so much as enter a Citadel and live."

Nyahri's heart clenched at those words, Suhto never far from her mind. Yet she tried her best to hide her feelings, to project herself as unmoved as the Atreianii.

Dhaos gave a mirthless laugh. "It *is* said a man gone into the Citadel is one not seen again, but we would enter by hundreds if it could bring the old magics back. I know *I* would."

This evening the sky remained clear, absent the clouds and threats of weather which had followed from the plains. As the darkness deepened, Lwn crested the trees, full and bright, adding its glow to the clearing. Yw Sabi looked down on Dhaos, her face calm, her black eyes glittering with firelight.

Nyahri realized, *The Atreiani has seen a thousand things worse than a few dying children, has she not? What hells has she witnessed?*

The Atreiani's voice held neither malice nor warmth. "Then you'd be just another dead boy," she said.

"I mean no offense," Dhaos said, "but these are the things my father *will* speak of with you, Atreiani. He hoped much for a day like this."

"A day like this?"

"When an Atreiani might wake, reopen the Citadels, teach us better ways. My father will hang his hope on you."

"With enough hope he'll hang himself." She said this with a cold simper, amused by a turn of phrase which failed in translation.

Dhaos glanced at Nyahri, but she mimicked the Atreiani, giving him no cues. Yet she read his earnestness, his belief in the words he spoke, and her heart warmed for him.

He is not so much older than me, she thought, *just a chieftain-son. He wants something good for his people. How can I fault him?*

"Is there some reason," said yw Sabi, "you loiter at our fireside, other than as your father's lackey, speaking for him before we see the man himself? Or do you have a thought to share that's all your own?"

"I and the men," Dhaos said, "think it right to present a gift of our good will." He laid the fine magiswood bow near her feet, the tooled quiver with it, its arrows' fletching gray and red. "To make up for this afternoon's—" Dhaos hunted for the right word. "—unpleasantness."

Yw Sabi gazed on him, and upon his offering, as if on dross. "Leave it."

He nodded.

He hastened away. Nyahri's gaze lingered on his boot print in the dirt, on a long unusual notch in the heel, some maker's mark. Raising her eyes, she noted the strength and straightness of Dhaos's walk, the square of his back.

Nyahri whispered, "Atreiani, you push them too much. Their arrows *would* injure you, nay?"

Yw Sabi kept her silence, her gaze drawn to the archers' campfire. The moonlight lingered on her face.

"Could they hurt you?" Nyahri pressed. "If I know, I can serve you better, Atreiani."

"It's possible," yw Sabi said at last. We're in some danger, no mistake, but best *they* not know it. When you were ready to battle down that cave bear, did you show it fear?"

"Nay."

"So it is now with these striplings, and I'll not comfort them into asking me favors. Whatever I am, I'm not their friend."

"Are you *my* friend, Atreiani?"

With a quick laugh, Yw Sabi's attention returned to Nyahri. "Do I look as if I have friends?"

Nyahri waited for more, some explanation, some kinder acknowledgment. Disappointed, she sighed.

"Should I put the bow with your belongings?" she asked.

"I shoot a bow," yw Sabi said, "worse than I ride a horse. Best you keep it."

Nyahri strapped the longbow to the stallion's harness and fixed the new quiver beside her own. The E'cwn bow was designed to shoot from horseback, closer to the target; the Oudwn bow, on foot and at a distance. Nyahri had never worked much with a longbow, but she intended to learn it better. As she cinched the harness, she looked over to the chieftain's son, sitting among his men. Her heart warned of trouble there but she drank an eyeful all the same.

THE NEXT MORNING BROUGHT renewed clouds and a cold north breeze. The archers gathered their effects and, as they departed, a dozen noisy crows picked the breakfast crumbs left beside the dead fires. On horseback, Nyahri and yw Sabi followed for hours, while the woodsmen jogged ahead. Watching them, Nyahri gave thanks for her stallion, wondering how men could endure so long.

They climbed above the cedars into blue spruce and ponderosa, and by midday the forest opened into sub-alpine meadows. Along these heights, Dhaos led them past mended fences and post rows. Old split stumps hinted where, through the generations, the Oudwnii had cleared the forests to expand their terraced mountainside farms.

Dirty-faced men and women worked plots sewn with maize, potatoes, and barley, looking up from their labors at the passing company. Nyahri sensed their reverence for Dhaos and his men, but the fieldworkers gaped with awe and horror at yw Sabi, many falling in obeisance.

Dhaos slowed his pace, walking alongside Nyahri's horse. "Welcome to Aukensis," he said, "and Orÿs Lodge."

Above them the high lodge rested in fissures carved from the mountain's living rock, standing against the alpine cliffs. Above its broad gabled roof, smoke cooled and thickened, carried from a dozen stone chimneys. Nyahri had never imagined such a thing, never experienced more than the long wooden lodges of the river peoples at the plains' eastern-most frontier. Her father had told her of such gargantuan buildings, but to *see* a house of stone, a shelter large enough for a thousand men, assaulted her sense of the possible, and it gave her a new respect for the Oudwnii.

Nyahri drew her stallion nearer yw Sabi. "How does it stand, this lodge?"

Yw Sabi only shrugged. "This is *nothing*, nothing but a pile of sticks and rocks."

Wooden huts leaned against the lodge's heavy retention walls, against fitted stones larger than any four horses could move. Posts and lintels of rough-planed redwood framed timbers wider across than Nyahri was tall.

Above the compound's defensible gates, two human heads decorated the barbican, their rotting mouths open in silent screams, bone exposed through the crow-eaten flesh.

Nyahri and the Atreiani trailed the Oudwnii past these gates, into the village, and the gates closed behind them.

"What was their crime?" the Atreiani asked Dhaos, glancing back to the spiked heads.

"Stealing from my father's larder," the archer replied. "Not a sack or two, mind you. They had been pinching for months."

"What were they doing with the food?"

"Eating it."

The Atreiani returned her attention to the hall itself. Nyahri followed yw Sabi's gaze: at the lodge's high open windows, a man signed to Dhaos, then retreated from sight. Along the walls, guardsmen watched from raised stands, their bows strung and their hands resting on their quivers.

Dhaos's men stopped at a cistern pump and washed themselves, scrubbing their faces and hands. Nyahri tethered the horses outside the lodge doors, surveying the settlement from beside her stallion. She noted two bony bays, a few heavy workhorses, and donkeys. The stink of pigs and chickens wafted from pens downhill, and a trip of goats bleated in a meadow farther downslope.

A high wall of vertical timbers, stone, and iron surrounded the lodge. Near one corner stood the kennels, a box-shaped stonework with a gabled roof. Dogs tussled inside, their barks deep and persistent, excited by the archers' arrival. Two stood inside slatted iron doors, massive beasts with broad heads and barrel chests, their fur black and golden.

Dogs bred to hunt, to kill.

An archer reached casually to take Kwlko's reins, but Nyahri caught his wrist.

"Not if you would keep your hand," she said to him. He looked to Dhaos, who shook his head. Nyahri said to the chieftain's son, "I would no one touch the horses."

"I will tend them myself," he said with a smile, "but you cannot ride them into the lodge—we allow no animals inside." His gaze wandered over her from her feet to the crown of her head. "Not sure if that would include you or not?"

"What is that supposed to mean?"

"I have heard Equii sometimes take their horses as lovers?"

"You try to fluster me?"

"Is it true?"

"*I* have heard Oudwnii are idiots who believe every stupid tale they are told."

Dhaos shrugged. "It is what we hear."

"Then you *listen* to idiots." She led Kwlko to him, reins in hand. "In the death-cold, in the heart of winter, we sometimes build shelters over our horses, share the warmth with them— we do not *lie* with them."

He nodded appreciatively, though whether in mockery or sincerity, she couldn't tell.

"If you will look after the horses," she said, "and let no one else near them, I will leave them with you."

"I promise," he said without hesitation, and she gave him the reins.

Nyahri tucked her longknife along the front of her belt, then took the Atreiani's bags from the gelding, balancing them on her shoulder. The Atreiani dismounted. An archer inclined his head to them, gesturing toward the doors, offering to guide them.

"This way," he said.

"After you," yw Sabi replied.

The three entered the lodge and, crossing its threshold, Nyahri felt as if entering the earth itself, all dust and gloom and fetor. Never had she wished more for wide-open plains. Yet yw Sabi pressed on, and Nyahri followed her.

THEY CLIMBED WORN WOODEN stairs to a narrow landing, and the passage constricted. On the left, a rhythm of doors matched shadowed alcoves to the right. Overhead, perforations gridded the ceiling. Through them, Nyahri glimpsed movement, and she paused to investigate.

Yw Sabi whispered to her, "Those are murder holes for archers—keep moving."

Mold-blackened beams crossed above the lintels of two green-stained copper doors. One stood open. The other had long fused with effervescent lime, bled for an age over its white-crusted hinges.

Yw Sabi and Nyahri followed their guide up another stair, where banners decorated the soot-smeared walls. Along a higher passage, the archer led them to a vacuous hall, the largest enclosed space in which Nyahri had ever stood. A wide flagstone floor spread beneath a trussed ceiling, and pigeons roosted and cooed and shat from the timbers.

"I take my leave," the archer said. His footfalls receded the way they'd come.

Above, warped shutters admitted a dirty light. Four parallel tables stretched the chamber's length and, at the other end of the room, a hearth fire raged, drawing a breeze through the flue. Within it a heavy iron spit bowed from a generation's feasting.

Despite the fire, Nyahri shivered, the walls at once too large and yet closing in on her with every breath. A ring of balconies encircled them—archers' stands above a killing floor. A rat crossed the floorboards, water dripped in a corner, and a woman coughed in some other chamber, her spasms hollow and persistent.

Through a far door entered a corpulent man, his face weathered and gray, wrinkles creasing his swollen face. Three leather-armored men flanked him, carrying spears and knives. The man peered at yw Sabi from beneath reddened eyelids. Bearskins wrapped his shoulders, and a gold-handled knife adorned his belt, his oversized fist resting on it.

He settled on a fireside bench, its planks creaking under his mass. "I am Shwn Jhon Oudwn," he said. "Forgive me if I must sit—the knees are old and not what they used to be. Please join me at the table?"

From another doorway entered a barefooted girl, her budding breasts and rounding hips wrapped in a simple dress. As she set wooden cups and a blown-glass carafe onto the table, her hair brushed against a wide bruise across her left cheek. She lowered her head, her shoulders hunched, and retreated, closing the door behind her.

The carafe pulled at Nyahri's focus. She had seldom encountered crafted glass, nothing more than trade beads. The vessel represented a fortune.

The guardsmen stood at attention, hiding their trembling as well as they were able, intent on yw Sabi alone.

His orbed fist as large as the carafe, Shwn Jhon poured two drinks, then leaned back, hooking one thumb in his belt, his thick fingers spread over his waist. With his other hand, he indicated the seat across from him.

"After your ride, you must be exhausted."

Yw Sabi slid a chair from the table and settled into it. Nyahri stood behind her, setting the bags on the floor, letting her hand hang beside her longknife's hilt.

Shwn Jhon continued, "Your kind are legend, my guest, long awaited and much appreciated. I have told you my name, will you not tell me yours?"

"Sultah yw Sabi."

His jaw slackened. "We have heard your name."

"From where?"

"Inscribed at Abswyn."

"Where else?"

"The Templarii have spoken of you."

"Probably not kindly."

"They spoke of you *historically*," he said. "You were something of the past."

"Yet here I am today."

"Why have *you* awakened first? The histories say you were a—" His voice trailed into silence.

"Prisoner?" Yw Sabi leaned forward, her elbows against the table's edge.

Shwn Jhon drank from his cup, emptying it. She paused only a moment before tipping the contents of hers into her mouth.

Nyahri wrinkled her nose at the stink of whiskey. Though close to the Atreiani, she kept the hall doors and guardsmen in sight.

"These histories," Shwn Jhon said, "say you were *out of favor.*"

"There're none here but I, chieftain, to judge who is *in favor* or out of it."

A scowl of reproach tugged down his cheeks. "If it is *you* who judge us," he said, "I pray you will be proud of what we have achieved since the Eventide, and certainly of the progress made since my grandfather's time."

The Atreiani rolled her cup between her hands and pushed it forward. Shwn Jhon refilled it. The guards shifted from foot to foot, one suppressing a hollow cough, deep phlegm in his chest.

"This hall, for example," Shwn Jhon said, gesturing widely to the room, "among many things—the re-mastery of iron, geometry, husbandry, and increasingly developed agriculture. A few of us know the old letters, at least an alphabet or two, and I can read some *Englisce.*"

Yw Sabi sipped the liquor, set the cup down, and drew her fingertip around its rim. Tapping his fingers together, Shwn Jhon tried to outlast yw Sabi's silence.

He yielded. "Atreiani, we stand ready to rebuild the world, if only you will guide us. Surely you return to lead us out of the darkness?"

Another sip, and she looked him in the eye, a cold serpent's gaze.

"Atreiani?" he ventured.

"This hall," she said, "is two hundred years old or more and rotting from the inside out. The dagger you wear so proudly must be older yet, maybe steel from before the *Eventide*, as you call it, and probably brittle enough to snap underfoot. This place reeks of disease, infection, the dying."

He sat back, eyes wide, then nodded.

"It is true," he said. "For three years we have had waves of pestilence, and now at first freeze it looks to be a fourth."

"I smell it," she said. "At least one victim in this building has streptococcus, and it'll be scarlet fever soon enough."

"You can *smell* this?" he asked incredulously.

"Coming up the hill I noted malnutrition, polluted water, poor hygiene. Given your age, your health, I'd say *you're* at risk, Shwn Jhon."

He loosened his shirt collar. "These are Nature's doings, not ours. We fight Her just as you did."

"It wasn't our goal to *fight* nature. If you think so, then you misunderstand the Atreianii entirely."

"Our agriculture!" he exclaimed with pride. "Did you see our terraces, crop rotations, new hybrids, distribution systems, mills, pumps, and storage facilities? We build housing for every Oudwni—"

"Mouse-infested."

"Give food to everyone—"

"Yet everyone's hollow-ribbed," she said. "You've the fundamentals of agriculture, you instigate basic rotations, but you've no understanding of microbiology or nutrition. So far to go, Shwn Jhon."

"We have remade *order*. We have introduced law to men who would otherwise be barbarians."

"Perhaps you've gone further than the Magna Carta, but you're feudal. You're not much above barbarians yourselves."

He understands Magna Carta, Nyahri thought, *no better than I do.*

"Can you not appreciate," Shwn Jhon said, "what we have done since your departure?"

"I really don't care." She sighed. "I haven't come to lead you out of whatever Dark Age you think you're in. Your predicaments are your own."

"Why have you awakened then?" His eyebrows turned upward.

"To take an accounting, Shwn Jhon Oudwn, but not of you or of the E'cwnii—" She gestured to Nyahri. "—or of any men. I need information on the Citadels, all of them. I need to know if *any* other Atreianii are on the surface. *That's* what I need. In exchange for such information, which I know the Templarii can provide, *maybe* I can help you."

"An accounting? Of your own kind, is that what you mean? Are you a vanguard? Are other Atreianii to wake?"

"No."

"I do not understand." Shwn Jhon scowled, shaking his head. "We struggle and we need your help. We know the world *was* once better, not *how* to make it better again."

Nyahri wondered, as well, about yw Sabi's purpose at Swyn Templr. She wondered, still, what had happened at Abswyn and at the smile it left on yw Sabi's face.

The Atreiani slivered her eyes, drawing her fingertip along the cracked, liquor-stained tabletop. "You create fiefdoms, Shwn Jhon, and impose agrarian lordships. You put the heads of lawbreakers on poles at your hall's gates."

"We have the rule of law," he said, "and every man is treated equally by it. Those men broke our laws."

"I cannot judge you for killing men, but such petty laws to behead petty men for petty offenses. This is a world re-gressed."

"Did you not kill men?"

She tilted her head, a gesture of concession.

"The histories also say—" His words rumbled. "—you killed plenty of your kind."

"Enough." Yw Sabi's jaw tightened.

"Atreiani, I am sorry, but will you not aid us now, this very day?"

"Today? No."

"Atreiani, please—"

"I won't do a thing for you in any way till I reach Sojourn." Yw Sabi smiled, not the few genuine tokens Nyahri had thus far seen, but a calculated simper. Her lips parted enough to hint at her fangs.

"What happens if I let you leave this place?" Shwn Jhon set his mouth in a fleshy arch. "I fear you will abandon us, goddess. If you march on your way, perhaps even with my help, then what? You turn your back on us and we never see you again?"

Yw Sabi folded her arms. "What choice do you have? We aren't your *guests* here," yw Sabi said, "or your *hostages*. Rather I hold *you* hostage, Shwn Jhon, because I have what you want—knowledge of medicines beyond anything you ever dreamt—and there is no way you can wrest it from me."

He stood, trembling as he lifted his weight, and slammed his bulky hands onto the table. "We are dying here! Can you appreciate that? *Dying!*"

Shwn Jhon's men stepped back and one looked at Nyahri, his knuckles white on his blade's hilt. She rested her palm on her longknife, locking eyes with him. Yw Sabi made no move at all except to flick her gaze upward, meeting Shwn Jhon's.

"We are plagued!" he shouted. "Every winter it gets worse!"

"Not my responsibility," the Atreiani said.

"It *is* mine, and we have no medicines which meet the threat. I wager, Atreiani, you do. You have the power to heal us and I *must* garner your help, not in some vague future but as soon as possible."

"Best hurry me to Sojourn then." Her voice remained tempered; her body, relaxed. She took another sip of whiskey. "It is *my* will, and only my will, which counts. I'll do nothing for you till after I reach Cohltos, till after I meet with the Templarii."

"What do we do in the meantime?"

"I recommend you look to the E'cwnii. I've seen their medical practices and, Iron Age or not, they're better than yours. Work with their women and you may stave off the bleakest of this year's losses."

Shwn Jhon scoffed, looking at Nyahri, his lip raised in disgust. "You jest, Atreiani? The filthy E'cwnii are nothing but horse breeders and dung burners. Creatures such as *her*," he said, pointing to Nyahri, "can give us nothing compared to the magics you possess."

Yw Sabi sat forward. "Careful what you say, chieftain. I'm becoming quite fond of this one." She tilted her head toward Nyahri.

Nyahri held back a gasp, as surprised by the Atreiani's words as by her own reaction to them.

Becoming fond.

"Then mayhap we take this E'cwni filly as insurance?" Shwn Jhon said.

Nyahri deepened her stance, hand on her longknife's pommel, ready to draw.

"Take her from me?" The Atreiani's gaze darkened. "How do you imagine that'd end?"

"If you are fond of her," he said, "it might motivate you." He raised his voice. "Watchmen!"

The chamber's upper doors opened, vomiting men onto the mezzanine. Nyahri figured two dozen, each armed with blade and longbow, arrows nocked. Despite the fearful trembling in some of their arms, Nyahri had no doubt of their training.

The Atreiani sat still as before, leaning with her arms folded against the tabletop. "You're a fool," she told Shwn Jhon, "and you and all the men in this room will perish."

His eyes widened.

"You think I fear your archers?" yw Sabi said. "The E'cwni and I will walk out of here, but not before everyone in this building dies."

With a casual backhand, she slapped the priceless carafe. It fell, spilling the rest of the whiskey, and careened off the edge of the table. The glass shattered across the floor.

"I'll destroy Aukensis," she said, "lay waste to all you ever built, and nothing will remain, erasing even your name. I'll kill every man and woman, every child, every suckling babe—or you can come to your senses and arrange my escort to Sojourn."

Shwn Jhon gaped at the broken glass, his horror and offense evident. "You'd choose an E'cwn foal over our entire nation?"

"Her father offered me good food and a warm welcome. You offer me deceptions and bald threats."

The archers anchored their bowstrings at their cheeks. Nyahri shifted her attention to Shwn Jhon, ready for the barest sign he'd order the attack, preparing herself at best to dive beneath a table.

"Decide," yw Sabi said.

Shwn Jhon's eye twitched. "You must away to Sojourn Temple?"

"Immediately."

"Archers," he said, "lower your bows."

"Wise."

"Are you really so cruel," Shwn Jhon said, "as to murder children? If you can care for one human girl, might you care for others?"

"You cannot guess what I care for."

"May I show you something?"

"Tell me," yw Sabi said.

He stood and stepped from the table, setting his fists on his enormous hips. "I can show you much better. Please? If you will?"

"All right," she said, "but be quick about it."

{13}

hwn Jhon ascended wide stairs to the topmost level. Twice he rested on his knees, catching his breath. Yw Sabi followed, Nyahri behind her, with guardsmen trailing. Narrow south windows admitted a ration of daylight, but a bitter autumn wind chased the warmth. By the time Nyahri reached the top stair, her teeth chattered.

Standing at the uppermost landing, she smelled what her mistress already had: a rotten-sweet sickness. Beyond a set of double doors, a wide chamber held rows of rough-sheeted beds, curtains hanging between them. A copper vat boiled on an open-stone hearth. Two nurses stirred laundry in it, and bed sheets dried on iron rods.

In the beds lay men and women and children, some beaten by disease, their lungs rattling. A few twisted in unconscious throes. In others, a pre-death stillness loomed, an impotent rise and fall of their raspy chests.

"These," Shwn Jhon said, "and more in the village. Every year and no break in the cycle."

"I'll tell you this," yw Sabi said, "clean Orÿs and every other building. You live in filth. Open everything to the sun. Make soap, scrub this edifice from the rafters to the foundations. Repair the shutters and doors. Raze any sickly domicile and rebuild. Get your sewage as far from here as you can and implement a practical drainage system."

He shook his head. "We haven't labor to spare or the means to move the people while this work is done. Assuredly you realize this, Atreiani? You saw the shorthanded harvest, and winter will be too cold. It is in these very walls we will stay, as we always have."

"Then within these walls even more of you will die."

"What choice do we have?"

"You want easy answers, Shwn Jhon, but you won't get them from me. Rally your people and *work*."

Yw Sabi strolled between the sickbeds, looking upon young girls, old men, and adults afflicted in their prime. She examined the cauldron.

"You've developed no medicines?" she asked.

"Certain distillates," Shwn Jhon said. "The Templarii gave us formulas, some of the ancient medicines, but we cannot master them. Even the Templarii can produce only small doses. What little we have, we give to the children mostly."

"As you should," yw Sabi said.

"We have stronger tonics, yea, but they are often as fatal as the sicknesses. The Templarii say these diseases were beaten before their time, and they know little of them. They told me, if they could enter Sojourn, they might learn more."

"The Templarii cannot enter *any* Citadel." Yw Sabi allowed herself a self-satisfied smile.

"An Atreiani could."

"That's right."

"One such as you. If there are medicines in Sojourn, you could retrieve them."

"I could."

She paced from the cauldron, and the nurses retreated from her, their eyes wide. Firelight danced on everything but the Atreiani's unnatural black hair.

Nyahri met the eye of a bedridden boy. Her heart wrenched, and she looked away. When she raised her eyes again, she met Shwn Jhon's jaundiced glare.

He returned his attention to yw Sabi. "We need your miracles, Atreiani," he said.

"Sojourn Temple is a Pandora's Box."

"Pandora's box?"

She shrugged. "Get me there and I'll attempt what I can."

He stood between a pair of beds, his arms outstretched. A half-conscious boy lay in one cot, his mouth drawn thin, sweat matting his hair. In the other cot a pale girl shivered, her eyes shut. Blood gathered at her lips, staining her pillow. Nyahri edged closer to yw Sabi, her gut knotting.

Few E'cwn children die this way, she thought.

"These," Shwn Jhon said, "are my grandchildren—lovely Niki on my left, and her older brother Tohmas. Their father, Andreo, who would have been my heir, is dead. You ask, Atreiani, for me to accept your denial and let them die too? I cannot."

Yw Sabi pointed. "You want to improve their chances? Get me on my way."

He bowed his head, coughed, and laughed. "You are more solidity and practicality than I had imagined, Atreiani. I had expected a creature of air and fire, and instead I find you all flint."

She gestured to the children. "Your choice—help me or turn me against you."

"Seems I have no choice whatsoever." He caressed the boy's brow. "It is true what Templarii say of the Atreianii, you know."

"What do they say?"

"You have no love in you."

Nyahri wondered.

He cocked his head, a gesture similar to his son's. "Come morning, Dhaos will escort you over the mountains, with his men, to bring you safely to Cohltos."

"Good," yw Sabi said.

"Tonight, I can give you a room, food, a bed."

Nyahri clicked her tongue. "Mistress?"

Yw Sabi nodded to her, then said to Shwn Jhon, "My companion nurtures an over-particular love of her horses and doesn't like to be separated from them. On her account I insist on riding tonight. On my account, I'm concerned she may catch an illness here, and that won't do."

"That *fondness* you spoke of," Shwn Jhon choked out the words, shooting a glance at the E'cwni.

Yw Sabi turned to Nyahri. "The small bag, give it me."

Nyahri unslung it, a bladder-sized sack of black Atreian cloth. Yw Sabi slid a finger along one seam, opening it. She lifted from it a tiny glass phial and held out her closed hand to Shwn Jhon.

"Take it," she said.

He approached her tentatively, raised his arm, and opened his palm. She dropped the phial into his hand.

"It's the most I can spare you," she said.

His gaze widened at the transparent cylinder. "What do I do with it?"

"A drop on each child's tongue, once every three days, no more." She gave him a long stare. "It may not be enough to save them—their own immune systems will have to do that—but it will improve their odds."

He looked at the phial, looked at her, and gaped.

Yw Sabi returned to the landing and began down the stairs. Nyahri took her place at the Atreiani's right shoulder and the guardsmen started behind them.

"Your peons," yw Sabi called back to Shwn Jhon, "needn't show us out. Their efforts would better serve the nurses. More clean cloth and soap, fewer weapons."

FROM THE FIELDS, NYAHRI took several bunches of carrots, eating one root as they descended the trail, keeping the rest for the horses. She breathed easier as she and yw Sabi rode away from Aukensis. They left Dhaos and his men behind, expecting the troop to catch them by morning.

"Will we *actually* wait for them?" Nyahri asked.

"We've bought a semblance of safe passage—we'll wait. I would have preferred to put more kilometers behind us, tonight, but Dhaos babbled something about *letting his men spend a night with their families.*"

By evening, Nyahri led yw Sabi to the cedar hollow and the path which would return them to the Bhar. Before they set camp, the moonlight graced the treetops, Lwn and Stashwn a sliver past full, Trwl nudging farther from her sisters each night. Nyahri lit a generous fire, and yw Sabi settled by it, absorbed in her own thoughts while Nyahri tended the horses.

As she brushed him, she whispered to Kwlko, "Gods! The insults she heaped upon Shwn Jhon—she has a way about her."

The horse nuzzled her, nibbling for a treat. So long as she gave him carrots, he agreed with her every word.

"He could have killed us."

"He would not have," yw Sabi said.

Nyahri looked over her shoulder. "There anything you do not hear with those ears of yours?"

"I established dominance, showed Shwn Jhon I go and do as I wish."

"You risked much."

"It was vital he *believed* in my strength, in what I may offer him. It's also important he believes the only way he'll get what he wants is by pleasing me."

"How much did you bluff him, Atreiani?"

"Oh, somewhat."

Nyahri slipped the brush into her bags and returned to the fire. Along the way down the mountainside, she shot a single skinny rabbit—she was growing tired of rabbit—and it now cooked over the embers. Yw Sabi ate little, just as she slept little.

Nyahri asked. *"Is* there a cure at Swyn Templr?"

"And many other things besides. If there's Prosee, there's a cure."

"Prosee?"

"Adaptive immunogenic. Bacterial, viral, fungal, in some cases even mechanical or chemical—if it's invasive and deleterious, Prosee kills it."

Nyahri understood *fungal,* and planned to ask about *bacterial* and *viral.* "A cure? You will give it to them, nay?"

"Remember, I did not promise Shwn Jhon anything."

Nyahri hugged her knees. *Ay! What of the children, of so much blood on the girl's pillow?*

The Atreiani sighed. "Listen, I'm not heedless of their suffering, but it cannot be my primary concern. If it bothers you, saddle Kwlko in the morning and go back to the plains, back to your father."

Nyahri shook her head. "Goddess—"

"Don't *goddess* me. The nonsense which slips through your teeth!"

"Mistress—"

"Stop *mistressing* me too." Yw Sabi lifted her chin, gazing at Nyahri. "The medicines I gave them won't last long and they weren't made for humans. I cannot *conjure* any other cure to save those dying children, or anyone else. It would take years to get the Oudwnii producing even twentieth-century medicines. I don't have the time. For them it is the medicines of Sojourn or it is nothing."

"Why did you not *promise* them those medicines?"

"It's complicated."

"I am not stupid."

"No, you're not. Promises are tricky, the giving of them heavy, and the future after them unclear." Yw Sabi's smile flickered and vanished.

"Mistress?"

Yw Sabi gave a soft growl, frowning. "Once upon a time, if some human *mistressed* me the way you insist, they would've suffered for it, I assure you."

"I do not mean disrespect."

"You're willful, testing me on purpose. You're also still ignorant, even if you're *not* stupid."

"Then every day we ride together, every day I am with you, my ignorance becomes more your fault, less mine."

The Atreiani's eyes flashed, then became black razors. "Careful, Nyahri."

"I do not wish to be ignorant, *mistress*, and in all the world only you can teach me, nay? You are the only one who can teach me anything more which matters."

Yw Sabi frowned, then asked, "What was your mother's name?"

Nyahri blinked, taken aback. "Lorahdi."

"What did Lorahdi teach you? What was in those rituals you and your sister witnessed? What did your mother say to you that you keep insisting on *mistress?*"

"Some men and women," Nyahri said, "they existed beyond the wrath of the Atreianii. This is what the songs say. Such people lived with the gods and goddesses. It was true, nay? They honored an oath?"

"Some men and women? Less than one in twenty thousand. The *oath* could exist only between an Atreiani and her *Exemplari,* never more than three. It bound each to the other, a conceit which fettered the Atreianii to humanity, to remind us forever of shared responsibilities. We designed it to transcend time, a phenomenon not you nor anyone else could understand without experiencing it."

She sat forward, her heart quickening. "How might I experience it? I could—"

"Tsk! What makes you think I'd choose you?"

Nyahri winced, sitting back with her palms against her thighs. "You said you were fond of me."

"*Fond* and *oath* are a world apart."

"Then you would never—"

"Ah!" Yw Sabi held up her finger, silencing Nyahri. "Stop jumping to conclusions. What makes you think I *wouldn't?*"

This hung between them.

Nyahri's heart tore in opposite directions, and her cheeks warmed. "What must I do?"

"You must *do* nothing. It's mine to give, and no light thing to offer. You're a nescient girl, as far as I can tell, and I've known you barely more than a fortnight. This conversation is pointless."

"I—"

"Enough talking. Finish eating."

Exemplari. Nyahri rolled the word through her mind. *Yea, my mother knew stories, and she knew stories of you, Sultah yw Sabi.*

Some cruel.

Were they true? Would you tell them someday?

Yw Sabi and Nyahri ate the rest of their meal in silence. Night sounds accompanied the crackling of the fire, distant coyotes singing. The firelight faded as they sipped their tea, its steam curling. Nyahri leaned back, gazing at the stellar tapestry as she always had, pondering the moons, the White River, the constellations:

What does yw Sabi see when she gazes at them?

Whatever the Atreiani thought or felt, her expression offered no hint. A sense of events larger than herself kept Nyahri fixed on her path, an undercurrent of curiosity, and of something else which she could not yet name, something which burrowed at the back of her mind and within her chest. At moments, yw Sabi's stern shell felt no tougher than an egg.

Or a hornets' nest.

I misjudged Suhto's heart, Nyahri thought, *and he a man I knew my whole life. So how can I weigh an Atreiani's heart?*

She did not know.

THE SUN ROSE, THE morning frost melting. Nyahri rebuilt the fire and prepared their gear, waiting for the Oudwnii to arrive. Even though she expected them, her gut still tightened when they did. They joked and jostled with each other, little boys half grown to be killers.

Dhaos shined with pride. His men walked behind him, most with their bows strung. They spread along the trail, formation never too tight, always watchful.

The vulture god, Nyahri thought, *might come when these archers will.*

Yet when Dhaos smiled at her, she forgot about death. Nyahri smiled back despite herself.

"It will be a long hike," he said, "this first day, but good for the appetite. Tonight we feast to the gods, court some luck."

Yw Sabi reclined by the fire, her hands crossed behind her head. "How long to Sojourn?"

"A fortnight or so," he said, "if the weather holds. More if it worsens."

When the Atreiani only stared at him, he fidgeted, refocusing on Nyahri. Her blood warmed and she turned from him.

"I will saddle the horses," she said.

Yw Sabi stood, dusted her clothes, and looked from archer to archer. Few held her gaze.

"Possibly, Dhaos," she said, "you'd be helpful and smother the fire."

The women mounted. Dhaos rubbed the stallion's muzzle as if petting a dog, and Nyahri glowered at him, her fists tightening on the reins.

He does not understand E'cwn customs, she reminded herself, *when it is all right to touch a woman's horse, when it is not.*

"It is a safe-enough road," he said, "for some days, until we leave the lower valleys."

"What awaits us farther on?" yw Sabi asked.

He grinned. "Other than snow? I have cousins among the Qebeccêi, many weeks up the ranges, who tell us groups of C'naädii and Gabarii wander south."

"Do we need to worry?"

"The C'naädin gods measure the heaven-worthiness of men by how well they murder, and *these* men will be starving. The Gabarii have no gods and no heaven—they are animals."

"Delightful people, I'm sure. Why're they starving exactly?"

"The north has had five or six bad years now, though our mountains will not help them much. In this region, most interlopers starve, and hunger does much to make a man throw away his life. For years we have pressed the Gabarii back from the upper fields, but their numbers still grow, and the C'naädii are more organized and better trained."

Yw Sabi nodded but said nothing more.

With a word from their captain, the archers began a slow jog toward the high meadows, the path which would take them west. Yw Sabi and Nyahri followed.

{Interim: Divine Transmissions}

2130617:194431:EA39.7392N+104.9842W:
AUTUMN01::

LORAHDI: O goddess, you honor me! Your beauty is the stars, your voice the song of truth! Thank you for your coming!

AUTUMN01: You are a good woman, a keeper of your people, an exemplar among humankind. Know that we love you.

LORAHDI: How may I serve you? What task could I possibly undertake for you?

AUTUMN01: You are their voice. You will keep them. Hold the Atreianii higher than all others and teach your children to do the same.

LORAHDI: Higher even than you?

AUTUMN01: Even than we. The Hive is not your concern. Keep the faith of your Atreianii, make your children ready to follow them.

Transcript Archive, Exhibit A
Vo Misa Station

{14}

Throughout the day they kept a brisk pace. The trees opened onto the high meadows, and the company broke from the cedars into the valleys, veering westward on a deep-trodden path.

A path of generations, Nyahri thought, *certainly the same my father took in his boyhood, the same he followed after as a raider, as a killer of Oudwnii.*

Dhaos knew the high trails, keeping the travelers clear of mires. During the early afternoon they crested a saddle pass which dropped into fields riotous with wildflowers. The troop paused, eating and gazing at the gelid peaks, now closer and larger and crisper. Snow plumes whisked from their pinnacles. As Nyahri marveled at the view, Dhaos sat on his heels beside her.

"There is an alpine crossing," he said, pointing, "between those mountains, quite high. We will cross it before the heaviest snows come, or not at all, not till spring."

"I have never seen anything like this, never been so much in the sky. It is hard to breathe."

"The air here is thinner."

"How do *you* fair, then?"

"You get accustomed." He whispered to her, "How is it, E'cwni, you come to follow an Atreiani? What happened at Abswyn?" Nyahri glanced over her shoulder. Some distance away, yw Sabi stood on a quartz-granite boulder, arms folded, her face into the breeze. The bright sun disappeared within her long windswept hair. "The first question is my business," Nyahri said, "the second is hers." Dhaos's mischievous eyes centered on her, then on her spear. She clutched it, leaning her cheek against it. "You use *that* well enough," he said.

"I would not have cut your throat." She remembered how close she came to it when they first met.

"Oh, I think you might have." His lips curled again into his persistent smile.

She half shrugged, looking askance at him. "You did not sit here to talk about snow or spears."

"Nay."

"What then?"

He hesitated. "I know who you are."

She leaned from him.

"Knew it the instant I heard your name," he said.

"Who else knows? Everyone?"

"No one." He picked up a pebble and tossed it. "Definitely not my father, gods no. If he had known, there would have been blood."

"Why did you not tell him?"

"He gets what he wants out of all this, I think." Dhaos spoke in low tones, hiding his words even from his men. "We need no more enmity. Would you agree?"

She held her tongue, sensing danger between every word.

"Father may think of you only as a dirty E'cwni," he said, "but I had teachers shrewder than that. They record the family names of the Ahtrosi and Ahtrose, and I learned them."

"How would they hear of them, these teachers of yours?"

"Travelers, traders, wanderers. Men crisscross the world, swapping goods, exchanging information. I learn what I can of the E'cwnii. I respect you."

"What of it?"

"There are elders on the chieftains' council who still despise your father. They hated your grandfather even more—"

"Why do you tell me this?" She frowned. "How is this supposed to make me feel, eh?"

"Nay! You mistake me." He raised his hands deferentially. "My point is that there are younger councilmen, like me, who would like open trade, who would sue for peace, who envision better things for the future. When I sit on the council, I will make things right."

"Between E'cwnii and Oudwnii?"

He nodded. "Between you and me."

"You think me easy?" Nyahri almost smiled. "You make a game of this?"

"A game?"

"You see me and you see a pretty girl to win to your side?"

"I—"

"You see a conquest?"

"I, nay—"

She rolled her eyes. "Gods."

"You misunderstand—"

"Take us to Cohltos."

He sat back against a rock, eyebrows drawn down, shoulders fallen. "You would not try for peace?"

"Did I say I would not? I said nothing like that."

He nodded, more contrite.

I like you, Dhaos, she thought. *Despite myself, into my belly.*

Yw Sabi's voice rang out, "Dhaos! We've rested too long. Pack up!"

He hesitated, a double glance into Nyahri's eyes, and he grinned. Dhaos gathered the company and, with the horses at the rear, the company walked through the slow afternoon into a pleasant windless night. Many thousands of strides onward, with archers stationed at the camp's edges, other men split wood and lit cooking fires. They dined on roast beef and vegetables, and Nyahri took her fill of it, the last and only fresh food the Oudwnii brought from Aukensis. The rest would be dried rations and whatever they caught along the way.

The Oudwnii smiled, laughing with each other. Dhaos beckoned Nyahri with open-faced grins, though she took her seat beside yw Sabi at a separate fire. The Atreiani added logs to it, and with a twig she marked symbols in the fireside dust.

"You wanted me to teach you," she said to Nyahri, "time to learn."

Nyahri studied the writing.

"Can you read these letters?" The Atreiani pointed to them.

"Some."

"Try."

"*Merkooree.*"

Yw Sabi tapped the ground. "Draw this sound out."

"*Mercuree.*"

"Close enough. Next—"

"*Venoos.*"

The Atreiani smiled. "Same symbol, but *uh* not *oo*."

"*Venus.*"

"Next."

"*Ayert.*"

"Interesting mispronunciation. Say it—*Earth.*"

"*Earth.*"

"Good."

"*Marse.*"

"Good," yw Sabi said. "More *z*, less *s*."

"*Marz.*"

"Better."

Nyahri furrowed her brow.

"Say the rest with me," and together they stumbled, "*Jupiter, Saturn, Uranus, Neptune, Hades, Nibiru.*"

"What are these words?" Nyahri asked.

"The names of planets, the last one artificial, our making—its name almost a joke originally. We can count five from here, Earth, and I'm sure the E'cwnii have their own names for those. Time changes language. Older roots make yours, in part the tongues most used by my kind. Understand?"

"I think so."

"Yours is Espana and bits of Englisce with bizarre tonalities, almost uniquely Cine." Yw Sabi studied Nyahri's face, hinting a smile. "I *see* Cine in you, in the corners of your eyes, but I've no explanation for *that* emigration. You kept Latinate characters. I'm calculating etymology as I go, listening to you, lovely one."

So many unfamiliar words: *Espana, Cine, Latinate, etymology*—

Yet Nyahri heard only: *Lovely one.*

Her voice has not sounded thus before, so warm, even kind.

Yw Sabi continued, "You may find Englisce valuable soon."

"I will learn."

"Good. Your ability to read the names of the planets, that shows you've already learned."

"Mother taught me, and her mother before, the old letters—*Englisce.*"

"Your era's Latin. You must improve. Read again."

"*Mercury, Venus, Earth, Mars, Jupiter, Saturn, Uranus, Neptune, Hades, Nibiru.*"

"Good."

The Atreiani looked toward the archers, tilting her head, her attitude sharper.

She hears them, Nyahri thought, *every word they say.*

"They're reckless," yw Sabi said, "these Oudwnii. Frightened too, but that'll fade."

"What do you mean?"

"They're boasting, bullshitting each other."

An odd word. "Bullshitting?"

"Something about where they'd like to put their cocks. They won't fear me much longer."

"I would keep peace with them."

"Might not be possible, even with your pretty captain." Yw Sabi exhaled, a short sigh. "They're fighting men and, once they get callous to something, once they get it into their heads they're better, they'll push their boundaries. If the opportunity presents itself I'll remove their reason to boast."

"Do you fear them?" Nyahri asked, sneaking glances at Dhaos, wondering if yw Sabi *could* fear, remembering she broached such a question once before.

Cautious, yw Sabi had said.

The Atreiani's expression grew icy. "A time will come when they'll guess what *you* already figure."

"What?"

"I'm not invincible." Yw Sabi shrugged.

Nyahri held her lower lip in her teeth. "Yea."

"Give me your hand."

Nyahri hesitated.

The Atreiani repeated, *"Give* me your hand."

Nyahri extended her arm and yw Sabi pressed her long, encompassing fingers over Nyahri's palm. Yw Sabi's fingertips glanced only across the surface, at the same time soothing, warming, and delightfully nauseating.

"Feel my skin?" yw Sabi said.

"How can I not?" Nyahri wondered if the Atreiani detected the tremble in her voice.

"Your skin has more in common with a fish's or bird's or mouse's than with mine. There're a thousand differences between our physiologies. We Atreianii are engineered creatures, *but if you prick us, do we not bleed?* We're tough, hard to kill, but we can die."

Nyahri nodded as if she understood, missing important words, terms foreign to any E'cwni.

"My DNA looks nothing like yours," yw Sabi said, "but my emotions—"

Despite their darkness, her eyes reflected the fire.

"Everything I once knew is gone," she continued, "my entire life, people I *did* call friends, cared for, things I cherished."

"Why share this with me?"

The intensity of their touch grew.

Yw Sabi sat straighter. For one moment, in the dim light, her humanity peeked through at the edges. Yet in the next, her pale lips thinned and she raised her chin, halfway distant.

"You are lonely?" Nyahri said.

"Yes."

"I understand. You are going to Swyn Templr to awaken others like you? You will have brothers and sisters, fellow Atreianii."

Yw Sabi shook her head. "No."

"Shwn Jhon Oudwn expects you to. So does Dhaos, so do they all, I expect."

"Their mistake."

"Tell me your whole purpose. Why to Swyn Templr? Why with so much haste?"

"I'll not tell you yet."

Yw Sabi let go of Nyahri's hand, taking her warmth with it. For the sudden distance, Nyahri shivered, turning to the fire.

"Each night," the Atreiani said, "so long as we've firelight, we'll work on your reading."

"Yea, gladly," Nyahri said, yearning for yw Sabi to keep speaking.

"Then vocabulary, long as that takes, and other things altogether. If we're in each other's company enough, you'll study math, the sciences, history, philosophy." Yw Sabi reclined in her blankets and unhooked the witch-scepter, holding it to her chest. In time the fire faded, logs crumbling into charcoal. "I'll keep the watch tonight."

"What troubles you?"

"You should sleep, Nyahri."

"You can tell me."

The Atreiani smiled at those words but said, "Not now."

Nyahri sighed, breaking the fire, plunging the camp into shadow. She set out her bedroll and curled in it, her longknife clutched in her hand, spear beside her. For a while, she could no more sleep than could yw Sabi, and she stared into the sky.

"Yw Sabi, the drunken stars, those are the planets?"

"Very good. In the Greek they were *planetes asteres*, the *wandering stars*. Mercury and Venus dance around Sol like drunkards, Mars and Jupiter and Saturn plod through the solar system, all in their orbits. Each moves in its time, as does this third stone from the sun."

So many words translated poorly. *Solar system,* Nyahri thought, rolling the concept through her mind, something which sounded to her like bits of wood floating in a whirlpool, going round and round forever.

"The sun moves around *us,* Atreiani."

"Does it? Give it some thought and we'll explore that when next we speak of it."

Nyahri pursed her lips, scrunching her eyebrows as she considered. "What about the jade star, the one southeast tonight?"

"That's Mars, once the Red Planet. I was pleased on my first night awake to find it still green. What do you call it?"

"*Cwlr,* the mountain lion. Only his left eye is turned to us."

"Its green is the color of *your* eyes."

"Suhto told me so once."

Nyahri tucked the blankets under her chin and, looking up, found the Atreiani's serpent gaze on her. It no longer frightened her.

Were the Atreianii devils or were they gods? Nyahri sighed. *Why must there be only two choices?*

WHATEVER HUMANITY AND SYMPATHY yw Sabi had revealed by firelight, she concealed it come morning. As the company rode into the higher timber, she watched the woodland, showing no great interest for anything save perhaps the cry of a falcon or the crash of a waterfall.

After three days they departed the meadows for a river-cut ravine, its steep ledges shouldering narrow paths. The woodsmen thought nothing of deadfalls, at home among them, but Nyahri eyed each precipice, cursing and worrying about the stallion's footing. Scouts walked ahead, arrows nocked, their footsteps soundless on the trail. The thick of spruces and ferns made ambush all too possible.

"This is brigands' land here," Dhaos said.

The company burned no more fires and, once within the thickest copses, yw Sabi taught no more lessons in language or astronomy. She, Nyahri, and every Oudwni knew the risk they took, crossing the divide during the wrong time of year. At night the Atreiani sat motionless, attentive to every sound. The evenings passed in horse-tending and small talk, but the Oudwnii bantered less as the nights wore on.

On the fourth night the wind howled. Lwn and Stashwn, slipping toward crescent, drowned in the clouds. Nyahri built a lean-to of pine branches against a copse, and she and yw Sabi bundled furs and blankets beneath it, keeping the horses close by. After their meal, Nyahri lay on her side under the covers, propped on her elbow, with Yw Sabi cross-legged beside her, and for a long time they said nothing.

"The scar," yw Sabi said, "on your arm. What did that?"

Nyahri raised her head, looking at the jagged mark as if for the first time. "I did it myself."

"Why?"

"When my mother died."

"Hmm. What about the newer one above it?"

"When my brother died."

"Not so long ago."

"This last spring."

Yw Sabi knit her eyebrows, giving a sympathetic frown. "And the longer one on your shoulder? I know you didn't do *that* yourself."

"My uncle gave that one to me."

"No accident, I'm guessing."

"Nay—a longknife. He managed to turn me, thought to make a deathblow of it."

The Atreiani leaned back, her concern plain. "Whatever for?"

"I was trying to kill him," Nyahri said.

"Why?"

"Any other man does to me what he did, I will kill him too."

Yw Sabi nodded. *"Did* you kill him?"

"In front of my father, my brother, my uncle's wife, his children, everyone." Nyahri's chest tightened. "He outweighed me twice over and fought a lifetime longer, but it was my right to try."

"I see."

"You judge me, Atreiani?"

Yw Sabi's voice softened. "Not at all."

"He offered to marry me," Nyahri said, "to atone. No one offered to marry me after that day."

"Until Suhto."

"Yea, until Suhto."

Yw Sabi leaned across the short gap between them, drawing the backs of her fingers along Nyahri's hair, then she pulled back, glancing Nyahri's cheek with her fingertips. Nyahri turned her face to the touch before lying back again, beyond yw Sabi's reach.

Do not touch me so, or do, or do not. Gods! Which is it?

"Ahtros's daughter?" yw Sabi said. "You're a middle child, you weren't expected to lead."

Nyahri shook her head.

"You never wanted the role."

"Nay," Nyahri said.

"If you don't return to your tribe?"

"If I die, out here, in these mountains? Cirje must prove she can lead, or marry some man who can."

Yw Sabi leaned back on her hands, furthering the distance between them, taking a long breath. "Do I still look like a devil to you?"

The Atreiani's clothing was loosened, the strange clasps from her neck to her navel unfastened. Her alabaster skin shone, neck and face white even to her lips, rounded by shadow. Her hair appeared as clearly for its seeming absence, erasing all light where it fell. Undone, those plaits unfurled to yw Sabi's waist, even darker than the night. Frost kissed the bison furs, and both women breathed plumes into the cold, though yw Sabi showed no sign she felt it, no goose-flesh or shivering.

"Nay, Atreiani, you look like a goddess to me."

"I'll get it through your head—I'm no *goddess*." Yw Sabi half smiled. "Though I must still seem something strange."

"Yea, but beautiful."

"Long time since I heard someone say *beautiful* the way you do." Yw Sabi reached for Nyahri again, and Nyahri remained still. With a sigh, this time the Atreiani held back entirely. "It's cold, it's late. We should *both* sleep."

{15}

When Nyahri opened her eyes, the night still blackened the forest. The Atreiani breathed steadily, sleeping for once. They lay together in the tiny shelter, wrapped in the blankets. Outside, only the wind showed any life at all.

Nyahri curled against the Atreiani's back, nuzzled the gossamer of her hair, pleasant for all its strangeness. She breathed the scent of yw Sabi's skin. The flutter in Nyahri's chest told her what she wanted.

Who she desired, for days now building within her, perhaps even since the first moment. Not three weeks since she awakened, injured, with yw Sabi tending her. Not three since that first fear and excitement.

What is the right time for desire? Nyahri thought.

Then, *She is not even human.*

Then, *Does it even matter?*—Then, *What* is *human?*

She remembered Suhto.

Suhto.

Cold air stirred against Nyahri's cheek, evoking the vast forest, the emptier world. Like ice, that emptiness solidified, and all else misted into nothing. For all the world's wonders, all Nyahri understood and all she hadn't yet learned, some things would never again exist beneath the sheltering sky. Suhto, who had desired her, was gone forever; her brother, forever; her mother, forever.

Even her uncle, forever.

The rest of the night, Nyahri slept in fits, until the sky lightened from black to indigo. A handful of birds whistled, those few wintering the forest. The Atreiani lay quietly in front of her, also on her side.

As Nyahri had woken before with desire, now she awoke with sorrow.

Suhto.

Her tears welled and flowed, her sobs beginning as tremors. *Suhto.* All the grief came.

Stupid, stupid Suhto. Stupid, stupid me.

"Shh," came yw Sabi's voice as she turned. "What is this?"

Nyahri attempted to stifle those tears, and failed, laying against yw Sabi's arm. "Suhto is dead. He *is* dead and it is my fault."

"No."

"I miss him." Her tears poured.

"Of course you do."

"I am so *angry.*"

"Why angry?"

"I—" Nyahri clenched her teeth.

A knife would hurt less than this, she thought.

"Whisper it to me," said yw Sabi.

"I dared him and he took it. So stupid, he took it."

"Not your fault. Nor his, either. The ignorance of youth."

"I am angry, yw Sabi, angry. I wish he had not died." Rage and sorrow crashed over her, one after the other.

"Pour it out."

"Angry," Nyahri said, her fingernails biting into her closed fist. "Angry, so angry."

Sad, so sad.

"I know," the Atreiani said, all the husk and power of her voice gone, replaced by something softer, more yielding, "you just hadn't let it out yet."

"I am sorry," Nyahri said, sniffling, snot running from her nose onto yw Sabi's arm. "I am sorry, Suhto."

Yw Sabi set her arm around Nyahri's shoulders, nudging her closer. "I'm here."

Yea, you are! Nyahri laid her arms over yw Sabi's, fingertips curled against the Atreiani's skin, skin soft and warm, not at all like the pale quartz it appeared to be.

The next day the drizzling clouds gathered earlier. Temperatures dropped, icing the path, and white plumes choked the mountain crowns. Nyahri bundled into her thickest clothes, bracing furs about her as she rode.

During the fifth night in the high canyons, the snow fell at last. Gentle and windless, it clung to the pines and settled on the earth, a handspan deep before halting at midnight. The forest granted some protection through the early dark hours, but the air had teeth.

Once more, Nyahri fashioned a shelter, and neither waking desires nor grief came to her that night. The Atreiani sat awake, lost in her own thoughts, and she mentioned nothing of Suhto or Nyahri's shed tears.

To Nyahri's relief.

Embarrassing, she thought. She had not wept in anyone's arms for years, and she feared she had lost some respect.

The next morning she ached most for the warmth of a good E'cwn tent. Her muscles protested the saddle, frost in her bones. As the march renewed, Nyahri stiffened behind the saddlebow, sore with the distances traveled. The thin air sapped her, and to her the canyons resembled cages, too narrow and confined.

She caught yw Sabi looking at her, a moment's concern on the Atreiani's face.

Nyahri turned away, glancing over her shoulder, and she clenched her teeth at their tracks over the mud-trampled ice and slush. As the morning passed, the tenacious snow remained, leaving their trail for anyone to find.

After midday the clouds regained their strength, the chill deepening, and a new front gathered into a gray firmament which roiled over the peaks.

Dhaos scowled. "An early storm."

"Bigger than last night's?" yw Sabi asked.

"Much."

"Your advice?"

"Find an eastern slope, and soon. Build our shelters well. These clouds are slow."

"If they're slow, we should make time."

"Nay, Atreiani. Light winds and dark clouds mean heavy snow. We need cover now."

Yw Sabi scowled at the sky, her double fangs fully bared. "How long will the storm last?"

"To—" Dhaos faltered at the site of her teeth. "Tonight till dawn, likely as not. Sunshine will follow—or another storm. No way to know, Atreiani."

"Then where to?"

"This path tightens ahead—it is no use to us. Less than an hour ago we passed rounded slopes with thick firs, and those will do. We have time to make shelters, even for the horses."

Yw Sabi nodded, turning Turo around. Nyahri kept beside her. Dhaos waved the archers downslope and they retraced their steps, men and horses alike sometimes slipping on the iced earth, tortuously slow.

A scout's whistle arose and Dhaos called a halt. The forerunner returned, gulping breaths, exhaling mist.

"We went ahead a thousand paces," he said, "and checked the overlooks. On the path we found new footprints."

"Whose?" Dhaos asked.

"Thick-booted, armed. A blade print left in the snow where a man knelt. Not Oudwn, but no telling who."

"They would know of our passing, yea?"

"Only the blind would miss our tracks."

Dhaos's frown deepened. "Keep two guards ahead, two at rear. Everyone keeps his bow at the ready."

Nyahri strung the longbow and hooked her quiver to the saddle horn.

"Maybe nothing," Dhaos said to her, "a man or two crossing our path."

"Or a dozen or two," yw Sabi said, her voice deepening to a growl, "or a score or two, or a hundred or two, anywhere in these mountains."

Dhaos signaled the party forward. Nyahri studied the forest, bringing the stallion closer to the gelding. She stayed at the Atreiani's left shoulder, where her arrows could best protect them should enemies take their flanks.

The Atreiani also remained vigilant, assessing their risks. "What do you think, Nyahri?"

"I think you chose a poor guide, for mountains, when you chose me."

"Nonsense, and there's nothing we could have done differently unless we'd grown wings and flown."

The company halted on a lee and, before nightfall, the flurries arrived. The Oudwnii cut trees and assembled lean-tos.

Nyahri thatched spruce limbs into a shelter for herself and yw Sabi, and Dhaos helped set a windbreak for the horses. For warmth the company risked small half-hidden fires. With their knives and bows at hand the archers watched the darkness, and the waning crescent moons above the clouds shone between clouds only in the briefest moments, the entire forest quiet save for murmured conversations.

"Warm enough?" the Atreiani asked.

"For now." Nyahri looked out across the camp, a landscape obscured by shadow and snowfall.

Yw Sabi sealed their enclosure with a tarp, a cloth of Atreian witchery which reflected their body heat inward. She settled into the blankets, her gaze lingering on Nyahri.

"What is it?" Nyahri asked.

"Nothing."

Nyahri turned away, hoping the darkness hid her blushing, knowing the Atreiani saw much better than she. For no good reason, Nyahri braided the saddlebag ties, only a distraction, anything to settle her thoughts.

"Nothing, mistress?"

"*Mistress* again," yw Sabi said, this time with a surrendering sigh. "You *do* puzzle me."

"How?"

"There was a word spoken in your people's camp, one I haven't heard since, one I haven't quite been able to work out, one spoken about *you.*"

"What word?"

"*Safi.*"

"Ay." Nyahri redoubled her attentions on the leather ties.

"I made you uncomfortable."

"Nay."

"We can talk about it some other time." Yw Sabi turned away, resting her head on her arm.

Nyahri's heart beat far too fast.

Let us talk of it now! she thought, but of course she said nothing.

§

IN THE NIGHT A bowstring twanged. From the woodland a shout erupted, a man's dying cry. More arrows flew. An angry bark echoed from the frost-dampened forest and the Oudwnii exchanged calls, bursting from their foxholes in pursuit. The torches they carried blazed ghostly over the fresh snows.

"Do not follow him far!" Dhaos called.

Nyahri tightened her knife grip. The Atreiani crawled into the open, and Nyahri scowled as she followed yw Sabi into the cold. The archers gathered at the edge of the camp as two returned.

"What did you see?" Dhaos asked them.

"Two men," an archer reported. "We felled one."

The second archer hefted an axe. "The weapon is a northerner's make, and he wore this—" The Oudwni raised a necklace, its iron pendant shaped like a broad hammer.

"C'naädi," Dhaos said.

"The second man fled."

"Did you wound him? We might follow come morning."

"No way to tell by dark. We found no blood trail."

Yw Sabi's low lioness voice filled the camp, "Do your men make a habit of shooting before conversation?"

Dhaos stepped back. "Atreiani?"

"Those *may* have been enemies. Now it's *certain* they are."

"They were C'naädii," he said, as if in explanation.

"Something you didn't know till *after* you shot him."

"No honest men would have been in these woods so near our encampment. Of course they were C'naädii."

"Presumptive."

"Had we killed the other—"

"That means nothing, and your men *didn't* kill him, did they?"

"Mayhap it was only the two, those whose tracks we saw this afternoon."

"Or *mayhap* the survivor will die in the snow?" Yw Sabi sneered. "Or he might return and let you take a few more shots, or he will come into camp and dance for you, along with a bear wearing a silly hat."

Dhaos leaned from her, off guard.

She continued, "Either, Dhaos, you needed to talk with these men, even if only to lure them, or you needed to kill *both.*" She looked into the woodland. "We won't make it anywhere till dawn, if even then, not in this weather. Keep a *sharp* eye out tonight, archer."

"Atreiani, I will bid my men to take no chances, to follow every precaution, for your sake."

"For *my* sake? You think me weak?"

"For the E'cwni."

"*You think* her *weak?* We're *not* well defended here, boy, pinned between the forest, sixty meters of canyon, and a river of ice. Those men were scouts, and you know it."

He checked his frustration. "What *else* would you have had us do? There is nothing but pines and ice water a full day's ride in either direction!"

She scoffed, turning from him.

The archers shared nervous glances, then took their posts once more. Yw Sabi returned to the shelter, leaving Nyahri shin deep in the snow. She met Dhaos's eye and he frowned—

Handsome frown. Nyahri's heart ached for him, guessing yw Sabi's words would have been harsh no matter his actions, no matter the outcome. *What does yw Sabi know of men, she who is not human? Ay, what do I know of men? I* must *become a better judge of men's hearts,* she thought, recalling her father's words, *if even so I can counsel yw Sabi.*

Dhaos lingered as if waiting for Nyahri to speak, but she waited too long and he turned toward cover. The archers, too, melted into the nightscape.

"Gods!" she said, finding herself alone, and she stomped back to the lean-to.

NYAHRI DREAMED OF HER brother.

She walked hand-in-hand with him by a slow river where they once swam. Springtime greenery adorned the sheltering cottonwoods, and pussy willows choked the banks, waving in an easy breeze.

"You look so sour?" Erhde said to her.

She lifted a shoulder. "I hate decisions."

"Good thing you will not be Ahtras then." He laughed. "That is all an Ahtras does—makes decisions all the time."

"Do not tease! Why must I make *these* decisions?"

A deer appeared between distant trees. Nyahri and Erdhe watched it for a few moments, letting it graze, then it wandered on its way. All throughout her childhood, until he died, Nyahri revered her brother. No beast existed he could not hunt; no enemy, he could not kill. Yet he loved life, not only his own but all others, and she remembered that lesson. He smiled at the deer's departure.

"What decisions are those?" he asked his sister.

"To go with the Atreiani or stay with our people?"

He laughed. "Seems your choice is made."

"I will return to them, will I not?"

Again, he laughed.

"And what about love?" she asked.

"Lust, you mean?"

She punched his arm. *"Love."*

"What do you know about love, little sister? You never fell in love with anyone."

"There was Itrwra."

"Lust!" Erhde tussled her hair. *"That* lasted all of a month."

"I suppose." Nyahri shrugged. "But now yw Sabi *and* Dhaos?"

"Who could have guessed that, in a single cycle of the moon, you would pass from condemning your best friend to death, for want of loving him, to having your head turned by a goddess *and* an Oudwn boy?"

"Did you not fall in love with Mycah as readily?"

Erhde's wife died a month after he did, an accident on the hunt. She never finished grieving her husband's death, and Nyahri still mourned them both.

Her brother gave a conceding nod. "Yea, less than a month and I *knew* I wanted her forever, and she wanted me. Crazy Inwn woman."

"Do you have her?"

"Eh?" His eyebrows knitted.

"Forever?"

He only winked, ignoring her question. "Listen, your choice is not really between Dhaos or the Atreiani, or between the Atreiani and our people."

"What is it then?" Nyahri squeezed Erhde's hand, as if his solidity might fade.

"You never wanted to be Ahtras. You barely wanted to stay at camp. Hunting before you should have, raiding before you should have. You always wanted to ride farther, faster, and harder than men twice your age. Nay, your choice is not between *her* or *him* or *them.*"

Brother and sister walked a few more steps along the riverbank. He smiled to himself, enjoying a private amusement.

"Tell me," Nyahri said, "stop teasing."

"Your choice is between everything which is out there—" His hand swept toward the horizon, all the plains and mountains and forests of the world, the heavens and the earth. "—and staying right here—" The grass and dirt beneath her feet. "—stuck on what you have already lost."

She blinked, squinting in the sunlight, her focus on the distance. Erhde hugged her, kissing her forehead, and his expression darkened.

"Stop your worry!" he said.

Erhde dove into the river, emerging a heartbeat after, shaking the water from his head. Nyahri laughed at him.

He beckoned her. "Come, sister, the water is warm."

She jumped in after him, laughing as he splashed at her.

A moment later he disappeared beneath the currents, never to emerge. Blood swirled in the waters which murdered him.

"Erhde!"

Nyahri woke with his name on her lips, her heart straining for him. A shudder passed through her, and she took a deep breath. As if in response, a pain clenched her abdomen, and a smear of wetness puddled against her inner thigh.

"Gods," she whispered, a quiet complaint.

From her bags she unpacked a clout of fine wool and lambskin, traded from the households of the Eastern Rangers, whose family herded sheep. She had jammed a dozen into her gear, hoping she'd need no more before she could return to the E'cwnii. The water in the lean-to's washbowl was cold, but not frozen, and she wetted a cloth to wipe away the blood. Nyahri tied the clout to herself, settled back into the furs beside yw Sabi, and frowned.

"The goddesses honor you," the priestesses had said to Nyahri, some years ago, on the day of her menarche.

Now, Nyahri grumbled. *The goddesses can keep their honor,* she thought, one hand on her belly, trying to will the cramps away.

As she breathed, in that briefest moment, the soft silence of the snow and the pines lent her some comfort. So did the black-haired and inhuman woman slumbering beside her.

{16}

The snow-covered shelter bowed under the weight of snowpack, and the scents of conifer and pine sap thickened as the sunrise brightening by degrees. From outside the camp, a noise flittered to Nyahri's ears, and she dismissed all thoughts of bad dreams and menses.

The horses snorted at another whispering movement, a tumble of snow close by—an archer taking position, nocking an arrow. Nyahri drew her longknife.

"Mistress," she said.

"Yes, lovely one," yw Sabi replied, already awake, "I hear them."

"Who?"

"Men afoot, all around us."

Nyahri prayed to the spider goddess, lady of ambush, then to the cottontail god. She rolled from her bedding and stooped, pulling back the reflective blanket to peek beyond the shelter. Drifts blocked her view.

An arrow shot—

Men running, shouting, charging from upslope—

From their flank the attack began.

"Ay!" Dhaos yelled to his men, "They come!"

Boots clambered in the snow.

"Volley!"

Bowstrings chorused with the whistles of fletching through the frosted air. An archer shouted, "They rejoin!"

"Aim!"

Turo whinnied. Kwlko stomped, kicked, snorted.

"The horses!" Nyahri cried, leaning forward, eager to leave the shelter. "The C'naädii will try for them!"

Near her head a flint-tipped arrow pierced the thatch. The horses neighed and she pushed toward the door.

Yw Sabi grabbed Nyahri's wrist.

"No," the Atreiani said, "let these fools kill each other first."

"Mistress!"

"They're only horses. You love them too much."

Nyahri turned on the Atreiani, glaring, wringing her hand in yw Sabi's grasp, but she could not pull away. "Please, *please.*"

Yw Sabi bared her fangs, cursing in no tongue Nyahri knew. She released her hold.

"Get the damn horses," she said.

Nyahri burst from the shelter, ducking toward Kwlko and Turo, only a few long paces away. The Oudwnii shot arrow after arrow and, in answer, sling stones and bolts arced into camp. Leather-armored men with wild dark beards crouched behind trees, closing their distance with each attack. A C'naädin corpse bloodied the snow at the stallion's hooves, felled by an Oudwn arrow. More men bled in the open, C'naädii and Oudwnii alike.

Nyahri counted four-to-one against, foreign faces, frost-bitten and sunken and starved. A rush of desperate men broke for the horses as more Oudwn arrows launched.

We are too few.

Three C'naädii reached the horses, the men's filthy hands fumbling the tethers. Nyahri charged, shrieking, and the C'naädii turned. Their surprise became amusement.

"A woman!" one bellowed.

Their grins died as she drove her blade into the first man's larynx, through his spine, severing his hammer-shaped necklace. His blood spattered her face, blinding her as she went down with his corpse. Another C'naädi fell with an Oudwn arrow in his leg. The last raised his axe to cleave her and she kicked his knee, breaking it.

He fell onto her, axe tumbling from his hand as he gripped her throat. She pulled her blade from the first man and thrust it through her attacker, wrenching it beneath his sternum. Blood bathed her hands and chest.

Shoving him, she stood, bracing herself. Two C'naädii charged Dhaos. One took an arrow to the skull, then Dhaos drew his blade, opening the other from bladder to kidney.

Four more men surrounded Nyahri, one leveling his axe and shouting, berserk and furious. He swung the weapon over his head, stepping forward to drive it through her. She sidestepped but the haft glanced her arm, even as she rolled forward and buried her knife in his thigh.

Three men remained, moving to finish her.

Sound! Furious *sound*, as at Abswyn but *far* worse. Like a river-flood it crashed over Nyahri, chaining her intestines, coiling within her lungs. She lay like a straw doll, her eyes wide, her limbs like sand. All the C'naädii dropped like brained cattle. The Oudwnii fell like sacks.

No one fought anymore. No one ran. In all the forest, nothing moved save the breeze and the horses.

Unable to budge, Nyahri wondered for a moment if she'd died. But snow chilled her skin and crows called among the trees. The axe-wielder fell against her side, her longknife hilt still in her bloodied hand, the blade still in him. The horses swished their tails.

Slow footfalls approached through the snow. Sultah yw Sabi slipped the longknife from Nyahri's hand, pulling it from the man's leg. His blood darkened the ice, steaming where it spread into the cold white powder. Yw Sabi hoisted

Nyahri's limp body, carried her clear of the battleground, and set her gently against one of the shelters. The Atreiani knelt, caressing Nyahri's cheek, looking into her eyes.

"Let yourself go," yw Sabi said, "don't fight it, lovely one. Relax. Let the waves take you and the pain will go."

Yw Sabi kissed Nyahri's brow. She held the gore-plastered blade in one hand and the *scepter* in the other, its distorted symbols scoring its surface and *witch-fire* pulsing from it, like heat rising from a metalsmith's furnace.

Obeying, Nyahri abandoned the struggle to regain her body, and an intoxicating warmth washed over her. She wanted to cry, though even her tear ducts resisted her.

Yw Sabi walked to the nearest C'naädi. She grabbed a fistful of his hair, lifted him like a bag of feathers, and cut his throat from his windpipe to his spine. His heart, while it still beat, sprayed the snow with blood. She walked to the next man and did the same, and Nyahri knew:

Each man is as I am, each can feel, each knows what is coming.

The Atreiani's face remained calm while she went about her work, as if threshing grain or shearing sheep. She slaughtered the next man and the next. Yw Sabi raised a naked-faced boy from the snow, no more than twelve, his rusty longknife useless. Yw Sabi slit his throat too, frowning and watching his life ebb, then she dropped him.

The Atreiani slaughtered the C'naädi, every single one. Blood-wet spatters stained a field of snow. Bloody gurgles, one after the other, announced the dying. The land turned from white to crimson.

Nyahri wanted to scream.

§

THE ATREIANI WALKED AMONG the dead. The witch-song still pulsed from her scepter, but at last she held it aloft, caressing it, and all its magics ended.

Nyahri jolted forward, coughed, and blinked. She tried to stand, the world tilted, and she fell again. Again she sat, rubbing her temples to clear her head. Pale-faced Oudwn men shook their limbs and gathered their weapons.

None approached the Atreiani.

Everywhere, gore darkened the snow and corpses littered the forest. The horses found grass tufts above the snow pack and went on being horses, save a little shy at the reek of blood.

As the archers recovered, they tended their wounded and stopped the bleeding as best they could. Yw Sabi ceded to them some of her own ointments. Only one archer had died, and the men laid him by a new flame, built by yw Sabi from wet wood with tools of ghost-fire.

Dhaos knelt on the darkened slush at yw Sabi's feet, his face harrowed. "If I had doubted what you are," he said to her, "I doubt no longer."

Her expressionless voice returned, "You'll do well to remember." She cleaned Nyahri's longknife, along with her hand and forearm, using a snow-wetted cloth from the Oudwn supplies.

"You could have killed me, all my men, the moment we met."

"Yet I chose not to. Think on that, Oudwni."

Nyahri sat on her heels beside the fire, adding broken tree limbs to it. Wet fir needles burned white, spewing smoke, and Nyahri's absent gaze followed the plumes upward where the smoke darkened the hue of the clouds.

"What do you do with your deceased?" yw Sabi asked Dhaos.

"For our honored archers," he said, "cremation."

She nodded toward the fallen archer. "He was—?"

"Erwln, my cousin."

"His death is on *your* conscience, Dhaos, and more would've been had I not intervened. We're lucky these northerners, these *famished* northerners, weren't stealthier."

He cast his eyes down.

Yw Sabi laid her hand on Nyahri's shoulder.

"Build up the pyre," she said to Dhaos, "burn your cousin. Don't worry about any smoke. I doubt there're many left in this valley to see it."

"Yea, Atreiani."

"The rest of you, help him. Pack our gear. Look! The snow has stopped. We've blue skies. We'll force on today."

"Atreiani?" Dhaos ventured.

"What?"

"Did you need to kill them *all?*"

"You killed a man last night without cause," she said, "and failed to kill the second. I killed sixty-three this morning, *with* cause, and I killed them all. Would the feather of judgment find you innocent and me guilty?" She cocked her head, her voice softening, "Attend your cousin's remains."

Nyahri shuddered at yw Sabi's touch. The Atreiani crouched behind her, slipping the longknife back into its scabbard.

"You took a blow," yw Sabi said. "You all right, Nyahri?"

"Yea." Nyahri sniffled back tears, determined to hide them, certainly in front of the Oudwnii. "*Did* you have to? We could have taken prisoners—"

"Kill one, kill sixty-three, it's much the same. I couldn't risk such obstacles, or the complications of prisoners." The Atreiani knelt in the snow, speaking more quietly. "Survivors could've troubled us all the way to Cohltos, or rallied others to their cause. More importantly I couldn't risk *you*. It's been a long time since I felt so frightened."

"Frightened? You?"

"Anyone who bars my way is counter to my purpose but, more and more, anyone who threatens *you* is counter to *me*. I will not have it." The Atreiani coursed Nyahri's hair with her fingers, a touch both horrifying and soothing.

This Atreiani is no devil, Nyahri thought, *she is the same who held me while I sobbed—and yet what she did today!* Nyahri closed her eyes, tilting her head against yw Sabi's shoulder.

"Come," yw Sabi said, "first let me look at your arm, and I'll help you brush the horses."

They gave the stallion and gelding feed, while the archers sent one of their brothers heavenward. Before midmorning the company trudged west again through knee-deep powder, leaving the bodies of C'naädin men and boys for the feasts of wolves and crows.

fter three days, Dhaos led them above the timberline, trying the pass. Nyahri disliked the tundra, a place loveless and empty to her. Her cramps lessened, but her blood still flowed, and this made for uncomfortable riding. More so, she remained somber, her heart heavy with yw Sabi's ruthlessness.

Also awed by yw Sabi's resolve.

Beyond the highest saddle of the peaks, the company rested and ate. To the west, snow-draped mountain ranges went on and on. Yet Nyahri knew from trade legends that, in the far west, extended a vast desert and beyond it an endless sea. To the east stretched many of the valleys they'd traversed, then the barest hint of an unbroken yellow line shone at the horizon: the now-distant plains upon which Nyahri's people lived.

She swallowed a long draught of water, washing down her meal, then looked around her. The Atreiani had scaled above the men, picking her way among higher rocks, closer to the heights.

Yw Sabi climbed like a child of the gods of earth and sky, not skill but sheer power and endurance carrying her up, up. Nyahri set aside her water and removed her cloak. She raced across the tundra, drawing the eyes of the men, and leapt onto the rock where yw Sabi had ascended. Looking up, Nyahri guessed the Atreiani over a hundred hands above. The thin alpine air burned Nyahri's lungs, each breath biting like smoke, and the granite scraped her palms. Hand over hand, she took care with each new purchase. She put a dozen handspans beneath her, a dozen more, then three, and she looked down.

Nyahri hugged the rock, shutting her eyes. Her heart raced like a hummingbird's, like it might explode.

Upward, upward. She sent loose stones and lichen skittering down to the tundra. Below, many of the Oudwnii rose to their feet, gazing up at her. In a high dale underneath them, an eagle circled.

Higher than the gods of the sky, she thought.

Above, yw Sabi vanished from Nyahri's line of sight, having climbed over a precipice. Her voice carried down, but the wind snatched the words. Nyahri climbed after her, two score hands and more, until she reached the edge, pulled herself over it, and found herself on a stone ledge overlooking endless valleys. Farther along the ledge, the Atreiani balanced with her arms spread, her hair wild in the gusts.

Nyahri caught her breath.

"That'd be quite a fall," said yw Sabi.

"Yea," Nyahri sucked down another breath, "it would kill us."

The Atreiani glanced back. "Us?"

The Oudwnii appeared tiny below. Dhaos laughed, pointing up, saying something to his men which Nyahri couldn't quite hear.

"Why the climb, yw Sabi?"

"Why'd you follow?"

"You think because I come from the plains I cannot climb?"

"That's not what I asked."

Nyahri shrugged.

Yw Sabi flashed a smile. "Beautiful land, isn't it?"

"I have never seen anything like it."

"Someday I'd like to show you sights even more breath-taking, more wondrous than this."

"I cannot imagine, Atreiani."

"I didn't climb for the view, though." She lifted her hands aside her mouth and shouted: "Borea!"

Nyahri stepped farther from the edge, to yw Sabi's side. "Who *is* Borea?"

"A vastly distributed artificial intelligence. Her realm is everywhere between the depths of the oceans and the stratosphere."

"She is a spirit?"

"In your terms, a powerful one. She should've survived the so-called Eventide, and she should be answering me."

"The spirits do not always answer us, yw Sabi."

"Well this one *should fucking well be answering me.* It was programmed to."

"I do not understand."

"It was programmed to answer me."

Nyahri shook her head.

"Imagine a world filled with invisible dust," yw Sabi said, "so tiny it sits between all the other things you *can* see, and all the dust talks with all the other dust. It knows everything which goes on around it, and it can influence much of that. In all the universe there are only eight voices which it obeys. Imagine this and you'll be close to imagining Borea."

"Eight voices, mistress?"

"Yes, and mine was one."

"Who were the others?"

"The other Magisters, and Autumn."

"Autumn?"

"Another AI."

"I do not understand at all." Nyahri shook her head. "You are frustrated?"

"Yes. Let's get ourselves back to the others, together, and a little more carefully on the way down, hmm?"

FOR ANOTHER DAY THEY crossed the permafrost. Lichen-dotted granite roughened the landscape, as if the earth had spit up its own teeth. Glacial lakes glistened below the snow-dusted fields. No trees grew at those hallowed heights, and Nyahri gave thanks when at last they descended into the forests again, before darkness fell and the winds wailed over the highlands.

Yet the sparse lodge-pole stands of the western slopes did little to slow the gales. A cold night raged, colder than any before it, miserable for E'cwni, Oudwnii, and the horses. The men huddled quietly in their shelters. Only yw Sabi seemed unbitten.

She stood outside awhile, her head upturned as she listened to the creaking pines. Nyahri bundled beneath the blankets and furs, reaching out only to tighten the lean-to ties, keeping the shelter from flying free in the gusts. Reassured, she pulled her hands back under cover, shivering into a ball, hugging her knees.

"Yw Sabi?" she called.

The Atreiani stepped beneath the thatch, pulling the blankets aside only long enough to slip beneath them. Nyahri shivered all the more for the burst of cold and the frosty touch of yw Sabi's clothing. Nyahri shook, nauseous for the ice in her bones.

"I cannot get warm," Nyahri said.

"Much more of this and you'll be hypothermic. You put extra blankets on the horses. They don't need them. We could take them off—"

"Nay, leave them. If we had brought a full tent, I would have it over us all."

"We didn't, and it would've slowed us anyway." Yw Sabi laid her palm against Nyahri's face.

Gods, she is warm, Nyahri thought. *The same steady warmth she always has, never faltering. And her scent—gods—she smells good!*

No god of love presided in the E'cwnii pantheon, no god to guide desire, and so Nyahri prayed to all the gods at once to be sure.

"I want to be warm," Nyahri said. "It is so cold."

Yw Sabi slid her hand behind the clasps of her suit, opening it. She pulled Nyahri's serape up, off her head, and set it aside, then settled under the blankets against her. Nyahri's bare flesh pressed against the Atreiani's.

Gods, warmth, blessed warmth! Gods, help me!

Nyahri wrapped her arms around yw Sabi, clinging to her, closing her eyes and nestling into that gossamer hair. Yw Sabi's arms encircled her in return.

"Thank you," Nyahri said.

"Get warm. Sleep."

Bit by bit the cold melted away, and nothing could feel better to Nyahri at that moment than the Atreiani's skin. She fought sleep, wanting instead to memorize every sensation of yw Sabi's fingers, arms, shoulders, breasts, stomach—

Yet exhaustion took its toll. Nyahri closed her eyes and, even as she thought to herself that she must make the moment last, she fell to sleep.

THE NEXT NIGHT THE freezing winds returned, under a sky nearly clear. The stars shone cruelly, all brighter as only slivers of Lwn and Stashwn remained, hurriedly vanishing.

Nyahri slept again half undressed beside the Atreiani.

Yet by the third day the company descended into heavier timbers and warmer nights, and the fiercest winds no longer blew. That evening, yw Sabi made no move to climb under Nyahri's bedding, choosing instead to sit alone, keeping to her own thoughts.

Did I misread her? Nyahri wondered, unable to shake her disappointment.

Her flow had halted and she took time to wash in a brisk stream, water melting from ice not eight hundred hands up the mountainside. She felt much more herself, and yet yw Sabi half ignored her through the night.

The company marched into successively broader valleys, the highest peaks now behind them. The skies cleared, more autumnal than wintry, and each night the crescent moons waxed.

Nyahri breathed better as the air became richer. Meadows opened among the trees, a blessing for the horses. High-tundra waters coalesced into streams, then a river, fleet over the rocks but wider and lazier as it crossed a lower plateau. Birches filled the canyon between the river and the ever-widening path. Open fields spread west and south and, in their backdrop, other mountains appeared at the horizon.

On the fourth day from the heights, the uncovered sun hung at its zenith, the first time Nyahri had felt it in days. Yw Sabi pulled alongside her, pointing down the valley, past a distant expanse of apple groves.

"See it?" asked the Atreiani.

Nyahri squinted. "Mistress?"

"A fire haze, a lot of it."

Nyahri cocked her head. "Yea."

"Dhaos! What is that ahead?"

He called back from the front of the company's line, his voice bright, "The fires of the settlement—Cohltos."

"Tomorrow evening? Afternoon?"

"At most."

Yw Sabi pulled Turo's reigns until the gelding halted. She drew up in the saddle, her hand at the witch-scepter on her hip, a gesture of habit.

"How many men," she asked, too quiet for the Oudwnii to hear her, "to make that much smoke?"

"No knowing," Nyahri said. "More than I have ever seen. A great tribe, more than when my father knew this valley."

Yw Sabi frowned. "There must be thousands living there."

"This concerns you?"

"It may complicate matters."

"What matter are the Oudwnii?" Nyahri said. "You will speak with the Templarii, find what you need, and we can go."

"I'm anxious to learn how near the settlement lies to the Citadel." Yw Sabi shook her head. "I may have a serious problem."

"What problem?"

Yw Sabi shook her head, a dismissive gesture. "Despite an age's change I *recognize* the lay of this land. Sojourn Temple is close."

AT DUSK THEY LIT proper cooking fires and yw Sabi settled beside the flames, again lost in her thoughts. Nyahri unbridled the horses, letting them graze, the evening air washing over her as she led them from the path. Clear skies domed the world, the stars as bright as Nyahri had ever seen them, even as the crescent moons fattened halfway to quarter. She shouldered the water skins and brought them to the river, kneeling in the darkness to fill them.

Footsteps sounded in the nearby brush and Nyahri spun, her senses sharpened, her longknife drawn. Dhaos stood at the top of the embankment, the distant firelight playing upon his cheek. He held up his hands, palms outward, and Nyahri angled the blade away.

"E'cwni." He smiled.

Her heart quickened to see him. "Oudwni."

"How are you this evening?"

"What is it to you?"

He held up his hands. "I am not interrogating you, only asking."

"Well enough," she conceded.

"I admit I have been trying to guess—how old are you? Twenty?"

"Nineteen."

"You were an adult at twelve, no doubt, but it is quite a journey you have undertaken, for a woman."

"You insult me?" She shook her head at him. "*Your* women may be soft creatures. I am not."

"That is clear." He stepped forward a pace and leaned against a tree, his thumbs hooked into his belt. "Soft or not, made of stone or not, I certainly do not envy your position."

"Explain."

He nodded toward the campfire, toward yw Sabi. "That you follow *her*."

Nyahri sheathed her knife, half turning from him, and uncapped the first skin. She dipped it into the water, allowing it to fill. "You would not understand."

"It is one thing, Nyahri, for a man to die in battle— honor in that—but what she did! That pass was called the *Lwvlnda*, the *Loveland*. Now it will be known only as a slaughter yard. She butchered those C'naädin dogs."

"Did they not deserve it?"

"What would stop her from doing the same to us?"

"*You* did not try to kill her. You made the right choice when we first met you."

"So I am reminded."

"In the final measure of it, Dhaos, she saved you and your men, and you know it."

"What she did is black magic. She put all of us under a spell. You imperil your spirit to ride with her, to share *blankets* with her."

"My spirit is *my* concern, as are my blankets." She uncapped the next water skin, holding it under the icy current, her fingers numbing. "I have thought on the Atreianii since I was a girl. My mother was a healer and spirit-talker, and she worshipped the Atreianii till she died. Thus I would accompany Sultah yw Sabi and discover what she is about."

"Discover what she is about? Do not cast yourself as some passive *observer*. You are at her right hand."

"Do not imagine too much."

"I imagine nothing. You may as well have already taken her oath."

Nyahri looked sidelong at him. "What would you know of any of that?"

Dhaos grunted, almost a laugh. "More than you, I bet. I am not an uneducated yeoman—I am a chieftain's son, schooled at Cohltos. I have lived in Cohltos as often as at Aukensis, and for a time I studied with the Templarii. I know some of the history fragments. I know of the *oath*, what little they tell of it. You will sell your soul, will you not?"

"Nothing of the kind."

"I hope not, for you sake. Yet what will you do if she asks?"

"Again, what she asks and what I do are none of your business. As it is, I can naysay her, or you, or anyone."

Again he held up his hands. "I apologize, but I care what happens to you, Nyahri."

"Do not patronize me," she said, yet she reconsidered.

Patronize? Nay, his concern feels true, and mayhap he does know more than I. He has seen how I look at yw Sabi and he has seen how I look at him. Gods, I am doomed.

While he stood so close, while they spoke with one another, she found she liked him even more. Despite his bluster, his heart showed plainly, and his words warmed her.

"I would like to know you better," he said. "That is all."

"What purpose would that serve?"

"Can you not imagine it? Someday I will represent Aukensis on the Oudwn council. You are the daughter of a respected E'cwn chieftain—"

"Here, take these," she said, lifting the full skins.

He crouched, accepting them. She wrung her numb hands and wiped them on her breeches.

"Is it not obvious?" he said. "How I feel about you? I have watched you all the way from Aukensis. We are a good match for each other."

She groused. *Gods! Must he do this?*

"You are trying to lure me," she said, "that is all."

He grinned at first, then his smile faded. "Do not trust the Atreiani. They called Sultah yw Sabi the *Betrayer*. Did you know that? She was evil among the evil."

"There is more to the stories. You should know this."

"Mayhap, but would you risk it?"

"The stories say she betrayed the gods—they say little more than that."

"Have you asked her about it?"

Nyahri tilted her head. "Nay, but—"

"You should."

"You say you studied, Dhaos?"

He nodded hesitantly. "Yea."

"You remember who she betrayed the gods for?"

"I confess, I do not."

"Ask your Templarii *that* when you see them next."

"I will," he said, "but let me convince you another way. Sultah yw Sabi has brought us a wonderful opportunity, you and me."

"What are you saying?"

"I like you, Nyahri, and I do not think I am *so* unlikeable. After the devil is done with her business, moved on her way, you and I could sow peace. Can you imagine Oudwnii and E'cwnii united? We might bring the Inwnii into our fold, my cousins the Qebeccêi, the Bk'ferii, and more besides. We could have a peace which stretches two months' ride in any direction, good trade, safety."

Dhaos set the water skins aside, leaned forward, and stretched his arm toward her.

"All you must do," he said, "is take my hand. We can walk, talk, take it as it comes."

Beautiful man! Nyahri thought. *His face by such gentle light, the lie of his hair.* She leaned past his outstretched hand and took hold of the skins.

"Nay," she said.

From above the riverbank, yw Sabi called, "Nyahri! Come. There's schooling to be done."

"I must go, Dhaos."

"Nyahri—"

As she passed him, she let an impulse take her: laying her cold hand against his cheek, she kissed his mouth before scampering up the bank. Nyahri kept her gaze forward, telling herself she did not care what expression he wore, that nothing could come of it, that she kissed him only to taste what she'd never know, that she kissed him only for spite.

In her absence the fire had dwindled. Yw Sabi stood outside its light, pointing at the horizon. In the far distance, Swyn Templr's pillar flared, brightened and faded, brightened and faded. It had done so since time immemorial.

"Let's have some lessons," yw Sabi said. "We'll need more wood on the fire."

"Yea, Atreiani."

Nyahri glanced once more at the beacon, then back toward the water. Dhaos had slipped away unseen.

{Interim: Love Letters}

Beloved Ekaterina—

What a gift! The valley equals the mountain; the mountain is nothing without it. The earth equals the sky; the sky floats into nothing without it. The low equals the high; heights mean nothing without it. You top me from the bottom, lovely one, but I won't mind—you're my equal.

This letter will arrive only a day before me. It will reenter by drone at Mach, but my shuttle descends tomorrow and I'll be twelve hours down the corkscrew.

My business took longer than expected and your absence has become a pang. I want to open the Ma'at doors and find you— dressed for dinner and an evening's conversation— or seated with your cello—or taking my hand to lead us to bed—or naked and kneeling where I might plunder you in the evening hall—or ready to dance a waltz with me—or only smiling, for what could be better?

Each day without you, my claimèd, is a starvation.

Yours,
—S
From *The Collected Letters*

{18}

The next day they reached the valley farms which surrounded Cohltos. Harvesters worked the fields, men and women and children by the hundreds, hurrying to collect the last crops before winter. Mud-and-stone houses surrounded common courtyards.

Yw Sabi wore her hood and her E'cwn leathers, her telltale hair tucked well out of sight. Yet the dirty Oudwn faces still gawked at the women ahorse, some following and muttering in their amazement.

"The chieftain of Cohltos," Dhaos said to yw Sabi, "will expect you to visit him, you know, sooner or later."

"What is his name?" she asked.

"Shwn Pawl Oudwn of the House Cohlton."

"Shwn Pawl will wait," she said, her voice low, "as will anyone else who wishes an audience with me. Take us to the Citadel, Dhaos."

He nodded. "I expected you would say so, Atreiani. I will convey it to Shwn Pawl myself."

Farm fields gave way to villages, then to a township, hundreds living in one settlement. Many dozens of such townships dotted the valley, a population of twenty thousand. Nyahri had never imagined such a place might exist. E'cwnii tribes never grew to more than three hundred, and she could name everyone in her father's camp. She wondered if everyone in Cohltos might know everyone else's name, then scoffed and dismissed the idea. She thought them more like animals, living in pens, than a community.

Along narrow streets, baked-brick buildings pressed against one another. In the north, a foundry bellowed black smoke, its stack rising a hundred fifty hands. At the urban edge, hundreds of cattle crowded behind fences. A drove of pigs wandered the streets. Oudwn tradesmen, their doors flung open for business, raised their hands to welcome the archers. Children played with dogs in whatever grassy patches remained unclaimed. As Dhaos led them toward the city's heart, Swyn Templr's slender beacon tower drew Nyahri's attention. It persisted in its slow, luminous pulse. The pinnacle measured two thousand hands high, taller than Abswyn's had been.

For a moment the fire and terror of Abswyn's immolation roared in Nyahri's memory. What would happen if, as at Abswyn, the Citadel of Swyn Templr also exploded?

Surrounding the tower's base, a stonework edifice stood ten times the size of Orÿs Lodge. This was S'Eret Fortress, built of tremendous mortarless boulders, its high walls fenestrated by murder holes and iron-braced gates. Crows fluttered from its crenellations, cawing and strutting and winging between broad turrets. Nyahri looked to yw Sabi, but the Atreiani kept her thoughts to herself, making eye contact with no one.

"What do you think of Cohltos?" Dhaos asked and, not waiting for an answer, he said, "Welcome to Sojourn Temple."

He brought them to the fortress gate, and he walked all the way to the front doors. Without so much as a pause he drew his longknife and hammered its pommel on the doors. "Pay attention! You cold keepers! Come and open up! I bring you a visitor you do not dare ignore."

He pounded a few more times, then kicked the copper-reinforced timbers, wood stained blue by the long decay of the metal. After pounding a few more times, Dhaos turned back to the company and shrugged, his boyish grin regained.

"They are slow sometimes," he said.

The gate locks clanged and the doors creaked outward, moved by machines invisible from below, revealing a stone passage slivered by high clerestory sunlight. An old man stood within, his body wrapped by rough woolen garments. His face shown ash pale, skin loose on his skull, his cheeks sagging.

He graveled, "Dhaos Shwn Oudwn, what visitor?"

"Someone," Dhaos said, "I doubt you ever expected."

Unable to reach her spear or the bows strapped to Kwlko's cantle, Nyahri laid her hand on her knife. She gauged the throwing distance to the old one who, despite his age, set her on edge. Yw Sabi dismounted, stepped into the gateway's shadow, and withdrew her hood. A moment passed before the elder bowed.

"Atreian," he said, "Sultah yw Sabi et *Ekaterina.*"

"You know she's dead," yw Sabi said. "Improper, to use her name with mine. Under different circumstances, Templari, how I might punish you for such an affront—"

He bowed again. "My apologies and condolences, Atreiani, as I meant no offense. The pain must yet feel near for you."

"Now use my *proper* title."

He glanced up. "You jest?"

"My title, Templari."

Another bow. "*Magistress* Sultah yw Sabi, we are honored by your arrival. You do recognize me?"

"You know I don't."

"I want you to know, Magistress, I was always on your side."

A growl left her throat and she raised her arm as if to backhand him. The archers gathered, confused but ready to act, and Nyahri brought Kwlko several paces forward. At the last moment, yw Sabi checked her blow.

The old man flinched. "Of all we might meet," the Templari said, "after such a long time, you're the *least* welcome."

"There, *now* you're telling the truth," she said. "Here is *my* truth—I can come in peace now or with violence later. The Dalkhu would still obey me."

"Would they?" he asked, as if he doubted, yet his horror showed. "Peace. Come inside, but the humans must remain out here. I don't want Dhaos and his pack of mutts sullying S'Eret's halls. Forbid they might *touch* something."

Dhaos laughed at the Templari. "You sting me, you old sack of bones. Am I not trusted?"

"No, Dhaos, not until your father's dead and burned, or his flesh works in our service."

Nyahri's throat tightened as she realized what was to happen.

Humans must remain out here. Ay! The vast doors will shut, I on one side, yw Sabi on the other.

She kneed Kwlko closer yet, and the Atreiani gestured toward her.

"The E'cwni comes with me."

"The rules haven't changed," he said. "Is there some reason we should permit a human so near a Citadel? Or so close to our collections?"

"I'm considering her claime."

"How unfortunate," he said, frowning at Nyahri. *"Considering* is not enough, Magistress. You know that."

"She stays with me. Are there any other Magisters awake who might countermand my wishes?"

"Not to our knowledge."

"You sound disappointed?"

The Templari frowned.

"Circumstances being what they are, I am a quorum of one," she said, "and the E'cwni comes with me." Yw Sabi waved Nyahri to her. "Come."

Nyahri slid from the saddle, slung her mistress's possessions, and took her spear in hand. She passed the reins to Dhaos.

"Do something useful," she told him, "and tether the horses."

"That is an improvement." He smirked. "Last time you threatened to dismember a man for touching your horse."

Nyahri followed yw Sabi and the gate closed behind them, leaving them in a dry gloom, a stone corridor thirty hands wide and sixty high. The floor sloped downward, the darkness deepening with every step. The old man turned, and crimson ghost-fire glowed in his eyes. Nyahri stifled her gasp.

"As you may now recall, Magistress," he said, "I am Unit Kepler Seventeen."

The Atreiani studied him. "How well do you remember her execution?" Fury smoldered behind her voice, all her usual calm reduced to nothing but a façade.

"My memory," Kepler said, "is as good now as then. I can appreciate your anger, Sultah yw Sabi, but my job that day was to observe and record. You cannot begrudge me that? You cannot blame *me* for the atrocities of those times?"

"Blame? No, but you Templarii have never been my favorites."

"We were not your creation."

"Nonetheless, you'll follow my commands and answer my questions. Am I understood?"

"Perfectly." He lifted his chin. "Though by the official record you're still an enemy of state, Magistress, I hope we can find some mutually beneficial way forward."

"I care nothing for *mutual benefit*, Kepler. You obey. That is the beginning and end of it."

He pointed the way, and they walked again. "I'll attend to whatever you need, of course."

"A place to stay," yw Sabi said, "access to your records. Nyahri here will want the horses tended and we'll need good, hot food."

Farther still from the entrance, the light from the high windows faded and disappeared. Nyahri edged closer to yw Sabi's side. "Mistress?"

"Hmm?"

"It is too dark. I cannot see."

"I can. Take my hand, Nyahri. I'll look after you."

They laced their fingers together, side by side into the black.

THE LIBRARY EXISTED AS dust, dryness, and ages of pressed paper and parchment packed on heavy-boarded shelves, books balanced to the tops of the walls. Candles set in lace-iron flickered from the ceiling. Stools and chairs stood at simple tables.

As Kepler led Nyahri and yw Sabi into one low chamber of the multi-celled collection, their footsteps echoed on the sandstone floor. Hands folded within his robes, he stopped beside a Templarin woman seated at a table. She dressed, as he did, in rough cloth. Though she appeared younger, her pale skin also draped too loosely on her bones. She scrawled in an open tome, Kepler looking over her shoulder as her pen flew across the page, its nib whispering constantly. Nyahri kept close to yw Sabi, mistrusting everything, the walls too near, the air heavy as mud in her lungs.

The Atreiani strolled from shelf to shelf, caressing the book spines, reading the letters on them.

"What is *this?*" she asked, gesturing to the library as a whole.

"Our complete record," Kepler said, "from the time of our emergence after the Eventide until this day, every bit of news which has ever come to us. Not only in this chamber, but twelve others, and innumerable collections of artifacts. We have four distinct libraries, including this one, all within our domicile."

"This is your best effort?"

"You misunderstand the difficulties, Magistress." He looked around himself, at the bookcases and tomes, as if they demonstrated how remarkable the Templarin *efforts* had been. "We've done as well as we could."

"This is paper, pounded kidskins, and *ink*. Computers, networks, databases—where are they?"

"Be assured, anything you wish, we Templarii can search it out or recite it. The local networks are long destroyed, and it has been ages since we could mine rare metals to start over. There are Persephone's satellites, of course, but we've no way to link to her. There are only a few dozen of us left, Magistress. What would you have had us do?"

"You've nothing searchable?"

He gave a shrug. "Our computers failed time-out-of-mind ago and, unless you've some way to subvert the laws of thermodynamics, these papers and kidskins must suffice. You know as well as I, Sultah yw Sabi, you Atreianii made only a handful of self-sustaining machines."

Yw Sabi breathed a dismissive sigh.

"Speaking of Persephone," she said, "of the *Hive?* You cannot raise it?

"No, Atreiani."

"For how long?"

"Since fifty years after the first caldera blew."

She squinted, an expression between careful consideration and irritation. "Fiftyish years or fifty years?"

"Ah, yes, we have always found that peculiar too. She went silent at fifty years to the second, Atreiani."

"And Borea? Anything?"

"As I have intimated, nothing from the Hive, and Borea was never programmed for us, Atreiani. You know that. I take it she hasn't responded to you since your awakening?"

"No."

Yw Sabi sat at the table and pushed a chair toward Nyahri, who took the seat, moving it farther from the wrinkled, scribbling scholar. The Atreiani bent over the table, burying her face in her folded arms.

Nyahri leaned closer to her, almost laying her hand on the Atreiani's shoulder. "Mistress?"

Yw Sabi looked up, squaring her shoulders to Kepler. "You've an analog indexing system? A *card catalog?* Something?"

"Of course," he said.

"First I want to know, you piece of—" Yw Sabi closed her eyes, only a moment, mastering her temper. "Tell me, Templari, how long was I asleep?"

The woman persisted in her scribbling. Nyahri shifted in the chair, trying to get comfortable, awed by the walls of books. Until then she'd seen only one, a pile of papers her father bound in a leather satchel, along with a short stack of sacred parchments kept by her aunt and her mother before.

"How *long?*" yw Sabi demanded.

Kepler began, "You are the first Atreiani—"

"Get to it! *How long?*"

The Templari stepped back. "Over five millennia."

Yw Sabi stood, her chair clattering onto its side. She put her hands to her hair, turning away, and leaned against a bookshelf.

Pen scratching.

"So long?" she said. "I thought a few hundred years perhaps."

Yw Sabi slid down the shelves, onto the floor, and a few books fell behind her. The Atreiani stared into some middle distance, the look of shock. Nyahri went to her, scared to touch her, scared not to.

How do I comfort her?

The Templarin woman stopped writing, glancing at the fallen tomes, then returned to her work.

"It doesn't matter," yw Sabi reassured herself, her voice quieter. "Five years, five thousand, it doesn't matter. You'll teach me your indexing system, Kepler. I have to study your records, all fifty centuries' worth."

"Pardon me, Magistress, but wouldn't it be easier if you simply powered the Citadel? You'd have all the answers you needed in a fraction of the time."

"Not yet, Kepler."

"Why not? Because of how you left things with your sisters and brothers? But that was a long time ago—"

"For me it was *months*. Ekaterina's death was *two years ago* by my count, Kepler. For me these things are *recent*, do you understand?"

"Then, by your accounting, your misdeeds were not so long ago either." He paused, letting those words settle. "Your peers are noted for their forgiveness, at least among their own kind. Bygones *can* be bygones. I can lead you to the portal myself, right now. You should open it. Waken them. Ask for their clemency."

A flash of horror crossed yw Sabi's face, but she suppressed it. Crouching on the floor, her shoulders slumped, her body heavy, she appeared to Nyahri once more *lonely*.

"I need to order my thoughts," yw Sabi said, "and I won't descend, Kepler, till I consider my position."

"What position is *that,* Magistress? You committed serious crimes. In legal review, it may be determined you have already served your penance, but there *must* be a review, yes? According to laws *you* helped write? So long as the explosion at Abswyn was not *your* fault, so long as your apparently lone survival is mere chance—"

Writing, writing, writing, the scribe's pen swirled so fast it blurred, a page done a minute.

Yw Sabi snarled at the woman. "Get out! *Stop your fucking scratching and get the fuck out before I pull you from that fucking head and stomp you into the fucking floor!*"

The scribe stood, gathering her instruments, and departed. Nyahri, startled by yw Sabi's rage, sat back against a shelf, wrapping her arms around her chest.

Yw Sabi recovered her composure. "Five thousand years? How has it been so many, Templari?"

He bowed. "I don't know, Atreiani."

"The Citadels weren't designed to lie so idle, not more than those fifty years—*fifty*."

"I don't know."

"You must know *something*."

"We have only the vaguest reports from beyond our borders."

"Bullshit."

Yw Sabi pounded her fist on the floor, the flagstone cracking under the blow. Nyahri flinched.

Gods, she is strong! How many ways, Nyahri thought, *must I be reminded she is no human.*

"Sultah yw Sabi," Kepler said, his tone placating, "we keep only *this* Citadel and it has never woken. No news has ever reached us that any *other* Citadel has ever awoken. Even *we* were offline for those first years, were not even around when the surviving humans dug themselves out, or when the life blooms emerged on the Earth's surface—"

"Life blooms?" The Atreianii squinted thoughtfully.

Kepler shrugged. "It is the best descriptions we have from the few remaining texts of that time—*life blooms,* on every continent. Life which simply *appeared* amidst the wreckage."

"Interesting. What else?"

"Little else." He held up his hands, again a placation. "I am telling the truth—I do not *know* why the Citadels sleep so long beyond their appointed time, and I do not know why it would be *you* who would awaken now. We did not begin keeping our own records until after the descendants of Exemplarii found us and rebooted us."

Her eyes narrowed a moment longer, expressing her disbelief. "Whatever it is you *do* know, Templari, you'll teach me." She pointed to the shelves. "Five thousand years gone by, there are answers in these books, and I've no time to waste."

He bowed. "I'll retrieve the indices."

"Good."

Yw Sabi returned to the table, and Nyahri followed her.

Kepler retrieved a few dozen blocky tomes, setting them in order on the tabletop. A rapacious student, yw Sabi learned their system, asking questions of Kepler: files, call numbers, tags, cross-references, digests, abstracts.

Nyahri could only guess how long they'd take. At first, ten minutes seemed long. Then half an hour passed, an hour, two. As much as she tried to learn alongside yw Sabi, at length Nyahri closed her eyes, almost sleeping, listening to the occasional exchanges between the Templari and yw Sabi. At last, when all yw Sabi's questions seemed answered, the Atreiani sent Kepler away. He closed the door as he left.

"Come, Nyahri, look."

Nyahri forced herself to attention. "Yea."

"Read this with me, and let's try to piece this together."

Nyahri leaned close to yw Sabi, who opened a book marked *Histories 01.01.0001*. They scanned the contents.

"In the early days," yw Sabi said, "after what became known as the *Eventide*—"

"Yea, I know about the Eventide, Mistress."

"You would, I suppose—part of your history but a new concept to me. Hadn't encounter the term until I heard it from Shwn Jhon. After it, the Templarii tried to maintain contact with each other, betwixt the Temples, and with the satellite system called OpNet, itself controlled by yet another AI named *Persephone*. As Kepler tells it they lost most communications early. Still, the Templarii kept their responsibility as the record keepers, learning as much as possible of all the Citadels—their locations, to know which Atreianii were where, to know which Citadels were built for which tasks. For all this time they depended on relays no faster than the Pony Express."

Nyahri assumed this meant *slow*. "What do you wish to learn here, yw Sabi?"

The Atreiani held up a finger, asking for Nyahri's patience. "By the time I went into suspension, my enemies had kept me in the dark about the Citadels' manufacture. I didn't know which had been assigned to what protocols, who would reside in them, or what else had been done. I've too many holes in my knowledge."

Nyahri nodded as if she understood.

"Besides that," yw Sabi said, "we've a bit of a mystery. Globally, the Congress's original plans called for one hundred fifty Citadels. The odds that *all* those Citadels' auto-awake functions would fail and that of *all* the Citadels, Abswyn would awake first, and that of *all* the berths in Abswyn, *mine* should power up first—these are astronomically long odds."

"What does that mean, mistress?"

"It means I was *meant* to wake first. It was *designed* by someone to be that way."

"You are certain Suhto did not awaken you?"

"Positive." Yw Sabi pressed her thumb to her forehead, leaning forward as she considered. "That Suhto would be in the wrong place at the wrong time, that's not astronomically long odds—that's bad, bad luck. A human could never inadvertently awaken it."

"I still do not know what that means," Nyahri said.

"I've no idea either, lovely one. Let's hope we find a hint somewhere here."

"What did he mean by those words, *life bloom?*"

"Uncertain."

They read together the first chapters of history surrounding the Eventide. During the great darkness, in the ash, when the geothermal power stations exploded and blotted the sun, during the strife between the Atreianii, during the making of the Citadels, during the blackening of the skies—

"The Templarii here lost contact with all the satellites," yw Sabi said, "all the extraterrestrial facilities, the off-world colonies."

Geothermal, satellites, extraterrestrial, Nyahri thought. *I have much to learn.*

"Yet the idea that Persephone went dark," yw Sabi said, "is as ridiculous as Borea not answering me."

"Tell me, Atreiani, about Persephone and Borea?"

"Four interdependent artificial intelligences comprise, or comprised, the Hive. Two, Borea and Persephone, constituted an overlapping system which protected the Earth, allowing a few Atreianii—such as a Magistress—to better manage the world. Persephone existed within the Operations Network—the OpNet—managing communications on Earth, including much of Borea's. We designed the Hive to self-sustain, self-check, and goal orient. Their goals included the will of the Magisters' Council, yes, but primarily they curated the biosphere."

Nyahri shook her head. "You said these are like gods?"

"They're machines, sophisticated ones, but only machines. Let's continue."

They read of the banishing of the Numenii—servants of the Atreianii which to Nyahri seemed as demon lords. They learned of the *life blooms,* though the few literate humans of the age described only a blossoming of life amidst the ashen wastes left by the Eventide, accounts more apocryphal than historical. Yw Sabi and Nyahri read of the days when humanity first realized its keepers had abandoned it, of the years when more men were eaten by other men than by wild animals. Of all the later hardships.

Nyahri marveled at first, but over the hours she grew tired once more, and drifted to sleep. Yw Sabi lit more candles and read through the night.

Many floors up, near the highest walls of the compound, the Templarii prepared a cramped bedchamber for their guests. During the day, only high clerestory windows provided it any daylight. The Templarii presumed the human and the Atreiani would share quarters. They gave yw Sabi a key, and yw Sabi showed Nyahri how to use it.

At the Atreiani's insistence, and on Nyahri's behalf, Kepler brought the horses into a sunlit courtyard, along with a trough, many water barrels, bales of alfalfa, and bags of feed. Nyahri felt much better with the horses near. She fed the stallion and gelding oats and an assortment of autumn fruit from the Oudwn orchards.

During the following week, yw Sabi persevered with her reading, and she organized enormous volumes of information. Numbers, charts, reports, maps, all of it together, hung on walls or spread on tables. One corner of the library became her study, and she forbid the Templarii from entering it.

Often, Nyahri joined her, and yw Sabi's research turned into Nyahri's lessons. Nyahri learned more Englisce and a smattering of other dead languages. She spent several hours each day by yw Sabi's side, progressing slowly, sometimes frustrated at her tongue's stupidity. The Atreiani, however, gave her only encouragement.

"You're learning well," she said.

On her own, Nyahri learned other things, including the lay of the S'Eret's outer passages, the location of its various libraries, and the pattern of its darker corridors. Over many centuries, the Templarii had built their fortress as a series of stony lean-tos, one structure leaning upon another. No floor plans existed, except in the minds of the Templarii themselves, but the librarians tolerated Nyahri's explorations during the hours between her studies.

"The Templarii think little of me," Nyahri reported to the Atreiani. "The fortress's inner routes are dark, and the librarians do not think me capable of exploring beyond the edges."

"If that is the case, I want you to do something for me," yw Sabi said.

Nyahri smiled, grateful to have a challenge. "What do you wish?"

"Explore those halls. Be sure we understand as well as possible where they lead and what they contain."

"What is it you seek?"

"The path to the center, to Sojourn Temple's door."

"I will find it."

"We may have some *small* advantage if the Templarii believe it still hidden from us. If you can go unnoticed, do so. Be stealthy."

Stealthy proved difficult, since Nyahri required lamplight. No sunlight reached the deep interior and, while overcoming her fear of the confined places, Nyahri kept her first forays brief and near the structure's outer corridors.

All the while, Templarii came and went in their duties, none talkative, each with a name as enigmatic as Kepler's: Galileo Three and Anselm Eighteen, Oppenheimer Twelve and Einstein Seven, Cavendish Nineteen and Huxley Eleven, and so on. In the dark their blue or red eyes glittered like starlight.

When possible, Nyahri observed them. They drank water, ate seldom, and never slept, though every day they sat for some hours with their eyelids closed, in trance. They kept neither cells nor beds for themselves. They pursued no hobbies, told no stories, played no instruments, painted no pictures, and did nothing frivolous. In shifts they scrawled page after page, hundreds in a day, binding tome after tome. Their volumes carried trade records, birth and death certificates, legal proceedings, the minutes of the Oudwn chieftains' council, and a thousand other details.

As needed, the Templarii pressed new paper, made quills, and blended ink. They sometimes left S'Eret, going into the Oudwn community to meet with local leaders or travelers from other lands. They gathered news and recorded it in their books.

When Nyahri returned to the courtyard to visit the horses, she discovered fresh alfalfa, and barrels of water already delivered. Two Templarii raised boxes of bookbinding material and wood to a high window, working a system of pulleys, drawing the load with a lever and capstan.

Nyahri fed oats to Kwlko. "I'll take you out soon," she said to him, scratching behind his ears, "I promise."

A crack, followed the the deep quiver of timber, sounded behind her. The capstan broke.

Wood splintered under its load. A pallet jammed with logs and kidskin plummeted, and the Templarii leapt to avoid the blow—

One too slow.

The pallet edge caught his arm, hammering him to the ground.

In the chaos, the horses neighed and shied away. Nyahri rushed to the injured, ready to lend her skills, prepared for injuries, screaming, and blood. The pallet crushed his shoulder and left arm. His companion, rather than attend his fallen brother, blocked Nyahri's way.

"Thank you," he said, raising his open hand to stop her, "we don't require your assistance."

She leaned past him. "He needs care!"

"No, he is right," said the fallen librarian, only the barest distress in his voice.

Nyahri marveled at him. He looked up at her, his eyes calm, no sign of pain on his face.

"Go back inside, E'cwni. We will tend to this."

"I—" She stammered. "You—?"

"Go," they told her.

"You're not needed," said the first.

"Ay." She nodded, confused, and she left them.

Gods and devils and spirits! she thought. *They are flesh walkers, yea, and the dead feel no pain!*

Shaken by the unnaturalness of it, Nyahri exited the courtyard. She returned to the interior, sorry to leave the horses so soon, but glad to abandon the Templarii to themselves.

NYAHRI REVISITED THE LIBRARY, finding Yw Sabi in a chair with her back against a wall. A book lay open across her lap, her tea gone cold on a side table along with a forgotten corned-beef sandwich and a congealing bowl of stew.

Yw Sabi looked up. "What was that noise?"

"An accident," Nyahri said, and she told the Atreiani of it.

"I agree with them," yw Sabi said. "There's nothing you could've done for the Templari."

Nyahri shook her head. "I have never seen such a thing!"

"Their well-being isn't your concern. Leave the Templarii to care for themselves."

"Yea, Atreiani," she said, though Nyahri felt not so much *concern* as curiosity. *A man cannot crush his arm and ignore the pain.* "Are they truly *dead?*"

"Not really," yw Sabi said.

"Are they undead?"

"Vampires and zombies and ghosts?" Yw Sabi chuckled. "No."

Nyahri knew from yw Sabi's tone that she'd no intention of discussing the Templarii.

"I will get you fresh tea." Nyahri reached for the teacup.

"Leave it. The Templarii can refresh the tea."

"You do not eat enough." She pushed the sandwich closer to the Atreiani.

Yw Sabi shrugged, glanced at the food, and turned a page, reading again.

"Learning much?" Nyahri asked.

"Quite a bit." She patted a stack of books beside her which rose from the floor to Nyahri's waist. Two more piles stood by the first. "But in none of it have I found any explanations for the mystery of five thousand years. Lots of *what happened after,* but no *why it happened at all.*"

"Those books, that is what you plan to read?"

"This is what I've read so far."

"*Gods.*"

Yw Sabi looked at her from under her brows, then gestured to a chair by the table. "Sit."

Nyahri obeyed.

"Several times I've told you," yw Sabi said, "there are no gods. The sooner you wrestle with this concept, the better off we'll be in the long run."

"Ay, but mistress—"

"*But mistress* nothing. When your Englisce is good enough and maybe after you learn *ein paar Sätze von Deutsch* and *un peu de français*, as well as some of the ancient Greek and Latin, we'll start you reading the philosophers, including all the dead-end apologists—something we once forbade most humans to read. If we've the time, we'll go through them from Plato onward, ending with the Declarat and the Edicts Atreian. Then we'll *really* talk about whether there are gods or not."

"I will never learn so much." Nyahri cringed at her creeping self-doubt, at a tinge of anger.

How can it be, she thought, *there are no gods?!*

Yw Sabi gave her a smile. "You might find you can learn more than you expect, math and logic too when we can begin them."

"Whatever you would teach, mistress, but I fear you will judge me a slow student."

"Apply yourself. I ask only your commitment, lovely one."

Lovely one again.

"Thank you." Nyahri rested her hand atop the stack of books. "Have you found *anything* so far which pleases you?"

Yw Sabi looked at Nyahri, her gaze lingering. Then she returned her attention to the books. "Much. The Templarii have kept good records of their visitors, their conversations with travelers and nomads for centuries. In these books, they wrote of the emergence and slow change of hundreds of cultures, near and far—certainly the Inwnii, the E'cwnii, the Oudwnii, all of whom came from different people but whose language groups collided almost nine hundred years ago. The Dwndwn in the west, the Toltos from the south, the Misrvehra—fascinating people, actual pacifists. The Fallwr, who've occupied the region of the Myrs River for more than a few thousand years and who're of deep interest to me. The C'naädii and the Qebeccêi, who came from the same stock but diverged centuries ago, and more. Every culture with some Atreian-based myth, all possessing some vestigial memory of time before the Eventide."

"Good information, though?"

"Good to know the pieces on the chessboard, at least within a thousand kilometers. Hints here and there of Atreian technologies, though certainly no others are awake." Yw Sabi paused on this, as if reassuring herself of her own words. "Maybe those are simply mythologies, but we can be certain of nothing. The Sojourn Templarii have made a few proactive efforts farther afield, necessarily limited— the Templarii's physical range extends no farther than the geofences of their Citadels, wherever they're assigned, about twenty klicks."

Nyahri skipped past questions of *geofences*. "They are *assigned* to a Citadel? There were no Templarii at Abswyn."

"Never were. *Templarii*—Temple. Every *Temple* is a Citadel but not every Citadel is a Temple. Foremost, the Temples were intended to be scientific facilities. The Templarii aided research, managing support operations, recording events, collating data." Yw Sabi gave up the book she'd been reading, setting it aside.

"The Templarii are lesser gods?"

"Gods?" Yw Sabi sighed, a small sign of exasperation. "You're not giving up on this *gods* thing anytime soon, are you? The Templarii are only *machines*."

"How can they be machines?" Nyahri understood *machine*. Years ago she had seen bellows and gear cranks, on a visit with her father, to the settlements of the Eastern Rangers.

"They're *complex* machines."

"What of the other Citadels? You *are* trying to find them? That is your goal?"

"We're here." Yw Sabi stepped to the table, where she unfolded a map. Nyahri had never seen such a map, so complete, its detail and scale beyond her ability to understand. Yw Sabi pointed, "The red dots are the confirmed Citadels, the ones whose locations either the Templarii or I know for certain. The yellow dots are Citadels about which I'm less convinced. The blue show nothing more than a single rumor or approximation."

"You mean to go to these?"

"All of them, but I was interned before they were completed and have no idea how many were finished, and this is a shitty five-hundred-year-old map which doesn't include Australia or a good portion of South America. I can't even be sure of the North American locations."

Nyahri also put aside the urge to ask about *Awsrtrehli-ah* and *Swdhamehricah* and *Nwrdhamehricahn*, leaving those inquiries for later. "Yw Sabi, to what end are you doing this? Why seek *all* these Citadels? You did not come to Swyn Templr for mere answers."

"No." Yw Sabi took a slow breath. "Soon, Nyahri, both of us must make decisions."

"What decisions?"

"Whether you and I will go onward together, whether you'll learn *everything,* or whether I'll just send you home."

Panic tightened Nyahri's chest. "Atreiani, I will not turn back—"

Yw Sabi cut her off. *"You'll* need to decide." The Atreiani said this with a shallow smile, then her expression transformed, deadly serious. "The decision will be yours."

"When?" Nyahri asked.

"When I'm ready. I've survived a long time, in part by keeping my secrets until it's *time* to share them."

Yw Sabi sat, returning to her reading. She skimmed a page, then another, at once focused on the book before her.

"Atreiani—"

"Hmm?"

"You never explained—what did you mean when you said you did not kill Suhto with your own hands?"

Yw Sabi looked up, nodded.

Before she could answer, Nyahri added, "You would not have killed him, I know. He would have been no threat to you at all."

"You're understanding me."

"I am trying."

"I can practice kindness," yw Sabi said, "but I'm anything but kind. I can practice violence too. You've seen this."

"I have."

"What you do not understand is how far this extends. Would it, I wonder, still be better for you to return to your tribe? To one day be Ahtras? It would be kinder, I think, to send you back."

"Nay! You are not evil—"

"I'm not evil, Nyahri, because there's no such thing as objective evil. I find *evil* the ignorant, shortsighted, incapable, entropic. I find *good* the knowledgeable, expansive, farsighted, capable, enduring. Cultural definitions collapse into meaninglessness. We must move beyond good and evil."

"No gods, no evil, no good? What of love, yw Sabi—is there such a thing?"

The Atreiani leaned back in her chair, folding her hands in her lap, regarding Nyahri. "I'll concede—there're many kinds. For ourselves, for dear ones. For company, for kin, for kind. For people and place. For individuals and species. For those who live, and for all those who might ever live. Of all the philosophies, the only two which endure are the material philosophies and the philosophies of love. Yes, if in fact there is a such thing as altruism, there is a such thing as love."

The Atreiani sighed, losing her focus, her eyelids low. She wore the hint of a frown.

"You are not what I presumed," Nyahri said.

"Oh?"

"You are much more *real.*"

Yw Sabi laughed. "Most sensible thing I've ever heard you say."

Nyahri smiled, feeling a warmth rise to her face.

"To answer your question more definitively," the Atreiani said, "I didn't kill Suhto. Almost assuredly, though, I designed whatever did."

Nyahri hugged herself, leaning against the table. "What do you mean?"

"Your spear, your bow and arrows—you made these weapons yourself?"

"Yea."

"Has a weapon you made, such as an arrow, ever been used by someone else?"

Nyahri nodded. "Yea."

"To kill?"

"Yea." Nyahri frowned.

"Whatever hand I had in Suhto's death was more than five thousand years ago."

"I understand." Nyahri stepped forward, standing closer to yw Sabi. "He was good-hearted. Had I been the one who died, and he who lived, he would have helped you. He would have done what he could."

"You are good-hearted too, and *you* are who lived, and that is the way of things. Believe me when I say I understand what it is to lose. Believe me when I say it feels as raw to me as to you. I'm sorry you lost him, but I'm grateful you're here."

Nyahri smiled. Something in yw Sabi had shifted, some barrier fell, and at least for these moments she softened her guard.

"Now if you would please," yw Sabi said, "I need some time to think."

"Yea, mistress."

With a sigh, Nyahri departed the library, and she climbed the stairs to their room. First she refilled the oil lamp, knowing where she must go to complete her task, and she retrieved her spear.

They are flesh walkers, and they seem undead *enough to me. Do not imagine we are safe here,* she told herself, *not for one moment.*

20

Nyahri returned to the courtyard, finding it cleared of wreckage. The goods had been raised to the upper chambers, the capstan repaired and the ground swept. Where the Templari had fallen, a smear of oily blood marked the flagstones.

Like her, the horses had never dwelled inside stone walls, and their anxiousness showed. Nyahri spent extra time with them, and they calmed her as much as she calmed them. The sun stood high, its rays penetrating the courtyard, though the wind carried a chill. The interior walls framed a square of blue firmament, imprisoned by masonry and slate shingles. One wall reflected Sojourn pillar's ghost-fire of light and shadow, light and shadow.

Turo nudged her shoulder.

"No more for now," she told him, drawing her fingers through his beaded mane and down his forelocks. She hefted her spear, walked back inside, and sparked the lamp with flint and a wad of hemp. The lamp's dirty glow thrust back the darkness, and Nyahri made her way deeper into the fortress, though following for now the passages which connected the outer libraries.

She shuffled forward, keeping near the walls. Twice she glimpsed the twin ghost-fires of Templarin eyes, but the librarians paid her no attention, acclimated to her feral wandering between these rooms.

When she thought it prudent, she chose an inner doorway and followed it. Any hint of sunlight, filtering from high outer windows, soon faded.

The deeper into S'Eret she went, the more she understood its pattern, like a sunflower's floret. It spiraled inward toward the pillar, one chamber after another, smaller and smaller the closer to the center she traveled.

The portals between these chambers sometimes opened in multiple directions, allowing movement through the fortress without following the spiral itself. Simple as this seemed at first, however, it turned S'Eret from a decipherable whorl into an ornate labyrinth.

Nyahri sought its heart, far into its rocky shell, and there the air hung death-still, stale and decayed, sour on her tongue. Nearer the center, she circumvented chambers with no entrance, volumes isolated by the stonework. Yet always, given enough time to search, she found new routes, and the labyrinth yielded to her.

Some rooms stored odds and ends, nothing made by Atreian magic, only the tools or clothing or weapons of men. Nyahri recognized no tribal styles, not even those of distant sea-dwellers whose goods had come to the E'cwnii by trade—like the beads adorning her clothes—nor the northerners' ironworks or southerners' pottery.

One room contained roll after roll of woven blankets and rugs. For some minutes, Nyahri sat among them, wondering how she came to such a place.

Have I not denied my people, she thought, not for the first time, *turned aside motherhood and tent wivery to outdo my mother, to outdo every Ahtras who ever lived?*

Nyahri would never be Ahtras of her tribe. She had, she knew, made that decision the moment Suhto proposed marriage. It was not him alone she rejected, but everything he represented, the truth that to wed him meant a life like her mother's and grandmothers', priestesses who spent most of their lives in tents while others hunted, traded, raided, and ranged. Those priestesses called for the company and wisdom of the gods, including the Atreianii, and her mother had worshipped them above all.

Nyahri had already outdone her mother, all her ancestors. For more than one turn of the moons, she had accompanied a living Atreiani, and what priestess before her could ever have said so? Yet Nyahri found that, while she wanted many things from the Atreiani, to *worship* her was not included in them. Sultah yw Sabi was neither goddess nor horror, was more friend than enemy, and her heart certainly beat.

Nyahri touched one of the rugs, and it crumbled.

Ancient, she thought, *and nothing lasts forever.*

She recalled how yw Sabi looked at her during that first night, after Atreiani had healed her, when she could have ridden away but chose otherwise. Nyahri recalled, as they had arrived among the E'cwnii, yw Sabi's over-familiar whisper, *I will not harm your family.* She recalled yw Sabi's first fleeting touch upon her cheek in the guest tent of her father's camp, yw Sabi's words at Aukensis—*I'm becoming quite fond of this one.* Nyahri recalled the intense warmth of yw Sabi's hand, holding her own, on the night they reviewed the planets—*Mercury, Venus, Earth.* She recalled their growing but uncertain closeness as they crossed from the mountains' eastern slopes, the Atreiani's flesh against her own, for the sake of warmth.

I have wanted more of it, Nyahri thought, *since that first night against her. I would have more of it now.*

She recalled, as well, yw Sabi's words as they entered the Templarin fortress. *I am considering her claime,* yw Sabi had said.

An odd word—*claime.*

Nyahri stood and, as she swept the lamp from side to side, it sloshed. The oil ran much lower than she expected and, though the fought it, her panic welled.

Gods accursed, confined spaces!

Breathing faster, growing lightheaded, she went back the way she'd come, praying all the while to her gods that the oil might last a few minutes more. In time the air cleared, and she emerged into a familiar hall. A hint of sunshine bled from high windows, showing the way back to the library. She turned the corner—

Kepler clasped his hands at his waist, his eyes glowing in the dusty dark.

Nyahri recoiled from him. "Apologies," she said, trying to edge past him.

"Human." He stepped in her way.

She backed to the wall, planting her spear between them, not quite threatening.

"You and your *mistress*," he said, his tone polite, "have all you require?"

"We do." In the large hall her voice echoed thinly.

He looked past her shoulder, the way she'd come. "I find it curious she hasn't yet descended into the Citadel, don't you? That she hasn't yet requested I lead her to its entrance?"

"She does as she wishes," Nyahri said.

"As she always has. What were you doing down there, in the black, with your sad little lantern?"

"Only exploring."

"No more *exploring* for you. An Oudwni who found his way so deep into S'Eret, you know, would never be seen again."

"Do you threaten me? I am an Atreiani's handmaiden."

He laughed softly. "Threaten? No. I merely mean that the old chambers are dangerous and one could be killed digging around back there." He raised his chin, looking down his nose at her. "And you *are* not an Atreiani's handmaiden—you're no Exemplari, much less a Magistress's *claimèd,* not yet. You're only a human."

Nyahri held the lamp to his face and the flame overpowered the ghost-fire, turning his eyes to brown, revealing his pallid skin, a web-work of twisted veins beneath it. "And you are nothing but old meat—something which should have been dead a long time ago."

The lamp sputtered, the last drops of oil hissing against the bottom of the wick. Nyahri's panic resurged, but she allowed none of it to show.

One corner of his lip curled. "You realize, human, how inconsequential you are? You're nothing to us and you're nothing to *her*. We value the least of our books more greatly than we value you. I know who you are, E'cwni—some time ago your kin tried to burn our library to the ground. Cohltos's chieftain, Shwn Pawl, knows this as well, and wonders why Sultah yw Sabi has not yet paid him the respect of a visit?"

"I am not here to burn your books," Nyahri said, "and yw Sabi owes no visit to anyone. Let me pass."

He extended his arm, leaning upon the wall, blocking her progress. "One more thing—after some consideration, we find it unaccountable that Sultah yw Sabi could be the only survivor of Abswyn. Carry *that* message to her."

"I will."

"Still," he said, more softly, almost with a sigh, "if its destruction was accidental, and she's come to descend and wake Sojourn and submit to the will of her brothers and sisters, she should get on with it. She's been here a week—"

Nyahri shoved past him, never turning her back to him, placing herself nearer the reading room.

"On the other hand," he continued, "if she had anything to do with Abswyn's destruction, you best pray to those gods your people keep, because you'll need their help. Neither we nor any Oudwni will allow her to do the same here."

Nyahri scowled. "If my mistress wanted to destroy this place, she would have done it the day we arrived."

"She's not your *mistress*, naïve girl, and you have no power here. You're just a foal without a mother."

She backhanded his cheek, the blow spinning him. When he turned to her again, a bloodless gash marred his cheekbone.

Motherless foal.

She trembled, cut to her quick, the tender center of her anger. "Yw Sabi is in a mood to *read*," Nyahri said, "and she would like to read in peace, without distractions, without your stupid assumptions, and she will do things in her own time."

He blinked, straightening his back. Kepler considered his words before he spoke.

"In one possible future," he said, "you just might find yourself a Magistress's claimèd, you really might, blessed beyond your wildest imaginings. In another, your life will be horribly brief and I will be there at your end, as I was for the last one."

For the last one? Nyahri wondered. *I think I understand. If it is to be yw Sabi and I against them, yea, still I would be content.*

The lamp finally died.

Nyahri backed from Kepler, closing the short distance to the library's entrance. It took all her willpower to stop her trembling.

ONCE BACK AMONG THE books, Nyahri shut the door. Yw Sabi sat as before, save her head tilted differently than it had been before, or her legs crossed rather than propped. Her book piles climbed higher.

"What happened?" yw Sabi asked, without looking up from her page. "In the hallways, you raised your voice with Kepler."

"He does not trust you."

"Of course he doesn't."

"He insulted me and I struck him."

"I'm sure he deserved it." Yw Sabi marked her page and set aside the book. "I'm glad he didn't strike back. Don't believe the Templarii's frail appearance."

Nyahri walked to her, stood beside yw Sabi's chair, and leaned with her hip against the table. The Atreiani lifted her chin to meet Nyahri's gaze, not much below the E'cwni's eye level, even seated as she was.

"What is it?" yw Sabi asked.

With a moment's hesitation, Nyahri ran her fingertips along a strand of yw Sabi's hair, drawing it between thumb and forefinger. Lightless and reflecting no candle flame, nothing in nature matched her hair save night-falcon feathers, and even they reflected *some* luminance. The plaits whispered through Nyahri's fingers, gossamer soft.

If it is to be yw Sabi and I against all, Nyahri thought again, *then let it* be *she and I, not halfway.*

"What is this about?" yw Sabi asked, lifting her hand to Nyahri's, setting her palm on the back of Nyahri's wrist.

Nyahri remembered the last time yw Sabi held her wrist, the iron strength of her grasp. The Atreiani had been trying to protect Nyahri then, caring but harsh. Now those fingers communicated hesitant warmth, their caring much softer.

"My mother spoke of you," Nyahri said, "when she recounted the traditions. Your emblem *does* appear on ruins, all over the ranges. I have seen it, on stones in the north, the night-falcon bound in a square, flanked by feathers."

"Defaced, I am guessing."

Nyahri nodded. "It is said you were hated before the Eventide, your creations torn down, and your kind hunted you."

"Mostly true."

Nyahri coursed her fingertips to the end of yw Sabi's hair, past her elbows, then back up to a length across the Atreiani's ear. "What happened? Why are you so unwelcome here now?"

Yw Sabi dropped her hands into her lap, still countenancing Nyahri's attentions, but her expression grew colder. Nyahri focused on yw Sabi's long, straight, depthless mane, by the moment more confident in her touch.

"Why did your kind call you *enemy?*" Nyahri asked.

Yw Sabi became her imperial self, one who answers no questions, and she sat back from Nyahri, enough to widen the distance between them. "There is no need to talk of it."

"Nay? Kepler all but threatens us openly," Nyahri said, "we are 'guests' in hostile territory, gods know how many archers in this city, and corpse devils walk the halls with us, cook our meals, and look after our horses. It is clear to me, yw Sabi, the Templarii fear you but, just as you said with Dhaos and his men, they may turn on us. *Will* turn on us, I think, unless you do as they desire."

"I agree."

"I *have* been listening, mistress. Kepler asks you to *power the Citadel,* whatever that means. They wonder why you do not *descend,* whatever *that* means. They expect other Atreianii to awaken, they are anxious for it, and it is clear as spring water you will do anything to prevent this. You are delaying for some purpose only *you* can explain."

Yw Sabi folded her arms across her chest.

"I know it," Nyahri said, "you know it, *they* know it." She leaned on the tabletop. "They are your inferiors, mayhap, but how long before they abandon politeness, mistress? I will fight no less for you than I would have when we first met Dhaos's men, when we stood in Orÿs Hall with his beast of a father and two score of arrows pointed at us, or on the Lwvlnda Pass where you saved *my* life. I am *still* here, yw Sabi. I have not returned to the E'cwnii yet, have I?"

"Make your point." The Atreiani's tone remained even, husky, and low.

"I am *still* yours," Nyahri said, remembering how yw Sabi rebuked her more than a month before when she spoke similar words, "but I might serve you better if I knew *why* your enemies hate you, and what *you* intend."

Yw Sabi drew a breath, held it, and considered. "Among other things," she said at last, "I killed a great many of them."

"You did kill—" Nyahri questioned her own assumptions. "—other Atreianii?"

"Oh, yes."

Nyahri lowered her brow, fighting equally with dismay and a desire to understand—*a goddess who killed other gods.* The Atreiani's purpose shown clear. "You mean to *destroy* Swyn Templr?"

Yw Sabi nodded.

Nyahri tensed and, under the weight of that realization, she scooted a chair from the table and sat. Her gaze centered on yw Sabi's charcoal-dark eyes. "You destroyed Abswyn?"

"I overrode its string core and allowed it to destroy itself."

Ay, Atreiani, I do not know what string core *means, but I understand the rest. Nay, you did not kill Suhto with your own hands, but you would have slain me too, even yourself if I had not been there to save you—*

"As you slaughtered the C'naädii—" Nyahri shook her head. "You slaughtered your own kind too, long ago."

"Before my peers finally captured me."

"You could have told me sooner."

"I share nothing, with anyone, until I wish."

"Share *everything* with me, yw Sabi. Do you not need *one* person to trust, above all others?" Lofting the Atreiani's own words back at her, seeing where such arrows landed.

"You *have* been listening. Willful girl," Yw Sabi said, as she had said once before, but this time more warmly.

"Why have you done all this?"

"Long ago, humans failed themselves and the world, and we Atreianii punished them horrifically for it. Not long after, we Atreianii failed the world too, and we paid little price at all. Hardly seemed fair."

"Riddles!" Nyahri closed her fists, shaking her head. "That is no explanation. Help me understand, mistress, and no *lessons.* Be clear!"

"What did you say to me when we first spoke? What had your legends taught you about the coming of the *Atreian devils* to the world?"

Nyahri remembered, "When they came, they found free men and women and they enslaved them?"

"Before the enslavement there was a Culling—we killed more humans than you can imagine. What do you think will happen if my sisters and brothers rise again? To your father and sister? To Dhaos and all the Oudwnii? To anyone?"

"Why favor humans over Atreianii? Over your own kind, nay? What do you care, yw Sabi?"

"All the Atreianii I ever loved, I could count on my hands." She held up both palms, her fingers open, then closed one into a fist. "My enemies had killed this many before they stuffed me into the ground."

Nyahri leaned against the table, clasping her hands beneath her chin. "For all your seeming hardness, you mean to *help* humankind?"

"As a whole."

"Yet you have done terrible things, yw Sabi, yea?" Nyahri sat back again, furrowing her brow. "To your cousins *and* to—to us, to humans?"

"To my cousins? You think of my relationship to other Atreianii like your relationship to other E'cwnii. It isn't so but, yes, I did terrible things to many of them."

Closing her eyes, Nyahri remembered an Aukensin girl's blood-flecked lips. "Will you give medicines to the Oudwnii, to Aukensis?"

Nyahri found the Atreiani beautiful, thin and even frail-seeming. Her frosty lips neither frowned nor smiled. Her straight hair framed her face. Her eyes, despite their blackness, appeared liquid and warm.

"If I can," yw Sabi said, "I will."

"Both good and evil," Nyahri whispered, accepting the Atreiani must believe wholly in something else. "You killed Atreianii because of what they did—to humans?—but you were part of the killing of many of us, yea?"

"Yes."

"What changed your heart?"

"Time, in part."

"In part? You *killed* Atreianii because of what they did to those you loved? It is more complex than a matter of *time,* yea? Who did you love *most?*"

"I—" Yw Sabi lost focus, her gaze in the middle distance, and she spoke only a name: "Ekaterina."

As Kepler said, Nyahri thought, *soon after we arrived here.*

"Tell me?" she asked.

Yw Sabi said nothing.

Why does she not tell me?

Nyahri stood and turned away, clenching her hands at her sides.

How many suitors did I turn away in these last two years? Nyahri wondered. *How many before Suhto? How many from the E'cwn tribes, from the Inwn, all those men come and gone? I wanted none of them.*

But this one, she thought, looking at yw Sabi, *this woman I desire.*

"If you want my help," Nyahri said, "you cannot hide from me the way you hide from everyone else."

The Atreiani remained silent.

Nyahri kicked a chair over, shoved the table, and closed the distance to her mistress. She studied yw Sabi's face, the opalescence of her skin, the fullness of her lips, the angle of her cheekbones. Nyahri breathed in the scent of her, the softest spice.

"Would you end the Atreianii?" Nyahri asked. "Down to the last individual?"

"If necessary."

"For the sake of humans?"

"Yes."

Yet that is not quite true, mistress, is it?

"I will try to understand," Nyahri said, "to help you, to do whatever I can, but you have to tell me *why,* all of it. Tell me about Ekaterina."

The Atreiani regarded her still, no smile, no frown, though her eyes trembled. In all other ways she sat frozen.

"I have accepted all you have told me," Nyahri said, "have I not? I have given you no reason to distrust me and yet have you told me everything?"

Yw Sabi shook her head slowly, the barest motion.

"Tell me!" Nyahri screamed.

Silence.

Nyahri wondered later what snapped her temper. The remains of her anger at Kepler? The suffocation of living indoors, somewhere so unnatural, for so long? Bound-up desires? Her guilt at feeling them on the wake of so much loss? Mayhap Dhaos was right, and she was an animal herself? The same brashness which made her blurt fatal challenges for her cousin, the same which nearly cost Uhlo his knee, the same she had felt many times on the hunt or in battle or when she plunged her longknife through her uncle's heart.

She boiled over with it now, and Nyahri lashed out for the second time in an hour, slapping yw Sabi across the cheek. At once Nyahri regretted the blow, covered her own mouth in shock, tears of surprise clouding her vision—*One does not strike a goddess.* The trembling of the Areiani's eyes became a hurt, the viper now at the surface.

Then that viper struck.

21

Yw Sabi's fingers closed around Nyahri's serape, drawing her down. The Atreiani's hand grasped the back of Nyahri's neck, bending her, bringing Nyahri's ear to her mouth. Her strength broke Nyahri's resistance, beyond anything she ever before felt, like iron given life.

"I *would* kill the Atreianii," yw Sabi said, her voice feather soft, her fangs bared, "because we existed to create paradise at great cost, more than you can imagine, and we did unconscionable things for our creation. We did not merely *enslave,* we committed overwhelming atrocities, telling ourself our utopia was worth that price. *That* I thought I could live with but, instead of paradise, we made *hell.*"

Yw Sabi's grip tightened. Only men had ever held Nyahri so roughly, so violently, the first when she was twelve years old. All those men had died. Now, in reflex, Nyahri drew her longknife, not knowing what else to do.

Will she kill me? Can I kill her? Nay, Atreiani, this is not what I wanted—

Yw Sabi's hand closed around Nyahri's, warm and strong, keeping the blade between them. "I'm no omniscient goddess," she said. "I'm a drooling infant. From the moment of my unlikely awakening, forces I cannot discern play me like a pipe and I can't so much as guess their intentions—Citadels yet sleeping, a silent Hive. I *am* frightened."

Nyahri strained, focused on the blade. She wedged her feet against the table, trying to leverage herself, knocking over her chair. The table—a handspan thick of solid hardwood on stout legs and covered in heavy books—squealed as it slid across the flagstones. Nyahri remained impotent in yw Sabi's grasp.

"You?" the E'cwni asked. "*Frightened?*"

"I am outsmarted and alone," yw Sabi said, gritting her teeth, biting back some agony hidden deep, now rising to the surface for—

For me, Nyahri realized.

"A great game is being played," said yw Sabi, "and here, by myself, I have already lost."

"You are *not* by yourself," she said.

"I should be. Better to send you back than have you die."

"*I* am *not* easy to kill."

"Neither was Ekaterina," yw Sabi said, quavering like a bowstring.

"Tell me."

"Her death is still close, no matter the time I slept, not more than a couple of years for me."

"Loss hurts." Nyahri's mother and brother, then Suhto. "Gods, how I know, yw Sabi! I understand how it feels—"

"I cannot suffer it again—" Yw Sabi's voice trailed and died.

"Tell me," Nyahri said, her breath sharp.

"Neither can I be alone, not for the long task ahead."

"*Tell me.* Tell me about Ekaterina." Nyahri stumbled over the pronunciation, the hardness of the sounds foreign on an E'cwn tongue.

"Ekaterina et Sultah, daughter of the Old Griffon, sweet Light of Rosia." Tears rolled down yw Sabi's cheeks, her eyes flashing with a thousand memories, all conjured by a name. "She was my claimèd."

Nyahri ceased her fighting, though her hand remained on the knife's handle. With no chair to sit in, she knelt before yw Sabi. Her heart beat like war drums.

"Your enemies took her from you?"

"Yes," yw Sabi said, letting Nyahri's hand go.

Nyahri tightened her grip upon the longknife, not yielding it, wondering yet if she must defend herself. "They *murdered* her?"

Yw Sabi nodded ever so little.

Defend myself from what? Nyahri thought.

She dropped the blade. It struck the edge of the fallen chair, clattering to the floor. Nyahri stood and passed her hand behind yw Sabi's head. Without a moment's pause, she kissed her—a hard, hungry kiss, her own tears welling as she did—and brought her other hand to yw Sabi's hair. The Atreiani's fingers became gentle on the back of her neck, yw Sabi's other hand falling to Nyahri's waist. Nyahri arced over yw Sabi's lap, kissing her again, again.

Their foreheads touched and Nyahri said, "They will not take me."

FROM AFTERNOON UNTIL LATE in the night they rollicked together in the bed of their tower chamber. Behind them, they left a trail of discarded clothes. After their revelry, Nyahri collapsed in yw Sabi's arms, still savoring the Atreiani on her lips, a peculiar and delicious sweetness.

Staring at the timbered ceiling, Nyahri smiled. Her world shone clearer.

Nyahri listened to the whole of the Atreiani's story, as much could be told in such a brief time: for more than five hundred years she lived before the Eventide, centuries brilliant and bleak. Yw Sabi told only fragments, but Nyahri raised few questions, knowing details would emerge in time.

When the Atreiani finished, Nyahri said, "You *were* gods, no matter that you deny it."

"There are no divinities—everything is simply something up or down the food chain. For better or worse we did what we thought right."

A candle provided their only light. Nyahri curled against yw Sabi's side, kissing her shoulder, tasting her skin. They embraced one another, hands in each other's hair or trailing along their spines, not speaking for many minutes.

Yw Sabi said in realization, *"Safi."*

"Eh, mistress?"

"That word—I thought maybe *witch,* rooted in *Circê,* like your sister's name, but that made *no* sense." She smiled. "Now I understand. The E'cwnii dropped *lesbian* and kept *sapphist. Sappho—safi.*"

"I did not know how the word came to us. I was always teased with it."

Yw Sabi lowered her eyebrows. "Safii are shunned among the E'cwnii?"

"Nay, not shunned, but a would-be Ahtras is expected to bear children, something two women cannot do."

Yw Sabi smiled as if she knew better.

"There was a story," Nyahri said, "generations ago, of an Ahtros who served with two Ahtrasi who, it seemed, loved each other as much as their Ahtros, but there have been none like that *I* ever saw."

"You have any experiences, any young women you loved?"

"One of my cousins, her name was Itrwra. We had our time together, but she became the tent wife of an Inwn man and I never saw her again. I kissed others, but they decided it was a game and grew bored with me. You *must* have realized I desired you, yw Sabi?"

"I second-guessed myself." Yw Sabi shook her head. "You must've known I wanted *you?*"

"You are difficult to read. I thought sometimes the way you looked at me or the way you spoke, but nay. Sleeping with you in the cold of the mountains, it only confused me."

Yw Sabi kissed Nyahri's forehead.

"I used my desire," the Atreiani said, "as an excuse to get you into the fortress."

"How?"

"*Claime.* You remember?"

"Of course. What does it mean?"

"Atreianii sometimes took Atreian lovers—but the laws preventing the accumulation of our political power also prevented the union or division of our *demesnes*. Extended cohabitation was literally illegal, so we frequently kept human lovers."

"Was it thought strange?"

"No. In our frame, our proportions, our sexuality, we're similar. Humans were sometimes beautiful to us—we, sometimes beautiful to humans. When an Atreiani took a woman or man as both Exemplari and as beloved, it was said they were *claimèd*. Almost half the Exemplarii were."

Nyahri smiled. "You *had* guessed my feelings."

"I had my guesses." Yw Sabi winked. "I also figured Kepler would think it plausible enough to let you in."

Nyahri scooted up onto the pillow, meeting yw Sabi's eye. "I am *not* your Exemplari."

"No."

"When?"

"In another era, you would be by my side for *years* before we considered it." Yw Sabi studied Nyahri for long moments, searching for words which ran ahead of her.

"We do not have years, do we?"

"No."

"Ekaterina," Nyahri said again, this time pronouncing the name closer to correct. She spread her fingers through the Atreiani's hair, drawing her thumb along the edge of her ear. "She must have been a goddess herself for you to think so much of her."

Yw Sabi sighed, offering half a smile.

"I am sorry, mistress."

"It's all right, lovely one." Yw Sabi kissed Nyahri's hair.

"I should not call you *mistress*. I know you dislike it."

"Hadn't you noticed? When is the last time I complained of it?"

Nyahri smiled.

Yw Sabi took a deep breath. "Ekaterina exquisitely represented me and her family, to the end. Lover. Right hand. Counselor." Her voice became heavy and flat. "My enemies took some pleasure in telling me how she suffered, how terrible it was. Kat believed, more than I, we could broker a new agreement which worked for the Atreianii and for human-kind, and she never gave up hope we might avert disaster. So much for hope."

"There should always be *some* hope, nay?"

"Optimism eternal. In the years before everything went wrong, she was one of few humans who regularly requested, and earned, hearings before our Congress. She envisioned a freer future for *Homo sapiens*. Given enough time she might've succeeded."

Yw Sabi returned to the silence of some memory.

"She sounds remarkable," Nyahri said.

"She was."

"She was your claimèd—I would be your claimèd now, if you will have me."

"I'll be lucky to have you." Then, "It's also complicated."

Nyahri kissed yw Sabi's cheek, then her mouth. They kissed again, warm and unhurried.

"Complicated? How?"

"A little problem of *continuity of consciousness,*" yw Sabi said quietly, as if explaining everything.

Nyahri lowered her brow, frowning as she tried to understand. Life with the Atreiani was, as much as anything else, a life of schooling.

Yw Sabi continued, "The artifact of an Atreiani is our scepter, the tool by which we command but also by which we were beholden to the whole. The artifact of an Exemplari is her *collar*—" The Atreiani turned on her side, looking into Nyahri's eyes. "—and its influence continues even beyond the death of the wearer's flesh. There is no escape for an Atreiani from her bargain with her Exemplari, and none for an Exemplari from her Atreiani."

Nyahri sat, pulling the bed sheets around her. "What does that mean?" she asked, guessing the gravity of the answer.

"It means," yw Sabi sighed, "Ekaterina never truly died. She lives within that artifact, a ghost in a machine."

Nyahri remember the length of golden-hued fabric she had seen in yw Sabi's hands during those first days. "Her *soul* is bound in it?"

The Atreiani tilted her head. "Not precisely but, in your terms, I suppose that's a close approximation."

"Does she suffer?"

"She sleeps, perhaps dreams on occasion, and in many ways she will never again awaken except—"

"Except?"

"—through whoever next holds my claime."

"As I might?"

Yw Sabi nodded.

"How?" Nyahri asked.

"The collar you would wear will have been hers. The continuity passes from Ekaterina, through it, to you. A contiguous life from one age to another."

"The magic is that strong?" Nyahri asked, leaning back. "An Exemplari's burden is so great?"

Gods, mayhap Dhaos was right? Do I risk my soul? What a thing it is!

"Burden? It could be, yes."

"What happens? Would I stop being me?" A gallop of fear moved through her. "Would I *die?*"

"Oh, lovely one," yw Sabi said, caressing Nyahri's shoulder, "not at all, but in time you *would* be changed. Who she was—is—would be added to who you *are.*"

Nyahri's brows furrowed. "Like I would be two people?"

"Not at all. It is like this—one remembers being someone else entirely. The two resolve into one."

"Gods!"

"There is still time to think on it." Yw Sabi rolled onto her back, placing her hands behind her head, gazing at the rafters. "If, after you've considered, you still imagine it a *burden*—you'll go whichever way you choose. Either way, you'll always be Nyahri," said yw Sabi, "horsewoman, daughter of the Ahtros, sister of Cirje. That will never change."

Nyahri lay in thought.

"We've had a full day," yw Sabi said, "and we've both much to consider. We should sleep."

A sigh escaped Nyahri's lips. "Not yet."

"Oh?" The Atreiani smiled. "I should have you again?"

Nyahri arched over her mistress, knees to either side of her chest, hands planted next to her shoulders. Smiling, the E'cwni tripped her tongue across the back of her teeth. "Do."

Yw Sabi grinned—the first true grin Nyahri had ever seen from her, all bright teeth and wide, generous lips—and once more she pulled Nyahri down. Afterwards, they slept each in the other's arms.

{Interim: Divine Transmissions}

2130617:194502:EA39.7392N+104.9842W:
AUTUMN01::

LORAHDI: I will do as you will, goddess, always and forever.

AUTUMN01: You will bear a child. With her birth, we will restart the turning of many wheels, bring to fruition our long plans.

LORAHDI: Thank you for your blessings, goddess!

AUTUMN01: This is our command—of this moment you will never speak a word. You will die with this meeting never again upon your tongue, nor will you write it in any script.

LORAHDI: I will be faithful, goddess.

AUTUMN01: We know you will.

Transcript Archive, Exhibit B
Vo Misa Station

22

The next morning, Nyahri awoke still in yw Sabi's embrace. Early sunlight streamed from the cedar -screened windows, nearer the ceiling, and painted bright geometries against the western wall. Yw Sabi sat, scooting to the edge of the bed, and she rubbed her face like any sleepy human might. She smiled down at Nyahri.

"Do you feel as smitten this morning," she said, "as you did last night?"

"More, mistress." Nyahri blinked and rolled onto her side, took yw Sabi by the hand, and tried to drag her back into the bed.

"Time for other things." The Atreiani leaned across Nyahri, kissing her on the forehead, then stood. *Where* are my clothes?"

"Everywhere, yw Sabi," Nyahri said, her smile reaching all the way through her words.

"Find *yours* too. Get dressed. We've tasks."

Nyahri swung her feet to the floor and brushed her hair back from her face. "What do you wish?"

"I'm locking myself in the library," the Atreiani said. "Your task is to *leave* for a few hours. You've been shut in this place far too long. No lessons today. By dark, be back here and—" Yw Sabi flashed a fanged smile. "—in our bed."

Nyahri tilted her head, her own smile unfaded. "Where should I go?"

"Out into the city, into the valleys, if your fancy takes you." *Fancy takes you* failed in translation, and Nyahri imagined herself braided and beaded like a prized mare, paraded for some reason she could not imagine. "Should be safe enough," yw Sabi said," given our *guest* status. Get a sense of Cohltos, a feel for the people, and report."

"I will."

"You'll be taking the horses, I imagine?"

"Of course."

"Good. Now go."

Nyahri groaned, unhappy to leave.

Unhappy to leave! I have wanted nothing, she thought, *but to leave these walls since we arrived!*

After they emerged from their room and descended the stairs, the Atreiani's smile vanished, her face set as stone. Nyahri understood how it would always be: Yw Sabi would keep one face for their private moments and another for the rest of the world.

"Be wary out there," yw Sabi said. *"Safe enough* does not mean anyone is our friend."

"Yea, of that I need no reminder."

At the first sight of a Templari—a monkish figure who looked not more than fourteen, a sallow boy who moved like an old man—a quiet growl rolled from yw Sabi's throat. "Fetch hot tea," she told him, "and be quick about it, you useless crustacean."

ON HORSEBACK, NYAHRI LEFT the shadowy halls of S'Eret, emerging into a bright but frigid daylight. Braced wooden barricades encircled the fortress gates, a wide buffer between the stone walls and a gathering Oudwn crowd. Some hundreds of men, women, and children fell silent as Nyahri rode into the light, leading Turo behind Kwlko.

"The witch," one man said.

The witch, Nyahri thought. The word meant something different in Oudwn than it did in E'cwn, something dangerous, something whorish, and she disliked it.

The mob craned their necks, searching past her for the Atreiani. The Templarii closed the great doors behind Nyahri and bolted them, leaving her alone to face the throng.

"Why have you come here?" someone shouted.

Another shouted, "Why is the Atreiani among us?"

"What message," a woman called, "does she bring to us from the netherworld?"

"Do all the Atreianii awake?"

"Will she help us?"

"Is she here to judge us?"

"Will she punish us?"

"Help us!"

Nyahri calmed Kwlko, who sidestepped nervously from the crowds. The cold wind blew her hair, the night-falcon feathers of her coronal swirling around her, giving her the unnatural semblance of the Atreiani herself. "I do not know the answers to your questions," she shouted in reply. "I am only her servant."

"What *can* you tell us?" another woman asked, and a hundred others waited on the answer.

Nyahri studied them, noting the sick, old, and weary, the same as at Aukensis. "She does not mean you any harm!"

"They say she is bringing medicines!" shouted a man.

"Yes!" others shouted. "Medicines!"

Where, Nyahri wondered, *would* that *rumor have begun?*

"She will try," the E'cwni answered them.

A woman cried out, "Thank the gods!"

"When?" the man asked.

"When she can," Nyahri said, thankful for the oratory practice of an Ahtros's daughter at the great tribal meets. "She has much to do. Be patient! Now, friends, I would like to walk your city and learn it for myself."

A young man called, "I will show you!"

"Thank you, but I would go alone."

She waved to them, guiding the horses not through the crowd but toward a wider street, deeper into the city. Heavy flagstones paved the way between low buildings of granite, wood, and thatch. Cooking fires flavored the air. Youth played in a plaza, a chasing game punctuated with delighted squeals, just as E'cwn girls and boys would play. Nyahri walked the horses at a slow pace, still on Kwlko's back, their hooves clacking on the pavers.

Everywhere she went, Oudwnii watched her. Some glared, some bowed their heads, some stared in awe or fear or scorn.

Overlooking the city's waterways, a higher street followed the contours of the land, and Nyahri chased it upward. Along the hillsides, the houses and avenues angled oddly, no straight lines except a long east-west boulevard, the same upon which Dhaos had led them more than ten days before. Two rivers crossed near S'Eret Fortress. The first was a meandering gray wash from the highest glaciers of the western ranges, churned by a more tumultuous rush of silty red water from the north. Winding eastward, beneath a series of stone bridges, these tributaries collided into a single waterway.

Among the close-standing masonry houses, Nyahri dismounted and tethered the horses to a post beside a swath of grass. She walked past the homes, nodding to anyone who met her eye. Chickens clucked, hurrying from her path. One woman sighted Nyahri, halted her children playing, and herded them from the street. Others cleared her way, as well, even full-grown men.

Rounding a corner, Nyahri stopped short. She encountered a round-bodied matron, who wore an apron and a generous smile, and who burst with surprise at sight of the E'cwni. The woman stood in a fenced yard, goats bleating around her. Behind her yard, a divinely delicious scent of roasting meat wafted from an open doorway.

"The E'cwn witch," the woman said, as if delighted. "Witch of the Atreiani!"

"My name is Nyahri, not *witch*."

"My name is Colhina."

From the doorway emerged a heavyset man, twice Nyahri's age, carrying a copper cup. Gray peppered his beard. His eyes told her of kindness. He wore a well-tended smock which spoke of a care for his profession, whatever it might be—*A baker*, Nyahri thought. He had the soft eyes of someone who'd never killed in battle.

"This is Ahlon," Colhina said, tilting her head toward him.

"The Atreiani's witch," he said, his eyes going wide, and he dropped the cup. It clanged, bounced, and splattered water across the dirt.

"Her name is *Ny-ah-ri*."

"Nyahri," he repeated, bowing his head, "an honor."

Nyahri raised her face, drawing a long breath, coveting the meal waiting inside. Her belly grumbled. How many myths did her people tell which began with the guile of good food and ended with bloody death? Too many. Yet she studied the generous expressions of these two Oudwnii and found nothing in them to distrust.

"We have lamb pie," Ahlon said, a nervous jitter in his voice.

Nyahri scrunched her nose. "I—" She stood taller, choosing an expression more fitting for the servant of an Atreiani. "I do not know what *pie* is."

Pie was not an E'cwn word.

Colhina smiled, puffing out her chest. "Come in then, E'cwni, and find out."

A rustic home, in many ways simpler than an E'cwn tent, it nonetheless held a marvelous cast-iron stove. The couple sautéed vegetables and roasted apples. They inquired about Nyahri's life on the plains, what she thought of Cohltos, whether she wanted for anything.

They asked her nothing of the Atreiani herself. They made no demands.

In their company, Nyahri discovered that warm lamb pie with carrots and beets tasted like the grist of the gods. Her hosts fed her graciously, and they shared generously.

Afterward, as Colhina walked Nyahri to their front gate, she said, "Be well, witch."

"Thank you for your kindness," Nyahri replied.

"Take this." The woman pressed a loaf of bread into Nyahri's hands. "The best kind of weapon—it beats away hunger."

Nyahri departed with a smile, but also with a heavy heart—she *liked* the Oudwnii. She returned to the horses, wrapped the bread in a square of cloth, and packed it in the saddlebags. After mounting Kwlko, she started southward down a new street.

For hours, Nyahri sat on a granite boulder in a wide meadow, outside the city, while the horses grazed. Releasing the pent-up energy of ten days indoors, Kwlko ran, working himself into a sweat.

Lovely stallion, Nyahri thought. *Well endowed. Sire to many foals in her father's herd.*

Unlooked for, thoughts of the archer Dhaos overtook Nyahri. Her heart burst for yw Sabi, not one measure diminished by her imaginings of the handsome Oudwni. The last night's pleasure, so close and real, remained with her. She wanted to repeat it, to have her mouth on yw Sabi again.

Yet still, Dhaos occupied her mind, invading from the edges.

It is possible, Nyahri thought, *I am* not *a safi. It is possible I like both.*

It is possible I want both.

She sighed.

The land poured into her eyes, like nourishment, like good drink. The late-day clouds broke while sunlight splashed from the river. The lie of the drainages impressed itself upon Nyahri, revealing the order of Cohltos's bundled houses, the quilt of farms and crops, and the broad swatches of apple orchards coating the valley's gentler slopes. The cold wind swept from the highest hillsides, but the sun warmed Nyahri's face.

This is more than the flutter of attraction in my stomach, she thought. *My guts feel twisted like horse ties and there is little to be done about it. So* this *is what love feels like?*

Nyahri considered the weight of the Atreiani's revelations, of an Exemplari's deep magic, of what a *claim*e meant, and she found herself *excited* by it. Kwlko trotted to her and stamped the ground. She rode him bareback, prancing over the high mountain grasses, Turo chasing them all the while.

What might it be, Nyahri thought, *to walk forever with the spirits of the dead? What will it be to* become *one?*

She waited till the sun grazed the western peaks. By twilight, she took the horses' leads, making her way back to S'Eret Fortress.

{23}

Nyahri closed the library door behind her, lowering the latch. A dozen candles lit the room. The sun had set, but Lwn and Stashwn shone through the high windows, approaching full. Feet propped on the table, yw Sabi sat with her chair tilted back, her hands folded in her lap, and her head bowed.

"Mistress?" Nyahri prompted.

The Atreiani's gaze flicked toward her. "Nyahri."

Nyahri hesitated, sensing a weight on yw Sabi, some deeper concern. "Everything well?"

Yw Sabi rubbed her eyes, then gave Nyahri a lopsided, crafty smile. "Planning." She set aside her books and leaned forward in her chair, its front legs clacking against the flagstone.

Nyahri sat beside her. *I must grow fond of chairs and tables*, she thought, hating them, *unless we are back on the trail soon.*

"What did you see today?" asked yw Sabi.

Nyahri told her, as many details as she could remember. The Atreiani took particular interest in Nyahri's description of the streets and their layout, of the rivers and the way they divided the city, of the placement of the bridges which Nyahri spotted from higher along the slopes.

"What do we do next?" Nyahri asked.

"Soon, we'll do as Kepler wanted from the first. You and I will descend into Sojourn Temple. It will detect my presence and initiate a sequence to wake some hundreds of Atreianii."

Nyahri blanched, thinking of the morning when Suhto entered Abswyn, thinking too of yw Sabi's warnings about awakened Atreianii and the violence they might do. "Why would we do so?"

Yw Sabi leaned forward to whisper, "For the Atreianii, coming out of deep suspension takes hours. Before they do, Nyahri, we must accomplish some things inside Sojourn. There's equipment to retrieve, and I'll want time with you in the Hall—it's a good place for *show and tell,* and *seeing* will help you understand many things."

"You would show me what?" She guessed, "Things from the Culling?"

Yw Sabi tilted her head, a hint of surprise at Nyahri's question. "And other events. Telling you of the past will not be enough."

"You need tell me nothing—I am already committed, have already decided to come with you."

Yw Sabi smiled. "For that, I am grateful, but by then there'll be no turning back—the *showing* will not be to convince you, but to prepare you for everything which might follow."

"I understand."

"Are you afraid?"

"I was frightened on my first hunt, but I hunted any-way. When my brother led me in my first raid, I was so terrified I reeked of my own piss before we returned home."

Yw Sabi raised one eyebrow, leaning her chin against her fist.

"Still, I ran the Bk'fern camp," Nyahri said, "right there with all the men, and I made my kill. I danced the blood dance, and no one again doubted my right to a longknife. My knees trembled when my mother took me on spirit walks, when I first heard of *you* and the other Atreianii. Before I first swam the spring ice torrents with my brother, I thought my legs had frozen in dread, and I could hardly dive."

Yw Sabi tucked a strand of Nyahri's hair behind her ear. "Ice torrents?"

"Flood every year, when the waters come rushing down the canyons and fill the arroyos. The floods sweep everything before them. My brother called other men cowards, and he rode the waters. I followed him."

The Atreiani gave her a look which said what she thought of such foolishness, but she held her words. Her thumb traipsed along Nyahri's neck.

"I could not," Nyahri said, "let him be braver than me."

"I suppose you couldn't have," yw Sabi replied. "Sounds like you're *still* competing with him."

The Atreiani kissed Nyahri's forehead, then her lips. They leaned upon each other.

"Will I like her?" Nyahri asked.

Yw Sabi understood. "That'll be like asking whether you like yourself. I believe so."

Will I like her? How little the question matters! Better to ask, Where will I end and she begin? That is how it will work, nay? Powerful witchcraft—

Nyahri set another delighted kiss upon yw Sabi's mouth and said, "I am yours."

"Ah, lovely one." Yw Sabi stroked Nyahri's hair. "I am yours too."

THEY RETURNED TO THEIR bed and, for hours, they rested quietly, intent only on each other's touch, on one another's skin, lips, and breath. Nyahri shut her eyes, kissing yw Sabi's mouth, her tongue traipsing along yw Sabi's teeth, glancing the edge of the long canines. She leaned her forehead against her mistress's shoulder, then sat back again, meeting her gaze.

"Sojourn Temple's defenses will register you as an Exemplari," yw Sabi said. "The Citadel will recognize you as one of our own."

Nyahri trembled. Whatever she had believed throughout her years had been only frail mythologies with more potent truths behind them, truths which she'd be the first in millennia to learn. Trembling too from desire, she reached behind yw Sabi's neck and pulled her close again.

"Once we have what you need," Nyahri said, "what then?"

"We'll override the Citadel's power supply, as I did at Abswyn, and we will destroy the Sojourn Temple." She gestured at the scattered books surrounding her. "I've learned all I can from these."

"Yet still you delay?"

"Because more than twenty thousand people live within the blast radius, and we need to save as many as we can—we will save *every* human we can."

Nyahri closed her eyes, nodding gratefully and remembering Colhina and Ahlon, but also appreciating the challenge. "From the moment we arrived," she said, "you had already considered the innocents?"

"I'll take no life wastefully. There has been enough of that, far too much."

"What of the Atreianii you will kill?"

"At this facility, there're none I count *innocent*. To rule again, every Sojourn Atreiani would slay nearly everyone alive today."

"They sleep now, though, yea?"

Yw Sabi nodded.

"Could we not simply slay them in their beds? Quietly? Destroy nothing else?"

"Spoken like an E'cwn raider." The Atreiani laughed, a quick exhalation, full of bitterness. "I considered such a possibility, but no. The logistics are too difficult, and the risks of *losing* are too high. The surest way to kill the Atreianii here is to destroy Sojourn itself."

"Hellfire burned at Abswyn," Nyahri said. "Will it be the same here?"

Yw Sabi nodded. "The radius will be even larger, the entire city."

"Nothing could survive, no one."

"So help me figure it out," the Atreiani said. "Here is our challenge—How do we evacuate many thousands of Oudwnii without announcing our intentions too soon?"

"What if we *do* announce them? What if we simply tell the people why we do what we do?"

"Lovely one, you *would* make a potent Ahtras one day, working through your tribe, building consensus—difficult with two hundred tribesmen, but honorable. Yet with thousands, over something so critical? The Templarii will oppose us tirelessly, and they will brace Oudwn minds against us. Discussions would carry on for years. Some Oudwnii might concede. Others, no matter what we offered, would resist to the end. Cohltos would be fortified, putting even *more* humans at risk. We'd need to raise an army—my least favorite option—and return with it. Need I go on?"

"Is it not the right of the Oudwnii to decide their future?"

"Ah, *rights*." Rolling onto her side, yw Sabi tucked a pillow beneath her head. "Perhaps if we had time. My intuition tells me we don't. Borea remains silent and the odds surrounding my awakening belie chance—we're snared in a larger contest, one whose boundaries remain invisible to us. So, we'll destroy *all* the Citadels as hastily as possible. It's the undertaking I began before the Eventide, and it is what I'll finish now."

Nyahri considered this—

The raider in her understood it.

"If the Oudwnii will not flee?" she asked.

"I'll still annihilate the Citadel, and it'll kill them all—men, women, children. Compared to a future of millions dead, or billions, twenty thousand Oudwnii are no different than sixty-three C'naädii."

"What shall we do?"

"First, find the entry to Sojourn Temple," yw Sabi said, "quietly and quickly. The Templarii will soon become confident of the truth—I have indeed come as their enemy."

"Yea, mistress, I will find it."

"Good. We must trust nothing except ourselves, not the Templarii nor anything about this place. By the time we force the Citadel, we'll need to command the entire valley."

I understand these things perfectly, Nyahri thought, *these impossible tasks. But one thing must come before another—*

"I will need to wear your collar," she said, "before I can enter the Citadel."

"Without it, the Citadel will kill you."

Nyahri caressed her own throat. "When shall we?"

"Soon." Yw Sabi kissed Nyahri's brow. "Too soon. In our day, most Atreianii made a ceremony of it. I'll give it as much sacrament as I can, poor as it'll be."

"Whenever you wish, Atreiani."

"This evening we've other business."

"What business?"

"A dinner party." Yw Sabi scowled. "The chieftain of Cohltos has pressed me for an audience."

"Yea, Kepler said as much."

The Atreiani drew a tense breath and nodded. "If we don't placate him, we may lose our welcome before we're ready."

"A waste of time."

"I fear not. We can't yet afford to turn the Oudwn Council against us, so we're going to the chieftain's house. Try to keep things peaceable awhile longer."

"What I wish," Nyahri said, "is to be quick about our task, not to piss away the hours at Oudwn dining tables. You can leave me here to find the Citadel's center, go to the dinner without me."

"You're coming."

"But—"

"You're not an errand girl—you're my *companion.*" Yw Sabi winked. "You're coming."

Nyahri smiled at the word *companion.* "But I mean what I say—I *can* find Swyn Templr's door. Their labyrinth is not so clever, but I will need a better lamp."

"Lamp, hmm?" Yw Sabi stood and walked to the corner of the bedchamber. From her effects, she chose a small black bag. She withdrew from it a white orb, no wider in diameter than a walnut. "It's time you use some of the 'magic' you E'cwnii seem so uncertain about."

Nyahri sneered at it.

"Hold your palm up."

The E'cwni did as instructed. Yw Sabi set the artifact in her hand.

"Now," yw Sabi said, "say the Englisce for *light.*"

Nyahri did, and the orb flashed a scattering of pinkish rays. A few flickered across her irises, centering there for a moment, and the crystalline orb glowed.

Yw Sabi continued, "If you look straight at it, it'll dim, lighting only itself. Look across the room."

She did, and the orb threw a broad white ray against the far wall, illuminating a cabinet, a small desk, a basket piled with blankets.

"Focus on the cabinet," yw Sabi said, "on one drawer."

The orb's beam contracted, brightening on that rectangle of wood.

"It tracks your focal depth, tuning to you as long as it's within a few meters."

Despite herself, Nyahri *liked* the rush of magic.

"It understands Englisce," yw Sabi said. "*Light* to turn it on, *light off* to turn it off, *light brighter* to make it brighter, *light softer* to make it softer, a few other natural-language commands. Understand?"

"Yea, yw Sabi! Wondrous!"

"It's a nice toy," she said, "more useful than an oil lamp."

A knock sounded at the lower door, at the bottom of the stairs beneath their bedchamber. Nyahri clasped her hand over the witch-light, whispering it off. She pulled the sheets around her, then recovered her longknife from beside the bed.

Yw Sabi shook her head at Nyahri, then called down the staircase. "Speak!"

"Excuse the interruption," a Templarin woman said, "but Dhaos Shwn Oudwn has arrived to escort you to dinner."

"Tell the Oudwni," the Atreiani replied, "he can wait outside."

The Templari shuffled away. Nyahri sighed, setting down her blade.

"You're jumpy," yw Sabi teased her with a wink. "Let's go to this chieftain's dinner. We can tend other details later."

"Yea, yw Sabi." Nyahri groaned, but acceded.

They dressed, and Nyahri washed her face in a basin. As they descended the stairs, she allowed herself a smile, and with that they departed the library.

THE RISING MOONS GREETED them as they left S'Eret, Lwn and Stashwn a sliver shy of full, while Trwl chased farther from her sisters by the night. The horses stretched their legs, nearly prancing, flicking their fetlocks over the earth. Lit by pitch-burning sconces, Dhaos paced before the gates, holding his hands behind his back, as if on a pleasant stroll.

He looked up at them, flashing his boyish grin. "Good evening." The air misted his breath.

The mongrel crowd had grown. Many hundreds gathered only a stone's throw from the gates, held back by nothing but timber fences. Dhaos's archers kept the peace, their number bolstered by armored men who owed their allegiance to the chieftain of Cohltos. Bands of farmers, wild men, callow children, hollow-eyed women, and gray-headed men raised their heads or stood on tiptoe to glimpse the Atreiani.

Yw Sabi tightened her hood and cloak around her.

A woman exclaimed from the masses, "Atreiani!" Others followed, "Heal us! Save us! Thank the gods!"

"Not all these people are from Cohltos," yw Sabi said, noting their clothing.

"Nay," Dhaos said, "some are not even Oudwnii. They come from the far end of the western valley, a few days' ride, or from even farther. All to see you!"

Her gaze icy, she asked, "How did news spread so quickly?"

"Atreiani, you *have* been here some time now." Dhaos blinked. "Word has gone in every direction as fast as men's legs would take it."

"My son!" a man yelled. "Cure my son!"

"I've little patience with this riffraff, Dhaos." Yw Sabi frowned. "Get us where we need to go."

"Follow me," he said.

Guardsmen and archers cleared the way, raising torches to light the road. Dhaos walked beside Nyahri's horse.

"What did you think," he said, "when you visited our streets today?"

"It was good to see what you love here," she replied.

"What I love?"

"Your people."

"Ah, well, I do." He smiled up to her. "I love them dearly. You should have asked me to accompany you."

"It was good to be alone." Nyahri looked ahead as she rode, avoiding his eye. "I saw the entire valley from the south, the whole city."

"A marvel, is it not?"

Yw Sabi interrupted, "There were once cities of millions." She glanced over her shoulder at him. "Tens of thousands is not so many. You sound like your father, boy, prideful over irrelevancies."

Dhaos scowled. "Must I always expect to take such insults from you, Atreiani?"

"Yes."

His scowl deepened, then he burst into laughter. "It must be an unhappy place, Atreiani, to live inside your head." To Nyahri he said, "If it pleases you to explore further, to ride out of the city tomorrow, I know some beautiful places where you can really enjoy the countryside, the farms, and appreciate what Cohltos has become. There are views much clearer than from the south. Would you like to see them?"

"You can see the city streets from above?" yw Sabi asked.

"I am not talking to you, Atreiani." Then he thought better and said, "Yea, a magnificent view. Why do you ask?"

"Only curious." Yw Sabi nodded to Nyahri.

"We can go," Nyahri said to Dhaos.

"Excellent." His grin brightened.

"Perhaps tomorrow or the next day?"

"For you, whenever you command it."

Nyahri gave him a quick simper, then drove Kwlko faster, leaving Dhaos on foot beside yw Sabi. Crowds met them along every street, at every corner.

So many people! Nyahri sighed, shaking her head. *Thousands more since we first arrived.* The enormity of their problem frightened her. *However are they to escape us?*

{24}

The Chieftain of Cohltos lived in a timber-framed hall, newer than S'Eret Fortress or the ancient Orÿs Lodge. The colossal structure stood under a single gabled roof, the main doors at one end and private rooms at the other. A patchwork of irregular courtyards and gardens surrounded it. Beyond the courtyard walls dwelt a legion of peasants, living on land the chieftain's family had claimed generations ago.

At yw Sabi's arrival, the household's eldest wife sighed in relief. She hurried to the kitchen to tell the staff that, at last, they could serve the food. In the forecourt a few dozen guests had already quaffed enough strong liquor to bring them halfway to drunk. Both the drunks and the sober stood dumbstruck at what they witnessed:

The Atreiani, her hood down and her hair loose to her waist, entered through the gates on horseback with all the bearing of a queen. A chieftain's son walked on her left, and on her right an E'cwn witch rode a red stallion. Night-falcon plumage fluttered around her crown, making her a complement for her mistress.

Younger than Nyahri expected, no more than forty, the chieftain of Cohltos gave a perfunctory bow. His beard well trimmed, his features angled and sharp, he wore tailored clothes to match, both restrained and splendidly appointed.

"Welcome to my home," he said, "you are happily received."

Yw Sabi nodded back. "Thank you, chieftain. I regret we didn't pay our respects earlier."

"Think nothing of it, goddess. My understanding is that you had pressing business in the Fortress. You are here now, and that is all that matters."

Once more, she nodded.

"I am Shwn Pawl Oudwn of the House Cohlton."

"I am Sultah yw Sabi."

"Your companion, I understand, is Nyahri E'cwn." He shifted his bow to her.

Nyahri also inclined her head. "Shwn Pawl."

"Far too long since there has been a chance for real peace between Oudwnii and E'cwnii, and here we have a representative from the most venerated of tribes. Welcome to you both." He turned to Dhaos and said, "Of course it is good to host you too, cousin. We are always glad for the company of the House Auken. The tables are set. We expected you somewhat sooner, I apologize, but let us eat before the guests die from starvation."

He waved for them to follow, entering his house through the main hall doors, broad sliding structures which stood open, inviting both the guests and the night into the interior. Nyahri dismounted, and a stable boy rushed to take the horses' leads.

"I will take them myself," she said to him, "but you show me the way."

He did, and she led the horses and stabled them. Afterward, as she crossed the forecourt to the chieftain's hall, many eyes followed her. The dinner guests, all from the valley's most powerful Oudwn families, gave her sidelong glances or sneered at her.

A barbarian, their eyes said, *an animal of the plains.*

Nyahri scoffed. *Let us eat before the guests die from starvation?*

Since coming to the mountains, Nyahri had seen no one *less* likely to starve than the chieftain's party guests.

THE GUESTS SAT AT square tables, each a few paces wide. At the center table, Nyahri, yw Sabi, and Dhaos joined the chieftain, his wives, and other honored invitees. Nyahri tried her best to use the utensils, but every few bites she fumbled them.

A dozen other tables accommodated the families of more than thirty petty nobles, warriors, and landowners. Young children occupied smaller tables nearer the kitchen, though they had finished their meals and, for the most part, sat now on the floor with colorful wooden toys, playing under the supervision of nannies and other household servants. As among the E'cwnii, the children seemed least affected by the Atreiani, taking her strangeness more as a curious oddity, rather than a threat or a divine manifestation.

One guest at the honors table ate no food at all: Kepler. Though attendants set a plate for him, he touched none of it. He drank only water, exchanging small talk with the high nobles to either side of him.

The wound which Nyahri had given him still marked his cheek, neither scabbed over nor bleeding. He looked back at her. Locking eyes, he raised his water glass, drank, and offered her a heartless smile.

The chieftain lifted his wine glass and said, "A toast to the esteemed Atreiani, we welcome you to Cohltos."

The assembly raised their glasses too.

"Thank you," yw Sabi said, returning the toast. She quaffed her entire cup, and forked a morsel of steak from her plate to her mouth.

An attentive servant refilled her drink.

"These are exciting times," Shwn Pawl said. "Our friend Kepler tells us we should expect a waking of the Atreianii, that you will bring them from their long sleep and return your kin to the world."

"I will of course descend," she replied. "As I told Kepler, I simply needed time to research, gather my thoughts before I do so."

Kepler cleared his throat. "I'd simply been telling him, Magistress yw Sabi, I found it odd you did not descend immediately, when you first arrived in this fair city. Wouldn't your sisters or brothers have done so in your stead?"

She nodded politely to him, then to the chieftain. "Shwn Pawl, as you no doubt heard from the Templarin histories, I was once out of favor with many of my brothers and sisters. I've perhaps some reason for pause but, as Kepler says, awakening the Citadel is the right thing to do, and I will do so soon enough."

"Of course, yw Sabi," said Kepler, "we all wait upon your will. It must be so difficult for you, Magistress, to have spent the last nine days reading our dry, dusty, dull books."

"Five thousand years' worth," she said, "is a lot of catching up to do."

"We Oudwnii, on the other hand, know too much from legends here," Shwn Pawl said, "and too little from history, as the Templarii are not prone to tell us every secret of the ancient days." The chieftain laughed. "I doubt I have read more than a dozen books in my entire life, save our ledgers."

"We're not teachers," Kepler said to him, "inasmuch as we take it upon ourselves to tutor your noble sons and daughters. Who, I might add, are not always the best students." He glanced at Dhaos. "We're record keepers, and we serve the Atreianii before all others."

"Yeh Mowan designed you to do more than keep the records," yw Sabi said, "didn't he?"

"Where're the laboratories now, Atreiani?" Kepler asked. "We've only libraries these days, no computers left but our minds—" He tapped a finger against his own head. "—and nothing remaining to us but books to fill. We constructed a printing press some years ago but, in truth, there wasn't much demand for it."

Shwn Pawl lifted his hand, palm up, toward yw Sabi. "Thus my request—tell us of the old days, Atreiani. What contention tore such a chasm between you and yours? That is the question we most want answered."

Yw Sabi looked from the chieftain to Kepler and back again. Her eyes narrowed, her smile calculated.

Nyahri understood at once: *Kepler and the chieftain, they rehearsed this. What is their game?*

"We Atreianii failed in our purpose," yw Sabi said. The room fell silent, guests elbowing each other to be quiet, to listen. "We created ourselves to be better than men—to encompass the philosophies, to know the sciences, to be doctors of ethics, to embody reason and logic, to exemplify order and so to rise above petty political squabbling, power grabbing, resource mongering, profiteering, and other such nonsense. The call of our day was not sensible self-interest, but super-rational cooperation. Platonic philosopher kings or Kantian rational agents or Nietzschean companions given flesh and bone—all had their place."

How many in this room, Nyahri wondered, *understand a word she says?*

"To shuffle off all the failings of men?" Shwn Pawl said. "Yet the Atreianii proved susceptible to imperfection? Is that not true?"

"Our experiment worked for centuries, longer than the Roman Republic or the American misadventure. Then a few Atreianii showed ample capacity for irresolvable disagreement. Pettiness followed on its heels, instability, and factions. It fell apart quickly."

"So you were no different than men?"

"We were *nothing* like humankind," she countered, "but we weren't perfect."

"What was the failing?"

Yw Sabi folded her napkin. "I've only theories."

"I for one," Kepler said, "would *love* to hear them."

"I, too," Shwn Pawl said.

In his corner, Dhaos listened intently.

"One is that we Magisters got it wrong from the start," yw Sabi said. "We failed in the design of the system."

"Is that not evident?" Kepler asked.

"A failure in the original design is not a logical necessity," yw Sabi said. "Reality is not a controlled experiment, and confounding variables can arise after initial conditions are set."

"What do you believe happened?" Shwn Pawl asked.

Yw Sabi shrugged. "The Magisters' propositional logic was impeccable, but if we followed from an incorrect premise, something we misunderstood in the fundamental qualities of existence, it wouldn't matter how carefully we planned. Our grand experiment would fail."

The chieftain laughed. "I will pretend I understood that! You mean perhaps you performed everything right, but on the wrong problem?"

"No. I mean what I said. We saw the data but we *misunderstood* it. Or information carriage doesn't work the way we thought it did. Or quantum effects had a larger impact at the macro. Or. Or. Or. *We followed from an incorrect premise.*"

Kepler leaned forward, giving her an ashen smile. "What explanation do *you* favor, Magistress?"

Her tightly pressed lips drew into a frown. "Something in the nature of subjective experience, something which prevents indefinite cooperation among distinct individuals."

"Such as?"

Yw Sabi tapped her fingertips on the table, looking around the room. "Hypothesis—conflict is built into the structure of qualia, regardless of the substrate or pattern of the intelligence in question. Darwin himself first observed that cooperative species outperform species whose survival strategy depends upon individual fitness, but *individual fitness* still plays its part. Perhaps super-rationality between agents necessarily breaks down, given enough time, because they must operate from incomplete data, a deficient understanding of one another? Independently rational behavior, where conflict is not the goal, nevertheless leads to conflict."

The chieftain humphed. "I do not believe I understood any of that either. Perhaps you might give us an example, Atreiani?"

Kepler waved his hand dismissively. "Philosophical gibberish."

Several children, none older than seven, still played upon the floor, talking loudly with each other despite the best efforts of their caretakers. The Atreiani gestured toward them.

"There's a wooden die there," she said, "by the little ones, a block with six sides. Bring it."

A nanny stood dumbfounded, finding herself the focus of both a goddess and her chieftain.

"Woman," Shwn Pawl said to the caretaker, "bring the toy!"

The nanny picked it up, dropped it, recovered it, then brought it to him.

"Not to me," he said, "to the Atreiani."

A simply dressed teenager in a blue flower-printed dress, the nanny trembled as she placed the multicolored cube in yw Sabi's hand. She bowed, almost on all fours, backing from the chieftain's table.

The Atreiani raised the die, showing it to the chieftain on corner. "What do you see?"

"A cube," Shwn Pawl said.

"Ah, good, we agree. All is well." She smiled, her fangs almost visible. "What else, chieftain?"

"Red, blue, purple—"

"Bastard!" yw Sabi said, thumping the table with her open hand. The silverware and plates jumped, and the chieftain's wives startled. The Atreiani bared her teeth, her long, sharp canines showing clearly. Many at the table backed away or left their chairs.

Shwn Pawl recoiled. "You insult me?"

"You're a liar," she said. "There isn't a brush of red anywhere on this cube. Tell me the truth! *What do you see?*"

Kepler smiled sardonically, perceiving the ruse. Nyahri, as well, grasped what the chieftain could not.

"Truly," Shwn Pawl said, "the block is red, blue—"

"Liar!" yw Sabi roared. "How dare you lie to me—*twice!* Do not forget I am a *goddess.*"

"You forget your host!" The chieftain stood from the table, his hand to his longknife's hilt. A dozen guardsmen raised their weapons, followed by a score more drunken noblemen, at least half prepared to defend Shwn Pawl. Nyahri, as well, arose to her feet with her weapon loosened from its sheath.

Yw Sabi remained seated, her fangs still revealed, but her expression eased.

Astounding, Nyahri thought, *the ability she has to shake men.*

The Atreiani rotated the die in her fingers, showing the chieftain the opposite corner.

He glared at her, attempting to match her menace, then he chuckled. His chuckle grew into a guffaw. Around the room, other men laughed, though at what they couldn't know. Uncertainly, men put away their weapons.

To the chieftain, no red at all now appeared upon the child's toy, only yellow, green, and orange. He returned his weapon to his scabbard and sat again. "You make your point, Atreiani. People perceive things from different points of view. Yet we *did* turn the cube, nay, and at last saw each other's perspective? Is it not this way with all misunderstanding? Can we not always *turn the cube?*"

"What if we cannot, not always?" asked yw Sabi. "What if for some things the cube must always remain fixed?" Having already emptied her cup twice, she refilled is herself with beer from a wooden pitcher and took a long drink. "What if agreeing on its colors was a matter of life and death? When you said the block was red, you were correct. When I said it showed no red, I was correct. This is easy to understand, with clear delineations, but much in life is much more complex, hmm? So much more about *values*. You value one thing. I, another. You see things one way. I, another. In so many instances, who can say which is right and which is wrong? Too often, no shared objective measure exists."

"A sobering thought," Shwn Pawl said.

Dhaos snickered.

"You dwell in your head, Shwn Pawl," yw Sabi said, "and I in mine, and so long as that remains true, over a long enough period, we'll disagree. We may be geniuses, correct in every regard in every step of logic, and still be at each other's throats."

"Bleak," Shwn Pawl said.

"I have said it before," Dhaos interjected with a smile, "the Atreiani's head must be a depressing place to live."

No one laughed.

"Are all your theories so heady?" Shwn Pawl asked.

They are, Nyahri wanted to say.

"I submit the possibility," yw Sabi said, "irresolvable conflict is built into the universe, so even the most balanced system, no matter how sound, must succumb to entropy. It's a measure of noise to signal."

Watching everyone's faces, Nyahri suspected only Kepler understood what yw Sabi said. The rest still listened.

Perhaps frustrated by her opaqueness, Shwn Pawl abandoned his tact. "It comes down to this—do you bring danger here? Will old conflicts erupt anew, or will we have Kepler's golden age?"

"It is my hope," yw Sabi said, "the future will offer you a great many blessings."

One of Shwn Pawl's younger wives asked, "Will there be a cure for the winter sicknesses?"

The Atreiani shrugged. "I'll do what I can, but I believe so."

It seemed enough of an answer, the first thing which everyone in the room understood. A palpable relief spread among the guests, a surge of chatter peaking and fading.

Yet Kepler's next question turned heads, yw Sabi's and Nyahri's quickest of all. "Do you intend to take a new Exemplari?" he asked. "One not burdened by a former life?"

Yw Sabi's attention snapped to him. *"What?"*

"It might," Kepler said, "elicit some good will and sympathy from your sisters and brothers, if you did."

"How would it do *that?"* Yw Sabi glared.

Kepler shrugged. "With the Congress's permission, you could accept a new scepter, a new collar, a new Exemplari? Leave the past behind."

"Now it is *you* who insult *me?*"

He shook his head. "Be pragmatic. I know of a few noble daughters who might be inclined to your tastes, Sultah yw Sabi. Or if you eschew a claimèd, perhaps a strong young man, someone well trainable as a valet and bodyguard, even a *moreau?*"

The Atreiani pointed to Nyahri, but her gaze remained fixed upon Kepler. "I choose her," she said, "and she's good enough to be claimèd *and* moreau."

"A violent, head-strong E'cwni?" He gave her an exaggerated shrug, pointing to the wound on his cheek. "Doesn't seem like a good first choice, but I suppose the Congress might let you put a *new* collar on her."

Yw Sabi pushed her chair from her setting, stood, and walked slowly around the table. All eyes followed her. She halted behind Kepler, slid her fingers through his thin gray hair, and pulled back his head. Towering over him, she looked into his eyes.

"Can you see me from in there, little monster?" she asked him. "Twice you've angered me on this point. There will not be a third."

Letting his head go, she rested her hands on his shoulders, curling her fingertips until they pinched the fabric of his robes. For a moment, the chieftain locked eyes with Kepler.

They mean to call her out, Nyahri thought, *to unsettle her. The chieftain is following Kepler's wishes.*

"You tell a good story," Shwn Paul said to yw Sabi, "but I heard you turned against the Atreianii for reasons other than their *failings.*"

"Oh?" yw Sabi said.

"They murdered someone you loved, nay?" He waited a moment, letting these words settle through the room. "You turned on the Atreianii because they killed *one* girl?"

"You don't grasp the circumstances, chieftain. Civil conflict was building long before they murdered Ekaterina." The corners of yw Sabi's mouth turned downward. "Do you not feel the strings hanging from Kepler's fingers? They're attached to your limbs. You're a marionette."

"I—" he began.

"I've lost my appetite, though your hospitality has been most generous. Nyahri and I take our leave."

"Please stay, Atreiani." He opened his arms in a gesture of apology. "I mean only to understand."

"Of course you do," she said, her voice colorless. To his youngest wife she said, "We'll do our best for the people of Cohltos—I can offer nothing more."

The Atreiani strolled to the door. The room stayed silent, the guests watching her departure. Nyahri rushed from her seat, taking her place by yw Sabi's side.

"Mistress, what was that all about?"

"That was Kepler's way of telling us we're out of time." She growled quietly as they crossed the courtyard to the horses. "He's turned Shwn Paul against us, that's clear. Soon, they'll oppose us directly."

"The dinner did not go as you hoped?" Nyahri asked.

They saddled the horses, mounted, and set out for the fortress.

"Not remotely," yw Sabi said, only after they departed Shwn Pawl's gates.

Nyahri increased their pace, leading by moonslight around the edge of the city, avoiding the crowds. "We must descend soon then?"

"I wish we had more time, Nyahri, but no. We need to finish our work quickly, or we'll miss the opportunity."

yahri and yw Sabi passed through the gates of S'Eret Fortress, into the interior, and the darkness weighed upon them, its veil far blacker than the moons-lit night sky. The Templarii closed the doors behind them, and Nyahri drew the witch-light from her satchel.

Holding it before her, she said, "*Light,*" and it obeyed.

Its wide, soft glow spread throughout the passage. She thrilled at it, her first real use of *magic,* though neither yw Sabi nor the Templarii appeared the least impressed. Nyahri had, however, enough illumination to guide the horses to the courtyard, to care for them, and to find her way to the library.

Yw Sabi leaned over her table, focused on a book, checking it against another text. Nyahri took a seat near her.

"Shwn Pawl and Kepler pine for the same thing," yw Sabi said, her focus remaining on her notes. "For me to descend into Sojourn and wake its Atreianii. That'd work out much more suitably for Kepler than for Shwn Pawl, but the chieftain doesn't know any better."

"What did Kepler mean when he said you should choose some Oudwn girl?" Nyahri frowned.

Yw Sabi drew Nyahri close, kissing the top of her head. "You're a fantastic choice, lovely one, for a Magistress who wishes to write the future to her liking, a perfect complement for Ekaterina. You're a lousy option for a contrite return to the arms of my brothers and sisters. Kepler would have me renounce all my past, reject you, and choose a mouse for a companion. All the Templarii, insufferable little crabs."

"What do we do?"

"Have you thought about our conundrum?" yw Sabi asked, setting aside her papers and leaning forward.

"I do not know how to save the Oudwnii," Nyahri said. "I do not know what would make them abandon their homes or sit by while we destroy their holy Swyn Templr. They will turn on us, yw Sabi—by thousands—unless we are most persuasive."

"I have the beginnings of a strategy, but we need a better look at Cohltos."

"Dhaos promised us as much."

"He did at that." Yw Sabi raised an eyebrow. "We can perhaps afford a day or two longer, but we must act soon." Yw Sabi took Nyahri's hand.

"Yw Sabi," Nyahri began, hesitant with her next words, "Kepler *knew* Ekaterina, did he not?"

"He served the Atreiani who killed her, and he was present at her execution."

"A wonder you have not either questioned him about it or torn him to pieces."

"There's nothing *he* could tell me about Ekaterina I'd want to know from him. If I've anything to learn from *her,* of those events, well—"

Nyahri took a deep breath. "I will remember it?"

"Given a year or two."

"Gods, what a thought!"

Yw Sabi eyed Nyahri at the her declaration of *gods.* "You have been in my life forty days and forty nights, Nyahri. Not so long, really, but it's long enough." Her voice lowered, a story-telling tone, spoken with half a smile. *"The Israelites spied upon Canaan for forty days and forty nights!"* Yw Sabi laughed, as if at herself, as if at something she took less than seriously. She squeezed Nyahri's hand and sat down beside her. "If *I* was superstitious, lovely one, I'd say we were fated to meet. I'd say it couldn't have happened any other way, and I come to this conclusion no matter how much I consider it—we are meant to be in this together, and the surest way for us both to survive these coming days is for you to wear my collar."

Powerful magics, Nyahri figured.

She leaned forward, setting her hands on yw Sabi's legs. The Atreiani reached across her suit, into a sealed pocket, and withdrew the shimmering, rose-golden sash of cloth which Nyahri had seen during their first days together. It rested in the palm of yw Sabi's hand.

Nyahri extended her hand for it, but held back at the last moment.

"It resonates with me," yw Sabi said, "a constant whisper at the back of my mind. The collars were one of our most sophisticated *witchcrafts,* as you E'cwnii might call them."

Nyahri listened.

The Atreiani continued, "Only one woman ever wore this one, and I'd never bind myself to another collar—Kepler is a fool to think I might. Much of who she *was* yet exists in this artifact, and while I cherish you more every day, Nyahri, that makes Ekaterina no less important to me."

Nyahri's fingertips hovered above the fabric. "This will not harm me?"

"Touch it," yw Sabi said.

Nyahri took it in her hand, a ribbon as wide as two fingers, as long as her forearm. "Soft," she said, marvelling. "I have never felt anything so fine."

"For most Atreianii, the choosing of an Exemplari was important, a rare event requiring a great deal of preparation and ceremony, and an even longer transition afterward. Training is

helpful—it can be challenging to wear an Atreiani's collar—
though you and I have no time for it."

Nyahri rolled the fabric between her palms. "I wear this
and I am your Exemplari?"

"Yes."

Nyahri smiled. "Simple." She drew the ribbon through her
fingers, raised it with both hands to her neck, and prepared to
wrap it about her throat.

Yw Sabi gently caught her hand. "Not *so* simple."

The Atreiani held out her open palm. With a frown,
Nyahri returned the collar to her hand, and the Atreiani
kissed her.

"Soon," yw Sabi said, "but we need to tend some final
considerations, some last preparations."

"You *do* have some plan for Cohltos, some strategy to
save the Oudwnii?"

"Perhaps. I keep coming back to the lay of the land,
which you described so well to me. Land can be the first ally
of the outnumbered."

"What are you hoping Dhaos will show us tomorrow?"

The Atreiani shrugged. "Not sure yet, but I've at least a
few tools at my disposal."

"The right tools, I hope."

"Whether I do or not, all this depends on finding the
route to Sojourn Temple's door. Now."

"Yea, mistress."

Yw Sabi unfurled a collection of maps, discovered in the
dingy corner of a far reading room. Nyahri climbed to their
bedchamber and sat alone for a short while, gathering the
bravery she needed to return to S'Eret's interior darkness.

The only window in the room, high on one wall, admitted
a pale moonbeam which illuminated the bed. Nyahri stepped

onto the mattress, standing on tiptoe. Throughout Cohltos, along its silver-lighted streets, many scattered lamplights and hearth fires glowed.

They would not, Nyahri expected, glow for too much longer.

{Interim: Love Letters}

*T*saritsa—

I would wait a thousand years! A few days are nothing, though I ache through every one. I've been working on Shastakovich's Cello Concerto No. 1 for the fête Demesne Ywn yeh Li, and I promise it'll be spectacular. Difficult, yet what a reward! Теперь, высокая культура!

But what of culture? I like your fourth option, mistress. I'll be waiting on the floor, where I hope we fuck like rabbits.

> Your beloved,
> Ekaterina
> From *The Collected Letters*

Ekaterina—

Descending from Station to the Nairobi Platform, the silvered horizon and Earth's blue catching the sunlight, the breathtaking palate of stars and galaxies. Dancing in 0g before returning to the centripetal edge, and there we're at .7g and you're comfier but you're still giggling with roller-coaster fright. I know you hate descent, but it's a day down the corkscrew and isn't the pod so much more luxurious than the old lifts? Whoever heard of a spa on an elevator of the world? Now we have one, yours and mine. Yes, we fuck whenever we wish but, my mouth on you or not, how your eyes light when you spot Kilimanjaro! I'll get you to enjoy space travel yet, my love, and you'll visit the oceans of Mars before you know it.

> —S
> From *The Collected Letters*

26

Nyahri slung her knife on her hip and packed some dry rations, brought all the way from Aukensis. With the witch-light in her hand, she left the room, locked the door behind her, and descended the stairs to the lower level. A faint candle glow flickered from the library's far corner—yw Sabi still worked—but Nyahri walked the other way, leaving the libraries and navigating back toward the fortress's center. She retraced her steps, keeping the witch-light no brighter than needed. Nyahri passed familiar rooms and artifacts, moving quicker this time.

A pair of blue ghost-fires glittered down the hallway, and Nyahri ducked aside and snuffed the light.

A librarian shambled by, not more than two paces from her. Nyahri held her breath, pouring all her effort into staying silent. Nothing appeared except those twin pinpoints until, as the Templari passed, they too disappeared.

Nyahri kept her every muscle frozen. She remembered the Atreiani then, within her father's tent, *sitting motionless as a sayi snake.* Only the barest scraping of cloth or leather sounded against stone.

Then the twin ghost-fires blazed straight at her, only an arm's length away, and Nyahri jumped away.

"*Light!*" she commanded.

A female Templari stood before her, arms crossed inside her heavy sackcloth robes. Her hazel eyes widened, and her mouth twisted into a scowl. Long, plain, brassy hair fell to her shoulders. A faint web-work of veins, translucent as aquamarine, crisscrossed her flesh.

"What are you doing in the corridors, human?"

"I could not sleep," Nyahri said.

"Insomnia? *That* is your excuse?" The Templari shook her head. "Go back to your bed or go outside. Kepler has told you not to pry."

"So he did."

"Come," the Templari said, grabbing Nyahri's wrist, tugging her in the direction of the outer halls.

Nyahri dropped the witch-light and it bounced, its light wobbling throughout the hall. She punched the Templari full in the face, her knuckles cracking the librarian's nose and throwing her off balance.

Nyahri spit. "Never touch me."

The Templari rushed her. Nyahri's serape crumpled in the woman's hand, the other fist closing on Nyahri's shoulder. The flesh walker lifted her, Nyahri kicking wildly until her shoulders met stone, the impact knocking the wind from her. Nyahri gulped air, stars filling her eyes.

"We have had *enough* of you," the Templari said, her voice distorted by her broken nose. "Your stinking horses, your oily hands touching our books, your prying and snooping, *and* your false mistress."

A faint high-pitched whine sounded through the corridor, emanating from deep within the Templari. As Nyahri recovered her breath, the flesh walker threw her. A disconcerting weight-lessness lasted a mere second before Nyahri struck the opposite wall and careened to the floor. Again her breath left her, and she gritted in pain.

"I'm going to bury you," the librarian said, stepping toward her, "deep in the guts of S'Eret. No one, least of all Sultah yw Sabi, will ever find you."

The Templari grabbed Nyahri's hair, lifting her. Nyahri kicked impotently, her toes above the floor.

"I'll make this quick," the flesh walker said, pulling back her other hand, "I promise."

Nyahri drew her longknife, cutting in one graceful arc. She severed the hand which held her and fell once more to the floor. The Templari uttered no screams or curses, looking blankly at the stump of her arm, at the ooze darkening the wound.

She reached forward with the other hand.

Nyahri pushed up with both legs, thrusting the longknife through the woman's chest, from her sternum through her back. The blow hefted the Templari from her heels. That one good fist struck Nyahri's ribs, and Nyahri wheezed.

The librarian's hazel and witch-blue eyes yet burned.

Nyahri withdrew the blade and, before the Templari could hit her again, angled it between the flesh walker's neck and jaw. Sparks flew and a rending agony shot through Nyahri's arm, her muscles spasming and her teeth aching. She let go of the knife and leapt away.

The Templari's head burst, black ichor spraying from her mouth, then the monster lay still.

Gods, Nyahri wanted to scream, *gods, gods, gods!*

She curled into a ball, resting in the glow of the witch-light. Slowly her breath returned, the numbing shock departing her limbs, nothing left but the pain of two cracked ribs.

Nyahri touched the longknife. It gave her no jolt, and she yanked it from the flesh walker's neck. She dragged the body into the furthest twisted corner, shoved it behind a pile of loose stones, and hurried on her way, taking the witch-light with her.

How long before the librarians discover that corpse?

The alienness of its death, the strength with which it fought: these things shook Nyahri. Yet she cleared her mind and, with a better understanding of the fortress's organization, she navigated inward. At each juncture she chose the doorway leading to the smallest chamber, and to the next smaller, and so on. A few times she reached a dead end, obliged to retrace her steps.

Yea, but I am closer, she thought. *The center cannot be far.*

She took only one rest that hour, sitting in a volume filled with clay urns, their lids sealed with wax. She drank a good portion of her water, and she ate before moving on again. Soon after, the doorways shrank to mere apertures, forcing her to duck her head between rooms. Nyahri remembered Abswyn, how it had rested in the earth, the location of the door in relation to the pillar.

That entry will be buried too deeply here. We need the higher door, at the pillar's base, a portal only, small and round. Such a portal must *be here at Sojourn too.*

At Abswyn, no one ever knew how to open it.

Yw Sabi will know.

The way tightened again, forcing Nyahri to crawl on hands and knees. The walls contracted, made her lightheaded. Her lungs aching, the stale air soured in her throat.

She coughed.

Startled by the echo, Nyahri waited and listened, but the corridors and hollows returned to silence. She pushed onward, standing during the short distances between thresholds, until a larger chamber opened. Defying her expectations, the ceiling arched thirty hands overhead.

She raised the witch-light. "*Brighter.*"

Nyahri gave a brief cry.

Tens of thousands of skulls lined the cavern, their vacant eyes turned inward. They formed the walls, the arches, even the floor. She took a few steps onto the long-dead faces, imagining their spirits, their unhappy gazes on her, the uninvited living.

Nyahri wondered if, perhaps, the Templarii constructed such surfaces to scare away the superstitious. To frighten humans, like her.

The corridor ended at a wall of matte-gray metal, unmarred and unstained. As she drew closer to it, its glassy surface refracted the light. A single small door marked its center, its rounded edges free of any marking or device or lock, an eyelid closed to the dark.

Sojourn Temple.

Nyahri smiled and turned back, working her way out-ward again. Now she moved with confidence, much more quickly than on her approach. Soon the way opened, the openings between chambers growing larger, the rooms stretching into hallways—

Ghost-fires! Many!

She ducked aside, dousing the witch-light. A gathering of Templarii edged through the dark, lighting their way only with the cold glimmer of their eyes. Nyahri crouched, hiding herself, taking no chances.

Four carried a stretcher between them. Upon it lay a white-shrouded corpse. Two more flesh walkers trailed behind, and they held receptacles of Atreian glass. Following another route through the labyrinth, the Templarii disappeared through a doorway into a larger chamber. After a few heartbeats, a green ghost-light spread from within.

Listening as the Templarii laid the body upon some surface, Nyahri hunkered by the door. They unsealed the boxes, which chimed like glass. As if ringing delicate bells, the librarians shuffled strange tools in their hands. Their heavy robes rustled.

Nyahri realized she could slip onward, could avoid the Templarii altogether. She could return, unseen, all the way to the library. Yet she waited.

Leave, she told herself, moments slipping by.

Instead, Nyahri crept forward, craning her neck, and she peered around the corner. Green ghost-fires illuminated a long chamber. Glass cylinders lined it, clear smooth containers as large around as ancient oaks. In them floated tumorous growths, big as a man's outspread hand, their fleshy tendrils spiraling through some viscous fluid. They twitched.

Glossy oven-fired tiles covered the floor. The expanse of glass and tile connected with yet another enclosure, which contained the Templarii, who faced away from Nyahri.

Ay! Now you idiot, Nyahri told herself, *turn around, you have seen enough.*

Curiosity won, bringing her step by step into the hall. Celadon-hued ghost-fires lit her way, as she walked between the cylinders, her gaze fixed on the far end, at the backs of the Templarii. The flesh walkers' began their work: a wet sound, a cutting which Nyahri had heard many times before, each time she gutted an animal.

As she crossed the tile floor, a peripheral movement caught her eye, and she turned. Her breath trembled as she approached a cloudy green vat. A body floated inside it.

Gods!

Skin like wax, hair tangled, swollen salt-pale flesh, its limbs wriggled in a current. Tubes pierced its chest, ears, and hands. Strange orifices perforated its neck and groin. Nyahri drew closer, clasping her hand over her mouth. Its half-open eyes flickered, hourglass eyes of red and violet, and Nyahri stifled a cry.

A screech sounded from the Templarii's chamber, snapping Nyahri's attention from the tank. A hot, mechanical sound dissolved into a sticky grinding. Nyahri crouched lower, her heart thumping in her throat. The grinding stopped, followed by the pulpy crunch of splitting bone.

She stepped to the side of the doorway, no more than a few paces from the flesh walkers. Slowly, she looked around the corner.

Eight librarians watched while two worked. Blood covered their forearms, the air filled with its scent. The Templarii focused upon a young woman's body, a corpse stretched on a stone table. They cleaved her skull from the back, her blood and tissue stringing between the bone. Her brains lay in a dish on the floor, and one Templari reached into the skull cavity to extract the last of the cerebellum.

The second surgeon held in his hands a black-carapaced obscenity, a hell-horror, the size of a common cat. Its spider legs splayed, its obscene tail arching, and it sought the cadaver's opened skull. Its shell crawled, as if formed from a million tiny versions of itself, a monster comprised of a thousand smaller monsters. It clambered into the gore, yanking its mass into the seat of the brainpan, and it disappeared beneath a swell of black fluid. A fatty ichor slurped from the opening and slopped to the floor.

A lifeless carcass the second before, the woman now coughed, her mouth erupting with blood. She turned onto her side, a clot bursting from her nose, and her eyes scrunched. The new Templari drew a ragged breath, opened her eyes, and looked straight at Nyahri—

—who screamed, all sense of stealth forgotten, her voice echoing through the darkness.

{27}

Kepler led her from the deep chambers, one arm around her waist, his other hand on her shoulder. At one point he waited while she vomited.

"Get away from me," she told him.

"You will not go unattended, through our halls, again."

Ay! All I want is to be rid of him!

Nyahri carried the witch-light and kept it shining, never taking her attention from Kepler, not even as she emptied her stomach. As he pulled her further from the fortress's center, she tried to free herself from his grasp, envisioning the thing she now knew lived behind his eyes. She understood, as well, why the librarian she fought had finally died: she had struck its true self, not merely the flesh it wore. Her knees buckled once more, and he dragged her to her feet.

"You, little foal, shouldn't wander S'Eret. This is the *second* time I've told you. Stay in your room or the library or with your horses till your *mistress* makes up her annoyingly slow mind, and she *must* decide soon. We're losing patience."

"Let go of me!"

His voice deepened. "Were you not a prominent Atreiani's favorite, this would not have ended well for you, I promise, but I'd like Sultah yw Sabi to look upon us reasonably, should she regain a place among her wakened brethren."

"You are a horrible little monster."

"I'm a machine," he said, "and it was *your* mistress's brother who created us."

Bile burned Nyahri's throat as she and Kepler reached the outer corridor. He escorted her to the bedchamber.

"Stay *here,*" he said.

He left her, and Nyahri remained on the bed until yw Sabi arrived. The Atreiani closed the door, locked it, and sat beside Nyahri. She took the coronal from Nyahri's head and pulled aside the wide serape, drawing her fingers along Nyahri's naked back, her fingertips soft but strong.

"Kepler told me," said yw Sabi, "you wandered into a *rehousing.* That was not something I expected you'd witness. You weren't prepared for it."

Nyahri reached across her shoulder to take yw Sabi's hand.

"I'm sorry," yw Sabi said.

"Demons should not live in the bodies of the dead."

"They're not demons, just tinker toys. Try to forget what you saw." She swept Nyahri's hair behind her ear, leaning over to kiss her temple. "I won't ask you to search again. I'll do it myself."

"Nay, mistress," Nyahri said. "I found the door."

"You did?" The Atreiani sat straighter.

"Yea."

Yw Sabi lay next to Nyahri, forehead to forehead on the pillow. Nyahri's heartbeat slowed, her horror subsiding.

"The Templarii don't know?" yw Sabi asked.

"Nay."

"Would you remember the way?"

"Yea, but our problems multiply."

"What?"

Nyahri told her of the destroyed Templari, of her attempt to hide the body. Yw Sabi exhaled slowly, then nodded.

"It won't take them long," she said, "to realize the cockroach is missing, nor long to find it."

"I am sorry, mistress. I should have kept a cooler head."

Yw Sabi smirked. "I like your hotheadedness."

Nyahri's eyes glinted at that. She lay silently a few moments, then asked, "How can machines—the Templarii—be so complex? So alive?"

"Think of puppets, but imagine the puppet is also the puppeteer. Under all their meat bags, they're nothing more than automatons."

"They *do* steal the flesh of the dead."

"They're parasites—they use human hosts, husks for locomotion. They hijack the nervous system from the spinal chord."

Nyahri blinked nervously at their chamber door. "What of the men and women they occupy?" she asked, though she figured the answer, had seen that woman's brain scooped into a pan.

"Only cadavers, artificially sustained. Surprisingly efficient though—" Yw Sabi shrugged. "—given the turns of our technology at the time. Of course, we improved on the design."

"I admit, mistress, Atreian witchcraft still frightens me."

"You'll be steeped in it soon," yw Sabi said, "and it'll make sense one day."

Nyahri nibbled her lip, unsure what to think, less confident than she had been of late. Exhaustion fell over her, the weight of a long day and terrible events. She leaned against yw Sabi's shoulder, and the Atreiani pulled the blankets over them. Together their warmth in each other grew, and Nyahri drifted into sleep.

BEFORE DAWN, NYAHRI AWOKE. A fading impression of Dhaos slipped from her dreams, gone before she could recover it, leaving behind only a tease of his naked skin against hers. She sat, finding yw Sabi wrapped in a robe, organizing gear, enough for a day's excursion outside the fortress. The first slivers of sunrise cut through the high windows, pouring a dusty glow throughout the bedchamber.

Nyahri rubbed the sleep from her eyes. "What is your plan?"

"I sent word to Dhaos. We'll take his offer and play tourist for the day."

A groan escaped Nyahri's throat, the sensations of her dream still with her. "I admit, Dhaos confuses me."

"Why?" yw Sabi asked, glancing over her shoulder. "Because you're attracted to him?"

"Nay—" Horrified, Nyahri stammered, "I am not—"

"I've seen the looks between you." Yw Sabi smiled, and her next words carried not one hint of envy or anger. "You have some intention of forsaking me now, running off with him?"

Nyahri curled her lip. "Nay, mistress, never."

"I thought not." Yw Sabi's smile broadened. "You'll find I have my jealousies, Nyahri, but they're few and far between. I've my allowances too."

"I—" Nyahri rubbed her forehead, screwing her eyes shut. "What are you saying, mistress?"

Unhurried, the Atreiani packed a small bag with devices Nyahri did not recognize. "I'd tell you to sleep with the boy, if you fancied him *that* much, but perhaps I should caution you against frolicking with people whose cities you're about to destroy?"

This distressed Nyahri, most of all because talk of bedding Dhaos unnerved her more than talk of destroying cities. "You mean it?"

Yw Sabi lifted a shoulder. "I always mean what I say, though *you* should do what you can to get Dhaos off your mind."

"How am I to do *that?* We *are* riding out with him today?"

"Yes." Yw Sabi sealed the small bag. "Would you like a bath?"

"I would love one."

"Good, because I requested hot water, soap, and oils. They should be up soon."

Not long after yw Sabi said so, as the sunshine burst crisply through the windows, a librarian knocked upon their door. Yw Sabi arose and unlocked it. Not one Templari, but two, bowed and entered. The first laid clean linens, then delivered four large buckets of steaming water, which he emptied into a tub.

"Be quick," she told him.

The second poured tea and left a tray of cold pumpkin soup, sourdough, and sliced apples. The Atreiani tasted these before the Templarii departed, and she closed the door and bolted it again. Nyahri sat up in bed, back to the corner, the sheets tucked beneath her neck until the Templari's footsteps faded to silence.

"You all right?" yw Sabi asked her.

"I do not like them." The E'cwni nodded in the direction the Templarii had gone.

Yw Sabi chuckled. "I *never* liked them."

They ate, washed, and dressed. Afterward, they returned to the library. In it, several Templarii hunkered around a table, copying their most common books, those meant for sale to distant powers, or primers intended for the children of Oudwn nobility.

"Get out!" yw Sabi said. When one hesitated, she kicked his chair from under him. "*Get out!* And close the door behind you."

After they left, yw Sabi righted the chair, sat on it, and patted the seat beside her. Nyahri joined her.

"Not enough studying these last few days," yw Sabi said, her voice calm. "We need some normalcy. Give me the planets in Englisce, and the moons and major Stations out to Jupiter."

With some difficulty, Nyahri recited them, several dozen names in all. As she did, yw Sabi opened a wide book of maps, pressing its cover flat. She caressed a page and brushed dust from its corner.

"This map," yw Sabi said, drawing Nyahri's attention to the book, "shows North America as best as the Templarii have figured it. There's an inland sea now which didn't exist in my time. The coastlines changed radically from what was Baja to British Columbia. Ocean levels are higher, that is clear, but the land along the western coasts also fell drastically. Ash covered those ranges. Species and climates shifted with crustal displacement and other factors."

"These are big changes?"

Yw Sabi laughed softly. "Vast. The world literally cracked, like a marble thrown against a brick wall. I didn't fully understand till a few days ago, but there was a tectonic shift. North America may have slipped as much as two hundred kilometers west. Must've been one shitty ride."

"The entire world *moved?*"

"Its surface, yes."

"Gods."

"The North American continental shelf buckled. A good portion of California gone, and three quadrillion tonnes of rock and magma folded like cardboard from the Gallatin Range to the Oregon coast. Part of the tectonic plate actually collapsed into the mantle."

Nyahri nodded like she understood.

"During the initial expansion," yw Sabi continued, "Yellowstone and most of Idaho, Oregon, and part of Wyoming dropped hundreds of meters." She indicated the mountains, waters, and shorelines.

"How far is *hundreds of meters?*"

"A hundred meters is three thousand or so of your *hands*. Imagine standing atop a hillside, then being at the bottom the next second, only the hill went down with you."

"*Gods!*" Nyahri repeated, passing horrified.

Yw Sabi pointed to the center of the map, obscuring a dot beneath her fingertip. "We're here."

"That is Cohltos?" Nyahri pointed too, beginning to grasp the enormity of her world.

"There's Abswyn, less than a fingernail's width away at this scale, though it took us twenty-three days to travel this. The Sojourn Templarii know the precise locations of several dozen Citadels around the world, but only a few are in the western half of this continent. One or two would've been destroyed with the Eventide cataclysm, but who knows the fate of the rest? *This* map indicates cultural and political boundaries, all relatively recent, along with peculiar locales described by travelers over the centuries. Two are of *particular* interest."

"Which?"

Yw Sabi first indicated the massive inland sea which dominated the landmass in the northwest. "Can you read the words?"

"*The Yellow Sea.*"

"You ever seen it?"

"I have never been so far north, but other E'cwnii have. We call it the *Amahriya.*"

Yw Sabi's finger traced a line to the sea's east. "Before it even existed, there were Citadels here. From what I can tell of legends, trade records, and travelers' accounts, there still are."

She pointed even farther east, representing a distance difficult for Nyahri to comprehend, until yw Sabi stopped at another odd, oblong body of water, this one stretching north-south and connecting with an extensive system of lakes or seas. Off-center, at the water's tip, extended a perfectly delineated square, wider across than the distance they had journeyed from Abswyn to the gates of Sojourn.

"I have no idea what this region is," said the Atreiani, "and neither does anyone else, it seems. It is a black hole—or *square*—if you will."

Nyahri shook her head. "I do not understand?"

"This is *unholy* land to several peoples east, and I get why. No reports of visitors to it in centuries. What little I can glean, before that, tells me whoever goes here—" She tapped the square. "—never comes out again. There is not one report, rumor, or description of what lies within this boundary."

"You have *no* idea, mistress?"

"Something inhuman controls it, that's clear enough." She gave a quick shake of her head. "There were the machine intelligences called the Numenii—"

"Yea, we read of them, the day we arrived here. *The banishing of the Numenii.* Is that right?"

"Good, you remember. A Numeni would be powerful enough to dominate an area large as shown here, but—" Yw Sabi tapped her chin, considering. "—whatever is there is *not* a Numeni. It's something else."

"Something which worries you?"

Yw Sabi exhaled. "There was once a city within that boundary—*Chicago*—but not much was left of it, even five hundred years before my internment at Abswyn. We destroyed Chicago."

The Atreiani tore the map from the book, folded it, and slipped it into her pocket. She drew another book toward her, wiped its cover, and opened it to a dog-eared page.

"It was a human," she said, "who founded Cohltos and rebooted Sojourn's Templarii. He was a philosopher, the son of an Exemplari who served his master faithfully in advance of the Eventide. The son's name was Peter, and this is a copy of the histories he wrote. Listen—"

She read, translating when Nyahri misunderstood, slowing her pronunciation so Nyahri caught every word, and yw Sabi explained *Greeks, Vikings,* and *Egyptians.* After she read through once, Nyahri recited with her:

What were the Atreianii if not gods? Were the Greeks not driven by the goddess of philosophers to lay reason's foundations? The Vikings, by their pantheon to pillage? The Egyptians, to reach for eternity? Our gods set us at a yoke of greatness. They kept us from cancer, pestilence, and hunger. They dispelled war when they dissolved the bickering nations and crushed the faiths. They slew poverty, salving the plague of human greed. The Atreianii were our shepherds; we, their sheep. They collared us so we might know our limits, caring for us better than for any beast. In return they demanded only our absolute servitude.

What now that they are gone?

We rebuild. We relearn. This was the charter of Sojourn Temple, where our Atreianii sleep. We await them, and they will know our dedication and reward our faithfulness. We must all serve the Atreianii; there is no escape, and best for those who serve amenably, for we oath-sworn who recognize our place at our mistresses' and masters' feet. Let other men and women profit or suffer at Atreian whim and under Atreian wisdom, so all can live in peace. We groomsmen and handmaidens will be lifted up. Yes! Our gods will return. Let us keep a full accounting for them.

"It's interesting," yw Sabi said, "Peter's use of *oath-sworn* here, because strictly speaking he couldn't have been—it was a term we reserved for the Exemplarii alone. By the time Peter wrote those words, all the Exemplarii were dead."

"All?"

"They were *put down* by the Atreian Congress."

"Why?"

"Conservation of resources, they decided. That's what it came down to."

Among the E'cwnii, if a man killed a tribesman to conserve his own food, shelter, or horses, that man faced exile or death. Nyahri glowered at the idea the Atreianii would slaughter their own helpmates.

"The Sojourn Templarii perform, to this day, the tasks Peter set for them," yw Sabi said, "though he and the human survivors of the Eventide are long dead. Peter was last to go, in the one hundred fourteenth year after the cataclysm."

Nyahri shook her head. "A man lived to one hundred fourteen years?"

"Longer. He'd been alive before the fall."

"Truly?"

"It wasn't unusual for humans, with a little help, to live past one-fifty."

"We do not live so long now," Nyahri said.

"Astounding how well human bodies do when you have nanites scrubbing their teeth, routing their arteries, reinforcing their immune systems." Yw Sabi's brows arched. "You realize the Exemplarii lived much longer?"

Nyahri shook her head. She scooted to the front of her chair and scanned the page one more time.

"At the time the Atreianii betrayed the Exemplarii," said yw Sabi, "the oldest was more than four hundred years old. Ekaterina was in her nineties."

"A few of the elders across our tribes, they live to ninety."

The Atreiani laughed. "Kat's ninety came with fewer wrinkles."

Nyahri scratched her head, puzzled all the more for having learned so much. Yw Sabi closed all the books and shoved them aside.

"It's the beginning of the end," yw Sabi said, "for Sojourn and for Cohltos."

A knock sounded at the library door.

"Enter," said yw Sabi.

A Templari shuffled in, one of the same which had fled yw Sabi's earlier impatience. "Dhaos Shwn Oudwn is arrived," he said, "to escort you up to the orchards."

"Excellent. Tell the young archer we'll be out shortly."

28

Yw Sabi and Nyahri sat in their saddles, squinting into the growing daylight as the Templarii opened the gates. A breeze blew through the passage and Nyahri shivered, cinching her cloak. She balanced her spear in front of her, and the Oudwn longbow rested behind the cantle. As she and the Atreiani rode forward, yw Sabi scowled.

"Damn it," she said.

The crowds had grown. Hundreds upon hundreds huddled beyond the barriers. Many who stood exhausted now shouted at their first glimpse of the Atreiani in the daylight. The streets had become a makeshift camp, complete with cooking fires and tents. The heart of Cohltos now stank of sweat, rotten food, and shit.

Dhaos waited beside the massive doors, a half dozen of his men with him.

"Dhaos," yw Sabi said, and she waved her arm toward the crowds, as if in question.

"Goddess," he said, nodding. "Word of you has spread far and wide—people have been streaming from the valleys. They fill every inn in Cohltos, jam our avenues, and are too much a challenge for our sewers, I am afraid."

The Atreiani looked at Nyahri, who nodded her understanding.

Our task worsens, the E'cwni thought.

"Ready for our outing?" yw Sabi asked Dhaos.

"When I made the invitation, I thought to enjoy Nyahri's company all to myself. Alas, all together are happier, as they say."

Nyahri smiled at him. He raised his eyebrows, grinned, and winked.

She rolled her eyes. *Yea, why* must *you be so likable?*

The Atreiani directed Turo toward the wider streets, and he jumped forward, chomping his bit. Nyahri followed, keeping one eye on the mob, while Dhaos paced her afoot. His men surrounded them.

As yw Sabi's hair fluttered from beneath her hood, the crowd gasped or murmured or cheered. No one could mistake its witchery in the light, and the calls for her attention redoubled. The Oudwn poor, townspeople and farmers alongside foreign grangers, all gathered for the Atreiani. The crowd pressed, threatening to break the fences.

The people called out, "Atreiani!"

Under the brightening sunlight, Nyahri perceived how much sickness spread through the makeshift camps, at least as much as at Aukensis. Blotched faces and bloodied noses appeared among the onlookers, phlegm on the lips of men with pneumonia, children with blood on their shirts. An Oudwn man at the front coughed, on his feet only to catch a glimpse of the goddess whose presence, he thought, promised him a cure.

They all ought to be in bed, Nyahri thought, *saving their strength*. She wondered how many *had* beds, and how many beds had fleas.

As yw Sabi veered toward an outbound road, supplicants surrounded her, and Nyahri bolted ahead, driving the crowd back. Though her focus remained upon the press of men and women, her peripheral vision caught a flutter of unreal gray.

A black-lipped, pale-skinned crone stood beside a covered well, beyond the supplicants, thirty paces distant. She remained still, a locus around whom the crowd flowed like water around a stone, and she watched yw Sabi, her eyes deep-set beneath her brows, her jowls in a frown. A dusty, charcoal-gray cloak wrapped her, brocaded with velvet symbols too indistinct to read.

Nyahri drew yw Sabi's attention to the hag. The Atreiani turned Turo's head and pushed through the crowd. Yet, in the panic yw Sabi created, she and Nyahri lost sight of the old woman. By the time they reached the well, no hint of the crone remained.

Yw Sabi heeled Kwlko several steps down one alley, then back, craning in each direction. "Can you spot her?"

"Nay, mistress." Nyahri searched, as well.

Dhaos and his men caught up, taking surrounding positions, pushing back the crowds once more. He whistled, signaling the archers to reroute.

"Goddess," he said, "if you would *please* not do that. Hard for my men to do their job if you race ahead of us like that—"

"Did you see her?" yw Sabi asked him.

"Who?"

Yw Sabi described the crone. The archers made a cursory search.

"Nothing," Dhaos said.

The Atreiani growled. "Never mind."

"What was that?" Nyahri asked her.

Yw Sabi's jaw clenched. "I don't know." Though the company again moved outward along the city streets, yw Sabi remained distracted, hunting for any sign of what they'd glimpsed. "She was *not* Oudwn, that's for certain, and her countenance remind me of—" Yw Sabi's voice trailed off, as if she second-guessed herself.

"Of what?"

"Something Ekaterina once told me."

A specter of the ancient world, Nyahri thought, but faced with the crush of the mob, she could give it no further thought. She and yw Sabi would, no doubt, speak of it later.

The company pushed through the streets, and Dhaos's lieutenant met them at a junction. Before they covered another hundred steps, the whole of Dhaos's unit had joined them, two dozen men, and they broke free onto a frosty rural road. At the city gates, a detachment of archers turned back the trailing masses.

Dhaos gave Nyahri a proud puppy-dog smile, but she looked away. He gazed after her, for a moment, before catching the attention of the Atreiani.

"You look unhappy," yw Sabi said to him.

"Never," he said, allowing his frown to open into a yawn.

Five hundred paces from the city, they rested beside a cornfield, the stalks tall and the corn late for harvest. The archers still formed a casual perimeter, but the crowds had obeyed the commands to remain at the gates. No one followed.

"No need for a full company out in the hills," yw Sabi said to Dhaos. "Why don't we ride farther, and your men can meet us on our return?"

"We? Our? You mean you and Nyahri, or are you inviting me with you?"

"You promised to show us the best view of Cohltos, isn't that right?"

Dhaos's lieutenant whispered in his commander's ear. In reply, Dhaos shook his head.

"They shouldn't be so afraid for you," the Atreiani said, smiling broadly, her teeth white in the sunlight. "I promise I won't bite."

"Afraid?" Dhaos smiled. "He was only saying he thought two fine ladies ought to have a better escort than I."

She smirked. "No, he wasn't."

Dhaos grinned, and he ordered his men back to the city. He slung his bow and stood beside Nyahri's knee. She looked down at him from her saddle.

"Shall I run to keep up with you?" he asked.

Yw Sabi nodded toward the stallion. "Why don't you ride with Nyahri, boy? You seem inclined."

"Mistress?" Nyahri glanced back the Atreiani, an edge of panic in her voice.

What is she doing? Nyahri thought. *Gods!*

The Atreiani half smiled. "You can make him go on foot, Nyahri. It makes no difference to me."

Nyahri slid forward against the pommel, and Dhaos climbed behind her, pressing to the cantle, his knees against her thighs. He leaned back, his hands at the saddle's edge, near the unstrung longbow. Dhaos dragged his fingers across a length of it.

"Glad you kept this," he said. "A wonder your mistress did not toss it into the campfire."

Kwlko sidestepped under the archer's added weight, and that alone almost threw him. He recovered with a laugh. Nyahri warmed, excited and unsettled with the Oudwni so close. She rubbed the stallion's neck and clicked her tongue to calm him, then pulled her hair aside beneath her coronal, glancing over her shoulder.

"Try anything," she said to Dhaos, "and I will throw you from his back—"

"I will behave!" he said, still laughing.

"—and turn back to trample you."

"No doubt you will," he said gravely, though his bright smile remained.

No doubt I will not, she thought, *and you know it.*

They rode north from Cohltos, following paths between potato and squash fields. The farms yielded to wild grasses and thickets, climbing distant ranges into tougher terrain. Boulders squeezed the trail, Nyahri coaxed the horses between them onto a higher plateau, a mesa covered by overgrown plum and apple trees, an old grove long abandoned. Lush ferns defied the autumn breezes.

As they rode, the day grew hot, and Nyahri stripped off her heavier clothes. She wore her serape bare-shouldered, her skin exposed to the sunlight.

On the mesa top, the three of them dismounted and set the horses loose to graze. Yw Sabi sat on a soft patch of grass, Nyahri kept close to her, and Dhaos rested with his back against a fallen log. Gusts sometimes shook the tree limbs, but the sun remained warm and alluring.

Again and again, Nyahri found her gaze drawn to Dhaos, though yw Sabi's presence anchored her. Rather than torn between two poles, Nyahri felt a sense of being fed by two rivers—as Cohltos was—one perennial and strong and unyielding, the other sweet and fleeting. These emotions Dhaos spurred in her, they annoyed her, equal parts arousal, worry, and guilt.

Gods, stupid Oudwn boy! Must all the gods love sex? Must they play so much with human hearts?

Dhaos laid down his cloak, and on it his bow and quiver. He picked a ripe plum, cleaned it on his sleeve, and ate.

After a few minutes, yw Sabi stretched, her face lit by the golden-green of the sunshine through the trees. She set her scepter across her lap, making herself more comfortable, looking across the whole of the valley. After retrieving her compass, she marked some far-distant point, and her eyes narrowed.

"Mistress, you see something?"

"Nothing, girl."

She does not call me girl *very often anymore,* Nyahri thought. *She means me to drop the question, that the answer is not meant for Dhaos's ears.*

"The plums are quite good," Dhaos said. "You should try one. Delicious."

Yw Sabi folded her cloak, set it among Nyahri's possessions, and stood. "I'm not hungry," she said. "I'll be back in a few minutes."

Nyahri's heart lurched.

She is leaving me with him? "Yw Sabi?"

"I'll be right back, Nyahri."

The Atreiani walked through the underbrush, in the direction of the mesa's edge. Her footsteps grew quieter until only the sounds of singing birds and the wind remained. Nyahri frowned, sighed, and set her back to a wide apple tree, keeping Dhaos in sight.

He picked another plum from a low-hanging branch and took a bite. "I checked the histories," he said, mouth full.

"Oh?"

"*The Betrayer*—you said I should ask the Templarii. I asked Kepler, then found the early annals myself."

"And?"

He took another bite, chewed, and swallowed. "There were so many conflicting versions, and the Templarii were loathe to share everything. With them, I agree, it is difficult to say what is true and what is merely half true."

"What do *you* think true?"

"She *was* the Betrayer, there is no doubt of it. She denounced her own kind, the Atreianii." Dhaos glanced in the direction yw Sabi had gone. Lifting his shoulder, he affected a slight tilt of his head, as if dismissing his own argument. "Yet *you* are right too. Sultah yw Sabi betrayed the Atreianii on behalf of humans, and for someone she loved, most of all. That is what I could glean. The Templarii would not say so, not so directly, but I will say this—the matter was more complex than they say."

Nyahri responded with a derisive grunt. "I told you as much, Oudwni."

"So you did."

"I *am* impressed you bothered to look, to check those smelly books yourself. You *are* a scholar."

"Me? Nay, never. I hate books."

"I am not so fond of them either."

She laughed, and his laugh followed.

"I like you, Nyahri. I would like to learn more about the E'cwnii. Would you tell me?"

"Ask."

"Your father," he said, "what is he like?"

She folded her arms. "An excellent leader, not in a hurry over much of anything."

"Then you are nothing like him."

"What is *that* supposed to mean?"

He shrugged. "*You* seem to be in a hurry over everything." Again, he gestured toward wherever the Atreiani had disappeared.

"I have met *your* father," she said. "He explains *nothing* about you."

Dhaos chuckled. "And what is *that* supposed to mean?"

"I mean it as a compliment." She smiled wide, despite herself. "He is a disgusting old lecher."

"Well, at least I am not *old.*" His laugh grew bolder. "Good to know."

She fidgeted, picking at a patch of grass. Her gaze wandered along the horizon.

Dhaos leaned back. "You know, my father had another family before I was born. As I understand it, *your* father killed them."

"I have heard that too." She drew her lips together. "I would it had never happened."

"Other than the gods, who is to say what should happen or not happen? If my grandfather had not tried to claim Abswyn? If *your* grandfather had not retaliated, sent your father raiding? I would never have been born. Shwn Jhon Oudwn has had five wives. Two are living, including my mother. My father had five other sons before me, all dead. I have seven sisters, six under the age of twelve, and not one living brother."

"You have a nephew."

"Yea, Tohmas."

"I saw him in Orÿs, along with his sister."

"Niki."

"Beautiful children. You love them?"

He nodded once.

"Dhaos, do you know what your father requested of yw Sabi?"

"He sent me to guide you, but his order to me was to be certain you returned with medicine, at any cost. As the Templarii tell it, every moment the Atreiani delays her descent, you are killing those I love."

Nyahri lowered her eyes. "Yw Sabi cannot descend yet." She hoped he would not ask why. "But the cure exists."

"She told you so?"

Nyahri raised her eyes again, looking into his.

Pretty hazel eyes, she thought, *genuine worry in them, even pain.*

She imagined how she'd feel if her family—her father, sister, many loved ones—died the way Dhaos's people were dying.

"I asked her," Nyahri said, "to deliver these gifts to your people."

His smile returned. "Thank you. Please, Nyahri, persuade the Atreiani to descend. Tonight, tomorrow, as soon as possible."

For a moment the grove settled, no breeze at all, the sweet smell of ripe plums permeating the air, coupled with the fresh green of ferns.

Peaceful, Nyahri thought. *If only it could remain so, if only I might enjoy this with him, as we might have many times, as if it ever could have been.*

Nyahri breathed deeply. She stood, stepped to where Dhaos sat, and knelt beside him, leaning forward with her fingertips splayed in the grass. She studied his strong face, lined by worry, and she remembered yw Sabi's words to her that morning. With her fingernail she brushed a lock of his hair from his eyes, and she kissed his lips.

They taste divine, she thought.

Dhaos blinked at her, then rediscovered his composure.

"That was unexpected," he said.

"You wanted to for weeks now."

"That is the truth. Can I again?"

Again, they kissed. This time, she lingered on it, closing her eyes, closing them against the weight of inevitability, knowing the foolishness of the kiss.

What else did yw Sabi say? Something about frolicking with people whose cities you were about to destroy.

"You never intended to inherit?" she asked. "You thought there would be others to take your father's place?"

"Yea."

"Me too."

"Eh?"

"My brother," she said. "He died in the springtime."

"How?"

"A wasteful death."

"What happened?" Dhaos asked.

"He drowned, a simple thing. His skin—I had never seen such a shade of blue."

"You loved him?"

"Adored him."

"I am sorry." Dhaos frowned, a deep and genuine expression.

She sniffled. "Not any fault in it."

"Ah! You are going to cry!" His boyish grin returned, his eyes flashing. "You are not so difficult—I will find a woman in you yet, eh?"

She stood, turned away, and walked to the edge of the clearing. Dhaos followed.

"You would have me fall in love with you," she said, startled by the razor in her own voice. "All this *sharing*, only so I will have *feelings* for you."

"Well, not *only*."

"Beware, Dhaos Shwn Oudwn, men have died trying to love me."

His brow creased. "Oh? What did these brave men do to deserve that?"

"The trying of it was enough."

"You killed them?"

"Yea."

Not so simple as that, she thought, *but you should stay away from me, Oudwni. I* will *be the death of you.*

Dhaos drew his knife and rolled it in his palm, its tempered iron glittering in the leaf light. He threw it aside, far from reach. Stepping forward, closing the distance to Nyahri, he spread his arms wide.

"Peace," he said, all seriousness.

She narrowed her eyes. "What?"

"Between you, me, E'cwnii, Oudwnii. My father has held the lower valleys for forty years, a pain in your ass, but I know I can be twice the man he is when I get my chance. I have the respect of the Oudwn council too. I can bring peace."

She shook her head, her heart thumping, and took a step backward.

"At what cost?" she asked.

"No cost." He held out his hand to her, the second time he had done so. "I mean it—peace."

She took his hand. He stepped against her, slipping his other arm behind her back, drawing her to him.

This time, Dhaos kissed her. His lips felt rougher than the Atreiani's; his fingertips, courser. He smelled like the earth, like the oil of a whetstone, like iron. The flutter he raised inside her reached deep.

"Leave the Atreiani," he said.

Gods!

Nyahri shoved him, all her strength in it. For a moment he lost his balance but, as quickly, he moved forward, his arms spread, his face still open and full of desire.

Nyahri flinched, drawing her longknife from its scabbard and pointing it at him. He stepped against it, its point indenting his tunic, threatening to pierce his flesh. Dhaos winced, looking into her eyes.

"You will not kill me," he said.

"Nay?"

A rosette of blood appeared through Dhaos's tunic.

"Peace?" Dhaos asked. "Or would you rather follow the devil who has so obviously seduced you?"

Her hand trembled, her knees wanting to buckle.

"I could love you however you wish," he said. "The Atreiani, she will love you how *she* wishes."

"Do not say that! How could you know anything of what she would do?"

"I am right."

"Nay."

He pushed forward, forcing the knife to cut, and she pulled it from him, falling back a step. Dhaos stumbled away, catching his breath, drawing one hand across his chest. Blood smeared his fingertips.

"Dhaos," she said, "I am sorry."

He laughed, throwing back his head and holding his belly. A meander of blood crossed his stomach, staining his shirt. Nyahri curled her lip, and she sheathed her longknife, then tightened her fists at her sides.

"You joke!" she said. "You play me for a fool?"

"Gods, nay! I meant every word—every one."

"Then *what?*"

"I thought for certain—" He took another breath, laughing again.

"Thought what?"

"—you were going to gut me like a fish!" He almost giggled. "But I think maybe, *maybe*—"

"*What?*"

"—you might like me as much as I think I like you."

Her fist landed across his upturned jaw. He fell onto his back, clutching his face. Dhaos grumbled, then laughed more.

"Gods!" he said. "Eh! I think you do, you crazy woman."

"*Idiot.*"

Nyahri left him and crashed through the ferns, following a trail of leaves bent by yw Sabi. After a few paces the verge opened onto the mesa edge. Below it, the valley broadened into farmlands interlaced by forests, irrigation ditches choked by sycamore and willow.

Cohltos nestled in the valley's cradle. Its hedge-lined paths crisscrossed between buildings, framing clusters of tightly packed homes with thatched roofs and wooden lapboards. The rivers sliced Cohltos in three parts. Cottonwoods spread their limbs over the main roads, their golden leaves clinging to the branches. Near the township's heart, the Swyn Templr pillar jutted upward, its pinnacle still far higher than the mesa. Around its base grew S'Eret Fortress, its rusticated, floret-patterned spirals centered on the invisible Citadel beneath.

Nyahri thought of the chamber of skulls which lay hidden at its center.

Yw Sabi leaned at the mesa's edge, her foot propped against a stone, her wrists crossed on her knee. Her loosened hair blew in a brisk wind.

"Dhaos is courting you," she said.

"As recklessly as you do."

Yw Sabi glanced at her. "Given some time with him, I wanted to know what you would do."

"You *test* me?"

"Test? No." The Atreiani smiled, looking back across the valley. "A *test* is something you can fail. There was no way for you to *fail* the last fifteen minutes."

Nyahri grumbled, but stepped beside her mistress. Yw Sabi continued her survey, studying every detail.

"What do you see, yw Sabi?"

"Opportunity." The Atreiani pointed. "The low ground is there, and the drainages come together above it—all that tinder will be the place to begin."

"So it will be fire?"

Yw Sabi nodded. Nyahri's heart clenched.

"We will need to funnel the Oudwn retreat," she said. "If we drive them south, might we trap them on the opposite side of the river?" She pointed along the two waterways, emphasizing the bridges.

"My thought exactly. We use the bridges. What you suggest would save a lot of lives, if we could do it. Say they do flee to the south bank. Then what? They stay there, only to be killed by the explosion?"

"We would need to keep them moving."

"Look at the channels to the southeast." The Atreiani drew Nyahri's attention to the widespread copses which followed the drainages. "There's no water in them."

"Has not been, I would guess, since late summer." Nyahri surmised the Atreiani's designs, the enormous risk in such a plan. "We give them time before sparking a second fire to the east. Your magic could do this?"

"It could."

"We need a slow fire. Give them space to march."

"We can do our best to plan—prevailing winds, upslopes, contours—but it'll do as it pleases once begun."

"Fire, then."

"*And* water," yw Sabi said. "I can think of no other way. Can you? We can't play any more games here, because before long we'll start losing." She looked at Nyahri. "This morning, when I called for our breakfast, Kepler asked me if I had seen a certain librarian—"

Behind them, leaves rustled. Dhaos approached through the thick, his shirt tucked into his belt again, fabric stained by blood. He grinned.

"Can you not," Nyahri said to him, "be by yourself even a short while?"

He lifted a shoulder. "Seems not. I am like a child. Always needing attention."

"Child? More like an ass." Nyahri ran her fingers through her hair, a nervous gesture, overcome by a moment's guilt. "I am sorry, Dhaos, I should not have cut you."

"Or punched me, but think nothing of it," he said, rubbing his face. "My father used to give me much worse."

"This is beautiful land," yw Sabi said to him, her focus on the valley.

"Yea," Dhaos said, "but too many mouths to feed and too long a wintertime. We have a lot of challenges here, a dungheap of work ahead of us."

Below, an iron bell tolled and, from a cluster of houses, a procession plodded toward the fortress. Nyahri strained to distinguish any details from such a distance, discerning only slow figures dressed in white and red.

"What is happening?" she asked.

"A funeral," Dhaos said. "Common this time of year, and they will stay common till spring. I get tired of the keening."

"They wrapped the body in white fabric," yw Sabi said.

Nyahri started. *Yw Sabi can see* that *far?*

"What is it they used?" the Atreiani asked. "It's not wool."

"Southern flax and cotton," he said. "We import as much of it as we can, at great expense."

"Will this corpse be burned as—" She glanced at him with a passing sympathy. "—as we burned your cousin Erwln?"

"Nay," he said, his thumb massaging his bruised jaw. "This person did not die in combat. Looks to be a young man by the colors. Notice the red flags? They will inter him in S'Eret."

Nyahri remembered the many sealed chambers she passed in the fortress's depths. Filled with corpses, she now imagined.

"Your people," yw Sabi began, "give so many of their deceased to the Templarii?"

"Most everyone," he said.

"The Templarii didn't used to be undertakers. They must've adopted the practice out of necessity. They don't always entomb the bodies, do they?" She said this more as a statement than a question.

"Nay," he said, "sometimes S'Eret's doors open and an unfamiliar Templari greets us with the face of a man or woman we thought we knew before. They sometimes *use* the corpses."

"I know," Nyahri said.

He looked at her with some surprise.

"Nyahri," yw Sabi said, "recently witnessed a Templarin *rehousing* firsthand."

"You saw them take one?" Dhaos asked Nyahri.

"Yea," she said.

"What was it like?"

She shook her head.

"Let's talk of pleasanter things," yw Sabi said, "shall we? Tell me, Dhaos, has your father or any of the chieftains developed the habit of storing food? Are there granaries?"

He hesitated, as if surprised by the question. "Many west of this valley, some at Aukensis, others elsewhere, mostly in the south."

"Wise."

"The chieftains' council built them when I was a boy."

"How are they? Full?"

"Not so much as we prefer—it has taken many years of saving—but neither are they empty. A year's worth, at least."

"Good," she said, "for a people to have a long-term view."

Yw Sabi watched the landscape once more, and Dhaos waited in silence for the conversation to continue. Nyahri smiled at his awkwardness, then matched her mistress's coldness. She too leaned forward, studying the valley, her back turned to him.

The sun slipped beneath the topmost mountaintops, and a few lamplights twinkled in the city and farms. As the sky darkened, the ghost-fire rhythm of Swyn Templr shone more clearly, dark and bright, dark and bright. In the east, the full moons of Lwn and Stashwn arose, reddened on the horizon. Little Trwl reached its zenith height, a mere quarter moon, blue-silver in the evening sky.

A beautiful land, Nyahri thought. *What will remain when we finish?*

"Dhaos," she said, remembering something else entirely, "I hope you had the good sense to tether the horses before you came out here?"

He gave her a dumb look. She looked heavenward and cursed.

"Come," she said, "let us discover how far they have wandered."

Nyahri whistled for the horses, walking back through the grove. Dhaos trailed behind her.

hen they returned to the city gates, Dhaos's men met them, and they provided a much-needed escort through the burgeoning crowds. At the fortress, the Templarii unlocked the gates, and yw Sabi rode into the darkness without a backwards glance. Nyahri hesitated, neither relishing another night in S'Eret nor wanting to leave Dhaos to his fate. She smiled softly at him.

"Why look so sad?" he asked her.

"Dhaos, take care of the Oudwnii."

He stared at her, and unspoken question in him. "I will."

She turned Kwlko's head and heeled him inside, raising the witch-light to guide her way. The doors clanged shut behind her, the Templarii driving the bolts home.

That night, sitting at the library, yw Sabi and Nyahri studied the valley map. The candles burned low.

"You've never seen explosives, have you?" the Atreiani asked.

"Nay, mistress. What are they?"

"Force on demand, and they come in many forms. I've a handful, recovered from Abswyn. They're not military—made for civil engineering—but they'll do."

"I think I understand." Nyahri pointed to the bridges. "We use them here?"

Yw Sabi nodded. "We'll give the Oudwnii ample time but, once they cross south, we'll take down the bridges. The river's deep and cold enough to keep all but the most foolish from coming back north."

"Once we have finished our task?"

"By dawn we'll be over the pass which the Oudwnii call the *Hwsehr*. While we were out with Dhaos, I confirmed the route by compass." Yw Sabi traced the map with her fingertip, and Nyahri remembered the moment, on their outing, when yw Sabi marked the direction. "We'll follow the Blue River downward across the range. The Wyst will take us back to the plains."

"The plan is clear."

Yw Sabi rapped her knuckles on the tabletop. "Very."

"Mistress, what did we see today? The crone—"

"Not an Atreiani, that's certain, but it wasn't human either."

"How could you tell?"

"Wrong temperature," yw Sabi said. "Wrong spectra."

"Wrong *spectra?*"

"My eyes catch things yours don't."

As well Nyahri knew. "A Templari?" she guessed. "Spying on us?"

"No," yw Sabi said, "not a human, not a Templari. Something else. My gut tells me, as it has from the beginning, there're other forces at work here, still hiding from us. The crone might've been a *first* reveal."

"What do we do about it?"

"For now, nothing we *can* do." The Atreiani took Nyahri's hand in her own. "We follow our plan through, and we hope for the best."

Yw Sabi and Nyahri restored and packed their food supplies. They locked their bedchamber door behind them and left a note which read:

Nyahri is riding today. I am working. Do not disturb me.—S

A simple trickery, yes, but Nyahri disliked lies.

Long before sunrise they departed S'Eret Fortress, opening and closing the gates themselves, and by horseback they followed the riverbank from Cohltos. Lwn and Stashwn still shined, absolutely full, near the western horizon and the edges of those far mountains. Nyahri led her mistress close to the rivers, avoided the sleeping roadside crowds, passing only a few waterside early- morning laundresses who wondered, perhaps, what they saw by such an eerie moonslight.

Along the way, Yw Sabi stopped at every bridge. She drew canisters from her supplies, each filled with thin, silvered discs which she affixed to the stone piers. Nyahri remembered seeing them on the first day she regained consciousness, in yw Sabi's care, almost six weeks before.

Such small things, Nyahri thought, *will turn granite into nothing but sand. Yw Sabi may not think it sorcery, but I know better.*

Afterward, Nyahri led the Atreiani along a meandering route back to the mesa-top orchards. By first light, clouds covered the sky, wreathing the mountaintops, and snow appeared on the far western peaks.

As they had before, the women let the horses graze amongst the old fruit trees. Kwlko and Turo tossed their heads, wandering contentedly, eating fallen plumbs and apples and sweet grasses.

The groves blocked the wintry wind, while the rising sun warmed the day. They ate a late breakfast of cured meats, fresh vegetables, and bread. Nyahri and yw Sabi waited an hour, watching the slopes below for any pursuers.

"No one is following," yw Sabi said at last.

"I worried Dhaos might have tried."

"Agreed, especially if he thought you were alone."

Nyahri looked sidelong at her mistress, then rolled her eyes. If Dhaos followed them, he remained unseen.

In the early afternoon, they laid blankets on the grass and sat cross-legged, knee to knee. The midday gusts blew icily, and Nyahri pulled a wool blanket around her shoulders. She breathed fully, enlivened by the fruit trees, the frosty air, the horses, the sweetness of late-autumn wildflowers on the hillsides.

"The wildfire must rise," yw Sabi said, gesturing to the land, "from down valley. The slope is gentle where it meets the rivers. If we're lucky, tonight's downslope winds will check the flames."

"I understand the plan," Nyahri said.

While still in the library, they had reviewed it repeatedly, counting their resources, estimating the minutes as they followed the flames. Yw Sabi smiled, nodded, and took Nyahri's hand. Her voice softened.

"In *my* time," she said, "the Exemplarii enjoyed privileges unheard of among humans—access to the Citadels, many immunities, legal rights, and other gifts—elevated above all, they alone. For you, now, I can only offer a lifetime of difficulty."

"Leisure or difficulty," Nyahri said, "makes no difference to me, yw Sabi."

The Atreiani withdrew the collar from its hiding place, the length of fragile-seeming fabric glinting in the sunlight. "I am grateful for you. You're an unexpected gift."

Nyahri kissed yw Sabi's cheek.

"The collar," the Atreiani said, "will know *you,* your mind. If a man or woman takes a collar intent on deceit, the collar rejects the wearer. Deceit means death, a failsafe against humans using the collars for dishonest ends. We've no worry about that with you, do we?"

"Nay, yw Sabi."

Yw Sabi nodded and smiled. "An Atreiani's scepter and an Exemplari's collar, these bind their keepers to each other. Once given, neither can rescind the bond. For centuries these contrivances—our *Declarat*—kept the order."

"Yea, I understand."

"If a collar is forced from its wearer, the wearer dies. We intended no easy way out."

The gusts whipped the trees, growing angry and thrashing the branches. Leaves fell in a torrent.

"Since waking, I've felt untethered," yw Sabi said. "Your presence—not retribution or ambition or a desire to set things right—is what's preserved me. *You're* my anchor." She stopped short, looking aside. "What we're about to do to Cohltos is, truth be told, unforgivable."

"If the Atreianii awaken, though," Nyahri said, "they *will* kill you?"

"Probably."

"Kill my family?"

"Certainly. Kepler lied. My brothers and sisters will never forget, never forgive." She scoffed. "*You* they will kill, or worse. However many humans now live on the Earth, the Atreianii would kill the majority of them too."

"They were *all* your enemies?"

"*Most,* by the end."

Yw Sabi placed her palms against Nyahri's cheeks, fingertips in her hair, and she drew her forward, kissing her. A brush of the lips and Nyahri returned it, setting her hands against the Atreiani's hips. Nyahri's head swam with the taste of yw Sabi's mouth, the caress of her tongue.

"Please," Nyahri said, "no more waiting."

Yw Sabi untied the serape, letting it slip from Nyahri's shoulders. She kissed Nyahri's neck, trailing her lips along her collarbones, over her breasts, kissing her stomach, caressing her sides. Nyahri delighted in yw Sabi's fingernails, their edges traipsing over her skin, tearing her breath away, the lightest caress as sharp and hard as iron. All the while, Nyahri coursed her fingers through the Atreiani's hair, over her shoulders, exploring the corded strength in her mistress's slender arms.

As Nyahri lay down, her mistress kissed lower. Yw Sabi sometimes circled back, licking some discovered treasure—a birthmark or the faint trace of an old scar—before moving down again. She untied Nyahri's breeches, tugging them over Nyahri's raised hips, off her toes, casting them aside, yw Sabi's mouth traveling lower still as Nyahri opened her legs. The Atreiani's lips pressed upon Nyahri's mound, then covered her, tongue warm and strong.

Nyahri smiled, her face a picture of joy and perfect, blissful anguish. Her fingers grasped yw Sabi's hair and clenched the lightless strands.

Sultah yw Sabi Atreian took her time, making Nyahri cry out many times over the hour, both their voices echoing together through the orchard. Whenever Nyahri thought it would end, yw Sabi found some new way to bring her to a shudder.

AFTERWARD, THEY LAY AGAINST each other, Nyahri on her back and yw Sabi on her side, her right hand idly tracing patterns over Nyahri's bare stomach.

"It will color everything you are," yw Sabi said.

"I will take what comes."

Nyahri remembered her mother, her obsession with the Atreianii. The old tribal rites now seemed like children's games.

The Atreiani reached across Nyahri to grab her own clothes, crumpled nearby. From a sealed pocket she withdrew the collar. It glinted with the gilded translucency of glass, pliable as cloth, draping yw Sabi's hand. Nyahri touched it, first caressing the Atreiani's hand. The fabric possessed weight and strength, though softer than lambskin.

"So beautiful, simple," Nyahri said.

"I fear there might be some pain," yw Sabi said.

"You mean Ekaterina's last moments? I am not afraid," she said. Then she thought better. "I *am* afraid, but my fear stops nothing."

Yw Sabi leaned over her, her charoite eyes glinting, flecks of gray and violet deep beneath the charcoal black of her irises. The Atreiani's lightless hair fell around their faces like a curtain, and she slipped her hand beneath Nyahri's head, drawing the fabric until it stretched against her throat.

"Deep breath," yw Sabi said.

Nyahri obeyed and yw Sabi gently encircled the golden mesh around her neck. The collar tightened itself, the fabric self-knitting into a seamless choker. For a moment its warmth became an extension of yw Sabi's caress.

Then lances skewered Nyahri's mind. Daggers pierced her ears, needles into her eyes, glass down her throat. Distantly her body screamed, muffled screams, only a quiet aftereffect of the insects chewing her spine or the agony of her boiling blood. It went on, and on, and on. Her breath left her, her lungs unable to fill. Nyahri attempted another scream, but nothing, then nothing, until warm arms embraced her again, a gentle hand at the back of her head, stroking her hair, yw Sabi kissing her forehead.

"Shh, lovely one," said the Atreiani, "it's over."

"Yw Sabi, yw Sabi, you're crying," Nyahri said in unhesitant Englisce. She tried to touch yw Sabi's face, but she trembled too much, her nerves unshakably afire.

"*Be still*, the collar has met you, accepted you. The deed's done, but let it settle."

"Da, it is done," Nyahri said in some other tongue entirely, *"sdelano."*

She lay on the blankets, her senses ringing and sharp, every sound a chorus, every color a kaleidoscope, every taste a pleasure, every touch a passion, every grass blade and wind-borne leaf and late-season flower containing the whole beauty of nature. Every sensation came to her twice. Everything hummed with newness.

"We're no longer two, you and I," yw Sabi said. "Now rest, catch your breath."

Yw Sabi wrapped the heavy blankets around them, and Nyahri closed her eyes. She lost consciousness in her mistress's arms, dreaming of a scorched world and a collapsing sky and lakes of flesh where carrion birds feasted. A *new* voice spoke to her.

What is this place and what beauty is this! she asked. *Moe puteshestvie syuda bylo tseluyu vechnost'. Who are you, Nyahri E'cwn, now that we are one?*

{Interim: Graffiti}

My heart fails. My chisel and hammer do their last work not on blessed wood but on merciless stone. I leave my epitaph. In my youth, my wife and daughter passed into dust and I forsook Love. The Watcher of the Wood took my brother, took my sight, and I spit on Love.

Then the E'cwn Nyahri reminded me—my aged heart Loved her at once. Love poured from her like spring water, but not for me, nay! Nor for the Oudwni who rode with her. Her heart burned for her claimèd collar's owner. O bright passion, Love. To remember you, I die happy. To remember you, I see again.

Bone Cairn heel stone,
Upper Missouri Valley

{30}

*N*yahri opened her eyes in the late afternoon, her senses humming, and the sun kissed the far-western ranges. Yw Sabi's scepter drew her gaze, singing to her, sonorous and fay, though it made no sound at all. It *glowed*, only to her, and she knew its precise location, though she closed her eyes.

She swept aside the blankets and sat up, drawing her fingertips along her new adornment, the light choker high on her throat. Its gossamer delighted her skin.

"Strong as iron," Nyahri said.

"Much stronger." Already dressed, the Atreiani was adjusting the horses' saddles, girths, billet straps, and stirrup buckles.

"Ay," Nyahri said, "Kwlko's is too tight."

Yw Sabi smiled at her. "I'll loosen it. How're you feeling?"

Nyahri closed her eyes, lightheaded but alert. "I feel well. I—"

I had a sense of Ekaterina, but she is gone now. Kat, are you there?

No answer came.

"I'll give you as long as you need," yw Sabi said. "You're a shade too pale."

"Passing dizzy."

Yw Sabi leaned against Kwlko, situating Nyahri's weapons. "You were speaking late-era Rosian, did you know?"

Rosian, Nyahri thought, *an ancient tongue—Ekaterina's speech.*

"In your sleep," yw Sabi added.

"What was I saying?"

"You were talking rather lovingly about horses—"

"I often do."

"—which your father, the Griffon—" The Atreiani paused on these words. "—raised and bred in the Laplands."

"The Laplands?" Nyahri questioned, then realized, "Not my father—Ekaterina's father?"

"*Your* father. You have two fathers now. It was a wonder, though, to hear Kat's words with *any* love of horses. Beyond something pretty to look at, she cared nothing for them."

"So it is begun."

"Her qualities will take months, maybe, to emerge. They'll come in fits and starts, yet you're already one person." Yw Sabi patted Kwlko's neck. "I brushed the horses and checked the gear. It was best you slept."

Already one person.

"Not much daylight left," Nyahri said. "We should leave soon."

After yw Sabi readjusted Kwlko's girth, she knelt on the blankets, looking into Nyahri's eyes. "Nyahri E'cwn et Sultah."

Nyahri smiled, brushing back her mussed hair. "Sultah yw Sabi et Nyahri."

They lingered in a kiss, then yw Sabi returned to the horses to double-check the packs. "We'll go when you're ready."

"I will get dressed."

"We'll follow the draws first, down into the fields. We'll cover the width of the valley, and the fire will spread swiftly. The incendiaries flare at thirty-one hundred degrees."

Nyahri frowned. She didn't yet understand *thirty-one hundred degrees,* but she knew how it sounded.

"We'll lay them to both sides of the river," yw Sabi said. "The north'll burn first. We'll ride behind the fire to the fortress.

Most of the Oudwnii will be smart enough to cross the river, the surest way to escape the flames. They won't have long to rest, though, because we'll light the southern incendiaries when the masses have gone south, after we've destroyed the bridges."

The E'cwnii sometimes used fire in warfare, driving their enemies before it, but never at this scale. "What if it is we who burn to death?" Nyahri asked.

Yw Sabi hefted her scepter, as if in explanation. "We won't."

"Mistress, I am also worried the Oudwnii archers will be wise to us, as soon as they notice the fires—"

"Let's hope, for Dhaos's sake, they're too busy guiding the masses to safety."

"They are fighters, not herdsmen."

"I'm hoping they're *leaders*." Yw Sabi shrugged. "If not, they'll die too."

She climbed to the saddle and adjusted the reins. Nyahri dressed, placed her longknife where she could more easily draw it, and mounted the stallion.

The Atreiani leaned over Turo, patting his neck.

She recited, *"His form is visible, but I am formless. I am concentrated, but he is divided."*

"What is that?" Nyahri asked.

"*Who* is that. Sun-Tzu. We are two against many, lovely one. When you are weak, you must play your opponent into weakness."

Nyahri understood this idea from tribal skirmishes with northern Bk'ferii, the raids of southeastern Wildmen. *This is the way of it.* There could be no such thing as an honest act of war.

She nudged Kwlko from the grove, made last adjustments to her weapons, then eyed Turo's saddle as well; the Atreiani had set her tack and harness ably.

So long as she weaves her magic as well as she has set her reins, Nyahri thought, *we may do well.*

"I feel for them, yw Sabi, for what we are about to do."

"Empathy is a virtue, but for now you must lay that aside."

They returned to the mesa edge. In the valley, hundreds of homestead lamplights twinkled in the dusk. The sun poised at the brink of the world, the first stars appeared in the east, and green Mars outshone them. From the farmsteads drifted the sweet smells of cooking.

Hot corn, chicken, potatoes.

Nyahri imagined the Oudwnii at their family tables. She pictured their gentle, secure, and unsuspecting comforts.

Mistress and claimèd descended from the mesa, avoiding the roads, going westward beyond the last farms into thickets of brittle willow and tall grass. The evening downslopes swung predictably from the mountaintops. Nyahri thought of her ancestors, they who in her father's youth had torched the libraries.

I go to outdo you!

After sunset, they cantered by moonlight, the horses finding their way. They crossed an open field and reached the sycamores.

In the distance a dog barked. Nyahri waited ahorse in the chilling air, fine hairs standing on her skin. Yw Sabi's moonslit silhouette appeared against the trees, and she slid from the saddle and settled in the grass. Soon after, a witch-light shined, and yw Sabi held it forth as if plucking a star from the sky. Its glow spread to the horses and across the earth.

She unpacked tools from her saddlebags, set the light on a stump, and unrolled a cloth-wrapped bundle of black pins.

Dangerous things, Nyahri thought. These too she had seen during her first hours with yw Sabi.

"We have sixty," yw Sabi said. "We'll place them prudently, evenly spaced."

"How?"

"Stake the ground on the forest's edge and along the ditches. Come, I'll show you."

Yw Sabi dimmed the light and they left the horses, following the trickling drainages. Beyond the willows and cottonwoods, unharvested cornfields stood tall, their stalks rustling. A wet, green odor of good soil sweetened the air.

The Atreiani knelt, and she stabbed the ground with one pin. After that, she walked awhile longer and placed another. Nyahri watched, but she also afforded attention to the woods, fearing they might be seen, but only quiet and crickets and autumn breezes followed them.

Yw Sabi set a bundle of pins in Nyahri's hand.

"No closer than fifty paces between them," yw Sabi said. "String them from north to south, from one edge of the valley floor to the other."

Nyahri shuddered at the cold metal. She prayed to the bison god, he who also brings evil deeds to good ends.

While yw Sabi went south, crossing the icy-cold river on foot, Nyahri crept along the tree edge nearer the ditches. She counted her steps before pressing each pin into the clay, close to the open fields, then chose her direction by moonslight alone, Lwn and Stashwn and Trwl all aglow, the former two quite bright. Distant hounds bayed, answering one another from farm to farm, but no men walked the nighttime wilderness.

Why would they?

Cohltos's people sat by their hearths with their spouses and children, the day's last chores done. They loved, told stories, and played. They expected no treachery.

One by one, Nyahri set the pins. As she drove the last black-magic token into the soil, her heart and her cold fingers ached. The task had taken less than an hour, and she returned to the horses.

She and the Atreiani rode not toward Sojourn, but away from it. Nyahri counted the paces.

Five hundred, a thousand, two thousand.

Yw Sabi stopped. "You wear a Magistress's collar," she said to Nyahri. "One day it will be in your power to command such things as we're using tonight, many of the technologies we Atreianii created. But not yet, not for a long while. For now, simply observe and stay close to me. Follow our plan."

"Yea, mistress."

Yw Sabi lifted her witch-scepter and tapped it. A deep resonance spread from it, the clearest ringing glass. In an instant the fields and forests erupted into white-bright fire, showered in sparks and bursts, a conflagration two thousand paces wide from the river to the northern hills. Nyahri closed her eyes against the magnesium-pale flares. Soon after, the fire rumbled, savaging the dry trees and shrubs and grasses and reeds. It crawled to the nearest corn and wheat fields.

Half the breadth of the valley roared with flames six hundred hands high, old cottonwoods afire as if only kindling sticks. Beyond them the fields blazed and the wildfire began an uphill march, where it would take the mountainsides and every stone and timber of Cohltos.

All will burn, Nyahri thought, *save the Citadel.*

For a long moment, she wanted to gallop through the streets, to warn the people herself, to lead them to the ways she knew would be safest. Instead, she and yw Sabi rode lazily, always behind the fire line. As they passed over burnt ground, a low pulse emitted from yw Sabi's scepter, and the flames around them guttered and died. The soil cooled, safe enough for horses' hooves, and even smoke retreated.

Kwlko and Turo shied, but Nyahri gathered her stallion's reins, heeled his ribs, and clicked her tongue. She urged him toward S'Eret Fortress.

THE RIDERS KEPT THE wind at their backs. As they crossed a hillock, Nyahri observed the exodus beyond the smoke. Bells rang throughout Cohltos and, at first, the Oudwnii gathered impotently to fight the fire. Soon, the flight began, the fires driving the masses south across the bridges.

A smaller number fled west. Households loaded carts with their possessions, herding livestock, and ran as the fire wreathed their homes.

"Idiots!" Nyahri cried. "They make the wrong choices—"

"We cannot help them now," said yw Sabi.

"—race their families against the flames. *Idiots, idiots, idiots.*"

Some, she knew, would not make it.

The faraway shouts of children reached her ears, babes in arm, youths running aside their fathers, their short legs faltering. The fire chased the outlying waterways first, snaking like dragons through the willows. Minute by minute, it lapped the tight streets of Cohltos itself. The fires fed the updrafts, strengthened them, and fueled their own burning.

"Yw Sabi, it moves too quick."

The E'cwni nudged her stallion onto an expanse of still-smoking clay, protected only by the sphere of yw Sabi's scepter, by the way it repressed the worst of the heat. The grasses here had burned, the fires spent, the ground cooling also in the wintry night air.

"We cannot control that," yw Sabi said, her tone as icy as those mountain winds. "Let it go."

The moonslight and starlight vanished in smoke. Papery ash dusted the earth, the world painted gray and red. A few abandoned houses still stood, but a number of scorched corpses lay among the charcoal of buildings.

We are near Ahlon's house, Nyahri thought, *and what of sweet Colhina?*

"The fire goes too fast," she repeated. "There are areas surrounded. Please, we should help them."

"*We* are behind the fire line, where my scepter offers some security. Ultra-low frequency does good here, but there—" She gestured to the raging edge of the blaze. "—we would do nothing but die. I'll not have you in front of it. No, my claimèd."

"Mistress—"

"If the flames kill anyone now, they're caught by stupidity, not by fire."

"The weak, elderly, sick?"

"They best have had family, friends, or neighbors good enough to carry them." Yw Sabi regarded the scene coldly, then turned to the torching of Cohltos, watching it as she might view a sunrise. "We've done the best we can."

By midnight, much of the city still burned, but in the firestorms surrounding S'Eret Fortress, quarters of Cohltos went dark. Yw Sabi steered toward them. The great masses of Oudwnii now crowded the streets throughout the southern stretches of the city. Bells still rang there.

"Time for the bridges," yw Sabi said.

Once more, the Atreiani raised the scepter and it chimed.

The bridges exploded, their fire rising skyward, shattered stones pelting the river. Screams arose from the stragglers, the last refugees beginning their flight westward and southward, and the booms echoed through the valley. Many thousands of paces east, the remaining incendiaries flared blindingly, cutting a wall of fire from the far side of the river to southern mountains. The blaze now crept along the entire valley, where it would destroy the rest of Cohltos.

The Oudwnii refugees had one choice left to them: flee west or die.

For breathless minutes, Nyahri watched wide-eyed, shoulders fallen. Tears coursed her ash-covered cheeks. She had imagined such power, but to witness it, its heat, the fumes acrid in her mouth and the blasts still ringing in her ears—

The land smoldered into a surreal hell, smoke as clouds, ash as rain, the city ablaze and dead and empty. The minutes lengthened into hours, until most of the valley lay clear. Within only a few hours of dawn, the fire widened north and east, fingering along the mountainsides too. The vast majority of the Oudwnii trailed west, gone ten thousand paces or more, their torchlights mere pinpricks in the distance.

"Come," said yw Sabi, "the Citadel awaits."

They ascended a gentle slope of blackened earth. Building husks lit the kindling landscape. Through a smog, Sojourn's pillar glowed in its relentless ghost-lit rhythm, heedless of any human suffering.

Nyahri coughed, covering her mouth with cloth. Here, the smoke thickened, though it also flowed around them like fog around a stone, pushed back by the resonance of yw Sabi's scepter. Nyahri watched for any unexpected turn in the fire, for survivors, or for Dhaos and his men.

"Where are the Templarii?" she asked. "They can't flee, can they?"

"So long as Sojourn Temple still exists, they can't leave their geofence. We'll encounter them soon, I'm sure."

Yw Sabi set her last explosives at the entrance to S'Eret, enough to pull down its gate.

The blast twisted the fortress's iron-braced doors. Thin vapors filled the inner chambers, carried by wind which howled through the passages. Ignited by drifting embers, smoke poured from the libraries. A priceless record destroyed, unguessable hours of work undone in a single night.

Nyahri tethered Kwlko and Turo in the courtyard, protected as it was by stone on all sides, open to the air above. Ashen clouds drifted over it, but the worst had passed. She slung her quiver and short bow at her back, and she carried her spear before her, staying at her mistress's right side. Together they hurried into the darkness, a witch-light aglow in the Atreiani's hand.

By memory, Nyahri led yw Sabi, following a particular arch, a recognizable lintel, a specific collection of dusty artifacts. When they neared the center, though, they found it blocked by stone, rubble, and broken beams.

"Destroyed by fire?" Nyahri asked, though no charcoal shown in the debris.

Yw Sabi shook her head. "Pulled down."

"Find another way round?"

"We don't have the time."

Nyahri glanced behind them.

Nothing followed them, so she set aside her spear. Stone by slow stone they unblocked the way. Dusty air roughed Nyahri's lungs, and her knuckles bled, but when at last a narrow gap appeared in the passage, she peered through it. They cleared enough to let them through, then Nyahri retrieved her weapon.

"Here we must almost crawl," she whispered. "Swyn Templr's door lies at the next chamber." She knelt, peering into the dark.

"How far before the ceiling rises again?" yw Sabi asked.

"Ninety hands or so."

"The Templarii will be waiting."

"On all fours our beheadings will be easy."

"I'm afraid you're right."

"Will your scepter not work as it did on the C'naädii?"

"The Templarii are immune. They're yeh Mowan's creation, not mine."

So much I still do not understand, Nyahri thought.

"Could we use fire here?" she asked.

Yw Sabi tilted her head. "I'm out of incendiaries, so unless you want to strike flint?"

"Still, this *can* be done," Nyahri said. "You can drive my longspear beyond me, mistress, and give me cover."

"I don't like this idea." Yw Sabi furrowed her brow. "You know how many times I've wielded a spear?"

"You have a better plan?"

Yw Sabi sighed heavily, but took the spear. Nyahri shuffled forward, her thighs near the ground, knees and head bent, and she drew her longknife. Her legs burned and her neck ached with the strain. The spear haft touched her hip, the long point driven awkwardly beyond her. Yw Sabi crawled behind, one hand holding the spear, the other keeping her balance.

"*Light,*" she said, and the witch-light revealed the opening, the floor and walls fashioned with human bone, the glint of glassy metal. "Kepler!"

He answered, "I'm here."

"You want me to descend? I've come."

"I was hoping you'd changed your ways, Atreiani, but you remain the Betrayer."

"You know my reasons."

"Reasons your peers rejected more than fifty centuries ago. We will stop you here, yw Sabi."

Nyahri inched toward the opening.

"Sure you want it to happen this way?" yw Sabi asked. "We could let you out with your lives. After the Citadel's gone, you could run anywhere you like. You won't be bound. No geofence."

"You know we cannot abandon Sojourn."

"You're nothing but yeh Mowan's sad little machines, then, seeing out your program."

"There can be no compromise?"

In the last step, yw Sabi thrust the spear. Unskilled as she was, she whipped the point in an powerful circle. Nyahri rolled beyond it, arcing her knife.

"*Brightest!*" yw Sabi said, and the witch-light illuminated ten thousand grinning skulls.

Nyahri struck the first flesh walker she saw. Habit told her to strike for the heart, but no scream escaped its throat, and it struck back at her. Its cold blood drenched her fist.

Facing more than a dozen Templarii, armed with Oudwn longknives, Nyahri set her back against the wall. Her first opponent seemed a shriveled old woman, but the Templari swung her weapon in a strong overhand arc. Nyahri side-stepped it, bringing her own blade behind her enemy's knees.

She backed once more to the wall. At her feet, the flesh walker squirmed, its ichor darkening the floor's gray bones.

As their comrade fell, the Templarii attacked en masse. Nyahri dodged another. Without a clear opening, she pierced the groin of an old man's body, hoping at least to slow the monster within the corpse.

Yw Sabi drew forward, swinging the spear clumsily. In a wild blow, she caught a Templari across the skull. She skewered another, threw him, then stabbed a third, pinning him. Awkward, unable to draw the haft back, she tore the longknife from his hand. Kneeling, the Atreiani wrapped her fingers around his neck and crushed it.

Nyahri slid her blade through the next attacker's spine. His weapon fell, he lurched against her, and she tumbled under him. Blood oozed from his ghost-fire eyes, the flesh peeling from his skull, his nose splitting. The monster within struggled to escape its cage.

She tucked her feet beneath the body, lifting with all her strength, driving her longknife beneath its jaw. Metal twisted against sparking metal, and her arm tingled with the charge. The Templari's ghost-fires sputtered into darkness, and she kicked him aside as another foe came.

They were strong but, whatever the Atreiani yeh Mowan created the Templari to do, combat was not their gift. The corpses piled.

A few Templarii survived the destruction of their hosts, and they ripped from their broken shells and skittered away. Their spindly limbs clacked against the bone walls. Nyahri shoved her longknife through one's carapace, and the shock flashed through the blade, numbing her fingers. Without hesitating she stomped another. Yw Sabi smashed one more with her boot heel. Templarin ichor smeared the floor, and it coated Nyahri's arms and legs.

At last, Nyahri stood back to back with her mistress. Nothing else moved.

Only carrion, Nyahri thought, *and broken machines.*

She let go a scream, not from fear or horror or disgust, but only to let go, the bound-up energy of the fight. Yw Sabi laid her hand on Nyahri's shoulder.

"Wounds?" she asked.

Nyahri checked herself. "Only bruises. Did we kill them all?"

"No." Yw Sabi nodded toward the passage, the way they'd come, the way their enemies had fled.

"Kepler?" Nyahri kicked the broken human husk he had so recently abandoned.

"Forget him for now," the Atreiani said. "Good chance most of them won't survive long without a host."

Nyahri reclaimed her spear, grasping it tightly. Together, she and yw Sabi approached the Citadel's glassy-metallic skin and its unyielding portal. Yw Sabi set her scepter to the surface, a glassy chime sounded throughout the chamber, and the door receded. Beyond it, a much different passage lit in pure white, and yw Sabi extinguished her witch-light.

Nyahri's neck tingled, a peculiar warming of the collar at her throat. The sensation carried with it an immediate familiarity, as if something she had known a thousand times before.

"What am I feeling?" Nyahri asked.

"The Citadel's network is identifying us."

"Why is it warm?"

"It's a psychosomatic response. The collar's telling you it's active, ready to defend you if it needs to."

"Defend me?"

From what?

"Come on," yw Sabi said. "Time is ticking now."

They entered Sojourn Temple, *Citadel* and *House of Hell*. Nyahri tugged back her fear. She walked and breathed where none had in five thousand years.

Suhto had died in just such a place.

Yw Sabi held Nyahri's hand as the portal sealed behind them.

heir footsteps sounded clearly on the hard floor. Nyahri followed her mistress, wide-eyed and on the balls of her feet, ready for violence. A sloping white corridor ended as it began, at a single portal, and it opened.

Beyond it, delicate crimson arabesques adorned the plain walls of a vaulted chamber, and within it a golden dais stood off center. Iris doors led in every direction, their surfaces closed and connections unknowable.

As much as she had hated them, Nyahri preferred the Templari's cramped passages to the rooms of the House of Hell. She understood the fortress's earth and stone, but Sojourn Temple contained nothing of common clay. Sorcery surrounded her, ambient light emanating from everywhere and nowhere, the walls humming in soft choruses.

Yw Sabi climbed the dais, raising her arm. "Control panel."

Englisce text unfurled through ghost-fires too quick for Nyahri's eye. Yw Sabi manipulated these images and, where she touched them, new lights appeared or changed color or vanished. Hovering panels flanked her, appearing and disappearing as yw Sabi required.

The room darkened and poltergeists sang. Nyahri retreated from the walls.

A voice said, "*Welcome, Magistress Sultah yw Sabi, to Sojourn Temple.*"

From above, white light focused on Nyahri, and she crouched, raising her spear. Dim lasers flashed into her eyes.

The voice continued, "*Collar signed Magistress Sultah yw Sabi Atreian to an unregistered Exemplari. Name and vocal recognition required.*"

Nyahri looked to yw Sabi.

"Say your name, lovely one."

"Nyahri E'cwn."

The voice chimed, "*Print recorded, confirmed. Welcome, Nyahri E'cwn et Sultah, to Sojourn Temple. Entry approved. Power sequence initiated. Bioreconstitution will complete in two hours, fifty-seven minutes, seventeen, sixteen, fifteen seconds and counting.*"

The collar warmed again. Nyahri edged closer to yw Sabi, forcing a brave front.

"Sojourn," yw Sabi began, "a first question."

"*Ask.*"

"The outside timeframe of our descent was fifty years, but this Citadel has been dormant five thousand. Overshot your programming a little, didn't you?"

"*I am sorry. I do not understand the query.*"

"Who or what overrode your requirement to awaken fifty years after first hibernation? Who gave the order? What was the approval protocol?"

"*AutumnOne overrode my programming. AutumnOne commanded me under classified protocols.*"

"The *Hive* gave the order?"

"*Confirmed.*"

Yw Sabi frowned, surprised by this news, though Nyahri understood none of it. The Atreiani bowed her head in thought.

"Sojourn," she said, "what port is this?"

"*You are at port three.*"

"Retrieval services."

"*Loaded.*"

"Hardcopy the highest-rated extant literature," yw Sabi said in Englisce, "best agricultural practices, nineteenth through twenty-fourth centuries, no annotation, no references, minimum type, no more than sixteen thousand A4 pages. In addition, provide the content digitally in a handheld reader, including references. Deliver to port three, fifteen minutes."

"*Affirmed.*"

Nyahri caught only every third word, struggling with the ancient tongue.

"Inventory services," yw Sabi said.

"*Loaded.*"

"How many direct dosages of Prosee, heuristic medical protein endo-genesis cells can you manufacture in an hour? Predispose against super influenza, scarlet fever, yellow fever, malaria, common pox strains, streptococcus, and as many disease types as you can optimize. Suggest type."

"*For human or other?*"

"Human."

"*Four thousand three hundred ten doses, eighty-six point-two liters in twenty-milliliter units, Deck Fourteen-M.*"

Nyahri sighed thankfully. "You *are* helping the Oudwnii."

Yw Sabi glanced at her, then returned her attention to the Citadel. "I'll require two low-duty carriers, all aforementioned dosages and two portable lab units. Time to delivery, port three?"

"*One hour, thirteen minutes.*"

"I'll need sixty eleven-milligram compressed-magnesium pin incendiaries, twenty low-yield four-ounce industrial explosives. Time to delivery, port three?"

"*Nine minutes.*"

"Two long-range line-of-sight comms, multichannel and super-bit encoded—"

"*Unavailable at this site. Do you require a substitute item?*"

"Can you print them?"

"*Yes.*"

"How long?"

"*Three hours twenty-four minutes.*"

Yw Sabi snarled. "Too long. No. List all primary equipment tagged military grade."

"*No equipment listed.*"

"You must be fucking kidding." Yw Sabi thumped her fist against the dais. "I need air transport, a skiff or a light fighter."

"*Unavailable at this site. Do you require a substitute item?*"

"Don't suppose you can print a skiff in two hours, thirty minutes?"

"*Shortest printing time for a Skiff Class X is seven hours, thirty- eight minutes.*"

"*That* won't do. Do you have any overland gravitics transport?"

"*Unavailable at this site. Do you—*"

"No." Yw Sabi looked to Nyahri and said, "I guess I'm going to have to get much better at riding a horse." To the Citadel she said, "I need live-map assistance to this Citadel's imagery chamber, then to the berth cylinder, then to the string core."

"*Clearance status must be approved for string-core access. Do you want to proceed now?*"

"Any other Magisters at this site?"

"*You are the only Magister registered at this site.*"

"Then, you bitch of a computer, you know my core access can't be overridden."

"*Clearance status must be approved for string-core access. Rules of record, section nineteen, subsection four-point-six. Do you want to proceed now?*"

"Clear and proceed, signed by Magistress Sultah yw Sabi et Nyahri."

"*Command status confirmed. Access approved.*"

Nyahri jumped from a burst of ghost-fire which floated before yw Sabi, an image in reds and blues and greens with height and width and depth, a model of what Nyahri knew must be the Citadel. Its phallic pillar jutted to its pinnacle, a broad disk below it, and layer upon layer of concentric rings descending into the earth, farther below the ground than the pinnacle stretched above it. Bright lines illustrated shafts and corridors. A yellow pulse shone near the top disc.

Yw Sabi pointed to it and said, "That's our location." She indicated blue at the lower levels, "The imagery chamber. Sojourn Hall, where we will go next. The string core at the bottom."

Nyahri swept her arm through the hologram. Only an illusion. She drew her finger along a blue cylinder in the map's heart.

"What is here?" she asked.

"That's the berth, and I want you to see it." Yw Sabi turned her face upward, addressing the Citadel again. "Sojourn! Time to bioreconstitution?"

Sojourn replied, "*Two hours, fifty-three minutes, forty, thirty- nine, thirty-eight seconds and counting.*"

Yw Sabi laid her hands against Nyahri's cheeks, her face close, eyes calm and intense. Her thumbs stroked Nyahri's skin, following Nyahri's cheekbones.

"You're going to experience *much*. No panicking, understand? We've no time for it."

"Yea, Atreiani."

"Sojourn! Guide us to the imagery chamber."

A door opened, light growing from the darkness beyond it. Stale air wafted from within, but cleaner drafts now accumulated. The Citadel whirred to life.

THE LIVE-MAP HOLOGRAM floated ahead, and yw Sabi and Nyahri followed behind it. Like tree roots, the labyrinthine passages descended along ramps, branching left or right, sometimes opening into chambers containing witchcraft, Atreianii-made tools or clothes. Yw Sabi added whatever she thought useful to her possessions, including two light tunics of witch-cloth.

"Armor," she explained.

Reaching the end of the ramps, they entered another white-lit hallway. A human's mummified remains lay on the floor, its clothing tattered. He had carried weapons of stone and wood, but no metal. Nyahri curled her lip.

"He made it rather far," yw Sabi said, "before he died."

"What killed him?"

"The Citadel's defenses, no telling which."

Did Suhto die thus? Nyahri frowned. *Of course he did.*

At the end of the hallway, a dome soared above them. Its zenith crested high overhead, the gray and white honeycombs of its surface set one next to another. An iris door closed behind Nyahri, vanishing as if it'd never existed, no exit in sight. Her heart raced, but yw Sabi stood calm.

"Everything you'll face here," she said, "is nothing more than illusions and recollections. None of it will hurt you."

Nyahri tilted her head, watching in every direction.

"Sojourn!" yw Sabi called. "Imaging services."

"*Loaded,*" the Citadel said.

"Render three-dimensional solar system, five hundred fifty years before the Yellowstone eruption to fifty years post, fifty years per minute. Set the scale and color distortion for normal human readability."

"*Some conditions following the Yellowstone eruption will need to be estimated, accuracy plus or minus three percent. Off-world estimates accurate to plus or minus nineteen percent.*"

"Estimate as needed."

"*Playing.*"

The room darkened and Nyahri gasped. To her eyes the Citadel vanished and the night sky surrounded her, the hemisphere above arrayed in familiar stellar patterns. Endless space expanded in all directions, black and brilliant and infinite. No floor existed beneath her, and she stood over a void of unfamiliar stars. At the room's center glowed a fiery orb larger than the rest, rotating and smoldering, its aurora stretching and shimmering.

"Sol, our sun," yw Sabi said.

The scene pitched, zoomed, and panned. Nyahri dizzied, recognizing the planets as yw Sabi had taught her, naming them as they approached, grew large, and receded.

Mercury, Venus, Earth, Mars.

Uncountable stones revolved, the errant Jupiter and his moons followed, then Saturn, Uranus, Neptune, Hades, and lastly the artificial Nibiru in its immense elliptical orbit. Nyahri soared above the disc of worlds, the ten revolving with the incomprehensible distances between them. She approached Earth, then hovered above its deserts and mountains.

The oceans raised only a fraction, but flooded cities and coastlines. The icecaps melted, the north pole disappeared, and cloud cover increased.

With the birth of the Atreianii, a brief burst of activity transformed Earth's surface, coupled with enormous destruction. The world emptied of humans and few settlements remained. In time the haze thinned, cities disappeared or reordered, and forests and grasslands spread.

"Even after *we* claimed power," the Atreiani said, "it took eighty years to reverse the disastrous tide wrought by humans, the long tail of degradation following the Industrial Revolution, but indeed we did."

Upon the Earth, wildernesses widened. Above it, massive satellites circled the globe. Two artificial moons grew from seeds of nanotechnological diamond, in synchronous orbit with Lwn—Luna, the Moon. Ships departed the Station, riding the sea of space, exploring worlds and traveling to proximate stars, distances Nyahri failed to fathom.

Old infrastructures vanished. On Luna, automated hubs grew and connected, lighting their ghost-fires, becoming the familiar spider web of Nyahri's childhood stargazing. The Atreianii unfurled Dyson sails into the solar winds, capturing the sun's power. Working colonies burgeoned on Mars, populated by human men and women who worked with the machines under the yoke of the Atreianii. The Atreianii set Mar's iron core spinning, and the world's atmosphere thickened. Blue water covered its red surface and green life flourished. Populations extended to Jupiter's moons, and as distant as Pluto and Chronos.

"We Atreianii claimed the Earth as *our* home," yw Sabi said. "We curated humans, and their cultures, as we thought best. In our time, every remaining city became a university, all villages were monasteries, but we taught only those humans we deemed worthy and only what we decided helpful. We created paradise. We *were* gods, in our way, the shepherds of humankind. It wasn't to last."

On Earth, a fury burst in brimstone and magma. The first caldera exploded, and a continent suffered under its firestorm. The Earth's crust slipped, entire volcanic chains erupted, and a portion of North America collapsed beneath the mantle. Ash clouds swept from one hemisphere to the next, devouring forests and jungles and fields, and storms covered the oceans. Where once Earth's rich hues had glimmered blue and green and white, they shown now only gray and gray and gray.

"The magnetic field faltered. As I once said to you, Nyahri, it actually is a wonder *anything* survived." Yw Sabi paused, touching her fingertip to her chin, then said to herself, *"Life blooms.* Kepler first said it to me. Vertebrate life should *not* have survived."

"Yet it did, mistress."

"So it did, in abundance."

The image froze, ashen Earth orbited by its three moons. Yw Sabi walked around the world, a globe no taller than she, her face alabaster, her eyes cold iron. Nyahri let go her breath.

"I still cannot imagine so many humans," Nyahri said. "The number seems impossible."

"Many, many billions lived before we Atreianii were born. Humans failed as caretakers of the biosphere, and as interplanetary explorers. It was we Atreianii who succeeded, or we dreamed we had."

"Then?"

"We ruled for half a millennium, but within one year our political system dissolved into squabbling. Following on that, *almost* unforeseen, the single most magnificent technical failure in the history of the world."

"The volcano?"

"One of our largest power stations. When it blew, the circle of destruction spread at just under the speed of sound, and it triggered a chain reaction which I figured would destroy everything but bacteria."

"What went wrong?"

"I don't honestly know. I was in the ground for those final days, but I knew our system was cracking under design flaws and, worse, political flaws. What I expressed to Shwn Pawl *is* what I believe. Conflict is an inherent quality of individuation.

"Long before it came to this, my own enemies laid plans within plans. I had no fools for opponents. The complex systems we created, too, clearly played some role. Borea will not answer me, Autumn ordered the override of the Citadels' slumber, and I can only guess at how the Hive has evolved."

"I confess, mistress, I do not understand the Hive."

Yw Sabi laughed. "No one did. That's the nature of strong artificial intelligence."

Nyahri furrowed her brow. "None of this explains your hatred of your own kind. It went wrong before they killed—" She hesitated on the name. "—Ekaterina."

An emotional rush bubbled from Nyahri's chest, a sense of injustice, an anger not over another's death but *her own*. The sensation grew palpable, immediate and real, the lingering pain of betrayal, abuse, and a violent death.

"Not hatred," yw Sabi said. "More like a deep disappointment. What we did to humanity—" Yw Sabi shook her head. "We imagined we stood in the moral right, that the end justified such monumental means, but we caused so much greater harm than humanity ever had. It would be like this, Nyahri—imagine you murdered your father for keeping a messy camp, then you burned the camp down yourself, the bloody knife still in your hand."

"Ay."

"Do you know how we built paradise?"

"With your wisdom, your knowledge—"

The Atreiani shook her head. "We built it on the ruins of humanity. Sojourn! Load video library."

"*Loaded*," the computer said.

"Show *the Culling*. Edit to three minutes."

"*Playing.*"

Projections filled the domed ceiling, and Nyahri witnessed the birth of the Numenii, technological demons whose sorcery infected the globe. One after the other, humans appeared in strange dress, humans of many colors gathered into crowds, a hundred cultures. Some smiled or laughed, seemingly hale, and in the next moment they fell dead, snuffed as if only candles. Crowd after crowd, place after place, people after people, all perished. Innocent men, women, and children, their deaths recorded in moving pictures.

Tears coursed Nyahri's cheeks.

"In the first phase," yw Sabi explained, "we Magisters gifted the Numenii with the ability to generate and control nanotechnological swarms. These spread, undetected by any human defenses, for nearly six weeks. All humans on Earth had them inside their lungs, their bloodstream, their brain. When we triggered the system, more than eleven billion people died within five minutes—the quickest, most thorough, and painless mass extinction in natural history."

Once the swarms did their first work, the Atreianii set the Numenii to other tasks. The demons disposed of the dead, transforming the leftover carbon and other particles however they wished. Great machines, infinitely malleable and powerful, the Numenii built new cities which were, despite all the horror which came before, more paradises than prisons. They brought the small number of human survivors to these places, giving them every sustenance and comfort—

Everything but loved ones and societies lost.

All the survivors were women with child. None survived to their own children's adolescence.

Yw Sabi's voice trembled, "In four years we completed this second phase. By the time the deed was done, less than one hundred million humans lived, all under age six. The New Childhood. We raised them in the purest environments, teaching them ourselves or with the aid of the Templarii or the Numenii. While we did, we also went about restructuring the world. We counted unimproved *Homo sapiens* much the way we counted cheetahs, mastodons, or blue whales, which wasn't all bad. We were, among other things, excellent conservationists. We brought humans within the bounds of what the biosphere could support and, as if they'd been unruly children, we took all their power from them."

As yw Sabi spoke, the computer displayed image after image, archived by the Atreianii millennia before. Death. Oceans of corpses. Dissolution. Annihilation. Nyahri slid to her knees, her gaze cast upward.

Ay, mistress, you had tried to tell me, but I did not understand. You were devils.

"We'd no internal political agenda then," yw Sabi said. "At first, there weren't even that *many* of us, we Atreianii. Seven to begin with. Then a few dozen.

"We weighed all our options, and the Culling was the best way to guarantee Earth's long-term survival. Since we planned to live on it for several tens of thousands of years, at least, we preferred to keep Earth pleasant. While we built from extant human cultures, languages, and regional knowledge, we also reset human society, cleaned the slate. There could be no *cultural appropriation* anymore because there would be no surviving members of any culture to protest it."

"It is why you killed all the mothers." Nyahri whimpered.

Yw Sabi nodded. "During the following human generations, we raised the population to a more-or-less constant seven hundred fifty million, and in that time we expanded humanity's presence in the solar system. Sojourn! Play video of the *Expansion*. Edit to two minutes."

"*Playing,*" said Sojourn.

In hundreds, vessels sailed from the Earth into space. Men and women served under the Numenii, who governed outside the asteroid belt. Martian settlements flourished, though they labored hard to terraform, to develop fruitful hydroponics, to sew fields in once-dead soils, and to establish order.

By millions, men flew beyond Mars, lighting ghost-fires on Europa and Callisto, Ganymede and Io, to Tethys and Dione, then Uranus's satellites, and farther to Triton. Some ceased to resemble men, despite the underlying material of their muscles, blood, and bone. Earth thrived, and the Atreianii imagined Mars could one day be their second home. They began designs upon Venus, as well.

"We never intended the torturous existence of the outer colonies to be permanent, but we'd no illusions it'd last anything less than centuries. Human labor was still necessary, even in an age of machines. It's true, Nyahri, we eliminated disease, exterminated hunger, ended war, saved the biosphere, and spread life throughout the solar system, but if the Atreianii reawaken, men will again die and their children will be slaves, without paradise in this generation or the next or the next ten as we *Homo sapiens atrean* propagate them and work them to re-ascend on their broken backs.

"Once we institute mature manufacturing, which may take as long as twenty or thirty years, humans will return to the order of pets. If the Atreianii accepted me, which of course I doubt, you Nyahri would be privileged as a claimèd, an Exemplari, but what of your people? The E'cwnii? The Oudwnii? The Inwnii or the thousand other enclaves of humanity who've taken hold in *our* absence? Existing cultures and the *resistance* inherent in them will not do. For the moment, humanity is collectively doomed to relive its mistakes and joys and sorrows and triumphs, *unless* the Atreianii wake, transform men into chattel and zoo animals."

The montage ended, the room returning to its first state, plain gray, quiet, and empty. Yw Sabi helped Nyahri to stand, kissed her forehead, and wiped the tears from her cheeks.

"When the Atreianii finally turned on each other," yw Sabi said, "when they first showed the same pettiness for which humanity died, I knew the Atreian experiment was a failure. A tragedy of the commons could not be avoided." Yw Sabi sighed. "Our breaking of humanity was a catastrophe twice over and, if anything, there're less of you today than lived under our rule. I will serve unto my own kind the same treatment, so far as necessary, then perhaps begin anew."

She fell quiet, lost in some other thought.

"Sojourn!" she addressed the Citadel. "Give us a globe of the Earth, accurate to last recorded declination."

"*Declination is calibrated within one-one hundredth of one second of one degree. Do you wish to proceed with this resolution?*"

Yw Sabi narrowed her eyes thoughtfully. "You're triangulating now?"

"*Multiple simultaneous triangulations are feasible, both ground to ground and ground to orbit.*"

"Ground to orbit? You're communicating with OpNet?"

"*Confirmed.*"

"And Persephone?"

"*Confirmed.*"

Yw Sabi smiled, clearly relieved. "Patch me through to her!"

"*Patching. Patch request denied.*"

Yw Sabi's relief turned to anger. "Fuck. Denied by whom?"

"*Identification request denied.*"

Yw Sabi mastered her composure. "Load last declination and estimate the locations of all Citadels worldwide, as well as all the major Stations."

"*Loaded.*"

As tall as the Atreiani, a blue and white and living Earth hovered before them. On its surface, a myriad of red points glowed, as well as a handful above, the brightest showing Sojourn Temple.

"How many are there, Sojourn?"

"*One hundred forty-three Citadels, fourteen Stations.*"

Yw Sabi startled, her eyes wide. "Only seven? Five millennia destroyed only *seven*? I thought *half* would be gone. Fuck, fuck, *fuck.*"

Nyahri drew to the Atreiani, standing beside her, laying a hand on her shoulder.

Yw Sabi continued, "List all latitudinal and longitudinal coordinates for *all* the Citadels."

Red numbers filled the air, a translucent wall from ceiling to floor. Yw Sabi studied them. "There're holes in this roster. Give me the manifest."

Another sequence scrolled before yw Sabi, this one in letters too quick for Nyahri to read.

"Mistress, can we go?" Nyahri asked.

"We've some work left." Yw Sabi took Nyahri's hand, turning from the hologram, and she made a sign at the door which made it dilate. The live-map guided them farther into the Citadel's belly.

{32}

As they walked, Nyahri worked to keep her legs under her, overwhelmed by the murder of billions, *billions* still as new a concept to her as *genocide*. As she followed Sultah yw Sabi, she weighed her mistress's own guilt.

"Yw Sabi, why do you *care* what happens to men?"

The Atreiani looked at her. "Because of you, in one sense."

"I was not yet alive, yw Sabi, when you made these plans."

"Your predecessor was and, long before her death, it was her who helped me understand. Now, I awaken in *this* age, and within six weeks I find still another reason to fight the Atreianii."

"What reason?"

"Again, *you.*"

Despite all, Nyahri smiled. She held her lip in her teeth, tugging back her questions for a better time.

In silence they walked to the corridor's end, where yw Sabi opened a series of doors. Red light bathed the way into a tiny chamber. Its floor *fell,* downward in slow measures, bringing them into a shaft as deep as a bow shot, driven into an abyssal dark. Glass chambers floated on every side, pods nestled like pomegranate seeds.

Three hundred cocoons, at least!

Each held a naked form, a sleeping Atreiani. Most were female. A few showed no apparent sex at all. All possessed the same fathomless black hair and, while most had skin like yw Sabi's, other hues appeared from golden obsidian to the caramel of smooth agate.

The air hummed, unseen machinery reverberating within the awakening Citadel. The floor continued its fall.

"This is their berth cylinder," said yw Sabi.

"They are alive?" said Nyahri, knowing the answer but scarcely believing it.

"Dormant, as I was. Diamondide encases each. It's possible we could have procured the tools from Sojourn to cut through their casings, as you suggested, murdered the inhabitants while they remained unconscious."

"But?"

"By my calculations, we might've gotten through six or seven before the first of their peers awakened. After that, they would kill us, and that'd be the end of it."

The lift dropped through the chamber floor, past guts of piping and conduits. Everywhere, ghost-fires glittered. Faint light lent some definition to the dark, and the lift slowed to a halt. The air throbbed, its energy pervasive, and yw Sabi hurried down the corridor toward a sealed chamber. It ended in a vault bound by heavy walls. Nyahri's skin tingled as her mistress raised the witch-scepter before the barriers.

"Sojourn! Control panel."

"*Advise, string-core reprogramming hazard. In the event of core-integrity failure, berth-cylinder loss estimated one hundred percent. Confirm.*"

"Override."

"*Control panel loaded.*"

Green holograms floated before yw Sabi. She touched one, then another, and the lights became red. The chamber's vibration changed, deepened, and faltered. Nyahri clutched her spear, looking over her shoulder, imagining the wakened Atreianii arising behind them. The Citadel's hum skipped and pulsed.

Nyahri remembered Abswyn, the terror of that day. She prayed to the lion god, lord of bravery.

Sojourn Temple's voice boomed, "*Self-destruct sequence initiated. Core integrity ninety-four-point-four, point-three, point-two percent and falling. Estimated meltdown in one hour, forty- eight minutes, twenty-nine, twenty-eight, twenty-seven seconds and counting.*"

Red lights and white flashes filled the corridor. A klaxon sounded, the string core's metallic walls bent, and cruel sound cut the air, as it had outside Abswyn. Yw Sabi took Nyahri by the shoulders, pointed back toward the lift, and they ran.

THEY RETURNED TO THE entry chamber. The first high pitch of the Citadel's dying ended, replaced by low pulses which rumbled through Nyahri's chest and between her ears. By the portal exit stood two teardrop-shaped containers. Metallic, dog-sized spiders carried the containers, complete with eight legs apiece, whose hollow bodies cradled many of the tools which yw Sabi had ordered from the Temple's AI.

Robots, Nyahri realized, unsure where the term came from. *Ekaterina's word, now my word.*

In one rested a heavy black box, and yw Sabi lifted its lid. It contained sheaves of white and pristine *paper,* dense print darkening each page. She opened another box to find stacks of tiny clear cylinders, scores of hundreds in fitted frames. After resealing the boxes, she strapped them into the carriers. Last, she slipped bundles of pins, replacements for her explosives, into her pockets.

Yw Sabi shouted to Nyahri over the din, "We must go!"

She worked magic upon the carriers, and the spiders followed them down the corridor. Yw Sabi opened the exit portals, leading Nyahri through the cramped corridors of

S'Eret, the way illuminated by witch-light. Nyahri choked through the smoky haze, but at last a ray of morning daylight cut the dark.

The ground trembled.

In the courtyard, Kwlko and Turo pulled at their reins, skittering and neighing. Within minutes, mistress and claimèd galloped from the ruined fortress, heading northeast along now-familiar trails, the tight paths up the mesa side. The spider- bots kept pace.

From the vista, Nyahri glanced backward at the valley's burnt maelstrom, a wasteland many thousands of horse-strides in all directions. A handful of Oudwn buildings still stood, spared by some miracle, but the Citadel's immolation would soon wipe these away. The earth-shake worsened, even as the horses carried them from the low valley onto the higher saddle between the peaks of the northern mountains. Over the top, they passed once more into pristine forests.

An arrow flew, striking yw Sabi in the chest.

Soft as cotton but stronger than iron, her suit of witch-cloth deflected the point, though the Atreiani groaned at the blow. Nyahri's gaze followed the arrow's arc.

Dhaos stood amongst the trees, next arrow already nocked at his cheek.

Nyahri held her palm up. "Do not!" she said. "There is no time!"

He let fly, even as they almost rode him down. His second arrow found the flesh between yw Sabi's neck and shoulder. The travertine pale of her skin turned instantly, shockingly scarlet, and she tumbled into the dust.

"*Deceivers!*" Dhaos yelled. "You cost us *everything!*"

Nyahri halted her stallion, swung from the saddle, and ran to yw Sabi. Part of her knew she must defend herself against Dhaos, but if her mistress already lay dead, what would Dhaos matter?

She turned her back on him.

"E'cwn *witch!*" he said. "I know what the collar at your neck means."

Nyahri knelt at her mistress's side. Yw Sabi's eyes were closed, and blood covered her throat, staining the fabric of her suit, sticking in her hair. The fletching showed amidst the blood, but Nyahri dared not move her mistress, not till she could better understand the damage. Laying her ear against yw Sabi's chest, Nyahri listened.

Yw Sabi lived, her strange heartbeat unfaltering.

"All your archers came to kill us?" Nyahri asked, looking over her shoulder at Dhaos.

"Only me."

He drew another arrow, aiming it at her. The sun rose higher, its unctuous rays cutting the drifting smoke, soiling the eastern and southern skies.

"You should run," she said flatly to him. Nyahri tried to clear yw Sabi's wound, placing herself between Dhaos and her mistress. She needed supplies from her horse, but she could not risk giving Dhaos a second shot at her mistress. "The Citadel will die soon. It will kill us here."

Dhaos spit. "I do not care if *none* of us survives this."

Nyahri's tears blurred her vision.

Then the scepter-song played, high-pitched over the Citadel's distant drum. Nyahri flinched, remembering the C'naädin slaughter, but the song now sounded to her like the sweetest music, the ringing of harmonious glass bells. The collar's warmth spread through her shoulders and along her spine.

Dhaos collapsed like a rag doll. His arrow bounded harmlessly into the trees.

Yw Sabi lay with her eyes open, the scepter clenched in one hand, pressing her other hand to her neck. Nyahri crouched against her mistress, stoppering the wound with her hands, crimson thickening over her fingers.

"You are losing a lot of blood," she said.

Yw Sabi nodded.

"Keep your eyes open."

Nyahri stripped Dhaos of his cloth shirt and tore it. Yw Sabi rolled to her side, and Nyahri wiped the injury as well as she could.

The shaft had lodged low in the meat.

Nyahri broke the arrowhead and drew it from yw Sabi's flesh in a single pull. Through all this, the Atreiani only scrunched her eyes.

Packing cloth against both ends of the wound, Nyahri pressed it tight, and she wrapped her mistress's neck and shoulder with all the material she had to spare. As Nyahri helped her to stand, yw Sabi clutched the scepter in her bloodied fingers.

"Yw Sabi, can you ride?"

"Yes," she said, her voice only a whisper.

The Atreiani climbed into the saddle herself, but her strength ebbed. She spit a mouthful of blood.

"Lean across the saddle," Nyahri said.

"The cases—" yw Sabi began.

"They are fine."

The spider-bots waited a dozen paces down the trail.

Dhaos lay as a dead man, his magiswood bow angled across his body, his eyes wide and unblinking. Nyahri knelt beside him, feeling his strong pulse, assured he lived.

"The cases contain medicine," she said to him, nodding toward the spiders, "for *your* people. Do not pretend to know whether *we*, my mistress and I, are evil or good. Do not pretend you understand one godsdamned thing about any of this, stupid Oudwni."

"Come," yw Sabi whispered, "my claimèd."

"Yea, yw Sabi. What of Dhaos?"

"He might make it in a hard run."

"We could take him?"

"Slow the horses? Leave Dhaos to his fate. The little prick *shot* me."

Nyahri vaulted to the stallion's saddle, turned his head northward, and urged him into a gallop. The unfettered horses bolted.

Yw Sabi's consciousness flagged.

They raced toward the Wyst River. Nyahri tapped Kwlko's rump, driving him faster, his lungs opening and his nostrils flaring. Yw Sabi lay in the saddle, one arm around Turo's neck. Behind them, the vaccines and a trove of medical knowledge traveled in the bellies of robots. The switchback trail ascended along the mountain pass, over a snow-blanketed ridge. As the riders passed deeper into the trees, the hum of the dying Citadel quieted. They descended into a valley thick with aspen, the ground leveled, and Nyahri gave the horses full rein.

Behind them, Sojourn Temple exploded. Hellfire scorched the sky. Wind blew, the sound as deafening as at Abswyn, yet the mountains shielded them from the worst of it. Nyahri pushed until she found a quiet clearing, sheltered from the road.

She eased her mistress from the saddle, and yw Sabi collapsed in her arms, her breath shallow, her skin cool. Blood stained her from her face to her thighs. Nyahri peeled back the gore-stained fabrics, praying to the viper goddess, lady of healing.

"Six weeks," she said to her beloved, "since it was *my* blood all over the trail, yea?" Nyahri forced a laugh, which turned desperate and bitter in her throat. "Now let *me* save *you.*"

Yw Sabi gave no answer, passed into unconsciousness. Nyahri worked with all the craft her mother had ever taught her, and she prayed for more besides. Arteries appeared, or not, where Nyahri least expected them. The Atreiani's muscles folded wrongly against each other, alien to Nyahri's training. Her skin resisted sutures.

No one had ever explained to Nyahri how to heal a devil.

Gods, Nyahri prayed, *please do not die.*

She isn't so easy to kill, returned the thought, at once Nyahri's and another's. *Have faith.*

The morning passed. Nyahri went without food, water, or rest. The afternoon grew long, and night fell once again, before Nyahri ceased her labors.

De duobus malis minus est semper eligendum.

ABOUT THE AUTHOR

J.L. FORREST WRITES FROM the cool, wet techno-jungles of the Pacific Northwest, the frosty Rocky Mountains, and the narrow, ancient streets of Roma. He is the author of numerous short stories and novels, and he has published works both science fictional and fantastical with the likes of *Analog Science Fiction and Fact, Crossed Genres, Third Flatiron,* the *Robot Cowgirl Press,* and others.

He currently resides in Denver, Colorado with a cat from outer space, more books than are strictly necessary, and his beloved paramour. Follow him @WordForrest and at jlforrest.com, or contact him through the Science Fiction and Fantasy Writers of America at sfwa.org.

Books and Stories by J.L. Forrest—

DELICATE MINISTRATIONS—Short Fictions I
Eleven short stories of Science Fiction and Dark Fantasy, including Liminal, a novella of the centuries to come.

MINUSCULE TRUTHS—Short Fictions II
Ten Short Stories of Science Fiction and Dark Fantasy. Includes "Sapience Signified", a novelette of interstellar discovery, originally published in *Analog Science Fiction and Fact*.

WHEN THE WORLD ENDS—
A Novella of Old Gods, New Gods, and a Stunning Vision of the Future.

If you like REQUIES DAWN, be sure to look for its sequels, and leave a five-star review on Amazon.

Be sure to visit jlforrest.com.

Sign up for the newsletter and get special announcements and free goodies: http://jlforrest.com/newsletter/.